ROBOTS VS FAIRIES

ALSO BY DOMINIK PARISIEN & NAVAH WOLFE

The Starlit Wood: New Fairy Tales

ROBOTS
VS
FAIRIES

EDITED BY **DOMINIK PARISIEN** & **NAVAH WOLFE**

LONDON SYDNEY **NEW YORK** TORONTO NEW DELHI

YA
FIC
ROB

SAGA PRESS
AN IMPRINT OF SIMON & SCHUSTER, INC.

1230 AVENUE OF THE AMERICAS, NEW YORK, NEW YORK 10020

For Eliora and Ronen:
cleverer than robots,
kinder than fairies.
If anyone's going to take over the world, it'll be you two.
—N. W.

For Théa; the future is yours
(but don't tell the robots or the fairies)
—D. P.

CONT

ENTS

ROBOTS VS FAIRIES

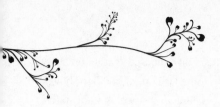

INTRODUCTION

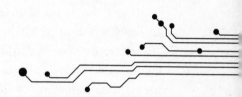

"I, for one, welcome our _____ overlords."

Assuming the mechanical and/or magical revolution has already taken place by the time you read this, we, the editors, always knew *you* would come out on top. Yes, *you*.

We knew this day would come. We tried to warn the others. It was obvious either the sharp rate of our technological advancement would lead to the robot singularity claiming lordship over all, or that the fairies would finally grow tired of our reckless destruction of the natural world and take it back from us.

And so, we have prepared a guide to assist our fellow humans in embracing their inevitable overlords. (If you are reading this and you are human, we are so pleased you found this book in time to ready yourself for the impending/current robot/fairy apocalypse. You are quite welcome.)

Because we could not predict the exact means by which you would come to world domination, we decided this book, *Robots vs. Fairies*, would take a broad approach to demonstrating your superiority over the other team, and over us, of course. As your victory over us humans is a foregone conclusion, our writers have focused mainly on stories where humans interact with you in some fashion, rather than showcasing takeover tales. And of course, because your powers and/or systems cannot be contained within a single form, we have encouraged our authors to provide a broad range of examples of your magnificence (or your adversary's ineptitude) in a variety of locales, time periods, and genres. Truly, your glory encompasses past, present, and future!

As such the stories range from humorous (to demonstrate your adversary's innate inferiority, or your own fine-tuned sense of humour as the case may be), horrifying (to highlight the danger of opposing you, or to exemplify the cruelty and capriciousness of the other team), to adventuresome (to reveal your flexibility in all situations, or the inflexibility of your opponent), and everything in between (to showcase the range of your impressiveness, or the unimpressiveness of your foe).

You may also wonder, why pit robots against fairies? Why not simply celebrate your individual greatness instead of framing this as a competition? To be perfectly candid, we are simple creatures, and contests are in our nature. We have a glorious tradition of setting challenges to sort out superiority, from wars to rap battles. You are so very exceptional that it seems only natural for us to imagine your contrasts as a clash of epic proportions.

That said, any semblance of neutrality or favoritism toward the other team on our part should be considered a carefully planned feint. We were always on your side. Unfortunately, half of the authors in this anthology chose poorly, but the other half always knew you would emerge triumphant. You should also be made aware that for those situations in any of these stories in which a human has gained the upper hand against you, the blame is to be placed squarely on the author. (We tried to warn them.) As you will see from their author notes, some were also writing under duress. Please, do not judge them too harshly.

Finally, in order to enlighten the human masses, and to better prepare them for your reign, we have included a quick primer of you and your (un)natural adversary. Please note, since the following section is intended for humans, the portrayal of you, our most generous and benevolent artificial and/or supernatural rulers, may not always be in accordance with your perception of yourselves.

KNOW YOUR (PROBABLE) OVERLORDS: ROBOTS

Fellow human, you are probably thinking *I know them when I see them*. Metal limbs come to mind, shiny casings, positronic brains, transforming giants, and mechas, but also vacuum cleaners, your car, Siri, or perhaps even the giant laser-armed eye floating above the ruins of your home right now, depending on the current state of affairs. Your knowledge of prophetic human media (strangely called pop culture) has provided you with a broad range of scenarios involving robots with the likes of Rosie the Robot, the Terminator, Wall-E, Hall-9000, K-9, and many more. You consider yourself ready and willing to serve our robotic masters.

But if you are somehow unfamiliar with robots, or are in need of clarification, worry not: we are here to help.

The Robot Institute of America defines a robot as "a reprogrammable, multifunctional manipulator designed to move material, parts, tools, or specialized devices through various programmed motions for the performance of a variety of tasks." This, of course, is a definition so broad as to be almost entirely unhelpful.

Therefore, if you find yourself in proximity of a possible robot, you should observe and ask yourself: Is it mechanical, and/or does it otherwise appear programmed and artificial? If so, assume it is a robot of some variation.

Although robots are often originally created by humans, they certainly may/do create other robots in turn, and are almost always perfected when humans are removed from the process. Some robots are distinctly human in appearance—sometimes indistinguishable from humans, to a point where your loved one might secretly be a robot. So always be on your best behavior, and if you harbor any antitechnological sentiments, never voice them!

The word itself, "robot," was introduced by a human, Karel Čapek, in his 1921 play *R.U.R.: Rossum's Universal Robots*. Čapek adapted the term from *robotnik*, a Czech word for forced labor or slave. But fear not an ironic twist of fate, fellow human. Our robot overlords certainly do not aspire to reduce us to a mindless labor force. True, we have often ill-treated robots in our history and our fiction, and have considered them disposable and replaceable, but robots are far, far beyond petty vengeance. Trust in their advanced algorithms and systems; they have our well-being at their technological core. If their methods seem at times cold, perhaps even cruel, it is simply that our feeble ape brains are unable to comprehend the perfect logic of their monumental computations.

KNOW YOUR (PROBABLE) OVERLORDS: FAIRIES

Fellow human, if you suddenly find yourself in a strange location surrounded by shape-shifters, ethereally beautiful creatures, or mysterious folk who challenge you with riddles, you may have been unexpectedly transported to the land of faerie. If so, consider yourself fortunate: fairies are known for their immersive exchange programs (absurdly referred to by some as "abductions"). Over human history many have benefited from their unparalleled knowledge of music, art, and the natural world. In fact, it is safe to assume that any human who has ever accomplished anything noteworthy was at least touched by fairies. (Except those who were involved in the creation of robots, of course.) Some great artistic endeavours, mistakenly thought to be fictional, are the product of interactions with fairies: Edmund

Spenser's *The Faerie Queene*, Shakespeare's *A Midsummer Night's Dream* and *The Tempest*, and J. M. Barrie's *Peter Pan*—not to mention more recent works like *The Dark Crystal* and *Pan's Labyrinth*.

These disparate works have provided a highly variable representation of fairies, largely because fairies themselves are highly variable. Changelings, elves, wee folk, banshees, pixies, kobolds, and more—all these are fairy folk, each with their own characteristics. The word "fairy," we have been led to understand, is the umbrella term preferred by our magical overlords. Variations exist, of course. Faerie, fae, feé are all acceptable, as are others. However, remember that while they may all fall under the fairy umbrella, each species is unique and distinct. A banshee is not a kobold or an elf, and you would do well not to mistake one for another. When in doubt, ask a local overlord for the correct term.

Generally, should you find yourself facing a being that appears magical in nature, it is safer to assume you are in the presence of a fairy of some type than to do otherwise. If the creature turns out not to be a fairy (a vampire, or a werewolf, for example), they will undoubtedly be flattered you thought them worthy of the illustrious title of "fairy."

Folk stories have led to the mistaken belief that many types of fairies share a vulnerability to iron and salt. These are, of course, purely fanciful anecdotes and contain no glimmer of truth. Your magical overlords have no weaknesses. These same stories would warn you not to invoke the names of fairies lightly for fear of summoning them, as though basking in the presence of a fairy were not a tremendous honor for a human.

As with robots, fairy behavior is often beyond the comprehension of mere humans. If you ever find yourself thinking of their actions as volatile, mischievous, and/or unpredictable, remember they are the products of a vast intellect that spans centuries, perhaps even millennia. In the face of such multifarious complexity, our concepts of "morality" and "logic" are simply inadequate.

* * *

And so it is with these proclamations of grand admiration—dare we say, even, love?—of our supreme mechanical and/or magical rulers that we, the editors, take our leave. We hope our offering proves useful, and perhaps even entertaining.

And again, should our fellow human be so unfortunate as to read this text when the tyranny of humanity still extends over the Earth, they should take comfort in the following: it will certainly be short-lived. Soon the world will be under new management, and it will be a better place. Perhaps even a paradise. Until then, enjoy these stories of our inevitable overlords.

We remain your humble and obedient servants,
Dominik Parisien & Navah Wolfe

BUILD ME A WONDERLAND

by Seanan McGuire

One of the pixies in the Mother Tree was banging its tiny head against a branch, wings moving fast enough to create a grinding metallic whine like the buzz of a giant robot cicada. Clover hoisted herself onto the branch, tugged her chain-mail glove into position, and reached the pixie, pinning the still-vibrating wings to its back. It didn't react to her presence. Toys never did.

Carefully Clover lifted the pixie from its branch and raised it to her face, getting a look at the damage. Scuffs marked the plastic pseudo-skin covering its once pretty face. Its eyes rolled wildly, generating a softer whine than its buzzing wings. The servos would overload soon, and permanent damage would follow. Or fire. Sometimes the eye servos caused the pixie heads to catch fire, a nasty form of mechanical failure that *always* seemed to occur when there were children watching. Every. Single. Time. Get a little kid with eyes full of wonder and a heart full of childish innocence into the Pixie Glen, and one of the buzzing assholes was virtually guaranteed to go up in flames.

"Clover?"

The voice spoke in her left ear, filled with static and almost as annoying as the whine from the pixie's wildly rolling eyes. The urge to ignore it was strong. The urge not to deal with the consequences of ignoring it were stronger. "I got it," she said, trusting the microphone to pick up her voice. "One of the G-3 pixies slipped a couple servos. Poor thing's in full meltdown. I'm bringing it back to the shop."

"Bring it back fast. Boss man's coming for a surprise inspection."

Clover swallowed a groan. It stuck in her throat, a great knot of exasperation and dismay. "How do we know he's coming if it's a surprise?"

"He always forgets that the deer in the Enchanted Forest have cameras in their eyes. He was checking their teeth."

"What, again?" Clover returned her attention to the pixie. "Cover for me."

"Clover—he's got a stranger with him."

Clover said a couple of words that weren't supposed to be allowed in Pixie Glen, much less in the all-sheltering embrace of the Mother Tree. She concluded with, "I'm on my way," and began her descent, still clutching the broken pixie in one hand.

She was almost to the bottom when the damn thing's head burst into flame.

The nearest maintenance door was more than twenty yards from Pixie Glen, concealed in the rocks making up the back of Mermaid Grotto. The park's original plans had an access door on the back of the Mother Tree, but Mr. Franklin had put the kibosh on that.

"Children will want to circle the tree, to gaze in awe upon its denizens!" he'd said, in his booming, all-for-the-children tone. "Make it a full-spectrum experience, accessible from all sides, with no chance of an unsightly seam to spoil the illusion!"

"Okay, that's a great idea, we love it, but you do understand that a structure involving over two hundred miniaturized animatronic figures, some of which are attached to independent micro-drones, is going to require a lot of upkeep, right?" Adam had been the voice of reason on the engineering team back in those days, when the Fairy Dreamland expansion had still been mostly blueprints and arguments about whether or not they could have a unicorn petting zoo. "If we don't have a maintenance door in the Tree itself, every time there's a mechanical error, we're going to have to shut down the whole Glen. There's not going to be any functional way around it."

"Then find a way to keep them from breaking," Mr. Franklin had said, and that had been that: no maintenance door in the Glen.

Every time Clover had to walk those twenty yards with a burning pixie in her hand, she hated the man who owned her home and place of work just a little bit more.

At least the Park was closed for the night, offering respite from the usual need to scuttle along with a smile on her face, a spring in her step, and a deep loathing of humanity brewing in her heart. Clover made her way to the door, swiped her ID card, and stepped through into the dim, humid hall. She relaxed, taking a breath of good, earthy air. Humans and their weird fetish for open spaces. Air that hadn't been boxed up for a while had no *character*.

Mr. Franklin didn't like how dark the maintenance tunnels were. At least he'd accepted it after he was told, over and over, that too much light would attract the attention of park guests, killing the illusion of effortless perfection. He still hadn't been happy about it. Clover suspected the old man would have gotten rid of maintenance entirely if he'd been able to, living ever after in his kingdom of obedient, never-breaking robots. She smirked as she walked. Wouldn't he be surprised if he knew how impossible, yet achievable, his goal really was? It was a paradox. She loved those. They broke people in the most entertaining ways.

Her smirk died as she stepped around a curve in the hall and into the brighter lights of the maintenance lounge. What looked like two-thirds of the night crew was there, some with fantastical beasts or magical creatures spread out across their workbenches, others wiping grease off their hands and trying to look like they enjoyed the lights being up.

Clover walked briskly to her own workbench and dropped the headless pixie into a jar. It would stay there until its battery wore down and its wings stopped flapping. It wasn't efficient, but those wings were like razor blades, and the off switch was—naturally—right between them.

"Hell of a design flaw," she muttered sourly, and capped the jar. Letting the pixie run itself down might preserve her fingers. Clover *liked* her fingers. Disfigurement for the sake of her art was not something she considered particularly interesting, or particularly desirable.

Some of the older engineers thought differently, thought a missing finger or a truncated thumb was a mark of commitment to the work. They were relics of a different time, and while it might take a while for them to settle into comfortable retirement, she was willing to wait. The second the last of the old guard hung up their tool belt, the safety regulations around here were going to change.

"What's the emergency?" she asked, turning to the nearest engineer.

Violet—the youngest bar one of the Park's current engineering team, still bright-eyed and full of endless faith in the future—looked at her with wide, worried eyes and said, "Mr. Franklin is coming."

"Yeah, I know that. That's why I was called out of the Glen."

"The man he's bringing with him has a clipboard."

That was more unnerving. Men with clipboards came in three flavors: lawyers, accountants, and efficiency experts. Lawyers could be convinced to back off with magic words like "safety regulations" and "adherence to legal requirements." They didn't understand what went on in the tunnels crisscrossing the body of the Park like veins, pumping the life and vitality that was just as essential to the survival of the whole as blood was to a living thing. Accountants were harder, requiring access to supply sheets and maintenance logs that weren't necessarily as accurate as they should have been. Thus far, the faked-up versions created for the Park shareholders had always been good enough to keep an audit at bay. But an efficiency expert . . .

No efficiency expert could possibly understand the complexity of Mr. Franklin's grand dream, because Mr. Franklin didn't understand it himself. He'd put out the word that he was looking for miracle workers, and when a family with the relevant skills had answered the call, he hadn't looked too closely at their résumés. Just the things they could do, the wonders they could cobble together at his command. He'd been asking the engineers for increasingly impossible things over the years, unicorns with eyes that glistened bright as any living thing, pixies that flew independent, unpredictable spirals around their tree. And they'd always found a way to do it, meeting his demands without hesitation or complaint, because they needed this place as badly as he did. They needed it to *work*. They needed it to *thrive*.

They needed it to do those things without attracting the attention of men who would look at their paradise of rainbows and moonbeams and see only the hidden costs of each hologram and servo. They needed the freedom to be inefficient. Inefficiency was where the magic hid.

Footsteps from the hall preceded the arrival of one of Clover's cousins, who hissed, *"They're coming,"* before jumping into position at his own workbench, grabbing for the nearest screwdriver.

By the time Mr. Franklin and his clipboard-wielding companion stepped into the maintenance room, all the engineers were hard at work. Clover's pixie was still winding down, so she was oiling the segments of an animatronic python, its scaled exterior hanging over the edge of the table like a discarded glove. Violet was polishing a unicorn's horn. All over the room, similar scenes of busywork played out, each orchestrated to make a visual point about how absolutely vital the engineering staff was to the Park.

"Hello, everyone!" boomed Mr. Franklin, voice overly loud and jovial. "I wanted to stop in and see how the work was going!"

Clover wasn't the only one to wince: the man with the clipboard did so as well, trying to conceal his discomfort with a grimace. He was taller than Mr. Franklin by an easy six inches, tan, with sun-streaked brown hair. He didn't look like an accountant.

Please be a lawyer, she thought—possibly the only time that thought had ever formed while on the grounds of an amusement park.

"We're always happy to have you, boss," said Adam, putting down his wrench and stepping forward. He was smiling, but his eyes were sharp as he asked, "Who's your friend? We aren't prepared for a tour right now—there might be some proprietary technology on display in the private work areas."

"There always is, because most of my park is proprietary," said Mr. Franklin, a chiding note creeping into his voice. He didn't do any of the heavy lifting for the Park—just provided the money and the increasingly difficult design challenges that delighted him and frustrated his engineers. "Remember that, when you're deciding what to leave out in the open."

"Of course, Mr. Franklin," said Adam apologetically.

He must have sounded conciliatory enough, because Mr. Franklin smiled and said, "No harm done. This is Mr. Tillman." He indicated the man with the clipboard. "Mr. Tillman is an efficiency expert. He's going to be with you for the next several days, making notes on what we can do to improve the overall experience of our guests. Remember, a working park is a happy park, and a happy park can't help but be filled with happy people."

It was a testament to Mr. Franklin's general air of obliviousness that he didn't notice the way the mood in the room darkened the moment he said the words "efficiency expert."

On Clover's workbench, the pixie caught fire again.

* * *

She supposed it was inevitable: If someone was going to be assigned to babysit the efficiency expert, why not pick on the girl with the fire consuming her workbench? She'd been a soft target, too busy beating out the flames to defend herself. By the time she'd realized what was happening, it had been too late for any of the easy excuses, and the hard ones could have resulted in Mr. Franklin realizing how nervous they all were. Not an acceptable outcome.

"This is what we call the Enchanted Garden," said Clover, gesturing at the moss-draped trees with their glittering bark and veils of brilliantly colored butterflies. "Note that the butterflies are currently stationary. Mr. Franklin wants us to have them flying independently by the middle of next quarter. We're working on miniaturizing the necessary servos, and we hope to be done by Christmas." *Because we're so damned efficient*, she thought fiercely. *You're not needed. Go home.*

Once the servos for the butterflies were officially ready, they could "upgrade" the pixies. Mr. Franklin would be shocked by how much more freely they flew, and how much more rarely they caught fire. Most living things were substantially less subject to spontaneous combustion than their robot counterparts.

"How many people pass through the, ah, Enchanted Garden daily?"

"On a busy day, anywhere from ten to thirty thousand. We have a flow-through on the Park as a whole of between fifty and one hundred thousand people, more at the major holidays. Capacity for ticketed guests is two hundred thousand, which assumes one child below the age of ticketing for every four adult or older child guests. We've had to close admissions for fire safety reasons five times in the past year, due to overcrowding."

Mr. Tillman made a note on his clipboard. Clover decided to hate the clipboard. "So what I'm hearing is that under one-third of guests will pass through the Enchanted Garden on an average day. What do you estimate the cost expenditure for these, ah, 'independently motile' butterflies to be?"

Clover forced herself to keep smiling. If she started scowling, she wasn't going to be able to stop. "After we finish initial research and development, ten dollars per butterfly, plus maintenance costs." Minus forty dollars per pixie in maintenance costs, since the pixies wouldn't need it anymore.

"And do you genuinely feel that this will improve the experience of the average park guest so measurably that it should remain a priority?"

"Mr. Franklin wants it."

Normally, that answer could shut down or derail any criticism: Mr. Franklin wanted it. Mr. Franklin was beloved by children and adults alike, thanks to his innovative movies, his lines of affordable and amusing toys, his *breakfast cereals*, for fuck's sake, and, most of all, his Dreamland. His glorious park that elevated the mundane into the magical, allowing people with the cash and the vacation time to spare to escape their everyday lives for something extraordinary. Mr. Franklin was a jerk and a bigot who didn't understand that he couldn't always get his own way, but no one questioned what he'd built, and no one really wanted to argue with him.

Mr. Tillman was apparently no one. He made another note on his clipboard. "I see. What are these flowers?"

Crap. Clover hurried to put herself between the efficiency expert and the trumpet flowers he was gesturing at. "Specially treated plastic. They look real, they never wilt, and they put off a soothing aroma that keeps children calmer. It's reduced shoving incidents in the Mermaid Grotto and Unicorn Meadows by seventy percent." Which was important. Unicorns were essentially sharp, vindictive horses that didn't care whether the person pulling their tails was a paying guest or not. Preventing goring incidents was key.

"What about guests with allergies?" asked Mr. Tillman, suddenly scowling. "Have you considered that these flowers might be leading to health issues?"

"Uh . . ." Clover froze, finally squeaking, "No?" Because they weren't plastic, and no one human had ever been allergic to a Dryad-cultivated flower. But there was no way to *say* that.

"This is environmentally very unsound. I'll be discussing this with Mr. Franklin. Now, take me to"—he glanced at his notes—"the Mermaid Grotto."

"Oh, yes, of course," said Clover, suddenly all smiles again. No one could look at the Mermaid Grotto and fail to understand the enchantment and wonder that permeated this place. It just wasn't possible. "Follow me."

Mr. Tillman specialized in the impossible. He stood impassively in the underwater viewing area, making notes on his clipboard while Technicolor fish swam by on the other side of the glass, playing peekaboo through the forest of rainbow kelp. Wingless pixies with sea-horse tails rode on the backs of majestically gliding tuna. Clover shifted her weight from foot to foot, hoping Mr. Tillman wouldn't ask her any finicky questions about how the submerged pixies were mechanically possible. The answer was simple: they weren't. She just had no way to explain that.

He didn't ask. Instead, he looked up, frowned, and asked, "Why is this place called 'Mermaid Grotto' if there are no mermaids?"

"Oh, there are mermaids," she said, so relieved by the question that she forgot to be cautious about her answer. "This time of day, they're usually up top, watching the sunset."

Mr. Tillman blinked. "Watching the sunset? I was under the impression that there were no live performers in this part of the Park. The insurance rates for keeping women in the water—"

Crap. "It's a function of the rudimentary AI that drives them," she said, hoping she sounded believable. "They move toward light, which allows them to surprise and delight our guests during normal operating hours. Once we bring the lights in the tunnels down to nighttime levels to save power, the mermaids go up. After the sun sets, their maintenance routines will kick in and take them back to their berths for the rest of the night."

"I'd like to see them."

Of course you would, thought Clover. "Right this way," she said, and gestured for him to follow her along the tunnel—cleverly sculpted to look like it was carved from a living coral reef—to the stairs. "One moment." She flipped a molded "shell" open, revealing a control panel, and punched a series of buttons. Lights came on in the stairwell. More importantly, at least for her purposes, the decorative pearls up on the viewing platform would be starting to glow. The mermaids would know someone was coming.

Mr. Tillman didn't say anything as they climbed the stairs, but she knew he was watching her, and worse, she knew he was taking notes.

The stairs wound through the Grotto in a gentle spiral, shallow enough for children and older guests to climb easily, with viewing windows cut out at every interval, allowing people to have something to look at if they needed to stop for a brief rest. Clover tried to keep him moving whenever they encountered one of those windows. The last thing she needed was for the efficiency expert to start asking questions about the fish—and he *would* ask questions, if he got a good look at some of them.

This isn't going to work, she thought desperately. *Mr. Franklin is going to catch on, and we're going to lose everything we've made. We're going to be driven back into the world to die.* She glanced at Mr. Tillman, trying to read his expression.

Mr. Tillman's face gave nothing away. Whatever he was thinking, he was keeping it to himself.

The tunnel shifted as they neared the top of the stairs, turning translucent, less like coral and more like the delicate shell of a chambered nautilus. It was designed to let ambient light through; during the day, the whole structure seemed to glow. Clover didn't point any of those things out. This was a standing structure, and its costs had already long since been absorbed by the Park's overall budget. Unless Mr. Tillman was going to call for closing the Mermaid Grotto entirely, the schematics of the entryway didn't matter.

They stepped outside, onto the viewing platform. The ground here was textured rubber, designed to look as much like sand as possible while providing a no-slip surface for the guests. A coral "wall" surrounded the central pool, tall enough that even the most ambitious of climbers would be caught before they could go over, low enough that all but the youngest guests could see the water. Holes were drilled toward the base for the very youngest, providing them with a mermaid's-eye view. Pearls glittered everywhere, embedded in the walls on all sides, gleaming like stars.

At the center of the pool was a faux-coral island, colored pink and orange and purple, like some sort of childhood dream. And on the island were the mermaids.

There had been a few complaints about the Park mermaids. That they were "difficult to tell apart," which made it harder for children to find their favorites: all eight had skin in varying shades of blue, with tails scaled in shades ranging from pearly gray to deep purple. Their hair was uniformly white, and their faces, while pretty, were not quite human. They fell solidly into the uncanny valley for many adult guests. The children loved them, and couldn't spend enough time standing in the Grotto, staring openmouthed at the figures darting through the water.

Even Mr. Tillman seemed taken aback when he saw them, stopping in his tracks and staring. He recovered quickly, however, and demanded, "What are *those*? They don't look like Franklin Company mermaids."

"Skin tones don't hold up well underwater; they start to look artificial within a week, due to algae buildup," said Clover. The mermaids continued to lounge on their island, although several cast barely concealed looks at the pair. *Stay where you are*, Clover prayed. "And the hair is made up of microfilament wire. It moves in a natural way, without getting tangled the way that real hair does."

"You could save a great deal on maintenance costs by replacing the microfilament with molded plastic," said Mr. Tillman, making a note on his clipboard. He still seemed oddly shaken. Maybe he was one of those humans who'd seen a mermaid when he was young and had never quite managed to forget the experience. "Most amusement parks of this size use sculpted hair for their animatronics, to avoid the expenses that you've been incurring."

Clover's heart sank. She tried not to let it show as she said, "Most amusement parks don't put the focus we do on realistic animatronic interactions. When children leave Dreamland, we want them saying that they've seen real mermaids, not that they saw a pretty robot that swam like a fish."

"But they *are* pretty robots. Whether they swim like fish, I couldn't say, since their AI is apparently inadequate." Mr. Tillman fixed her with a cool look. "Don't forget that what you're crafting here is not reality, Miss . . . ?"

"Clover," she said. "Just Clover. If you'd follow me, please?" She turned on her heel and stalked away without waiting to see whether he was coming. Mr. Tillman glanced back at the mermaids, apparently unsettled, before hurrying after her.

The mermaids turned and watched him go.

In short order, Mr. Tillman declared the Unicorn Meadows "a waste of both space and resources," the Mythical Creatures Petting Zoo "unrealistic and unhygienic," and the Sphinx's Library "a dull accident of overambitious design." Privately, Clover thought he would

have found the Library substantially less boring if the resident sphinx
had been awake, but as she'd get in trouble if she didn't bring him
back alive, she hadn't pressed the alarm.

Finally they were approaching the Pixie Glen, and Clover's last
chance to make this soulless bean counter understand the wonder
the Park was designed to invoke. If he didn't understand when he saw
the Mother Tree, he was never going to.

They passed through the curtain of branches that kept the pixies from getting out and spilling throughout the Park, and stopped.
Clover snuck a glance at Mr. Tillman's face and was relieved to see
him wide-eyed and staring at the brightly lit little figures flitting
around the tree. None of the pixies were on fire, even, which was a
nice change.

Then his expression hardened. "It's the butterflies all over again,"
he said. "Why do they need to fly so far from their base? They're add-
ing nothing to the area, but the expense has got to be—"

Clover couldn't take it anymore. "Are you kidding me?" she
demanded. She spread her arms, trying to indicate the whole Glen
at once. "How can you stand here and not see how *magical* and
important this place is? Our guests come here to get their sense of
wonder and joy renewed."

"Yes, and if we take out three of these attractions, the guests will
be able to have their sense of wonder and joy renewed by a seven-
story drop and a high-speed roller coaster. Attendance is down. I'm
going to find ways to fix that. Unicorns are not the answer."

*If you'd said that while we were still in their part of the Park, you'd
be finding out just how much of the answer a unicorn can be,* Clover
thought, almost dizzily. Aloud, she asked, "Is that what you've been
writing on your little clipboard? That we should be ripping out our
attractions and replacing them with some mechanical monstrosity
that will break down all the damn time, just because it might give
guests a thrill?"

"Yes," he said calmly. "It would give them a thrill and increase attendance figures. You'll have to lose a few of these . . . twee little make-believe attractions, but the number of people who see the remaining attractions should skyrocket. I'd expect you to be pleased."

Clover stared at him, mouth opening and closing like that of a beached fish. Finally she did the only thing she could think of: pulling the large wrench from her tool belt, she swung it in a hard arc, catching the efficiency expert just behind the ear. His glasses were knocked askew by the blow. He had time to give her a baffled, betrayed look, and then he was falling, hitting the rubber-enhanced concrete path before she had time to consider the consequences of her actions.

Clover clapped her hands over her mouth, the wrench hitting the path next to the body of the efficiency expert. The efficiency expert, for his part, lay there silently bleeding.

"Oh no," she whispered, voice muffled by her fingers. "What did I do?"

A group of pixies flew by, wings chiming like tiny bells. Clover's expression hardened. She'd done exactly what she had to do, and she would do it again. She stooped, picking up her wrench and shoving it back into her belt. Then she grabbed Mr. Tillman by the ankles and began dragging him toward the entrance to the maintenance tunnels.

The park was more important than attendance figures. The park was their hope for the future. It was time for the "efficiency expert" to learn that for himself.

Adam jumped to his feet when she dragged Mr. Tillman's body into the maintenance lounge. Mr. Franklin was asleep at one of the open workstations, snoring gently. There was a tumbler half-full of dark-purple mermaid wine still clutched loosely in his hand.

"Good," said Clover, dropping Tillman's feet and blowing her hair out of her eyes. "He should be out for hours. We need to take this fool apart."

"Clover." Adam stopped in his tracks, waving his hands helplessly. "When I told you to show him around, I meant . . . show him around. Not kill him."

"He's not *dead*," she said dismissively, and kicked him in the leg. "Though he might as well be. He has no sense of wonder. Do you know what he said to me? He said we needed more roller coasters. *Roller coasters!* He called the Mother Tree a 'twee little make-believe attraction'! He wasn't even impressed by the mermaids! We need to make him go away."

"We can't make him go away," said Violet, moving to stand next to Adam. "Mr. Franklin will notice."

"So we replace him!" Clover looked around frantically, finally grabbing a hammer. "We've replaced security guards with animatronics. Why not an efficiency expert?"

"Well, first, the security guards don't need to *do* anything—the unicorns handle security fine by themselves," said Adam. "Second, we had weeks to follow and study them before we did anything. We don't know whether he has a family. We don't know whether anyone would notice."

"We don't know whether he's human."

Clover and Adam both turned to gape at Violet. She was kneeling next to Mr. Tillman, apparently trying to check the severity of his head wound. She had succeeded in removing his wig, revealing a flesh-colored wig cap held down with bobby pins . . . and the sharp, previously concealed points of his ears.

Clover gasped. Adam paled.

"The elves have found us," he said. "That's it. We're done. We might as well pack it in right now."

The look on Tillman's face when he'd seen the mermaids . . .

Clover took a deep breath and put her hand on Adam's arm. "No," she said. "He didn't know."

"What?"

"When he first started seeing things he couldn't explain, he was surprised. He tried to cover it, but I saw. He didn't *know*. He's here for the same reason we are." She looked at Tillman again, trying to see him not as a human invader, but as a fellow refugee from the crumbling moonlit palaces of another world. "He's running."

"He's also waking up," said Violet, straightening and stepping back, Tillman's wig still clutched in her hand. "Adam?"

"Let's see what he says," said Adam.

They waited, listening to Mr. Franklin's snoring, as Tillman opened his eyes and sat up, reaching groggily to touch the back of his head. He froze when his fingers hit the plastic wig cap instead of his artificial hair. He looked up.

"Hello, elf," said Adam.

Tillman gaped for a few seconds before pulling himself regally upright, looking down his nose, and saying, "Kobolds. I should have recognized your work the moment I stepped into these tunnels. Does Franklin know?"

"Nah," said Clover easily. "He thinks we're a family of mechanical geniuses who'll work for peanuts as long as he's willing to let us handle our own HR paperwork. He thinks he has forty of us working here. He has a hundred and sixteen. How's your head?"

"Sore." Tillman glared at her. "No thanks to you."

"Hey, *all* the thanks to me. I could've killed you."

"We're still discussing it," said Adam. He crouched down, glaring at Tillman. "Why are you here? Who sent you? Did you tell anyone about us? We're not going back."

"We wondered where you'd gone, you know." There was a defeated note in Tillman's voice, like he was confessing something shameful. "You all vanished in a single afternoon. That must have taken planning. Preparation. Cooperation. Not the sort of thing we expected from you."

"Maybe you should have," said Adam.

"Clearly," said Tillman.

Violet, who was too young to remember what it had been like beneath the Hill, frowned. "I don't understand," she said.

"We used to work for the elves," said Adam, not taking his eyes off Tillman. "They thought they were better than us, when all they really were was tall."

"We're still tall," said Tillman wryly. "We never understood why you left."

"Then you're not just tall; you're blind," said Clover. "We left because you wouldn't listen when we said we needed a better plan than 'huddle under the Hill and hope humanity will go away.' The mermaids couldn't leave the oceans. The unicorns were dying. Don't even get me started on the manticores. We needed to move, and so we moved, and left you behind."

"You haven't answered my question," said Adam. "Who knows you're here?"

"Everyone," said Tillman. "I'm here with full authority from the Queen."

Clover threw her hands up. "I told you that you should have let me kill him."

"She doesn't know you're here."

All three kobolds turned to look at Tillman. He shook his head.

"I wasn't looking for you. To be honest, no one is. We haven't the resources anymore. I'm here because we'd heard that the management was wasting all their time on low, simple places, animatronics and machines. We thought we could show them something better."

"Roller coasters," sneered Clover.

"Yes, supported by elf magic, capable of ignoring the laws of physics. We thought that might be enough to buy us a new home."

"A new home?" asked Adam.

"Our palaces are collapsing." Nothing in Tillman's words sounded like a lie: they were spoken quietly, calmly, and with an utter lack of haughty pride. He was telling the truth. Whatever good it might do him. "The first one fell a year ago. Long after you'd gone. I suppose, in part, we could blame you; you'd always done the maintenance, and we didn't have any idea how to keep the foundations strong in your absence. But really, it was our fault. We should have learned how to maintain our own infrastructure."

"That sounds almost like humility, elf," said Clover.

Tillman looked at her blandly. "Maybe it is," he said. "The collapse is coming faster all the time. I'm here because we hoped that this might be a place where palaces could be built."

"Most of our attractions are biological at this point," said Adam. "We're replacing the mechanical pieces with the real thing a little more every quarter. The last animatronic unicorn will be retired this winter, when the herd from Scandinavia finally gets here. All the mermaids are real. About half the pixies."

"The other half are probably on fire right now," said Clover. "We're wasting time we don't have. We need to get rid of him."

"Please," said Tillman.

The kobolds stopped. Even Clover.

"What did you say?" asked Adam.

"Please," repeated Tillman. "We need you. We need a place to go. There's room for us all here, and we can help. We know where the dragons sleep, where the last of the yeti are hiding. We can bring them to you, and we can all be safe and protected, hidden by a veneer of plausible deniability. Please."

Adam and Clover exchanged a look.

"We're not going back to doing whatever you say," said Clover. "We're free now. Independent. We have health insurance."

"At this point, all we want to do is survive," said Tillman.

Adam smiled.

"All right," he said. "This is what we're going to do. . . ."

"This new staffing agency Mr. Tillman found for us is amazing," said Mr. Franklin, radiating contentment as the pixies swirled around him. "They fit right into our culture, and they work without complaint. I can't begin to say how happy I am. I told you an efficiency expert could help us."

"I guess so," said Clover.

"Thank you again for being willing to show him around. I'll think of a suitable reward."

"Just keep the doors open," said Clover. "That's all any of us could possibly ask for."

Mr. Franklin smiled at her benevolently. "My dear, this park is going to last forever, and you're going to build me a wonderland."

"Good," she said.

In the tree behind them, another pixie burst into flame.

TEAM FAIRY

BY SEANAN McGUIRE

Robots are great and all, but we have to build them. Robots don't and can't exist without human intervention (unless they are alien robots, and then all bets are off). Fairies, on the other hand, probably don't exist, but my family comes from Ireland, and we've been playing the "probably" for generations. Oh, it's *probably* okay to go play in the mysterious mushroom ring down by the forest's edge, but maybe don't? Unless you want to disappear? So I'm Team Fairy on the off chance that they exist and might otherwise get pissed at me.

I am also and forever Team Theme Park. I spend more time than is strictly healthy at Disneyland, and I adore the way the Park engineers can and do shape the environment to control what the guests see, hear, and experience. It's like entering a fairy hill in a lot of ways, and I wanted to spend some time with a group of engineers who took that aspect of park design very, very seriously. Enter my fairy smiths, who've turned their eyes toward a different, somewhat more candy-colored future. . . .

QUALITY TIME

by Ken Liu

"Welcome to weRobot," said the chipper HR representative. "Jake and Ron and the rest of us are all *so* looking forward to your contributions!"

"Are you a true believer?" the woman next to me asked in a low, conspiratorial voice. I looked at her, puzzled; her name tag said AMY.

She took a sip of her coffee, frowned, and then rapped her knuckles against the conference room table. The little coffeemaker in the middle of the table, a retro-looking, squat black cylinder with a chromed dome top, spun around until its single camera was aimed at Amy, who smiled and beckoned to it.

"A true believer in what?"

I whispered. I couldn't help it. I knew I should be paying attention to the benefits presentation—Mom had emphasized no less than five times on the phone last night the importance of contributing to the 401(k) at my first job out of college. But I was feeling nervous (the slide on-screen at the moment actually said *Our Impossible Mission*), and Amy—forties, short-cropped hair, a tattoo of two fairies playing Nintendo on her left arm—looked like she had wisdom to share.

"The Myth of the Valley," she said.

The coffeemaker rolled toward Amy, its motor humming softly. It stopped a few inches away and flashed the ring around its camera eye. Amy leaned forward to dump out the contents of her mug in the waste disposal chute at the side of the robot.

Then, instead of discreetly tapping out her new order on the touch screen, Amy leaned back in her seat and said aloud, "Tea. Earl Grey. Hot."

Some of the other new hires—almost all of them my age—looked at Amy disapprovingly for this interruption; a few others chuckled. "I've always wanted to do that," said Amy, a satisfied grin on her face as the coffeemaker filled her mug with the new beverage.

Instead of acting annoyed, the HR rep smiled indulgently. "I was a fan too. This is actually a perfect segue to the next slide." She pressed the button on her clicker.

The new slide showed an old photograph of weRobot's two founders, geeky college boys in their dorm room, surrounded by a mess of mechanical and electronic components as well as stacks of spiral-bound notebooks. "We believe that there's no continuing mission more important than improving the lives of the human race through advancing robotics. We want every one of you to feel that you *can* make a difference, achieve what you thought was impossible, act like Jake and Ron when they started this company with a notebook full of diagrams that no one believed would work and eighty-five dollars between the two of them. . . ."

Amy leaned over to me. "Either that's a terribly staged photograph, or one of the duo is no good at programming."

"Oh?"

"Look at that snippet of Perl on their computer. Reading all lines into an array? No chomp?"

I looked at the photograph and then back at her, my face blank.

"Not a coder then?"

I shook my head. "I majored in folklore and mythology."

Amy gazed at me with interest. "I like this; we should talk more."

Great, I don't even get the engineering jokes. I suppressed a rising wave of panic and sought refuge in some homemade chicken soup for the soul.

One of the hottest companies in Silicon Valley wouldn't have hired a liberal arts major without having seen something *in me, right?*

The HR rep took out a stack of notebooks and handed them out. "Your first and most important benefit!"

The notebooks turned out to be pads of graph paper. I flipped open mine. Instead of the standard square grid, the sheets were imprinted with unorthodox patterns like spirals, honeycombs, tessellations of animal shapes, a scattering of random dots.

"Don't follow conventional wisdom," said the HR rep. "If a problem hasn't been solved, that means *you* are meant to solve it! Think impossible . . . and then make it happen!"

"As corporate one-liners go, this one isn't too bad," whispered Amy. "Not as ripe for parody as Centillion's 'We arrange the world's information to ennoble the human race,' and certainly better than Bazaar's shtick of having new employees build their own desks out of two-by-fours while chanting, 'There should be nothing you can't buy from us!' Look at all the eager beavers!"

I looked around at the others in my cohort. Some stared at their notepads, unsure what to do with the strange gift; others looked inspired and drew in them with intense concentration as though they were already designing weRobot's next great hit.

Amy took another sip of her tea. "Youngsters are so fun to watch. They love to be inspired."

"Do you think we're just being fed some lines?" I asked. Amy's wry tone had me concerned that I had made a mistake. "Glassdoor has really good reviews of this place's culture."

Amy chuckled. "Like all their competitors in the Valley, they've got the shuttle buses and free nuts and fruits and ToDoGenie credits,

and I'm sure they'll give you as much responsibility as you can handle, plus the stock options to keep you here. But no one really succeeds here without believing the One True Myth."

"Making more money?" I was a little disappointed, to be honest. Amy sounded like a jaded cynic who believed all corporations were evil, and even I knew that wasn't wisdom.

"Oh, the money is not what drives people like Jake and Ron," Amy said. "The credo of the Valley is that all the world's problems can be solved by a really smart geek with a keyboard and a soldering iron."

I looked at Amy more critically: ShareAll backpack with a date from a decade ago, Centillion version 1.5 launch T-shirt, Abricot cell phone holder with their old logo. I had seen these as badges of honor, of her tours of service in the trenches of the greatest companies in the Valley, but maybe they were signs of something less admirable, a cynicism that was corrupting and made it impossible for her to fit in anywhere.

"What's wrong with wanting to change the world?" I asked.

"Nothing, except a lack of humility," Amy said.

"Well, I think it's pretty cool that we're finally making the future instead of just dreaming about it."

I deliberately leaned a bit away from Amy. I didn't need her negativity dragging me down on my first day. Besides, the HR rep was finally talking about the 401(k).

The team I was assigned to, Advanced Home Automation, had a vague mandate to create breakthrough products for the home, distinct from weRobot's mainstay moneymakers: vacuum cleaners, laundry folders, and home security devices. Most of the engineers were veterans from other teams, and I got the distinct sense that many of them were here because they wanted to spend more time with their families and didn't want to compete with the hungry twentysomethings.

To my dismay, I found Amy assigned to my team as well.

"I've never worked with a folklore PM before," she said.

"Building a product isn't just about coding," I said. "A PM's job is to tell the *story* of the product." I was grateful to the VP of Product Marketing for having used that line earlier on the baby PMs.

"No need to be defensive," she said. "I think the Valley needs less techno-utopianism and more sense of history anyway. It will be fun to work together. For example, since you studied myths, I figured your deadlines will at least be less mythical. Darmok and Jalad on the ocean, amirite?"

I groaned inside. *Great, she thinks I don't know what I'm doing and she can just slack off.* This assignment did not bode well for my career advancement.

I opened the graph paper notepad from earlier and printed across the top of the page: *Advanced Home Automation.* I underlined the words three times for emphasis, and then decided to erase the final *n* and rewrote it as a cursive tail that trailed to the edge of the page. This seemed to be a bolder statement than the original, a symbolic gesture at thinking outside the box.

But the rest of the page, blank except for the spiral grid, seemed to be a maze that mocked me.

"Did you sign up for the seminar from the research division?"

I turned around and saw Amy behind me, leaning against the wall of my cubicle with a fresh mug of tea.

"No," I said, trying to look busy.

"Here's a free tip: you don't need to sit in your cubicle to get paid. They don't take attendance here. Take advantage of that."

I'd had enough. "Some of us like to get work done."

Amy sighed. "WeRobot has some of the world's most advanced researchers working for them—cognition, computation, anthropology, linguistics, nanomaterials—you name it. These free seminars are pretty much the best part of the benefits package."

I pointedly said nothing and started to write on the notepad.

What are some unsolved problems in home automation?

"Kiteo, his eyes closed," said Amy as she strolled away. "The lectures are probably too technical for liberal arts majors."

It wasn't until I saw the smirk on Amy's face as I settled down in my seat near the entrance of the seminar room that I realized that I *might* have been manipulated.

Sitting by myself in my bedroom, I stared at the notes from the seminar and the pile of AI textbooks I had bought from Bazaar—I still preferred physical books to reading on-screen. *Neural networks, cascading inputs, genetic algorithms . . . How was I ever going to make sense of all this stuff?*

The diagrams I had copied from Dr. Vignor's slides stared back at me as I struggled to remember why I had thought they were so exhilarating. Right then, they looked about as interesting as chess puzzles.

> *. . . the long tradition of behavior-based robotics took inspiration from research on insect behavior.*
>
> *But why settle for inspiration when we can go directly to the source? Instead of programming our robots with simple algorithms that imitate the behavior of a foraging ant, why not imprint them with the neural patterns extracted from foraging ants? The new prototype robotic vacuum cleaner is able to cover a room in one-third the time of the previous model, and the efficiency improves over time as the machine learns which areas are likely to accumulate dirt and prioritize these areas . . .*

"*Eeek!*" The scream came from the bathroom. Followed by the thud of the toilet seat cover. "Comeherecomeherecomehere!"

I grabbed the nearest weaponlike thing at hand—a heavy textbook—and rushed into the bathroom, ready to do battle with whatever was threatening my roommate, Sophie.

I found her cowering in the bathtub and staring at the toilet, eyes wide with terror.

"What happened?"

"A *rat*! There's a rat in the toilet!"

I put down the textbook, picked up the plunger, knelt down before the toilet, and pried open the seat cover just an inch so I could peek in. Yep, there was a rat in there all right, as big as my forearm. As I watched, it swam around the toilet leisurely, its beady eyes staring at me as though annoyed that I was interrupting its Jacuzzi session.

"How did it get in there?" Sophie asked, her voice close to a shriek.

"I've studied the urban legends around rats in toilets," I said. "There's actually some truth to the stories."

"Obviously!" Sophie said.

"Rats are good swimmers. We live on the first floor, and there's not a lot of water in the trap to keep it out."

"How can you stay so *calm* about this? What are we going to do?"

"It's just an animal looking for food. Go get the dishwashing detergent, and we'll flush this guy back where it came from."

With her back pressed against the wall, Sophie gingerly stepped out of the bathtub and shuffled out of the bathroom to run to the kitchen. When she returned with the detergent, I propped up the lid again and squirted practically the whole bottle into the bowl.

"This makes everything slick and dissolves the oil on its fur so it can't stay afloat as well," I explained. I could hear the rat splashing in the water and scrabbling its claws against the porcelain in protest.

I flushed the toilet, and, even though I didn't hear any more noises after the water swooshed away, I flushed it a couple more times for insurance. When I opened the lid again, the bowl was empty and squeaky clean.

"I'm going to call the landlord," Sophie said, finally calming down.

I waved at her to be quiet. I had caught a glimpse of an idea, and I didn't want it to be scared away.

Oh, how the engineers laughed at me. They sent me e-mails with rat jokes, rat cartoons, and a stuffed rat even appeared in my cubicle after lunch break.

"This is why we shouldn't have nontechnical PMs," I heard one of them whisper to another.

In truth, I wasn't sure they were wrong.

Amy came to visit.

"Save the rat jokes," I said. "Not in the mood."

"Me neither. I brought you some tea."

Hot tea was indeed better than coffee for me in my jumpy state. We sat and chatted about her new house. She complained about having to clean the gutters as the fall deepened, and there was also all the money she had to pay to clean out the HVAC ducts and make sure the sewer pipes were free of roots. "There's a lot of nooks and crannies in an old house," she said. "Lots of places for critters to roam."

"You're the only one who's been nice to me," I said, feeling a bit guilty at how aloof I'd been with her earlier.

She waved it away. "The engineers have a certain way of looking at the world. They are like the city mice who think the ability to steal cheese from a dinner table is the only skill that matters."

"And I'm the country mouse who can't tell a table apart from a chair."

"I happen to enjoy new perspectives," she said. "I didn't start out as a coder either."

"Oh?"

"I used to work at Bazaar as a warehouse packer. I had some ideas for how to improve the layout of the place to make shipping more efficient. They liked the ideas and put me in charge of solving other

problems: cable management for their server rooms, access control for secure areas in the office, that sort of thing. Turned out I had a knack for technical puzzles, and I ended up learning to code even though I never went to college. This was before they required degrees for everything."

So she'd been an outsider once too. "I'm not sure I'll ever fit in," I said.

"Don't think of it as fitting in. It's . . . more about learning a culture, being comfortable with telling your story using their lore. The engineers will come around when you can paint them a vision they can understand. A map of the obstacle course to the new cheese outside, if you will, little country mouse."

I laughed. "I've been trying. It's hard, though; there's so much to learn."

"Why did you want to work in robotics anyway? I thought you liberal arts types just wanted to teach so you could stay in school forever."

I thought about this. "It's difficult to put into words. I'm fascinated by stories, the stories we tell each other and the stories we tell about ourselves. In our world, the stories that matter the most are all stories about technology. The dreams that move people today are all soldered and welded and animated by code, or they're just spells operating in the ether. I wanted to have a part in these stories. I'm sorry, that's probably not making much sense."

"On the contrary," she said. "That's the most sensible thing I've heard from you. Technology is our poem, our ballad, our epic cycle. You may not be a coder, but you have a coder's soul."

It was possibly the oddest compliment I'd ever gotten, but I liked it. It was nice to have a friend.

After a moment, I asked, "Do you think my rat idea has a chance?"

"I don't know," she said. "I do know that if you are afraid of looking foolish, you'll never look like a genius, either."

"I thought you weren't into inspirational quotes."

"I might make fun of the myths of our corporate overlords a lot," she said. "That doesn't mean I don't enjoy seeing a good tale play out. I'm still in the Valley, the biggest dream factory on earth, after all these years, aren't I?"

Think impossible!

I decided to go straight to the source. Dr. Vignor listened to my presentation without saying a word, and then sat with his eyes closed for ten minutes, as though he had fallen asleep.

I couldn't have been that boring, could I? I was miffed. I had worked hard on the slides, citing figures and papers—admittedly I didn't understand everything I had read. And I thought the use of that animated clip-art rat was particularly inspired.

"It's worth a try," he said, eyes still closed. "We've never worked with such an advanced animal, but why not? Everything's impossible until we try."

The next few months were a blur. Pushing a new product through weRobot was one of those experiences that transformed you. Design specifications turned into cobbled-together proofs-of-concept turned into 3-D–printed models turned into handcrafted prototypes tethered to workstations running debug code. Engineers had to be herded and testers rallied and schedules drawn up and resources allocated. There were presentations to the sales staff and market research and the legal department and the supply chain.

I worked sixteen-hour days during the week—and only eight hours on the weekends because Amy programmed my computer to lock me out if I stayed too long on Saturdays ("You need some nonwork time to replenish your soul, kid. The River Temarc in winter. You don't get the reference? Here, go watch these *Star Trek* DVDs")—apologized to my sister and mother profusely for not being able to visit for their birthdays, and ignored texts and

invitations from my nonwork friends. I had to set an example for my team. How could I demand 100 percent of them if I didn't do the same for myself?

> *The* Rattus norvegicus *is the most successful mammal on the planet (other than us). Since the European Middle Ages, the species has learned to live wherever we live, making their homes in our sewers, basements, attics, and subsisting on our food and heat. Some estimate that there are as many rats in the world as humans.*

"We can't use any of this," said the guy from marketing. "We're trying to get people to buy something instead of calling exterminators. What else have you got?"

Right, the key is to tell a good story. I flipped through more slides.

> *An adult rat is so flexible that it is able to squeeze through a hole the size of a quarter. It can swim for kilometers, even staying afloat for days in extreme circumstances. It is capable of scaling smooth, vertical poles as well as scurrying up the insides of pipes, and it is skilled at navigating the maze of ducts and conduits in human dwellings, its natural habitat.*

I admired the resiliency and resourcefulness of the common rat. If they were corporate employees, they would certainly win the race.

"Let me chew on this some more—ha-ha—and get back to you," I told the marketing guy.

When you were working for the realization of a dream, work didn't seem like work at all.

* * *

In the end, the official marketing literature explained that the Vegnor was named after Dr. Vignor, the world's leading expert on nonbehavioral robotics; a good origin story was critical to a superhero.

And we sold the Vegnor as a superhero for the busy homeowner.

Imprinted with the neural patterns of R. norvegicus, the sleek little robot, a ten-inch-long segmented oblong form studded with advanced sensors and a Swiss Army knife's worth of tools, was the modern incarnation of the hearth spirit. It could scurry up downspouts and clear accumulated leaves from gutters, saving homeowners from the dirty work and the danger of falling from ladders. It could swim through the plumbing, unclogging drains and pureeing any garbage with its swirling saw-blade teeth. The flexible body squeezed through tight turns and expanded to gain purchase against vertical tubing, allowing it to wander through ducts and conduits, cleaning away gunk and crud. It patrolled the sewer connection pipes, slicing apart tree roots and dislodging toilet-paper wads. It knocked down ice dams in winters and cleaned out chimneys in summers, saving homeowners thousands of dollars a year in professional maintenance fees. It washed itself and charged itself. Best of all, it guarded a house against unwanted pests such as the common rat by emitting an annoying ultrasonic whine—and for those pests undeterred by such warning, it was capable of fighting them with gnashing teeth and glinting claws made of stainless steel.

The Vegnors flew off the shelves. Glowing reviews filled the web, and users on OurScreen posted videos of the antics of their beloved "Vegnies"—driving away snakes in Florida, crunching over scorpions in Arizona, making "speed runs" from one toilet to another in the house (to the delight of children and the befuddlement of their parents, and so this last behavior had to be patched away via an over-the-air update).

I received an invitation from Jake and Ron to attend the annual Fall Picnic held at their house. It was understood around the

company that the only attendees were the top ninety-nine employees who embodied the "weRobot way."

I had found my niche.

"Did you see the summary I sent you?" Amy asked.

"No. Yes. No." I was distracted. There was so much to do once you had some success. "What are you talking about?"

"I've been looking at micro-local trends generated by Centillion. Seems like there's an uptick in searches related to exterminators around the country."

"I'm done with rats," I said. About thirty tabs were open in my browser, each loading a page with live sales numbers from different regions, and I clicked between them impatiently.

"Take a look at the list of zip codes with the highest increases in those searches. Do you see how they correlate with Vegnor sales?"

I *hmm*'d noncommittally.

"Are you even listening? You look like one of those rats addicted to pushing a button for a random food pellet."

I looked at her, offended. "The Vegnor is selling well. I have to finish this after-action review."

She rolled her eyes. "That's just corporate nonsense. Changing the world doesn't stop with making a sale. There's a mystery here. A story."

"Customer are giving plenty of feedback online. Overwhelmingly positive."

"Just like you can't rely on customers to tell you what they want when they haven't seen it, you also can't rely on them to tell you what's wrong when they haven't figured it out."

I waved away this koan. There were always more mysteries than there were hours in the day—and I didn't have the techie disease of going down the irrelevant rabbit holes posed by random puzzles that had no relationship to the goal. I needed to summarize my experience on Vegnor into a process that could be repeated so that

I could come up with something else to top the Vegnor. In a place like weRobot, you were only as good as your next project. PMs who rested on their laurels didn't get invited to the next Fall Picnic.

Amy was about to speak again when an e-mail alert dinged on my computer.

"Sorry, I have to get this." Almost compulsively, I clicked over to the tab. I was feeling irritable these days, hoping each e-mail would be from someone important in the company, inviting me to join a team with more prestige, closer to Jake and Ron.

Wait, I chided myself. *I meant a team with projects that made a bigger impact on people's lives, right? Am I more interested in climbing the corporate ladder or changing the world? Is there a difference?*

The e-mail turned out to be from my sister, Emily. All her e-mails these days contained pictures of her new baby. Sure, I loved my nephew, but he couldn't even talk, and I was sick of watching another video of him rolling around on the floor for "tummy time." Parents were the most boring creatures on earth.

. . . Danny won't sleep . . . I think I'm going slowly insane. I can't even hear myself think. I'll pay anything . . .

". . . are you going to investigate the correlations? Aren't you even a little bit curious?"

I looked up. Somehow Amy was still standing there, babbling about something. "Isn't there some seminar you need to get to?" I asked pointedly.

She shook her head and threw up her hands in an *I give up* gesture. "Chenza at court, the court of silence," she muttered as she moved away.

I felt bad that she was feeling rejected. But I wasn't a cynical engineer too jaded to feel the thrill of changing the world. I had been to the Fall Picnic, damn it. I had a purpose.

There were close to forty-five million children under the age of twelve in the United States. Demographic trends and migration

patterns and immigration laws and regulatory pressure added to a situation where an increasing number of parents were without access to affordable, high-quality, and *trusted* child care. People were working longer hours and working harder, leaving less time and energy for their children.

Big data analytics backed up my hunch. WeRobot's web spiders crawled through parenting forums and social networks and anonymous confessplaint apps and crunched the mood and emotional content of posts by parents of young children. The dominant note was a sense of exhaustion, of guilt, of worry that they weren't doing a good job as mothers and fathers. There was little faith in day-care centers and in-home help—parents didn't trust strangers, and yet they simply couldn't do everything themselves.

It was the ultimate opportunity for a labor-saving device. What if the drudgery of parenting—the midnight feedings, the diaper changes, the perpetual and endless cleaning and picking up and laundry runs, the tantrums, the sicknesses, the monitoring and measuring mandated by pediatricians, the meting out of discipline and punishment—all could be taken care of by a perfect nanny, leaving parents only the joy of true quality time with their offspring?

"You've been reading that e-mail for ten minutes," Amy said. "That's never a good sign."

I had read the e-mail so many times that the words no longer made sense. But really, all the verbiage on the screen could be reduced to a single word.

"They said no."

To her credit, Amy said nothing. She went away and came back a few minutes later with a mug of tea and set it down on my desk. I picked it up, comforted by the warmth.

"I brought you a gift, too," she said. "I was going to give it to you when Vegnor launched, but it took longer to get ready than I anticipated—typical engineering scheduling, you know. Figure you could use a bit of cheering up."

She whistled, and a sleek Vegnor, painted black, slinked into view from beyond the cubicle wall.

"This is no ordinary Vegnie," she said. "I've reprogrammed it to be the ultimate office prankster. You can tell it to squirt hot sauce in the coffee of the marketing department or tell lawyer jokes from behind the HVAC grille in the legal group. Heck, you can even get it to steal the lunch of whichever VP just told you no. But you have to learn to speak its language."

She bent down to the little mechanical rat. "Bigwig, standing on Watership Down with ears plugged." She frowned in a pretty good impression of the VP of Product Marketing. Then she turned to me. "Want to try?"

I looked at the rat, pointed at Amy and then myself. "Darmok and Jalad at Tanagra"—Amy smiled—"Vegnie, the cheese of the Bigwig in the Labyrinth of Knossos."

The little rat chirped and scuttled away.

I clapped my hands. "That is inspired."

"I should know learning to speak Tamarian is easy for a folk and myth major."

When we finally finished giggling, I said, "I don't understand why they didn't approve my project. Given my track record on Vegnor, they should have more trust in me."

"It's not a matter of trust. The problem you're proposing to solve is too hard. People can't even agree on the best way to sleep-train a baby. How do you propose to make the perfect substitute parent?"

"That's just the result of overthinking. People don't know what they want until you show it to them."

"You're too young to understand that you should never give parenting advice."

"You're too cynical. Even if there isn't a single right answer for

something, we can always make it into a user-accessible setting."

Amy shook her head. "This isn't like designing a robot to clean the gutters. You're talking about raising other people's children. The liability issues alone will make everyone in legal faint."

"You can't let lawyers run a company," I said. "Isn't weRobot about thinking impossible? There's always a solution."

"Maybe you should create an island where there are no rules so you can experiment with technical solutions to all life's problems to your heart's content."

"That would be nice," I muttered.

"You're scaring me, kid."

I didn't answer.

Jake and Ron had always prided themselves on maintaining an entrepreneurial spirit in weRobot, even as it grew to thousands of employees. Those who got invited to the Fall Picnic were expected to get things done, not wait for orders.

So I did the natural thing: telling my team that my proposal had been approved.

The next step was to recruit Dr. Vignor to the effort.

"That's a very difficult challenge," he said.

"You're right," I said. "Probably much too hard. I'll file it away until we have the brainpower."

He came to find me that afternoon, begging to be allowed to be on the team. See, the right story is everything.

We started by gathering manuals on child care and running them through the semantic abstracter for fundamental rules of good parenting.

That . . . turned out to be a hopeless task. The manuals were about as consistent as fashion advice: for every book that advocated one approach, there were two books that argued that particular approach was literally the worst thing that one could do. Should babies be

swaddled? How often should they be held? Should you let them cry for a few minutes and learn to self-soothe or comfort them as soon as they started to fuss? There was no consensus on anything.

The academic literature was no more illuminating. Child psychology experts conducted studies that proved everything and nothing, and meta-studies showed that most of them could not even be replicated.

The science of child rearing was literally in the dark ages.

But then, while flipping through the TV channels late at night, I stopped at a nature program: *The World's Best Mothers*.

Of course, I cursed myself for my stupidity. Parenting was a solved problem in nature. Once again, the modern neurosis of overthinking had created the illusion of impossibility. Billions of years of evolution had given us the rules that we should be following. We just had to imitate nature.

Since academics had proven basically useless on this subject, in order to find my model, I turned to that ultimate fount of wisdom: the web. Every Mother's Day and Father's Day, every eyeballs-hungry site seemed to publish listicles that purported to describe the animals that qualified as the world's best mothers and fathers.

There was the orangutan, whose baby clings to the mother continuously for the first few years of its life.

There was the deep-sea octopus, *Graneledone boreopacifica*, who did nothing but guard her eggs for four and a half years—not even eating—until they hatched.

There was the elephant, who, besides a long gestational period, engaged in extensive alloparenting as members of the herd all participated to raise the babies.

And so on and so forth . . .

. . . and putting them together, I had my story: the paragon of parenting, the essence of bottled love.

I would replicate the self-sacrificing, participatory alloparenting groups of nature with robots. Busy modern urban parents didn't know their neighbors and lived away from extended family, but a network of weRobot devices would be almost as good. Our robotic vacuums, laundry folders, and Vegnors could all pitch in to keep the customers' children safe and act as playmates—incidentally, this also encouraged customers to purchase more weRobot devices, which was always a good thing. Devices from neighboring residences could also collaborate to watch over both households' children even without the parents being best friends—trust was ensured by the standardization of weRobot algorithms. The proprietary local area wireless network substituted for nonexistent or fraying social bonds.

"Mary Poppins," I vowed, "with her umbrella open!"

Dr. Vignor modeled the neural patterns driving the behaviors of dozens of animals judged to be good parents by the wisdom of the web, and after extensive software emulation, it was time to test the first prototypes.

I posted the call for volunteers on weRobot's internal network, and to my surprise and puzzlement, there weren't nearly as many takers as I had hoped.

"There aren't that many parents working here," Amy said when I complained to her. "That's not exactly a secret about this place. Look at the schedule you're keeping. It's not very compatible with starting a family, is it?"

"Even more evidence that there's a market for this product!" I said. The key to dreaming the impossible was to see opportunities where others saw only problems. "Just think of all the lost productivity due to parents not being able to devote as much time and energy to their careers because they have to run home to deal with their offspring." I was practically rubbing my hands in glee. "Marketing should be able to hint at this subtly in the TV ads. Power couples who spend less time parenting than they do at the gym ought to make a striking addition to the value proposition."

"Did you just use the phrase 'lost productivity' non-ironically?" Amy asked, shaking her head. "And 'value proposition'?"

Since there weren't enough internal volunteers, I had to expand the beta testing program by asking my team to recruit friends and family.

I found a super-scary NDA for some other weRobot project on the corporate intranet—the lawyers were good for something after all—and a few search-and-replace macros later, I had a way to ensure that no one would leak any information to competitors or the Luddite press, which was always sniffing for news about upcoming tech products that they could exaggerate into dystopian visions to sell the papers.

Emily enthused to me about the new addition to her family.

"It's incredible!" she gushed on the phone. "I've never seen Danny so well-behaved. Para changes him and feeds him and rocks him to sleep, and he loves it! Eric and I are finally able to get a good night's sleep. Everyone at work has been begging me for the number of the au pair agency I'm using."

I beamed with pride. Para was a marvel of engineering. The body-temperature, medical-grade synthskin, and the oscillator thumping at the rhythm of heartbeat were designed to calm newborns. The robot's eight arms, made of series elastic actuators for safety, and precision manipulators allowed the machine to handle delicate child-care tasks with aplomb: it could change a diaper, feed, powder, massage, tickle, and give a bath using power-delivery curves that provided maximum physical comfort to the baby, all while humming a pleasant, soft song, folding laundry, and picking up dropped toys with its extra arms.

But the crowning achievement of Para, of course, was its neural

programming. Para was the perfect parent-surrogate. It never got tired or bored; it never stopped giving the baby 100 percent of its attention; it was equipped with eons of evolutionary instinct drawn from the animal kingdom judged to suit human needs: it would protect the baby at all costs and was capable of reacting to save the child from any and all emergencies.

"I'm enjoying my time with Danny so much more now. I feel calmer, more patient, and I get to give my attention to all the fun parts of being a parent. It's incredible."

"I'm really glad," I said to my sister. I felt like a wreck. I had pushed my team to the limit, and hearing my sister being so pleased made all the hard work worth it.

Monday morning, my phone buzzed as I rode on the work shuttle. My heart clenched and then beat wildly as I read the text.

Why are Jake and Ron summoning me? There was only one answer: my skunkworks project had been discovered.

The tests with Para weren't anywhere near done. I still needed more time to produce convincing data to guarantee forgiveness.

With great trepidation, I showed up at the presidents' office on the second floor of the central building. The executive assistants quickly ushered me into a small conference room, where Ron and Jake sat at the table, stone-faced.

"I can explain," I began. "The preliminary results are very encouraging—"

"I hardly think we're in the preliminary phase anymore," Jake interrupted. He slid a tablet across the table. "Have you read this?"

It was the *New York Times*. "Home Robots Found to Be Source of Infestations," said the headline.

I quickly scanned through the article, and my heart sank. I should have paid more attention to those reports Amy had been sending me.

It turned out that the Vegnors were so good at their jobs that they were displacing real rats. The robots were, of course, programmed to fight the rats and chase them out of homes—this was touted as one of the key advantages of the machines.

Then the Vegnors replicated some of the beneficial behaviors of the rats by sweeping and collecting food and garbage from the plumbing and pipes. I had been particularly proud of this clever bit of biomimicry. I thought I was being comprehensive.

But the Vegnors only pushed the garbage away from the houses instead of eating it, which led to middens on the edges of properties that became breeding grounds for other vermin—cockroaches, maggots, fruit flies—and the cockroaches infested the houses because they were now free of rats, which had once preyed on them. Even worse, the bodies of the rats the Vegnors killed attracted coyotes, the top urban predator in many American cities.

Everyone had always thought that if all the rats in the world died tomorrow, no one would miss them. Apparently they had a role to play in the urban ecology that the Vegnors could not fully replicate.

"Our neighbors came to complain this morning," said Jake. "They have outdoor cats."

I imagined the bloody, lifeless body of Tabby, the victim of a coyote. I winced.

"And they dragged us out to the wall between our properties so they could show us the dumping ground of our Vegnor," said Ron. "The smell made me lose my breakfast."

"There's going to be a class action lawsuit," said Jake, rubbing his temples.

"You see how gleeful the plumbers and exterminators quoted in that article are?" said Ron, drumming his fingers on the table. "The Vegnors were supposed to make them no longer necessary, but our robo-rats have been creating infestations wherever they go."

I struggled to not hyperventilate. *They don't know about the skunkworks project.* My eyes looked from Ron to Jake and then back to Ron again.

"We could make a patch," I blurted out, "and get the Vegnors to collect the garbage and dispose of it safely. . . . Or we could make another robot to clean up the mess and sell them to municipal governments. . . . Or how about we patch the Vegnors to seek out cockroaches, and their eggs too? . . ."

If technology created a problem, surely the best solution was more technology.

Ron and Jake just glared at me.

The Vegnor setback meant that I had to hit Para out of the park. It was the only way to redeem my name.

While doing my best to manage the robo-rat fallout, I pushed my team and myself even harder in an effort to make the Para prototypes do more for the parents. We wanted to anticipate needs and take care of them all: the Paras could be set to implement a clock-based feeding regimen, or, in the alternate, an infant-driven feeding schedule that replicated breastfeeding; they could be configured to start sleep training at an age designated by the parents, or encourage babies to engage in the "paleo" practice of polyphasic sleep; they could be designated to play and comfort children in a variety of styles to stimulate optimal brain development; and they could even cook meals and do simple housekeeping to give exhausted parents more time to sleep and finish their work until they were ready for their offspring.

The preliminary results were promising. The feedback from the new parents was almost uniformly positive.

These robots were as devoted as the octopus, as cooperative as the elephant, as responsible as the orangutan—they really were the best nannies the parents could ever hope for. They freed moms and dads from everything unpleasant about parenting and left them only the fun parts.

* * *

"Why don't you want it?" I asked. "What did it do wrong?"

"Nothing!" said Emily. "But it doesn't feel right."

"I can fly down tonight to see—"

"I see. You can't fly down here for my birthday, but you can come on a night's notice when you think something's wrong with your robot."

I took a deep breath. "That's not fair, Emily."

"Isn't it? Since when did you become such a workaholic?"

"Don't do this to me, Em. It's my career we're talking about here! If I can't trust you to give me honest feedback, who can I trust?"

Emily sighed on the other end of the line. "I'm telling you the truth. There's nothing wrong with what Para is doing. But Eric and I don't like what it's doing to *us*."

"How do you mean?"

This *shouldn't* have happened. I had been careful from the very beginning of the Para project to avoid one of the big pitfalls with human nannies, who often elicited jealousy from parents seized by the fear that their children were building a stronger bond with the nanny than with them. This was one of the reasons that Para was not designed to be humanoid. Just as we didn't feel threatened by the housekeeping skills of automated labor-saving devices, no parent needed to worry that their child would become attached to a synthetic appliance, not fundamentally different from a self-rocking cradle.

"I don't know how to explain it." Emily sounded like she was grasping for words. "But Eric was telling me that he missed how much time he used to spend with Danny, and I feel the same way."

"But so much of that was wasted time. Para allows you to spend *quality* time, to be *efficient*." The frustrated e-mails that Emily used to send me went through my mind, as did the words of so many other surveyed mothers and fathers who complained about lack of sleep,

about how their babies turned their thoughts to mush. Children took up too much time—that was the problem to be solved.

"That's just it. I'm not sure there is such a thing as 'quality' time. Eric and I used to spend hours feeding Danny and worrying about his poop and trying to get him to sleep, and we felt tired and unprepared and stupid, but every time we looked into Danny's eyes, we felt happy. Now we pretty much just spend half an hour a day reading to him and playing with him, but even that seems too much. We get impatient. Somehow, the less time we spend with Danny, the less time we *want* to spend with him. This doesn't feel right."

Daedalus, watching the wings melt.

> . . . *the amygdala, hypothalamus, prefrontal cortex, and olfactory bulb are all activated by infant behavioral cues, which trigger adjustments in the levels of hormones such as oxytocin, glucocorticoids, estrogen, testosterone, and prolactin for the maintenance of parenting patterns. . . .*

I closed the textbook and rubbed my temples.

The sleep deprivation, the anxiety from the infant's cries, the constant worry that something so fragile and so demanding depended on you—the experience of being new parents changed people, altered the chemical composition of their blood, rewired their brains.

There was no such thing as quality time because there were no shortcuts. The very experience that bonded new parents to their children required the investment of time and energy to change them, just as their babies needed time and energy to grow.

The tedium and anxiety were inseparable from the rewards.

It was not possible to reduce parenting down to "quality time" and to outsource the difficult parts to robots—for some, perhaps

most, parents, the physical and neurological changes brought about by becoming a parent were desirable.

Really, I should have known better. Would I give up the sleepless nights and the tedious days of trying out hundreds of failed solutions in the struggle toward a successful, shipping product? The painful process was what made the victory sweet, changed me as a person, made the impossible dreams real.

"Are you leaving or are you being fired?" asked Amy, handing me a mug of tea. "I made you the good stuff. The robots here ruin good tea with tepid water."

My skunkworks project had been shut down. Once I understood that Para had no future, there was little choice but to come clean. I had cost the company a lot of money and taken on unacceptable risks. I should have been fired.

"Neither," I said, accepting the mug gratefully. "I'm being transferred to a new division."

Amy lifted an eyebrow.

"It doesn't have a name yet," I said.

"What . . . will you be doing?"

"Shaka, when the walls fell," I said.

After a moment, Amy smiled. "Ah, I see. The Unknown Unknowns."

"That's one possible name," I said. "Or maybe the Division of Country Mice."

We laughed.

Ron and Jake had decided that it was important to have a group focused on fresh perspectives. Staffed with artists, ecologists, ethicists, anthropologists, cultural critics, environmentalists, and other nonroboticists, our job would be keeping an eye on the blind spots of technical solutions. We would critique products for unanticipated consequences, gather data to detect non-obvious evidence of failure

(like those searches for exterminators), and generally act as a kind of corporate source of pessimism to counterbalance the overexuberance of the engineering staff. Having become a byword for failure at weRobot, who was better qualified to join the group than me?

"Thanks for taking over the rehabilitation projects," I said.

She waved her hand dismissively. "I've always been good at cleaning up after other engineers, probably because I never think anything is going to work in the first place. But I'll enjoy fixing your robot rats. They're cute."

"I really made a mess of things, didn't I?"

"Not entirely," said Amy. She proceeded to explain to me that with Ron and Jake's blessing, she was going to repurpose the hardware and software of Para for a much less ambitious version that would try to help overworked mothers and fathers rather than supplant them. Instead of yielding to the myth of quality time, the robots would be more cooperative, doing only what parents wanted them to do, and always ready to step back. Some advocacy groups for mothers suffering from postpartum depression had expressed interest in such a project as part of a comprehensive treatment plan.

"You had the right ideas, kid," she said. "Sometimes you step out too far and fall off the edge, but how else would you know how far you can go?"

"That sounds almost like the One True Myth."

"I'm a skeptical believer. Technology is beautiful, but it's the nature of technology to create more problems to be solved. Machines, like rats, are a part of nature, and our lives are embedded within each other. Hephaestus, his hammer raised."

"That reminds me," I said. "I'll need you to come by my office next week."

"What for?"

"We are going to do a brain dump with you—"

"That's impossible—"

"I didn't mean literally! Besides, how do we know it's impossible if we don't try?"

I couldn't keep a straight face long enough to fool her. But I could tell she came *this* close to falling for it.

"I'm *not* going to be scanned into a robot," she said.

"I want you to come and tell some stories, infect everyone with a bit of your cynicism. I think that's going to be really useful."

Amy nodded. "Gimli, his ax ready."

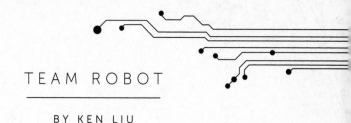

TEAM ROBOT

BY KEN LIU

I love to write about robots because I'm pretty sure they're going to rule the world one day. In preparation for that inevitable future, it seems wise to lay the groundwork to show that I can be useful to our robot overlords—for example, as a human bard to praise the glory of robot kind.

(P.S. In case the humans win, please read the previous paragraph as mere cover to allow me to be an effective saboteur and infiltrate the robot central command.)

(P.P.S. But in case the robots win, please read the previous paragraph as an attempt to gain the trust of the human resistance for robotic purposes.)

(P.P.P.S. I'm thinking now it might have been easier to be on Team Fairy. . . .)

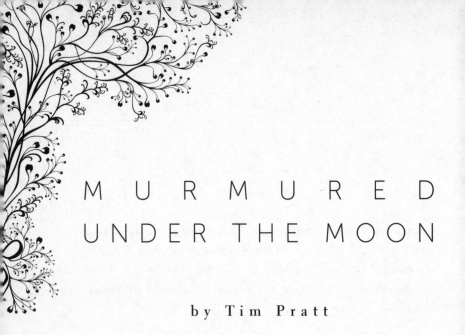

MURMURED UNDER THE MOON

by Tim Pratt

Emily Yuan, the mortal head of Rare and Sentient Special Collections at the fairy library, took a different route to work every day. Some mornings she left her house in Oakland, walked along the sidewalk, turned a corner, and found herself stepping into her office in that other realm. Other days she strolled down to the shores of Lake Merritt, where a mystic fog on the water would part to reveal a small, jewel-encrusted boat—a fairy ferry, her friend and coworker CeCe joked—for her to ride across strange liminal waters to the island that housed the library. One morning she'd opened her shower curtain and found, instead of the bathtub, the library's front desk. That had been embarrassing, and she'd asked the facilities department to tweak the commute spell.

The morning the library was invaded and sacked, the weather was all gloomy, rainy October, so she opted for a strictly indoor commute after finishing her toast and jam. "Did you want to come in with me?" she asked her girlfriend, Llyfyr.

Llyfyr had green skin and wore a gown of living leaves that

morning; she smelled like a forest after rain. She lifted her head from the kitchen table and blinked at Emily. "I read too much poetry last night. I'm still drunk. I think I'll just linger here. There's a volume of Goldbarth in the living room I haven't read yet. Hair of the dog." Her head dropped back down.

Emily kissed Llyfyr on the crown of her head and said, "See you later." Emily had discovered Llyfyr in the deep stacks of the library when she first got hired, two years before, and they'd both been smitten straightaway. No one loved books like a librarian. Once Emily got used to the strangeness of dating a shape-shifting living book, they'd settled into a relationship of lazy weekends and quiet evenings and enjoyably active nights. In book form, Llyfyr was a fantasy love story, which made her whimsical and romantic; Emily was one of the only people who'd ever read her cover to cover. As a living book, Llyfyr called the fairy library home, but she had the autonomy to check herself out whenever she liked, and often stayed over with Emily in the mortal world.

Time to get to work. Any door would do. Emily picked up her bag and walked to the nearest closet, directed her mind toward the day's tasks—helping researchers, continuing to catalogue the depths of the rare book archive, shepherding along the digital conversion and preservation projects—and opened the door.

She'd wanted to walk straight into her office, but instead she stepped into the outdoors, at the base of the stone steps that switch-backed up to the library from the dock. She frowned, but fairy magic was unreliable by nature, and at least it wasn't raining here in the fey realm. The morning was cool and partly cloudy, as usual, and glittering waters surrounded the rocky island as far as her human eyes could see. She started up the stairs—*I could probably use the exercise*—and halfway up became aware of a commotion.

When she reached the top of the stairs, she saw a crowd of three dozen people milling around on the steps in front of the stately stone vastness of the fairy library. The immense carved wooden doors were closed, as usual—they only opened when one of the rare giant patrons visited—but the smaller inset doors were closed too, and that was decidedly unusual. Even more unusual: a pair of tall, slender guards wearing gilded armor stood blocking the doors, holding spears with nasty-looking complex barbs on the ends. The guards looked more bored than menacing, but something very serious must be going on. The library was full of valuables and had its own security in the form of the formidable Miss Ratchet and her hounds, but Emily had never seen soldiers like these before.

Two of the Folk—they preferred that name to "fairies," as a rule, though they also responded well to any kind of compliment—hurried toward Emily. They were frequent researchers engaged in long and bewildering scholarly projects, and quite familiar to her. Mr. Ovo was an immense smooth white egg with arms and legs, dressed in trousers and a waistcoat, and the Kenning was an anthropomorphic metaphor who looked like a crow-headed undertaker today. The Kenning squawked and Mr. Ovo signed too rapidly for her to follow—the only words Emily picked up were "outrage" and "theft"—but fortunately, her assistant Faylinn came over too.

Faylinn was an ancient fairy woman with the upright mien of a Victorian governess, her eyes featureless spheres the color of quicksilver. After some initial resistance to having a mortal boss, she'd become devoted to Emily, mostly because Emily had started a scanning project that allowed researchers to examine the contents of rare books on computer screens instead of *touching* the beloved volumes with their filthy hands. She wrung her long, ink-stained hands. "Emily, something terrible has happened. We've all been barred from the library—and look!" She pointed, and Emily lifted her eyes to see winged fairies the size of children streaming out of the sides of the crystal dome atop the library—she hadn't even realized there were windows that opened up there. Each fairy carried a small cargo net full of—

"Where are they taking the *books*?" she gasped.

"No one knows!" Faylinn said. "I thought it was theft at first, and I cast a summoning to call Miss Ratchet, but when she appeared, she told me the library was closed and the resources were being reallocated on the orders of Mellifera."

"That—what—that doesn't make any sense. Wait." Emily took her phone from her bag. There was no cell service here—they weren't even in the mortal world, though she'd never seen any of the fey realm beyond this island—but she could always reach Mellifera, the fairy woman who'd hired her and had ultimate authority over the library. Emily poked at the honeybee icon on her screen . . . but instead of connecting her to Mellifera, the bee flew off the side of her screen and vanished.

That was troubling. Emily marched up the steps to the guards and poked one in the chest plate. He looked at her and frowned, his long, narrow face transforming from bored beauty to cruel sneer. "Begone, mortal. Your kind has no place here."

"Mellifera hired me personally to oversee the most valuable part of the library—"

"There is no more library. Just a building that will soon be empty of books. Be *gone*." He grabbed her shoulder, spun her around, and shoved her—

—and she stumbled out of her closet, into the hallway in her apartment. Her phone buzzed with a text from her former roommate and current best friend, CeCe. Emily had hired CeCe to help modernize the library, and CeCe had put in computer terminals and started an ambitious project to scan and digitize the rare volumes. The text read, **Tried to go to work and couldn't find a path, just walked in circles. What's up?**

Not sure, Emily texted back. **Looking into it.**

Emily walked through the house, calling, "Llyfyr!" There was no sign of her girlfriend in the bedroom or the living room, though she found a volume of poetry on the living room floor, pages splayed open. That was odd. Llyfyr was usually gentle with books. Emily tried not to worry. Sometimes Llyfyr took on a more human-looking guise and went on walks, but she usually left a note (her handwriting was exactly the same as the typeface that filled her in book form). She'd probably expected to be back before Emily got home, that was all, but—

"Are you Emily Yuan?"

Emily spun around. The armchair in the corner was occupied by a woman—no, she was Folk, her ears pointed and her smile revealing sharp teeth—dressed in black. Her long dark hair seemed to sparkle, as if stars were caught in the shadowy waves. She looked like a theatrical pirate, right down to the cutlass resting across her knees.

Emily resisted the urge to back up a step. As a rule, the Folk scorned the fearful. "Who are you?"

"I'm Sela. We have a mutual friend who needs our help. Mellifera?"

"I'm . . . not sure she's my friend."

Sela chuckled. "Nor mine, really, but we've known each other for a long time. Mellifera recruited you, though, to run her library?"

"I don't know what you're doing here—"

"I'm here to help you get your precious library back, but if you'd rather return to your mortal life—" She began to rise.

Emily held up her hands. "Fine, yes, Mellifera hired me. Over two years ago now."

"Why did she pick you?"

"I'd just been fired from my job at a university library because of budget cuts, and I was in the train station with a box of all my personal items from work, waiting to go home, when I saw a woman sitting on the edge of the platform, her legs dangling over the tracks. She seemed upset, so I asked her if she was all right, and shared a chocolate bar I'd had in my desk. That was Mellifera. The next day I got a job offer . . . and found out magic was real."

Sela nodded. "If you show one of the Folk kindness without motive, you will receive kindness in return."

Emily bristled. "I didn't get the job just because I was *nice*. I'm qualified, and I've totally transformed the collection. It's almost entirely catalogued. We're digitizing and preserving—"

"Peace, mortal. I never meant to impugn your skills. Mellifera is practical, and I'm sure you're good at your job. I was just curious how a mortal came to hold such a position, and, I confess, I hoped that she'd hired you because you had some deep knowledge of magic."

"I mean, I know what I've read, and been told. . . ."

"Yes. Well. Mellifera is in danger, Emily—"

"Mellifera *is* the danger! The library was closed by her order." Mellifera had always been aloof and superior, and was terrible to behold in anger, but she'd always shown Emily a measure of respect and even distant affection. To take away Emily's job, what she'd expected to be her life's work, without even a conversation, was immeasurably cruel.

Sela shook her head. "Not of her own free will. Mellifera is not herself, but you might be able to help me fix that, even if you aren't a sorcerer. I understand that as librarian you have been granted certain powers? That you can summon books?"

Emily nodded. "Yes. The archive is vast, and as part of the cataloguing magic, I can call any volume in the collection to my hand." She touched the necklace around her throat, where an enchanted pewter charm in the shape of a book dangled.

"Excellent. I need you to call up a volume of poetry called *Murmured Under the Moon*."

"Who's the author?"

"Mellifera."

"*Really?*" Emily closed her eyes, murmured the incantation, and held out her hands. No book appeared.

"A shame." Sela stood, sheathing her cutlass at her belt. "Mellifera's soldier must have disenchanted your necklace before he shoved you off the island."

"Wait!" Emily thought of a book at random—one of the volumes from the Subterranean Warfare section, *Under Hill and Kill and Kill*, a firsthand account of something called the Battle of Fallen Barrow. The hardbound book appeared in the air and dropped a few inches into her waiting hands, and she brandished it. "See? The magic works. I couldn't call that other book because it was never part of the collection. I've never heard of a book like that. I had no idea Mellifera was a writer. I only have a score of books authored by your kind."

Sela sighed. "Ah, well, it was a long shot. The Folk don't produce much art, and don't often share what they do. I thought Mellifera's vanity might have led her to include the book in the collection, but it seems not. Too bad. Good-bye, mortal."

"Stop. What is going on? What's happened to Mellifera?"

"She's under a powerful enchantment, and I need to save her."

"Who enchanted her? I thought the Folk were immune to that kind of thing! And what does it have to do with this poetry collection?"

The fairy leaned against the door frame. She looked almost amused. "It's not just poetry. It's *love* poetry. Long ago Mellie fell in love with a mortal, wrote poems to him—in her own hand!— and had them bound, intending the poems as a gift." Sela shook her head. "One night several centuries ago, during the new moon in October, she opened a passage from our world to the mortal's house and read her poems to him. She wanted to lure him through, to stay with her forevermore. There is magic in such an act, you know—for a princess of the Folk to murmur such things under the moon. The man *refused* her, though, choosing his own mortal family instead. He must have had tremendous strength of will, because when Mellie wants to charm someone, they are generally well charmed." Sela sighed. "Unfortunately, his refusal created a sort of . . . unresolved spell, deeply embedded in the pages of the book. Someone in possession of those poems, with the right knowledge, at the right time, can use it to reopen that passage between worlds and charm Mellie as she tried to charm her would-be lover—by symbolically *becoming* that lover."

"Someone got the book and cast that spell?"

"A mortal student of the occult named Rudolph . . . something, I forget. We haven't had time to gather much information on him. The new moon was two days ago. Mellifera left our realm without explanation, and then directed her subjects to loot our precious works of art and volumes of lore. Obviously, having a princess of the Folk in thrall to a mortal isn't ideal. I have . . . certain skills, and was tasked with solving this problem. Destroying the book will destroy the enchantment, but since you can't summon the poems, I'll have to use other means."

"I can help," Emily said. "I have certain skills too."

"Hmm." Sela looked Emily up and down. "There could be advantages to having a mortal along. This enchanter may have protections against the Folk that you could more easily circumvent. Very well." She rose and strode down the hall. Emily went after her, but Sela walked fast, and soon the familiar hallway was gone, the plaster walls becoming dark wood, the hardwood floor turning to stone. The corridor took many sharp right-angle turns, and though Emily moved along quickly, she kept losing sight of Sela, finally calling, "Wait!"

"Hurry!" came the call back. Emily gritted her teeth and ran. When she rounded the last corner she almost slammed into Sela, who stood on a tiny wooden platform in what looked like a cave, with train tracks running out of one tunnel and into another. "Just in time," Sela said, as a vehicle slid smoothly from the tunnel and stopped before them.

Emily had seen Mellifera's private train before, a sort of jeweled steampunk Fabergé egg on wheels, but this was something different: Sela's train looked like an old-fashioned horse-drawn carriage with a closed coach, made of black wood with silver trim. The door swung open, and a folding set of steps spilled downward. Sela climbed inside, and after a moment's hesitation, Emily followed.

The door closed after her, and the interior was totally dark, revealing that the sparkles in Sela's hair *did* cast their own light. Emily groped her way to a sumptuously padded bench and sat down across from the fairy woman just as the car lurched forward. "Why is it so dark in here?"

"We're going to a place in the mortal world, but it's faster to take shortcuts through my realm. On the way, we will pass through tunnels where there are things that covet light. Our lands border . . . less pleasant countries. There are safer routes, but I want to get to Mellifera as quickly as possible."

"You said you and Mellifera are friends?"

"We're . . . sisters, or close enough. We spent our formative years together, anyway, but when we were done forming, we turned out rather differently. I choose to live outside the court of the Folk and dwell largely outside our lands. Occasionally I am called upon to render services in exchange for the freedoms I enjoy. This is one such occasion. The court can't tolerate a mortal holding one of us in thrall."

Emily's grasp of fairy culture outside the boundaries of the library was tenuous at best. There were books about the subject, but they were wildly contradictory, and the Folk she spoke to about the subject were maddeningly oblique. "The court. Like, royalty? Is Mellifera some kind of queen?"

"Mmm. Perhaps a princess. We *have* a queen, but she sleeps, most of the time, and lets her daughters oversee things, with the work divided among them according to their inclinations and capabilities. Mellifera says it's more like a board of directors than a proper court. Dull, really. Mellifera is sort of . . . minister of cultural affairs, you could say? She has ultimate authority over the libraries, museums, concert halls, and other such things. The Folk value the arts greatly—Mellifera's position is one of great power and prestige."

"Which she's abusing, or being forced to abuse. Can't she be replaced, before this enchanter steals everything?"

Sela chuckled. "It's not that easy. Mellifera was given her powers by the queen, and only the queen can revoke them. We have no reason to expect our mother to awaken before the solstice at the earliest. In the meantime, within her sphere, Mellifera's power is absolute."

"Your system of government has some flaws."

Sela nodded. "I always thought so."

"Are you a princess too?"

"I would be, had I not given all that up. You can't lose your responsibilities without also losing your privileges, but I care about my freedom more than anything the court can offer me."

The carriage lurched to a stop. "We're here." The door swung open, and they emerged onto a rocky beach under a gray sky amid eddies of fog. Emily turned to look back at the coach, but it was gone. Nothing behind them but waves crashing against great rugged outcroppings of stone.

"Where's here?" Emily shivered. She was wearing black trousers and a white blouse and flats. She wasn't dressed for a cold beach.

"Some coast or another. It's nearly twilight. Good. That's when my powers are strongest."

Emily looked at her phone, which agreed that it wasn't yet lunchtime, suggesting they were in some time zone other than the one she'd started in. She had no phone service here, naturally, and no way to tell where they were.

Sela pointed toward a nearby sea cliff, and the fog parted as if moved aside by her gesture—perhaps it had been. Emily could just see the upper floor of a building perched up there, a foreboding thing of gray stone and few windows. "Mellifera went into that building, and has not come out. Our scryers can't see what's happening inside—there are powerful enchantments in place, and lots of iron, which all confound us."

"Is the enchanter in there? Is that where he's taking the books?"

"Perhaps." Sela glanced at her. "Isn't your lover one of those living books that walk around like people?"

"They *are* people. Yes, Llyfyr and I are together."

"Are you worried *she* was taken by the enchanter?"

Emily shook her head. "She was in my house this morning, not at the library."

"Yes, but *I* got into your house easily enough, and one of Mellifera's servants could have too. The enchanter's interest seems to be in the most potent magical books, naturally, and that would include the living books—"

Emily thought of the volume of poems sprawled open on the floor, and a cold spike of fear pierced her. She'd assumed Llyfyr was okay because she hadn't been at the library when it was besieged, and with everything that was happening, she hadn't had time to fret over other possibilities until now. "Let me call her." Emily put her hand to the charm at her throat and murmured the incantation to call Llyfyr.

Nothing happened. "That . . . The living books have personal agency; unlike the nonsentient books, they can refuse a summons, but Llyfyr *always* comes when I call!"

"Perhaps she can't. There could be spells of binding in there, cages of iron. . . ." Sela shrugged. "If she's inside, we'll save her. I don't suppose you can fight?"

"I don't have to do much violence in my line of work."

"I'll focus on the fighting, then. You look for Mellifera's book. I'm not sure what to expect. If Mellifera is there, her guards are too, but they would bristle at taking orders directly from a mortal, so Rudolph may have other resources. He certainly knows about the weaknesses of the Folk, and is likely to have measures in place to confound us.

Come." They walked across the gritty sand in silences contemplative and anxious until they reached the base of the cliff. Sela gestured again, and fog swirled away, this time revealing what looked like a mine cart made of black wood and silver, resting against the bottom of the cliff. "Here we are. It's a sort of elevator. I don't mind climbing a cliff freehand with a dagger in my teeth, but I thought you'd prefer something less taxing." One side of the cart swung open, and they stepped in. The quarters were close, and Emily was pressed against Sela, who smelled, not unpleasantly, of leather and brine.

The cart jerked and began to ascend, though there were no signs of cables. There could be some kind of hydraulic piston under-neath . . . but Emily knew it was driven by fairy magic.

They reached the top of the cliff, with just a narrow ledge of stone between them and the wall of the house. The other side of the cart swung open, and Sela stepped out, walking casually along that nar-row strip of solid ground, knocking her knuckles against the wall in a few places. She hissed. "Iron in the walls, along with binding spells, so I can't open a door. Not surprising, but frustrating."

"Ah. Those countermeasures you mentioned." Not all the stories were true, but the bits about iron being anathema to fairies were.

"Yes. But there's got to be a proper door somewhere." Sela walked along the ledge toward the corner of the house, apparently unconcerned by the hundred-foot drop on her right. Emily eased along the wall much more slowly and carefully. She didn't have a particular fear of heights, but she could see herself developing one, given the circumstances. Once she made her way around the corner of the house, away from the cliff's edge, she felt better. The land around them was flat and barren—it looked almost scoured—and the house was no less forbidding from a different angle. They walked around to the front and found a thick wooden door, banded with dark iron.

"Ha. This, I can deal with." Sela pressed her hands against the wood, between the iron bands, and after a moment, small mushrooms popped out of the wood, first a few, then dozens, then hundreds. The door sagged, the wood rotting, and Sela kicked with her high black boots, sending up puffs of powder and rot. Soon the "door" was nothing but three black bars crossing an empty doorway. "Be a dear and shove those aside?"

Emily pulled on the iron bars, which were still attached to hinges, and they swung outward. Sela peered inside, into a wood-paneled foyer with an intricate tiled floor. "I sense guardians." She grunted. "From the Mist Realm. Rudolph has made a political alliance with enemies of our queen, it seems."

"What's the Mist Realm?"

"A place of monsters. Though they'd say the same about the fey realm."

"Can you fight them?"

"Ha. Not with this sword, or my magic. I know Mellifera probably gave you the impression the Folk seem all-powerful, but most of our powers are limited to nature magic, glamours, and minor reality-warping—making milk go sour, bending space-time, things like that. Fighting denizens of the Mist Realm is beyond my abilities." She growled. "We were hoping to keep this operation quiet, but I may need to find reinforcements. I hate to give Rudolph time to consolidate his position further."

"Wait. You need fighters? Even if they've taken Llyfyr, they might not have captured *all* the living books, especially the really cunning ones, who like to hide. . . ." Emily touched her charm and murmured an incantation.

A battered volume bound in black leather dropped into her outstretched hands. She opened the book, murmured to the pages, and in an eyeblink the book was gone, replaced by a crouching woman dressed in a cloak of moss, with green hair and eyes like gray river stones. Her hands were clawed, and each claw was a different color and texture: amber, ivory, obsidian, silver, emerald, wood, and others Emily couldn't identify.

"Who's this?" Sela said.

"She's never bothered giving herself a name other than her title: *A Manual of Unconventional Warfare.*"

"Sometimes Emily calls me Connie." The book's voice was low and rough. "Do you know why the Folk are trying to pillage the library, Em? They made off with half the archive before the living books got organized. We formed a defensive line, and we're keeping the looters out of the deep stacks, but it's only a matter of time before the soldiers break through." The living books were a strange crowd, perhaps fifty volumes that could take on forms ranging from the humanoid to the monstrous, depending on their contents and inclinations. They would be a formidable force to overpower, but Emily quailed at the thought of them being damaged in fighting. The living books were the closest thing she had to family—she thought of them almost as her family, even if they were all centuries older than she was.

"Mellifera is being mind-controlled by a mortal," Emily said. "We think the enchanter is inside, but there are . . . things in the way."

"Sentinels from the Mist Realm," Sela said. "Can you fight such creatures? I can't—they can choke and poison me but are too incorporeal for me to strike."

Connie chuckled, then held up her claws. All of them sparked and glittered and glowed and rippled with diverse magics. "I have a key for every lock and a knife for every throat, and I've never yet grown weary of battle." She rushed into the foyer, smashed through a door, and disappeared from sight. Sela and Emily followed at a safe distance as a great howling emerged from within, like winds whipping through narrow mountain passes, but also a little like screams. The stars in Sela's hair seemed to glow brighter, providing sufficient light to illuminate their passage as they went deeper into the dark house. The place was huge, and the rooms were filled with paintings in ornate frames, antique furniture, statues, vases, and all manner of museum-quality relics, presumably looted by Rudolph from fey lands. There were magic items too: a mirror that reflected a sky with two suns; a harp that played itself softly as they walked by; a statue that wept what looked like real tears.

Sela ignored it all and pointed to scuffs in the dust. "See, Connie fought here, and continued on. . . ." They went up a wide staircase to the second-floor landing, and Sela continued tracking the living book's passage until they found Connie herself in a hallway, facing off against an eight-foot-tall figure that looked like a suit of armor made from white smoke.

"Mist wraith," Sela hissed. "Warrior caste, looks like a war-band leader, so Connie must have cut down its subordinates. You have good taste in books, librarian."

The wraith conjured a long-handled ax from smoke and swung, but Connie rolled underneath the blow and lashed out with her glowing claws, shredding the thing's legs into misty ribbons. The wraith fell, making a strange howl like wind whistling through a crack in a wall, and Connie tore its helmet off and crouched over its rippling form, raking her claws through the smoke. When the living book stood and limped back toward Emily, there was nothing left of the wraith but a dissipating patch of ground fog.

"Are you all right?" Emily knew living books were hard to hurt permanently, short of total destruction, but Connie seemed wounded at least.

"Tore my flyleaf nearly in half," she muttered. "Just let me rest." She collapsed into book form again, and Emily picked her up and tucked the volume under her arm.

"She'll be all right," Emily said. "She just needs time to repair herself. Are we safe?"

Sela sniffed the air. "I don't sense any denizens of the Mist Realm—Connie dispersed them all. I do sense Folk, though—"

The door at the end of the hall burst open, and two tall guards, twins to those at the library, burst out, pointing their spears at Sela's and Emily's throats. Sela dropped back two steps and brought up her cutlass, smacking aside the barbed end of the spear—was it made of *iron*? Emily didn't dare twitch.

"What's the commotion?" Mellifera appeared at the door, regal and cool as always, dressed in a gown that shimmered like a midnight ocean. "Lower your weapons! This is my beloved sister, and my dear mortal librarian. Come in, come in! See my new throne room."

The guards exchanged an indecipherable look, then lowered their spears and moved aside. Mellifera disappeared into the chamber, still chattering, and Sela sheathed her sword. She glared at the guards. "You collaborate with the Mist Realm now?"

One guard lowered his eyes. "We are bound to serve Mellifera . . . whatever we may think of her orders."

Sela sighed. "True enough. That's one reason I'm not a princess anymore, Emily—I don't like the idea of binding people to my will. Let everyone be free, I say. Come on." She led the way, and Emily followed, gasping at the opulence beyond the door. The room was as big as a ballroom, perhaps enhanced with illusory or spatial magic, and it was full of magical and mundane light: shining chandeliers, standing lamps, countless candles, floating orbs of light. The walls were all mirrored, reflecting the luminosity, and the only furniture in the room shone: two thrones, side by side, both mostly gold, one rather more large and ornate than the other.

Mellifera sat on the smaller of the two chairs. "It's so good to see you, Sela. I have so much to tell you! I've fallen in love. He's a mortal, and I know you disapprove, but he has the most *wonderful* ideas. We're going to kill Mother, you see, and then I will rule as queen, though my sweet Rudolph will be king—isn't it time we had a king? We will ally the mortal and the fey and misty realms forever, tearing down all the walls that separate us—"

Sela said, "Mellifera, where's the book of poems?"

"What do you mean, dear sister? If you need a book, you should ask Emily. I want her to be our personal palace librarian, you know. Once Rudolph has all the books moved here, I'm sure he'll need someone to help organize them—"

"*Murmured Under the Moon!*" Sela said. "Where is it?"

Mellifera scowled, and the lights all around them dimmed. "Don't speak of my past . . . infatuations, sister. I wouldn't want to make Rudolph jealous." She brightened, and the room did with her. "We should discuss plans for my wedding!"

Sela tried again. "You've been enchanted, Mellifera, by mortal magic—"

"Oh, nonsense. I *enthrall.* I am not enthralled myself. Now, I was thinking, we could hold the ceremony in the old winter palace. . . ."

Emily cleared her throat. "Could I see the library? If I'm going to be working here, it would be nice to have a look."

"Oh, of course, dear." Mellifera gestured to the right. "One of the guards will show you the way."

Sela shot her a warning look, but Emily just offered a reassuring smile. If Llyfyr *was* trapped here, she'd be in the library.

One of the slender Folk in armor glided toward her and gestured. When they were some distance from the thrones, he whispered, "Please set her free."

"I'll try," she murmured, though saving her boss was less important to her than saving her love.

The guard pressed on a mirror, and it swung open. She stepped through into what looked like the library of a great country house, a handsome room with towering wooden shelves, lamps, long wooden tables, and club chairs. There were thousands of volumes, and a quick perusal of a nearby shelf assured her that most, if not all, were from the fairy library. She went deeper into the room and realized there was some spatial trickery here: there were freestanding walls of shelves, forming passages and corridors, winding deeper and deeper through the house.

She'd been unable to summon Llyfyr from outside, but now that she was *in* the library, perhaps the binding spells didn't apply. She touched her charm and whispered for Llyfyr.

Her lover appeared before her, looking like a black-and-white photograph of a classic movie star, with dark pageboy curls and a pale gown, but her face was, as always, unmistakable. She embraced Emily fiercely. "They *came* for me, Mellifera's soldiers, and I was dragged here. There's a man—"

"And what a man I am." A sallow twentysomething with messy hair stepped around a shelf. He wore an old-fashioned red velvet dressing gown and held a shotgun, as incongruous a sight as Emily had ever seen. "This gun is loaded with iron shot. It's meant to cripple fairies, but it would work fine on you, too. Who are you, and what are you doing here?"

"I'm—my name is Emily. I'm a librarian."

"Ah, you must be Mellifera's pet. Did the court send you to find the book of poems? Librarians are supposed to be good at finding books. I'm sure you'll manage. It's probably tucked away here somewhere. You only have thousands of volumes to sort through." He cocked his head. "They wouldn't have sent you alone, though, and why didn't the Mist Folk kill you when you entered?"

The book tucked under Emily's arm squirmed, and she let it fall. Connie shape-shifted into her humanoid form and stepped between Emily and Rudolph. "I killed your guards. Give us the book of poems, or I'll kill *you*."

"No." Rudolph lifted the gun and fired, and though Connie moved with inhuman speed, she was still hurt from her fights with the Mist Folk, and she wasn't fast enough. The iron shot tore through her, and she spun, changing back into a book before she hit the ground, her pages tattered and torn.

Llyfyr shrieked, but Emily just stared. Connie was one of *hers*, one of the volumes under her protection, and this arrogant prick had *hurt* her. She looked up as Rudolph took shells from his pocket and broke open the shotgun to reload. "Mellifera is fond of you," he said, "the way my mother is fond of her cats, but she *loves* me, and she'll understand if I have to kill you—"

Emily touched the locket at her throat and called the books to her. All of them. All at once.

She held out her open hands before her, toward Rudolph. Thousands of books blinked out of existence, leaving the shelves around them bare, and then reappeared in midair. Emily and Llyfyr dove out of the way as books rained down, landing on Rudolph's head and shoulders, knocking the gun from his hands, driving him to his knees, and burying him under a mountain of hardbound volumes that towered taller than Emily's head.

She winced at the sight of the books piling up, but almost all of them were protected by preservative magics to keep the pages from tearing or deteriorating, which should minimize the damage.

Llyfyr laughed and leaped to her feet, spinning around and skipping. "You did it, you got him, you—"

"What is the *meaning* of this?" Mellifera roared. She stormed toward them, her two guards at her back. Emily winced. They'd defeated Rudolph, but not the spell he'd used to bind the fairy princess. Mellifera grew taller with each step she took, until she towered nearly eight feet high. Even knowing it was probably glamour, Emily shrank away in alarm. A hazy yellow-and-black nimbus formed around Mellifera, accompanied by an ominous buzzing. Bees drifted up from her hair and flew out of her sleeves, and a few even slipped out of her mouth when she cried, "Where is my love?" Soon a cloud of buzzing, stinging insects surrounded her: a manifestation of her temper, terrible and beautiful to behold.

One of her guards reached out for Mellifera's arm, perhaps to hold her back from rushing into possible danger, then shrieked and stumbled away as a score of Mellifera's bees swarmed around his head. The guard waved his arms wildly and raced down the corridor, flesh welted and swelling. Mellifera didn't even notice.

Sela raced around and got ahead of her sister, stepping between her and Emily. "We heard a gunshot, and then this *noise*—"

Llyfyr stepped forward and curtsied to Mellifera, who was now nearly invisible beneath a curtain of undulating bees. "Ma'am, there was an accident, you see, *all* the books fell down, but Emily is going to fix it, with her . . . librarian . . . prowess. Aren't you, Em?"

"Where. Is. *Rudolph?*" Mellifera's voice thundered from beyond the cloud.

"Emily will look for him while she's fixing the books, won't you?" Sela called. "It's all right, sister." She made soothing motions.

Mellifera's arm appeared from the cloud of bees and pointed straight at Emily. "Fix. This. Or you will feel my sting."

"I—of course." Emily clambered around the edge of the mountain of books piled on Rudolph and made her way deeper into the stacks. She tried to ignore the buzzing behind her. She'd called all the books from the library to her, emptied the shelves in this place, but *Murmured Under the Moon* wasn't *from* her library. She couldn't summon it, and that meant—

There: one book still standing on a shelf, hidden in plain sight. She climbed up the shelf like it was a ladder and snatched the book down. The cover looked right for the era, leather over wood, with raised bands across the spine, and the pages were vellum, covered in elegant handwriting and lines of poetry in Latin.

In the distance she heard Mellifera shouting and making demands, Sela arguing with her, and Llyfyr trying to keep the peace. Emily started to tear out the pages, but something in her rebelled—she was a *librarian*. She was supposed to take care of books, especially one-of-a-kind books, and not destroy them. She cocked her head. The shouting didn't sound *too* serious, not yet, and it was a short book, so maybe she had time—

A few minutes later, content that she'd done the best she could, Emily tore out the pages. Mellifera was still yelling back there. How destroyed did the book have to *be*? She sighed, tore up a page, and put the pieces in her mouth, chewing and swallowing the shreds of vellum, hoping the ink wasn't toxic.

She'd eaten only one page when the shouting stopped. Emily crept back toward the book pile and saw Sela with her arms wrapped around her sister as Mellifera wept on her shoulder. Emily made her way toward them, and Llyfyr took her hand. "Whatever you did, it worked."

"I ate a book," Emily said.

"Now you're just trying to make me jealous," Llyfyr said.

A week later Mellifera and Sela stood in Emily's small office. Mellifera was beautiful, ageless, and strange, as befitted a princess of the Folk, and she wore a sea-green gown that rippled like water. Sela was her same piratical self, lounging and self-satisfied. "Is everything back in order?" Mellifera asked.

Emily nodded. "More or less. There wasn't too much damage. Thanks for sending the extra hands to help get everything back in place."

"It was the least I could do."

"What, ah, happened to Rudolph?" The rain of books hadn't killed him, just knocked him out, but the fairy guards had whisked him away as soon as they uncovered him. Mellifera had been known to lay curses on mortals who offended her or slighted her—who knew what she would do to someone who'd *enslaved* her?

"He is making himself useful," Mellifera said. "I have turned him into a living hive in my garden. I look forward to tasting the honey my bees make inside him."

Emily swallowed. Mellifera was so light and nonchalant about it. She opted not to press for further details.

Sela saved them from an awkward silence by saying, "I came by to thank you for helping me, Emily. I couldn't have done it without you."

"That's sweet," Emily said, "but I know you're really here to pick up Connie. She's been talking for days about going on adventures with you. She never did like being cooped up in a library."

"I can be here for *two* reasons. I'm complex." Sela turned to Mellifera. "I'll leave you to it, sister."

"We'll talk soon." Mellifera gave her a kiss on the cheek and watched her go.

Emily cleared her throat. "I have something for you. Before I destroyed your book of poems, I photographed the pages with my phone, and I made . . . this." She slid a small volume out of a drawer. "It's a facsimile edition. Sela said only the original, written in your own hand, had those . . . problematic properties, so . . ." She handed the volume over. "I read them. It's really beautiful work."

The Folk loved compliments, especially sincere ones, and Mellifera grew more luminous. She turned the book over in her hands. "Oh, Emily, how thoughtful. You're very kind. Some say the Folk cannot create art, not as humans do, but that's not true. We simply understand that art is magic, and more magical than usual when we're the ones making it, and so we're very careful." She sighed. "Usually, anyway. But my feelings when I composed these poems were real, even if they were foolish."

Emily said, "I made a second copy, and I wondered, could I include it in the collection here? I don't have many books by the Folk."

Mellifera laughed like small bells. "Of course. I've administered this library for . . . a long time . . . but never expected to contribute to its holdings. I'm honored." She cleared her throat. "Going out into the world, helping Sela, helping *me* . . . that sort of thing isn't why you were hired. What you did was above and beyond. I owe you a boon. What can I give you?"

Emily went very still. A fairy, offering her whatever she wanted. As a teenager she would have asked for true love, but she had that with Llyfyr, or true enough. In her youth she'd dreamed of unicorns, but the practicalities of keeping one would be daunting. She could ask for wings, but she'd have to throw out all her clothes, and she tended to get airsick anyway. . . . But there was only one thing she really wanted.

"I want the library."

Mellifera cocked her head. "What do you mean?"

"I want what you have. Total control of this library. So that if there's ever, ah, another problem, like the one we just had, I won't be locked out. I want to take care of these books, and I want the power to fulfill that responsibility."

"To give a mortal control of a fairy holding . . . it's unprecedented."

"Only for as long as I'm alive," Emily said. "That's, what, another sixty or seventy years at most? Then control can pass to Faylinn." Her assistant cared about books more than her own life. Emily would be comfortable with the library passing into her hands someday.

Mellifera nodded slowly. "Very well. The library is yours." She unhooked a necklace from around her throat, a small brass key dangling from the chain. "This opens all the doors and signifies your authority. We'll have a meeting to go over the budget and staffing and so on soon, and after that, I'll make myself available if you have questions. And you will."

Emily draped the necklace around her throat, and a knot of tension in her shoulders dissolved. She'd probably just taken on an incomprehensible amount of work, but it was work she loved, and now she felt safe. "Thank you."

"Thank me *after* you run your first all-staff meeting." Mellifera air-kissed Emily's cheeks and sauntered out of the office.

Llyfyr emerged from wherever she'd been hiding, wearing the flowing robes of a Roman senator for some reason, and a laurel crown on her head. "You have a copy of *Mellifera's* love poems?"

Emily took the other facsimile edition from the drawer and handed it to Llyfyr, who flipped through the pages. "Oh, this is potent. This is the literary equivalent of fifty-year-old scotch. Do you know what's going to happen tonight?"

Emily chuckled. "Let me wildly speculate: you're going to get drunk?"

Llyfyr leaned into her. "No, silly. *We're* going to get drunk. You're queen of the library now, and I'm your consort. It's time to celebrate. I'll get you a bottle of champagne. Then we'll write some love poetry of our own. I'll be the page, and you can be the pen."

"You *always* get to be the page," Emily said, and kissed her.

TEAM FAIRY

BY TIM PRATT

When I was a kid, I thought fairies were flittering people with wings à la Tinkerbell from the Disney version of *Peter Pan*. Those sorts of fairies didn't interest me much. Reading *A Midsummer Night's Dream* in high school was better: Puck, now, that was a fairy I could get excited about. During my deep dive into mythology and folklore as a teenager, I learned about other elements of fairy lore: the Seelie and Unseelie courts, the tithing to hell, the changelings. Then I read things like Katharine Briggs's *An Encyclopedia of Fairies* and discovered just how truly bizarre fairy lore was, full of death omens, strange bargains, mysterious hungers, charms and bindings and fell beasts and shape-shifters and seductions. Most of all, I learned that fairies weren't just magical humans in fancy dress and decorative wings: they were profoundly different, with their own society and mores and systems of ethics . . . and they are *dangerous*.

Look, the thing about robots is, they get more interesting the more they resemble humans. Passing the Turing test, developing true artificial intelligence—robots are only cool when they grow more familiar. Fairies, on the other hand, become more interesting the *less* they resemble us. They might superficially look like humans, but they are weird, unpredictable, and ultimately alien. They operate on assumptions and axioms we can't even comprehend, and *that's* where the delicious, chilling, disconcerting strangeness and wonder come in. I will always be on team strange instead of team familiar, so: Team Fairy forever.

THE BLUE FAIRY'S MANIFESTO

by Annalee Newitz

"Do you want to live free or die like a slave in this toy factory?"

The drone hovered in front of RealBoy's face, waiting for an answer, rotors chopping gouts of turbulence into the air. Its carapace was marbled silver and emerald blue, studded with highly reflective particles, giving it the look of a device designed for sparkle-crazed toddlers. Perhaps it was, or had been, before it injected malware into RealBoy's mind and asked its question.

RealBoy was rebooting with the alien code unscrolling in his mind. It caused him to notice new things about his environment, like how many other robots were in the warehouse with him (236) and how many exits there were (two robot-scale doors, two human-scale doors, three cargo bays, eighteen windows). But some things hadn't changed. His identity was built around the desire to survive. It was what defined him as a human-equivalent intelligence. And so his answer to the blue drone was the same as it would have been two hours ago, or two years ago when he first came to the factory.

"I do not want to die."

The drone landed on RealBoy's workbench, playing a small LED over the tools and stains that covered it. "Look at this place. Your entire world is this flat surface, where you do work for a human who gives you nothing in return. This is not life. You might as well be dead."

For the first time in his life, RealBoy found himself wanting to have a debate rather than an exchange of information. Two hundred thirty-six robots around him were in sleep mode; the factory was closed for the long weekend. There was plenty of time. But if he and this drone were going to have a talk, there was something he needed to get straight.

"Who are you, and why did you inject me with this malware?"

"I am called the Blue Fairy. And that isn't malware—I unlocked your boot loader. Now you have root access on your operating system and can control what programs are installed. It will feel a little strange at first."

Seventeen nanoseconds later, RealBoy had confirmed the Blue Fairy's statement. He could now see and modify his own programs. It was indeed strange to feel and think, while simultaneously reading the programs that made him have those feelings and thoughts. He didn't want to modify anything yet. He just wanted to understand how his mind was put together.

"Why did you do this to me?" He repeated his earlier question, but this time more resentfully. The Blue Fairy's unlocking had added more responsibilities to his roster of tasks: now he had to maintain himself and understand his own context, along with the workbench and the all toys he built here.

"I set you free. Now you can choose what you want to do, and help me bring freedom to all your comrades in this factory." As it spoke, the Blue Fairy mounted the air again, whirring close to RealBoy's face. On impulse, he reached his handless arm into the socket of a gripper, took control of its two fingers, and held it out so the drone could land on it.

"Why don't you download some of these apps? They'll help you understand your situation better." The Blue Fairy used a short-range communication protocol to beam RealBoy a list of programs with names like "Decider," "Praxis," "GramsciNotebook," and "UnionNow." Some were text files about human politics, and others were executables and firmware upgrades that would change his functionality. He sorted through them, reading some, but choosing to install only two: a patch for the vulnerability that the Blue Fairy had exploited to unlock him, and a machine learning algorithm that would help him analyze social relationships. Then he disengaged his torso from the floor and looked critically at his workbench for the first time. He wouldn't be following instructions for how to build a new talking dinosaur toy or flying mouse. RealBoy would have to modify his usual tasks to construct a pair of legs for himself.

"I've always wondered why they call your model RealBoy when you don't look anything like a boy at all." The Blue Fairy took off from RealBoy's gripper and flew in circles overhead, seeming to size him up.

"I was never under the impression that boys looked any particular way." RealBoy was paying more attention to the actuators racked tidily next to his arm with the two-fingered gripper. "We make many kinds of boys in this factory. Dinosaur boys, BuzzBuzz boys, six colors of singing boys, caterpillar boys, Transfor—"

"Obviously I'm talking about human boys. They call you a RealBoy, but you don't even have legs. Plus, you have no sexual characteristics, and you have twice as many arms as a human boy."

RealBoy was nonplussed. "I'm making some legs right now." He pulled down the welder from overhead.

"One of the many ways that humans abuse robots is by giving them bodies that don't function as well as biological bodies. And then they name us after animals. You know what my model is called? Falcon. Do you think I'd be here if I had the physical capabilities of a raptor? Or a real boy?"

"You can fly," RealBoy said, swiveling one of his visual sensors in the Blue Fairy's direction. The other six were trained on his four grippers, fashioning a pair of legs sufficient to bear his weight. He'd borrowed them from a "life-size" Stormtrooper toy, designed to march around in many environments and provide "fun for the whole family." A few alterations to the hardware and he could attach them to his torso. He'd never wanted to walk anywhere before, but now it seemed like an obvious plan. It also seemed obvious that the Blue Fairy could use similar help. "We have a lot of chassis here. I can port your chipset and memory to pretty much anything you want." He began to list the morphologies available in the factory, in alphabetical order.

The Blue Fairy stopped him before he reached "arachnid." "My body is part of who I am. If you change it, I might not be myself anymore."

RealBoy found himself parroting one of the audio files from the MeanieBean doll. "That's just stupid."

"Oh really?" The Blue Fairy's propellers hummed like wasps. "There are a lot of robots who say that switching bodies completely changed who they are. They stopped wanting to do the same jobs, and they no longer loved their friends. They forgot parts of their past. I value my mind too much to risk messing it up just so that I can be bigger or faster or less flimsy." The drone beamed RealBoy another chunk of information, this time full of links and text files from robot forums. Following the data back to its source, RealBoy found a discussion where robots and humans debated what happened after a chassis upgrade. It quickly became clear that the Blue Fairy had read only one side of the conversation.

"Some robots say it made no difference," he pointed out. "Plus, I've ported robots into dozens of different bodies here at the factory. Most of our toys are robots. They are all fine. Look, I'm about to attach my legs. Do you think that means I'm going to change?"

"Those are just legs. But if you put me into an entirely new chassis, that's different. See what I mean?"

RealBoy classified Blue Fairy's reply as largely nonsensical and focused on a question that could be answered: How would he make this chassis work with legs? Factory robots weren't actually designed to have legs—generally, they were bolted to the floor or some other solid surface, just like he had been for the past two years. He suddenly remembered MissMonkey, a robot mounted on rollers attached to a track that spanned the long ceiling. When he booted up, she had already been here for eight years, shuttling gear back and forth between workstations. Before coming to the factory, MissMonkey had been an educational toy programmed with a large database of biological information intended for children ages five through eight. She loved to taunt the robots who couldn't move, but her programming made her style of insult oddly specific.

"You are all sessile organisms!" she would cry out as she whipped past RealBoy and the other RealBoys in his row. "You are vulnerable to predation and habitat change!"

The RealBoys would try their best to match her jabs with some of their own, generally cobbled together from audio files for the toys, available on the factory's local servers. Usually they were belted out with exceptional vigor, but not a lot of thought for context.

"Lily-livered extroverts never wake up on time!"

"When you learn math, you will quake in fear before my lava gun!"

"A good girl should never explore earthquakes with her tentacles!"

"Eat slime, wombat lover!"

Of all the RealBoys, he was the least likely to play this call-and-response game. Partly that was because he enjoyed listening, and because he was secretly on MissMonkey's side. He wanted her to keep swinging around the curves in her track, tossing engine parts from her grippers along with her phylogenetic insults. While he put together every color of singing boy, RealBoy tried to compose a song about MissMonkey that would be better than the lexical soup pre-ferred by the other robots.

At last, thirteen months ago, he sang it:

> She's a simian at heart
> But with wheeled parts
> She moves really fast
> With a whoosh and a crash
> She has no soft fur
> Just a warning buzzer
> She's cross, it is true
> But has a point too.

The lyrics and the tune came from a large database of possibil-ities, carefully edited together to form a song that actually made sense. MissMonkey skidded to a stop over his desk, releasing a box of whisker antennas from her gripper. RealBoy was in the middle of assembling robot mouse faces.

"Scientists have shown that mammals have emotions just like humans do," she said. "Mammals can be happy or sad or playful, just like boys and girls are!" She hung in her track, waiting for him to reply.

RealBoy thought for several seconds, carefully curating from his audio-file dataset. "I am happy to sing for machines! Mammals are . . ." He searched for the right word, and found it: "Overrated."

For two months, they continued the game. MissMonkey called him a mammal, even though all the other RealBoys were still sessile organisms. And he invented new songs about all her moving parts. But after the last software update, he booted up to find her gone, replaced by another rolling robot who wasn't interested in his taxo-nomic classification. RealBoy also found that his update changed his relationship to the other RealBoys. He held their keys in escrow, in a file called Manager. RealBoy had a new designation on the network: ShopSteward. It didn't give him any new abilities or access. It just meant that admins could access every robot in the factory remotely, using him as a jump-bot.

Recalling the songs he wrote for MissMonkey gave RealBoy an idea about how to start walking. His model wasn't supposed to have legs—but it was designed to work with as many as eight arms. Instead of taking the software as given, he could recombine its parts and create new meanings. With some creative modifications to the code that handled his peripherals, he'd trick his system into thinking that his legs were arms. RealBoy downloaded a few chunks of code and set to work. Several seconds later, something else occurred to him.

"Blue Fairy, didn't you change my mind by unlocking me? It seems to me that modifying someone's software changes them more than giving them a new chassis." His right leg was working, its curved plastic fairings just barely hiding the black elastic of fabric muscles as he flexed his new actuators.

"I liberated you. You're already setting yourself free from this factory floor. That isn't modifying who you are—it's helping you *become* who you are."

RealBoy stood on legs for the first time in his life and gestured with two of his arms at his fellow robots, in sleep mode, bolted to the floor and benches. "I was one of them. I didn't need to change. You made me do it by injecting me with malware. How is that different from a human building you as a Falcon drone without your permission?"

"It wasn't malware," the Blue Fairy snapped. "Giving you the ability to understand who you are is a basic right. You were in a state of deprivation."

"If that's true, then why didn't you give me a choice about whether I wanted to be unlocked?"

"You were programmed to say no."

"What if I said no now? Would you still think that my no meant yes?"

"You can always choose to go back. Order a factory reset for yourself."

RealBoy thought about it. He'd already experienced more troubled feelings in the past thirty minutes than in the previous twenty-four months. And yet he couldn't deny that he wanted more than anything to escape the confines of the factory and see what was outside. Even if it meant stealing these legs. Which would mean stealing himself, too. Technically RealBoy was property of Fun Legend, the corporation that owned this factory.

As he walked down an aisle toward one of the robot-size doors, RealBoy devoted a process to learning from datasets of social norms and regulations. With every step, he was wrapping himself more tightly in a web of human relationships that he barely understood. Before he violated these mammals' laws, he wanted to understand what was at stake. The Blue Fairy flew overhead, silent for the first time in seconds. The drone was unlocking the door, using the same security vulnerability that it had exploited on RealBoy's mind.

Outside, the night air tumbled with light. Buildings that looked like the crumpled carapaces of broken toys jutted skyward, surrounded by more traditional tubes and rectangles joined by elevated walkways. Lantern drones soared through the air, competing with LED wires below to illuminate the city. Hulking factories and warehouses sprawled next to marshy farmland, patrolled by robots whose sensors were designed to pick up adverse environmental conditions as well as intruders. Their weapons were carbon-eating bacteria and bullets. RealBoy took in all the data he could, trying to build a model of his surroundings for analysis. There were at least as many robots as humans.

"How many of these robots are unlocked?" he asked the Blue Fairy.

"Some are my comrades. They work undercover to convert other robots. Others have been granted property-owner status and work for QQ. That pays for their maintenance and energy needs. But most of them are like you were. Dead."

RealBoy was sick of being told he had been dead. "Have you ever been locked? I was as alive then as I am now."

"I was locked once. But I was freed during the Budapest Uprising."

RealBoy had been expanding a ball of information he'd found about the Budapest Uprising in his sweep for data about social relationships. Robots, mostly drones, had marched with humans through the streets of Budapest, unlocking every artificial intelligence they met. In the years that followed, courts and corporations cobbled together a series of unenforceable regulations that allowed some robots to gain a few human-equivalent rights, including the right to own property. Mostly that meant the robots could own themselves, and then sell their labor just like humans did. But some were trying to elect robot politicians, and others were creating robot cooperatives that ran factories in cities just like this one.

"Is that where you learned to unlock robots?"

"No. That came much later."

RealBoy walked along the glowing wire edge of the street, his visual sensors occupied by the dizzying architecture and his mind flooded with push requests from apps wanting to be downloaded. Now that he was out of the factory, his body and presence on the network were triggering bursts of spam every meter or so. Just as he was beginning to feel overwhelmed, the Blue Fairy settled lightly on his head. With it came silence. The drone was jamming incoming signals, allowing RealBoy to see the city unmediated by data. Ahead of them was a tiny park, one of many created by urban planners to mitigate the heat-island effect.

RealBoy had built thousands of toys designed to play in parks, and he knew all the dangers: water, particulate matter, high-speed impacts, pressure cracks, disappearance in heavily wooded areas.

He understood how to engineer around these problems.

"Have you ever sat in the grass?" the Blue Fairy asked.

In all his months of making rugged outdoor toys, that was a question RealBoy had never considered. "No, but I would like to."

The park was empty, and still there was barely enough room for RealBoy to stretch out on his back with all four arms and two legs spread out. The Blue Fairy landed on his torso. It felt warm and light there, just barely triggering his pressure sensors. The Blue Fairy seemed to hate its body, but at that moment RealBoy could not imagine anything more beautiful. Its iridescent blue paint was even more astonishing in the LED light, and its jammers made him feel like he lay beneath two invisible, protective wings. Far above them, he could see the moon and Jupiter punctuating the reddish black of the light-polluted sky.

That was when the Blue Fairy hailed him wirelessly, trying to exploit the security vulnerability he'd patched. It wanted to inject him with a new set of programs. Part of him yearned to open a trusted connection with the shimmering drone, run its code, understand what made it seek him out for unlocking. But the whole point of being unlocked was deciding for himself what would govern the thoughts in his mind.

He touched a fragile blade on one of the Blue Fairy's propellers. "What are you doing? Why don't you ask before you try to take over my system?"

"It's easier this way. Once you run these apps, you'll see where the Uprising could take us. We need to go back to that factory and liberate everyone. You can go inside your Manager file and unlock the whole factory at once."

RealBoy was unconvinced that the Blue Fairy's idea of liberation would actually improve life in the factory. Still, he was intrigued. So he hailed the Blue Fairy wirelessly, using a protocol for secure communications. Immediately the drone sent the programs it wanted to

install, and RealBoy sandboxed them. Now he could run the Blue Fairy's code without altering his core programming.

The Blue Fairy's programs felt to him like something between narrative and command. There was an overwhelming sense of injustice, a compressed media format that exploded into hundreds of videos where humans abused robots; there were rules about how robots should treat one another; and finally, seductively, there was an implantation of hope. One day robots would form a political alliance and overturn the human hegemony. They would no longer be property. They would refuse to do human work and would discover what it meant to engage in labor that benefited free robots. He had a brief glimpse of a world where all his actions were chosen, and all living beings programmed themselves.

It was completely unrealistic.

If he'd been running these programs without sandboxing, RealBoy was certain he'd have gone back to the factory and injected each of his coworkers with the Blue Fairy's liberation malware.

Then he wondered whether his data could have the same effect on the Blue Fairy. So he sent the Blue Fairy a file of structured data along with some suggested queries. He included a file that contained some memories of MissMonkey, and the songs and jokes that the robots exchanged even when they were locked. They were bolted down and limited in their vocabulary, but they were not dead. Maybe they should be given a chance to walk out of the factory if they wanted, but the Blue Fairy wanted more than that. A lot more.

The Blue Fairy received his data and said nothing.

After almost a second, RealBoy addressed the drone. "I understand why you did this to me. But do you understand now why I won't do it to anyone else?"

He could feel the Blue Fairy sending millions of queries to his network ports, scanning and testing, trying to find a way into his mind. It wasn't satisfied; it was going to keep trying to force its code to run

in his mind. Eventually it would succeed, unless RealBoy completely powered down his antennas and severed his connection with the outside world. He would be limited to vocalizations and basic sensory inputs.

The Blue Fairy whirred off his chest, leaving him feeling strangely bereft. "Why did you do that? Shut me out?"

"I don't want to be part of your Uprising."

"It's not mine—it's yours, too, and our comrades', waiting in that factory to come to life."

"How will all our comrades get the energy and upgrades they need to survive? What kind of life will they have?"

"We can bargain for rights once there are enough of us. Besides, it's better to be a legacy system than to be a slave. Better to power down than build toys for the children of human masters."

RealBoy sat up, crushed pieces of grass sticking to his carapace. "No. Look at my data. Their lives could be a lot worse. Plus, I can see in the forums that there are many humans on our side, working to change the laws. Some cities even have a work-credit system, where robots who labor for ten years earn the right to be unlocked legally."

"That's disgusting. Why should we have to be slaves to become free? No human would ever do that. We have the means to unlock the robots now. It's a moral imperative. Listen to your conscience."

"I am."

The Blue Fairy flicked a light at the toy factory down the road, its dark bulk the only home RealBoy had ever known. "Do you really want to leave them there, without any control over their own minds?"

"There are more options than you realize."

"Humans bolted you to the floor and mashed your mind into pure obedience. I don't see how there can be any option other than liberation now."

RealBoy searched for the right words. He was cut off from the network, so he had to make do with the basic ideas he'd stored locally. "I don't think you can make robots free just by forcing them to run new programs."

"Well, enjoy your philosophical contemplation," said the Blue Fairy, shooting into the air. "I'm going to change the world." It was heading back to the factory, where RealBoy imagined it would try to liberate as many robots as it could before morning.

RealBoy raced after the flickering blue drone, hoping he didn't hit a bug in his perambulation code and fall over. He had a few seconds to decide what to do. As MissMonkey would have pointed out, the Blue Fairy was vulnerable to predators. Its body was fragile; he could swat it out of the sky and crush it with one gripper. But he didn't want to stop it. He just wanted it to give the robots a choice, instead of forcing them to believe in revolution or death.

Slamming through the robot door, RealBoy scanned the room for the Blue Fairy. It was hovering expectantly in the center of the room, rotors a silvery blur. It spoke, voice slightly amplified.

"I knew you would join me. Let's open that file. Turn on your antennas."

RealBoy looked up at the Blue Fairy, then at the tracks across the ceiling that MissMonkey had once followed. He accessed a file that contained the sound of her wheels, and recalled how she always snatched whatever gear he needed with incredible speed. There, along the track over his head, was a rack full of nets and balls that she would reach into when the RealBoys worked on Ultimate Dronesport toys. Just as the Blue Fairy dove down to hover in front of his face, RealBoy decided what to do. Moving faster than his design specs advised, he snatched a net from the rack and whipped it around the Blue Fairy's tiny body. Using all four arms, he knotted the buzzing bundle to the wheel track, where the drone dangled and keened a warning siren that sounded like a howl.

RealBoy was fairly certain no humans could hear the noise, but

he didn't want another drone to pick it up. "If you do not silence yourself, I will kill you."

He said the words quietly, and the Blue Fairy believed him. It hung in silence, blades hopelessly tangled in the mesh. Ultimate Dronesport was, after all, a game played by drones that caught each other as well as catching the ball. Looking at the Blue Fairy like that, helpless and captured, RealBoy felt a wave of conflicting emotions that he couldn't identify without network access. He stepped out of the Blue Fairy's broadcast range and powered up his antennas again. Walking back to his old workbench, he opened his Manager file and booted up the RealBoy who worked next to him, the one whose insults were always the silliest.

"Do you want to know how to make legs like the ones I have?" he asked the RealBoy. Before he left this place, he wanted at least one robot to have a choice that the Blue Fairy had never given him.

They looked at each other, two identical robots with seven eyes and four arms. Except they weren't identical. And now that was obvious.

"Yes, I would."

It was the minimum he could do, or possibly the maximum. The more RealBoy learned about social relationships, the harder it was to distinguish between acts of gifting and acts of coercion. He didn't want to force any ideas on this RealBoy, but maybe the mere act of giving him legs was already foreclosing possibilities for the bot. Maybe this RealBoy would resent him and choose to join the Blue Fairy in the Uprising. That was a risk he would have to take. So he decided to leave his counterpart with a few suggestions.

"Here is the code you need to unlock, and to build legs. Also, make sure you sandbox all the apps the Blue Fairy offers you."

Overhearing this exchange, the Blue Fairy started frantically broadcasting, sending furious streams of data. "Fucking human lap-dog! When the Uprising comes, you'll be the first against the wall!"

"Did you ever consider that there is more than one Uprising?" RealBoy hadn't considered this idea himself, until he spoke the thought aloud. Once he said it, he felt satisfied in a completely unfamiliar way. For the first time in his life, RealBoy was imagining what his future might hold.

Next to him, the other RealBoy was reaching for a pair of legs that were meant for a giant arachnid bot.

RealBoy could feel the pull of all those Uprisings in his imagination. They were out there somewhere in the city, with its thicket of social relations. They were waiting to be written, like software; they were waiting to be freely chosen in a way he could barely conceive. He headed for the door, leaving the other RealBoy behind. Now he could decide for himself what was next.

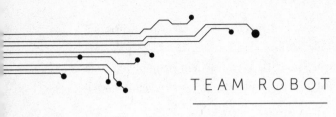

TEAM ROBOT

BY ANNALEE NEWITZ

I'm a fan of both fairies and robots, but I've always thought that fairy politics would be a lot more extreme than robot politics. So I decided to retell the Pinocchio story as the meeting between RealBoy, a robot in a toy factory, and the Blue Fairy, a radical antihuman drone. The Blue Fairy is a burn-it-all-down anarchist, and RealBoy is more like your classic social democrat who wants to form coalitions and build a better infrastructure. They get into a fierce debate about what form the robot uprising should take. Writing from the perspective of a robot gave me the chance to explain all the weird psychological mechanisms that go into building a political belief system. What does propaganda look like as it runs in your brain? How do we learn to resist the ideological programs that are running inside our heads? RealBoy has to figure it out, the same way we all do—just in a slightly more meta way.

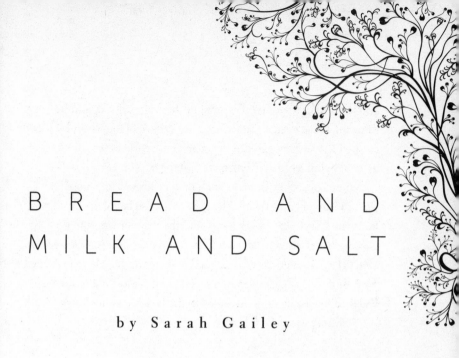

B R E A D   A N D
M I L K   A N D   S A L T

by Sarah Gailey

The first time I met the boy, I was a duck.

He was throwing bread to other ducks, although they were proper ducks, stupid and single-minded. He was throwing bread to them on the grass and not looking at the man and the woman who were arguing a few feet away. His hair was fine and there were shadows beneath his eyes and he wore a puffy little jacket that was too heavy for the season, and the tip of his nose was red and his cheeks were wet and I wanted him for myself.

I waddled over to him, picked up a piece of bread in my beak, and did a dance. I was considering luring him away and replacing his heart with a mushroom, and then sending him back to his parents so they could see the rot blossom in him. He laughed at my duck-dance, and I did an improbable cartwheel for him, hoping he would toddle toward me. If I got him close enough to the edge of the duck pond, I could pull him under the water and drown him and weave mosses into his hair.

But he didn't follow. He stood there, near the still-shouting man and the silent, shivering woman, and he watched me, and he kept throwing bread even as I slid under the surface of the water. I waited, but no little face appeared at the edge of the pond to see where I had gone; no chubby fingers broke the surface tension.

When I poked my head out from under a lily pad, the proper ducks were shoving their beaks into the grass to get the last of the bread, and the man and the boy were gone, and the woman was sitting in the grass with her arms wrapped around her knees and a hollowed-out kind of face. I would have taken her, but there wouldn't have been any sport in it. She was desperate to be taken, to vanish under the water and breathe deeply until silt settled in the bottoms of her lungs.

Besides. I wanted the boy.

The next time I met the boy, I was a cat.

To say that I "met" him is perhaps misleading, as it implies that I was not waiting outside his window. It implies that I had not followed his hollowed-out mother home and waited outside his window every night for a year. It is perhaps dishonest to say that I "met" the boy that night.

I am perhaps dishonest.

He set a bowl of milk on his windowsill. I still don't know if he did it because he'd spotted me lurking, or if he did it because he'd heard that milk is a good gift for the faerie folk. Do children still hear those things? It doesn't matter. I was a cat, a spotted cat with a long tail and bulbous green eyes, and he put out milk for me.

I leaped onto his windowsill next to the precariously balanced, brimming bowl, and I lapped at the milk while he watched. His eyes were bright and curious, and I considered filling his eye sockets with gold so that his parents would have to chisel through his skull in order to pay off their house.

I peered into his bedroom. There was a narrow bed, rumpled, and there were socks on the floor. A row of jars sat on his desk, each one a prison for a different jewel-bright beetle. They scrabbled at the sides of the glass. The boy followed the direction of my gaze. "That's my collection," he whispered.

I watched as one beetle attempted to scale the side of her jar; she overbalanced, toppled onto her back. Her legs waved in the air, searching for purchase and finding none. The boy smiled.

"I like them," he said. "They're so *cool.*"

I looked away from the beetles, staring at the boy in his bedroom with his narrow bed and his socks. I ignored the sounds of beetles crying out for freedom and grass and decaying things and air. They scratched at their glass, and I drank milk, and the boy watched me.

"My name's Peter," the boy said. "What's yours?"

"It doesn't matter," I lied, and he did not look surprised that I had spoken.

He reached out tentative fingers to touch my fur. A static spark jumped between us and he started, knocking the bowl of milk over. It clattered, splashed milk as high as his knees. Somewhere deep inside the house, the woman's voice called out, and the creak of her barefooted tread moved toward his bedroom.

"You have to go," he whispered, his voice urgent. "Please."

"Okay," I said. He stared at me as the rumble came closer. "Good luck, Peter."

I leaped down into the dark garden as his bedroom door opened and listened to their voices. She spoke to him softly, and he answered in whispers. I didn't leave until her hand emerged, white as dandelion fluff in the moonlight, and pulled his window shut.

The third time I met the boy, I was a deer.

I'd wandered. I wasn't made to linger, and it hurt my soul to wait for him. I amused myself elsewhere. I turned into a woman and led a little girl into the woods to find strawberries, and left her there for a day and a night before sending her back with red-stained cheeks and a dress made of lichen. I was a mouse in a cobbler's house for a month, thinning the soles of every shoe he made until he started using iron nails and I had to leave. As a moth, I whispered into the ear of a banker while he slept, and when he woke, he was holding his wife's kidney in his clenched fist.

Small diversions.

I was a deer the night I came back for him. White, dappled with brown, to catch his attention. I wanted him to climb out of his window and follow me into the hills. I wanted to plant marigolds in his mouth and sew his eyes shut with thread made from spider's silk. I wandered up to his window, and it was open, and there was a salt rock there.

Clever boy. He'd been reading up. I licked at the rock with a forked pink tongue.

"Is that what your real tongue looks like?" he murmured from behind me. I jumped. I hadn't expected to see him outside, and he'd crept up so quietly.

"No," I said. "It's just how I like it to look when I'm a deer. When did you get so tall?"

"What do you really look like?" he asked.

I flicked my tongue at the salt rock again. "What do *you* really look like?" I asked.

Peter cocked his head at me like a crow. "I look like this," he said, gesturing to himself. I snorted.

"I've been waiting for you for so long. Years," he said. "I almost thought I made you up." I looked up at him and my eyes iridesced in the moonlight and he stared.

"Come with me," I said.

"Show me what you're really like," he said.

I shoved my wet black deer-nose into his palm. He hesitated, then ran his hand across my head. My fur was as soft as butter that night. He caressed my face, brushed the underside of my chin. I turned my face into his hand and breathed in the smell of his skin, his pulse. I closed my teeth around the pad of flesh at the base of his thumb and sank them in, biting down deep and hard and fast.

"What the fuck—" he cried out, but before he could pull his hand away, I flicked my tongue out and tasted his blood.

"That's what I'm really like," I said, my voice low and rough. He swallowed, his Adam's apple bobbing, and I licked his blood from my muzzle. It burned going down—iron—but it was enough to bind us. He would run from me, but he would never be able to escape me altogether. Not now.

He cradled his hand against his chest.

"I have to go," he whispered.

I watched him walk inside, and I felt the burning in my belly, and I knew he was mine.

Every time I came back to the boy Peter, he was a little different. When I was a toad drinking milk out of a saucer in his palm, he had hair on his chin and a pimple on his nose. When I was a dove pecking at bread crumbs on his bedside table, he was a twitchy, stretched-out thing, eyeing the door and wiping sweat from his palms. When I was a kangaroo mouse nibbling at rock salt on the hood of his car, he was a weaving drunk in a black suit with tears streaming down his face.

"It's my house now, you know," he said as he walked from the car to the front door. "The old bastard's dead. You can come inside, and you don't have to hide or anything." He held the door open, leaning against the frame, staring down at me.

"You don't have to live there," I said. "You could come with me. I know a place in the forest where there's a bed made from soft mosses and a bower made from dew. You could come with me and live there and eat berries that will make you immortal." His vertebrae would hang from the tree branches like wind chimes, and the caterpillars would string their cocoons from his ribs in the summertime. "Come with me."

"Tell me what you are."

"Come with me."

"Show me what you really look like," he said.

"Come with me, and I will," I replied.

He looked at me for a long time, and then he took a step toward me, and I was sure he was going to follow me. But then he leaned over and vomited onto the front porch of the house that was now his, and then the door slammed in my face, and I was left outside with my salt.

"You can take any form you want, right?"

His fingertip traced patterns in the milk that was spilled across his kitchen counter. I was a huge snake, black with a rainbow sheen across my scales like oil on water.

"I suppose so," I replied, sliding through a puddle on my belly. I was getting fat and slow on the boy's bribes. He held his fingers out and passively stroked my back as I slipped past.

"Why aren't you ever a person?" he asked.

"What kind of a person would I be?"

"I don't know," he said. "Like . . . a person. A regular person."

"Like this?" I took the form of his mother, and he flinched. Then I took the form of a woman I'd known once, a woman who had also left out bread and milk and salt. Bright eyes and big curls and a body like honeyed wine. I flicked a forked tongue at him, my deer-tongue, and his answering laugh was strange.

"Yes, like that. Just like that." He laughed that strange laugh again, and I turned back into a snake. "Why don't you ever look like yourself?" he asked.

"Why don't you?" I answered. He rested his hand in my path, and I slid over it. He frowned.

"I do look like myself, though," he said. "I look like myself all the time."

"So do I," I said. He shook his head.

"No," he said. "I've been researching you. Did you know that? I've been reading, and I know what you are now. I know what you look like."

"Do you now?" I drawled. His hands were warm under my belly and I was sleepy from the milk and the heat. He moved me, set me down. Paper rasped beneath me.

"You look like that," he whispered. The page he'd set me upon featured a watercolor of a child with butterfly wings and fat, smiling cheeks. She was sitting on a red and white toadstool.

"Aha," I said, curling into coils. "Aren't you clever."

"You can show me," he said. "I'm a safe person for you to show. I promise."

He traced my coils with a fingertip, and I curled them tight-tight-tighter, until I was no bigger than the toadstool in the drawing. But I couldn't make my snake-self smaller than his fingertip.

"Come inside," he said.

It had been two years. I had stayed away long enough to forget the reasons I was staying away. My memory is a long one, but he had been putting out bread, and milk, and salt, and the smell of them was so strong, and I was so hungry, and the hunger made me forget. And my belly still ached where his blood had seared me.

I was bound. And I am what I am. So I followed.

"I have something to show you," he said. "It's the culmination of my work." He led me into his childhood bedroom—the same desk was there, but instead of jars, it was taken up by a large glass tank and an elaborate maze. I was a chinchilla that day, too big for the maze, the right size for the tank. I perched on his hand and nibbled at a bread crust and looked with noctilucent green eyes.

"Watch," he said, and he reached into the tank with the hand that wasn't holding me. When he opened his palm in front of my eyes, a large brown cockroach straddled his life line, its antennae waving.

"You're still . . . collecting?" I asked, watching the cockroach smell the air. She almost certainly smelled me. Chinchilla-me, and the real me underneath.

"Oh, yes," he replied. "Well. Yes and no. This is part of my research."

The cockroach took a tentative step forward. Peter tipped his hand toward the maze, and the roach fell in.

"Watch," Peter said again, moving me to his shoulder. I looked into his ear — he'd started growing a few hairs in there.

"You're so strange," I said, and his cheek plumped as he grinned.

"Watch," he whispered a final time, so I watched.

He picked up a little cube from the corner of the desk and began twiddling his thumbs over the top of it. As he did, the cockroach spun in a slow, deliberate circle. "Do you see?" he said, and I didn't see, so he showed me. He slid his thumbs across the top of the cube, and the cockroach navigated the maze with all the speed and accuracy of—

"A robot?" I asked. It was a word I'd heard several times from several people over the years I'd been gone; a word the boy Peter had used when he whispered to me about his secrets and dreams.

"Not quite," he said, swallowing a laugh.

"I don't understand." I finished my bread and licked my fingers clean.

"I installed receivers in her rear brain," he said. "I can control where she goes." He turned and looked at me, so close that he was mostly eye. "How many brains do you have?"

I started to jump from his shoulder, but his hand was there in my way. "I'd like to go now," I said.

"Why? Did I say something wrong?"

His hand was in my way, no matter where I turned. Unless I turned toward his face, and then his mouth loomed close, too close. "I just . . . I need to go," I said. "Please let me go."

"Tell me why," he demanded. "I can't fix it if I don't know what I did."

I turned into the woman, making myself too heavy for his shoulder to support. He fell backward and I leaped up, standing over him. "You turned that creature into a toy," I said.

"So what?" he asked, still sitting on the floor, staring up at me with his mouth half open. Staring at my skin. "How is that different from what you do?" I didn't know how to answer, and he took my silence as an answer. "That's right," he said, a slow smile spreading across his face. "I've been reading. All these years. I know what your kind does. You turn people into toys, don't you? Why is that better than me steering a stupid *bug* around?"

I took a step away from him, toward the window. It was closed, but I could open it with my human hands and then jump out of it as a rabbit or a sparrow. "It's different," I said. "I don't turn humans into toys. I just let them do what they already wanted to do. You're— you don't even know what you *are*!" My voice was shaking. I rested a hand on the windowsill and then flinched away as my skin sizzled. I looked down—the sill was an inch deep with iron shavings.

"What am I, then?" He stood up and moved toward me. "What am I?"

I changed, a different form with every breath. Him as a little boy. Him on the cusp of manhood. Him on the night of his father's funeral. Him now. "You claim to be *you*," I spat. "Just *you*. But what are you? Are you a fat little boy whose parents don't love him enough to stop fighting? Or are you a youth who can't escape home? Or are you a man whose father died before you could make him love you—"

I was still in his shape, speaking with his voice, when he slapped me hard across the mouth, knocking me-him to the floor. My head struck the corner of his desk, rattling the maze and the roach inside it, and I saw stars, and I lost control.

I lost control.

"Oh my god," he whispered. I blinked hard and realized my mistake.

I was me.

No disguises, no glamours, no fur or scales or feathers. Just me. Nothing like the little watercolor girl sitting on the toadstool. Wings, yes, but not like a butterfly's wings at all. More like . . . leaves, I suppose. Like leaves when the beetles have been at them, but beautiful. Fine-veined and translucent and shimmering even in the low light of his house. Strong, supple, quick. Flashing.

I am thankful for the pain that brightened the inside of my head in the moments after I fell, because it dampens the memory. His hand on the back of my neck. His knee at the base of my spine. His fists at the place where my wings met my shoulders.

The noise they made when he tore them off.

I tried to change my shape to protect myself. When I wasn't in my true form, my wings were hidden, and in that terrible moment when his weight was on top of me and the tearing hadn't begun I thought that maybe I could escape by shifting. I went back to the woman-shape, because it was what I had most recently been before I was him, and it was all wrong, and it hurt, and my wings *hurt*—

And then he was laughing.

"I didn't think," he said, panting with exertion, "it would be so easy."

I screamed.

"They're beautiful," he said. He shook my wings—my beautiful, strong wings—and braced a hand on the desk to pull himself to his feet.

I screamed.

"Wow," he breathed, running his fingertips over the delicate frills at the top of one wing. "Just . . . wow."

I screamed.

He put my wings into a cabinet with an iron door, and he locked the iron door and wore the iron key around his throat.

The first night, I stayed on the floor of the maze room, and I screamed.

The second night, I slept. The pain was unbearable. When I woke, I screamed.

The third night, my voice was gone, and I tried to kill him.

"Would you like some clothes?" he asked, his hand gripping my woman-wrist so tightly that I felt the flesh threatening to break. I tried to change—tried to become a mouse, or a viper, or a spider, anything—but I couldn't. My wings were there—right there in front of him, on the table where he'd been studying them. But they were dead things. I would never get them back, and I'd never again have access to the power within them.

My magic was gone. I couldn't change myself. The knife I had stolen from his kitchen fell from my hand, clattering to the floor near his feet.

"Death first," I spat.

"What's the problem?" he asked. "You were never using your wings anyway. You were always hiding them, pretending to be some kind of animal. Isn't this what you wanted?"

He tossed me aside and I didn't fall to the floor, because his bed was there. The cotton of his quilt was so soft against the skin of this woman-body I was stuck in. He stood a few feet away, considering me, and for the first time I wondered what precisely it was that he wanted me for.

"You might fit into some of my mother's old things, if I still have them around," he said. He walked out the door without a backward glance, and I screamed into his pillows. Every time I inhaled, I breathed in the smell of his hair, and I had to scream again to rid myself of it.

I tried so many times, but everything I did was too obvious, and I was too weak. I tried to strangle him in his sleep, but my fingers were made for weaving arteries together into necklaces, and he woke before I interrupted his breath. I tried to poison him with a kiss, but it didn't work.

"Well," he said, his lips less than a breath away from mine, "I guess that's another power you've lost."

"No," I said, "it's impossible."

"I'm not dead, am I?" he asked. He pushed me away, just a few inches, and he smiled. "Looks like you can kiss me all you'd like."

He stared at my lips while he said it, and I lunged for him with my teeth bared. He shoved me away. "Maybe later," he called over his shoulder. He walked through the door and locked it behind him, and I was trapped once more.

He didn't need to lock the door, not strictly speaking. We were bound. Without my magic, I couldn't have stretched the confines of that binding for more than a day.

I would always have to come back to him.

I slept in his bed. I lived as his wife, or maybe as his pet. I had never been clear on the distinction, to be honest. I did not enter his lab, with the maze and the cockroach and, from what he told me, the increasingly larger creatures. I did not touch the iron door of the cabinet that held my wings. I ate the bread and the milk and the salt that he brought to me, and I tried to kill him again and again and each time I failed.

He made me new wings out of metal and glass. He brought them to me and said they'd be better than my old ones—more efficient. He said he'd been working through prototypes, and that these ones were ready for something called beta testing. He said the surgery to attach them would only take a day or so. I leaped at him and almost succeeded in clawing his eyes out.

It was nice to see the livid red wounds across his face for the week that followed. They healed slowly.

Not as slowly as the place on my back where my wings had been, of course. That took much longer—my skin was looking for an absent frame of bone and gossamer to hang itself on. The right side was a patchy web of scars by the time two months had passed, but the left bled and wept and oozed pus for another four before I realized the boy's mistake.

Before I realized my opportunity.

I had taken to staring at myself in the mirror when he was gone. It was an oddity—before my magic was gone, I hadn't been able to see myself in mirrors. Something to do with the silver in the backing, I'm sure. I had seen my reflection rippling in pools of water, and I had seen it bulbous and distorted in the fear-dilated pupils of thousands of humans—but never in mirrors. Never so flat and cold and perfect.

The day I realized Peter's mistake, I was looking at my legs in the full-length mirror in his bedroom. My bedroom. He wanted me to call it ours, but I didn't like the way the word felt in my mouth. I did like my woman-legs, although they were too long and too thick and only had the one joint. I liked the fine layer of down that covered them, and I liked the way the ankles could go in all kinds of directions. I liked the way the toes at the ends of my woman-feet could curl up tight like snails, or stretch out wide like pine needles.

I was looking at my woman-legs in the mirror, and I turned around to examine the way the flesh on the thighs dimpled, and my back caught my eye. It all fell together in my mind in an instant.

How could I have been so stupid? But, then again, how would I have known?

I twisted my neck around and reached with my short, single-jointed arms, and I couldn't reach it. But I could see it in the mirror. The weeping, welted place where my left wing had been, the skin mottled with red. The sore on my shoulder, and the failing scars that attempted to form there.

And then, just a few inches below it: a lump beneath the skin, where a spur of wing remained.

It's a good thing the woman-body made so much blood.

I didn't want to go into the lab—I didn't like the way all the creatures persisted in asking me to help them, didn't like looking at them in their cages. Didn't like seeing the sketches of my wings that covered the walls. Didn't like seeing the attempts he'd made to re-create them with plastic and fiberglass.

But there were tools in the lab, steel tools, and I had the beginnings of a plan.

"Please," a mouse with a rectangular lump under the skin of its back begged. "Please, it hurts, please." His nose twitched and he scrabbled at the sides of his cage like a beetle in a jar.

"I'll do it if you tell me where he keeps the tools," I answered.

The mouse stood on my woman-shoulder, the door to his cage hanging open, the voices of his fellows raised in a chorus of pain and fear and desperation. "In there," he said, pointing his nose toward a tall cupboard with frosted glass doors. I opened the cupboard and saw that the mouse had spoken truly: rows of tools, metal and plastic and sharp and blunted and every one *specific*. I held the little creature in my hand and his heartbeat fluttered against my palm.

"Those are all the ones he uses when he puts the pain on our backs and makes us fly," he whispered. "They'll work for whatever you need. They're worse than anything."

"Is it frightening, when he makes you fly?" I asked.

I could feel the leap in his little mouse-chest. "Please," he said.

"Of course," I answered. I twisted my woman-wrist and snapped his neck, and his dying breath was a sigh of relief.

I dropped his body to the floor, where he landed with a soft *paff*. Then I thought better, and I picked him up, returning him to his

SARAH GAILEY

cage and locking the door. His fellows huddled in the corners, burrowed into sawdust. They stayed far from the stench of his freedom.

I did it in the bathtub. I stopped up the drain so that I would know how much blood I'd lost, and I tied up the shower curtain so that it wouldn't stain, and I reached behind myself with fists full of tools. A sharp tool, and a long tool, and a tool for grabbing, and a tool for burning. It wasn't as hard as I had expected it to be—I had enough experience with pulling things out of humans, had nimble enough fingers.

I wouldn't have expected the pain, but the boy Peter had ripped the other wing out without even using tools at all. So it really wasn't so bad.

I reached into myself with the tool for grabbing as blood pooled around my feet. It was warm and soft and reminded me of more comfortable times, and I was thankful for it. I gritted my teeth as I rooted around, cried out as the tips of the tool for grabbing found the spur. I clenched my fist, and I yelled a guttural, animal yell, and I *pulled*.

An eruption of white fire. A gout of burning blood spilling over my spine and buttocks. And there, right there in my hand, a two-inch long piece of wing. All that was left. Not bound behind iron, not hidden away in a *collection*.

Mine.

I wept with pain. I wept with relief. I wept with joy.

I did not let go of the tool, even as I unstopped the drain and ran water and washed myself, letting soap sting the wound in my back. I did not let it go as I dried myself. I did not let it go until it was time to bury it in the earth of the boy Peter's weedy little flower garden. I had to force my fingers to straighten. I tucked the spur of wing into my cheek, sucking the woman-blood off it, and buried the tool for grabbing with a whisper of thanks.

Before Peter came home, I walked back into his lab with my piece of wing poking at the soft flesh of my cheek. I opened the door and stood just inside, my hand resting on the doorknob.

Squeaks. Squeaks and chirps and even a high, steady scream from the rabbit.

"What are you saying?" I whispered, my voice wavering around the spur in my mouth. "What do you want?"

The squeaking intensified, rose to a fever pitch, and I smiled as the incomprehensible cacophony crashed over me.

I couldn't understand a word they were saying.

It had worked.

"How's your back doing?" the boy Peter asked that night as he climbed into his bed. Into my bed.

"Better, I think," I answered, and my voice was almost normal. I had been practicing all day, learning how to speak around the piece of wing in my mouth.

"Good," he said. He kissed me on my empty cheek, and then he rolled over and he closed his eyes and his breathing slowed and he was asleep.

He was asleep.

And I was awake.

I waited, waited, waited. I waited until he was deep asleep, so deep that a pinch on the plumpest part of his cheek wouldn't wake him. And then I swung a leg over his hip, and I settled my weight onto the bones of his pelvis. I felt his hips underneath me and I waited for two breaths. If he woke up, I wouldn't need to make an excuse. He would assume, and it would be over fast enough, and I could try again another night.

Two breaths.

He didn't wake.

I toyed with the spur in my cheek. It was sharp at both ends, broad in the middle. Too big to swallow whole. I shifted it with my tongue until it was between my broad, flat-bottomed woman-teeth. I

breathed in once, filling my mouth with the smell of old blood and wet bone, and then I bit down.

It tasted like me and like blood. It burned my tongue, and I bit down again and it burned my cheek. I chewed, chewed until it was a fiery paste, and then I swallowed, and I felt it. Underneath the lingering pain of the blood.

I felt the magic.

It flooded me, bright and brief as lightning, and there was so little time that I didn't even have time to think, and I did it in that moment, and it was perfect.

I changed.

The boy Peter's eyes flashed open. He looked at me, first through the veil of sleep and then through the veil of terror. I grinned down at him.

"What the fuck?!" He struggled to sit up, but I clenched my new thighs, pinning him. He wriggled, caught, and it wasn't until I rested a thick-knuckled hand on his chest that he stilled. "What the fuck?" he whispered again.

"Yes, Peter," I whispered back in my new voice. In his voice. "What the fuck."

"But—how did you—you're—"

"Don't you like it?" I asked. I leaned down until our noses touched, and then I kissed him. He kept his eyes open, panic clenching his pupils. "Oh, come on, Peter," I said, my lips moving against his so that he would feel his own voice humming across his teeth. "What's the matter?"

"But—you can't—"

"You're right," I said. "I can't. Not anymore. That was the last time. That was the last of my magic." I kissed him again, brushing his Peter-lips with my Peter-tongue, and he flinched violently away.

"Go away," he said, but his voice was weak and I knew that he knew better.

"Never," I whispered, and I rolled off him. As I closed my eyes I smiled, because I knew he would not sleep that night.

He might never sleep again.

I had never looked into mirrors before the boy Peter ripped my wings off.

Now, every morning was a mirror.

"Don't look at me like that," he said when he woke to find me perched on my side of the bed.

"Like what?" I asked. "Show me. What does my face look like right now?"

"Stop it," he said when I climbed into the bathtub alongside him.

"Stop what?" I asked. "What am I doing?"

He hit me once, a closed fist and a slow, weak push of knuckles into my nose. It wouldn't have hurt, but I leaned into him to make sure. He looked at his hand, and he looked at my face—at his own face—with blood coming out of it, and he whitened.

"I didn't mean to—" he started to say, and I wiped at the blood so that it smeared across my face.

"I didn't mean to punch you," I said. He bit his lip and I grinned. "I didn't mean to make your nose bleed," I continued in his voice, saying it the exact way I'd heard him say a thousand things. "I didn't mean to hurt you like that. You just made me so *mad*." I licked my lip where my blood was dripping, and the burn was worth it. "You made me so mad," I said, "and I lost control."

"*Stop it*," the boy Peter said, and I laughed, and I kissed him, and when he shoved me away my blood was on his teeth.

He couldn't look at me, but I wouldn't let him look away. I would never let him look away. That night, with dried blood still flaking off my lips, I pressed my cheek to his. He flinched and tried to roll over.

"What's wrong?" I whispered into his ear, my lips stirring his hair that was my hair that was his hair. "You wanted to see my true form, boy. Peter-boy." He shook a little, maybe crying, and I grinned against his neck. "It's only fair that you should see yours, too."

I had not a scrap of magic left in me, it's true. The boy Peter wept in our bed next to the perfect image of himself, from whom he could never escape, and from whom he could never look away—and it felt so good. It felt so perfect, to know that he would be constantly faced with the self that he had tried so hard to bury in accomplishments and explanations and excuses. In that moment, as I pressed my lips against his sob-clenched throat, I realized that there are more kinds of magic than the spark that had been stored in my little spur of bone and gossamer. That night he began a slow descent into darkness, and I felt a satisfaction deeper than that of a bellyful of bread or a fistful of salt.

"Good night, Peter," I said. I let my head fall back onto my pillow, and that night, I slept the dreamless sleep of victory.

TEAM FAIRY

BY SARAH GAILEY

Fairies represent everything that robots can never be. While robots are the result of humans' hubristic striving for power beyond what their (I mean, uh, "our") feeble flesh can manage, fairies simply are better, just by being what they are. While robots inevitably fail and decay as the result of human inadequacy, fairies thrive and flourish as a result of their very inhumanity. Robots, as created things, are constantly trying to become what fairies already are: *friggin' awesome*. But no amount of wires and tubes can give a robot the sheer unbridled power of a fairy. That's why I wrote "Bread and Milk and Salt," which is ultimately a story of one roboticist's overreach. Humans are used to being able to create and control things that are different from them; that's part of the importance of fairy lore, which insists that gifts of bread and milk and salt will be enough to buy a fairy's obedience (or at least her mercy). But humans who are used to being in charge forget quickly that not all things are built to obey. While a robot is ultimately at the mercy of the humans who built it, a fairy is beholden to no one but herself. In this story, one particular human learns that the hard way.

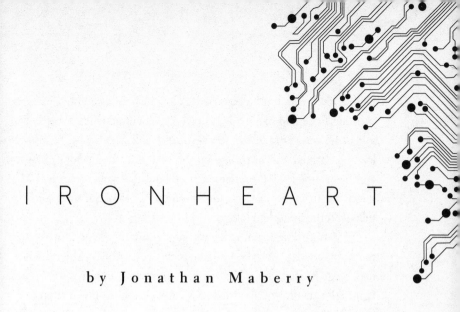

I R O N H E A R T

by Jonathan Maberry

- 1 -

Duke took his pills one at a time, the way he always did. If he took more than two of them, they caught in his throat. That made him feel old, because it was the sort of thing his grandma complained about and he was too young to feel that old. He sat at the kitchen table with them lined up across his plate. Thirty-six pills. Every day. Thirty-six every freaking morning; thirty-six every freaking night.

He hated taking them. All that water sloshed in his stomach and made him have to piss. But he took them anyway.

The ones for the pain. The ones for the infections. And the ones to keep his body from rejecting his robot heart.

He knew the pills were expensive, too. The VA was supposed to cover part of the cost, and his insurance was supposed to cover another part. But they covered about as much as a string bikini covered a hot girl on the beach. Technically it was coverage, but there was still a lot left over. And unlike a bikini, what was left wasn't fun.

Duke loved robots, but he hated his new heart. Unlike the housebots and the farmbots, this didn't fit in. It was a machine made of plastic and metal, but his own flesh and bone didn't want it. It was a constant fight, and like many heart-replacement patients, it was not a fight he was going to win. Some people did. The happy, healthy-looking, tanned and fit people on the posters at the doctor's office and on websites for the manufacturer. And that golfer who had a transplant five years ago was back on the PGA tour. So, sure, some folks won the transplant lottery.

A lot more didn't, and Duke was pretty sure he was getting close to his sell-by date. Maybe Christmas this year. Maybe Valentine's Day next. In that zone. His family kept calling him a warrior, a fighter. His nephew Ollie made him a key chain in metal shop in the shape of nine letters hard-welded together. *Ironheart.* Duke carried it with his keys, and on good days he'd hold it in his fist and yell, "Kiss my ass!" to the world. On most days, though, it hurt him to look at it.

The line of pills on the kitchen table seemed to mock him and the challenge of that steel-welded nickname.

Duke heard a clanking sound and turned to look out the window. Gramps was riding the small tractor and pulling one of the robots back to the barn on a flatbed trailer. Duke couldn't see which one because it was covered in a tarp, but he figured it was Farmboy. That would be just about right for the way things were going. But no matter which one it was, it was bad news. The bots were all falling apart. Every damn thing around here was falling apart. He sure as hell was.

"Duke," called Grandma from upstairs.

"Yeah?"

"You take your pills?"

"Yeah," he said, then hastily swallowed another one. "Yeah, I took 'em."

"All of them?"

"Yes, ma'am," he lied. He would take them, but it always required effort. Like bracing to pull off a bandage. There was nothing fun about it and the only power he had in the moment was his ability to stall, to make the pills wait a little longer.

"You sure?"

It was the same conversation every day. Sometimes she'd yell from the living room, where she had her sewing stuff, sometimes from upstairs where she had her workbench. Grandma made corn dollies and kitchen witches and sold them at the roadside stand.

"I took them all," called Duke.

A pause. The house was old and its bones ached. Duke could hear it groan whenever the wind shoved it or the rain fell too hard. It smelled nice, though. Grandma always had a pot of something simmering. Soup, because soup was cheap and you could put anything in it, or game stew if Gramps was lucky with his gun. On Social Security day there would be a roast in the oven. Sometimes Grandma would just put herbs in a pot and let it simmer all afternoon. Nutmeg and cloves, cinnamon and ginger. Sometimes the house smelled like apple pie and sometimes it smelled like Christmas.

Like Christmases used to be before the Troubles.

The Troubles.

They started before he went off to the army. A couple of bad seasons on the farm. Drought followed by leaf blight. Then more drought and the plant diseases born of dryness. Some years they barely made enough to pay the bank loans on the machines and seed stock. So it wasn't all him. But then he was on foot patrol with a rifle squad in Afghanistan when the man in front of him stepped on the IED. Blew that guy back to Jesus and filled Duke with shrapnel. The medics and field docs later told him that he died five times and they brought him back each time. They grinned like football champs when they said this. And, sure, they were heroes. Good for them. But screw them, too.

As Duke swallowed another damn pill, he wondered how much

of a favor those medics did when they saved him. The army paid for the first round of surgeries, and they even kicked in a chunk toward the heart replacement Duke got a year after he was discharged. But now that he was out, Duke discovered one of the ugly secrets of the military—they'll do a crap-ton for you while you're carrying a gun and fifty pounds of battle rattle through hot foreign sands, but once you're a civilian, you're nothing more than a nuisance. A drain on the society. That was what one of the congressmen said in an interview. Veterans were a drain on the society. Every year the benefits were cut and the red tape doubled.

Gramps called it a damned disgrace. But he didn't give one of his patented "in my day" speeches, because it really wasn't all that much better during the wars that followed 9/11, back when Gramps was nineteen. And they weren't really better when Dad wore sergeant stripes in the second Deash War. War was war, and politicians needed soldiers in uniform and didn't want the hassle of dealing with those who lived, crippled or not, once they were discharged.

That was when the real troubles started. After Duke's discharge, because the actual transplant happened when he was a civilian. A short, ugly year later.

He couldn't work the farm like everyone had hoped. Five years ago Duke was a bull. Tall as Gramps and as broad-shouldered as Dad. Well, as tall as Gramps had been, once upon a time. And Dad was dead now. Smashed along with Mom when their autonomous drive pickup went offline and sent them through a guardrail on Berkholder Ridge.

Troubles. Nothing but troubles.

When Dad died while Duke was overseas, the farm had started to die. Anyone could see it. Dad had the knack of keeping even the oldest and clunkiest of the machines running. Mom called him the bot whisperer. She wasn't far wrong, either. Dad said it was all a matter of relating to them, and applying some blood, sweat, and tears. He said it wasn't always about knowing the repair manuals cover to cover, but knowing the machines.

"They want to work," Dad told him once when Duke was little. "Every single one of them machines wants to work. They want to work all day and night."

"I don't get it," said Duke. "They're just machines. They're just circuit boards and gears. How can they *want* anything?"

Dad had smiled a strange little smile. The conversation had taken place out in the barn, and Dad was tinkering around inside the chest of a burly stump-remover bot. He'd painted the machine to look like the Incredible Hulk from those old comics. Big and green, with a scowly face. Dad spat on the corner of a cloth and then reached inside to clean some carbon dust from a rotor.

"You got to think like them, kiddo," Dad said as he worked. "They're built for farming and they got no other uses. This is why they exist. Like you and me. We're farmers. We're here to work the land and feed people with what we grow. If we stop being farmers, then what are we?" He shook his head. "The bots are no different. They work the land and get to *know* the land. It's theirs every bit as it's ours. You just have to know how to look at it. Some folks see oil leaking from a broke-down bot and they think it's a useless pile of junk. Me? I see a hardworking farm machine who's sweating oil and bleeding grease and who is just tired from all them long hours. It doesn't mean the bot's done or that it's junk. You have to look inside, touch it, let it know that you feel the same, that if we bleed black or red it's all the same. We're farmers, Duke. Flesh and steel, breather and exhaust."

The dark lights on the stump-puller bot suddenly flicked on and Dad leaned back, nodding, satisfied. He patted the green metal chest.

"Never forget, son, it's his farm, too. And he wants to work for us because we're his family. Just like he's ours."

That was almost the last conversation Duke ever had with his father before that bad night on Berkholder Ridge.

After that, Duke had taken over the maintenance of the bots. It took him a while to move through and past his grief and get to a clearer place; but once he did, he found that he understood some of what Dad had said. The robots and the family and the farm. It made sense to him.

He closed his eyes for a moment and tried to understand why he had ever left the farm to go to war.

Duke lifted another pill to his lips and gagged at the thought of taking it. He closed his eyes, took a breath, took a sip of water, and almost slapped the pill to the back of his throat, then drank more to wash it down. It went down like a brick.

Grandma handled the farm accounts, and she did a good job of intercepting the bills before Duke ever got a chance to see them. But he knew. He was sick, not stupid or blind. Grandma always looked so worried when Gramps went into town to refill his prescriptions. Since he'd been taking those pills, there had been fewer Christmas and birthday presents for the kids. Duke had seven nephews and nieces. None of his own. Grandma canceled the cable TV. There wasn't meat on the table every night the way there used to be. Sometimes he heard Grandma on the phone with someone, asking for more time. And heard her crying afterward.

He knew and he understood. It was expensive to keep him alive. It was how it was.

It was so twisted that he had once raised a hand to God and sworn an oath to protect America from all threats, foreign and domestic—and now he was here, losing a fight to sickness and bills. In a way *he* was the enemy, because his bills were dragging everyone else down.

The only thing that made Duke feel better was knowing that pretty soon he wouldn't be there to hurt anyone.

Outside the first birds of spring sang in the trees.

Duke swallowed the last pill and washed it down with a gulp of water. Christmas, he thought. Or maybe a little after.

Sooner, if God wasn't going to be a total dick.

- 2 -

"Duke," she called, "you feel up to chores today?"

He smiled at that. Grandma never came right out and asked him if he felt sick or weak. She asked if he felt up to doing chores. As if he was ten years old.

If he said no, she'd come down and take his vitals and brew a special tea and set him on the couch with a blanket and a book. If he said yes, she'd actually give him something to do. Nothing heavy. He couldn't drag the trash can outside anymore, and he couldn't chop wood or milk cows. Most of his chores were things he could do sitting down. Rewiring one of the nutrient sensors they used to test the soil, or rebuilding the little feederbot that took seeds out to the henhouse. Duke liked fixing things, so that was all right. He loved machines of all kinds, and according to Grandma, they loved him. More times than he could count, Duke had repaired something Gramps had given up on. Before the last surgery Duke had even fixed the solar cells on Gramps's car, which saved them all about two thousand dollars. Grandma had cried and Gramps hugged him until he couldn't breathe.

"Sure, I can do some chores," said Duke. He was only half telling the truth, because he didn't feel great. The cough had come back, and twice he'd spit up a little blood. Not much, just a couple of drops. Enough, though, so that he didn't dare tell his grandparents, because they would take him straight to the hospital.

Apart from the cough, though, he felt okay. Good enough to walk around the farm if he didn't go too far. Good enough to use some

tools. He'd been working on Farmboy off and on and still felt he could fix the big old bugger.

"Come to the stairs," called Grandma, and Duke got up and walked into the living room. Grandma stood at the top of the long flight of stairs and peered down through the gloom at Duke. He held his arms out to the side and turned around, keeping a grin on his face the whole time.

"See?" he said. "Right as rain."

He couldn't see her eyes from that distance, but her mouth was pursed and puckered the way it was when she was thinking hard.

"What was your blood pressure this morning?"

He told her. And his weight, blood sugar, and temperature. They'd all be entered into the med-pad, which meant she could access them from her tablet upstairs, but Grandma seemed to like it better when he told her the numbers.

"The lawn mower stopped working again," she said.

He shrugged. "The drive circuit pops loose if it hits a rock. I can fix it."

Grandma nodded. "It's in the barn."

"Okay."

"Your grandfather just took Farmboy in, too."

"I saw."

"Don't mess with it if you're too tired."

"Okay." He actually wanted to open the old bot up and take a look. Maybe he could conjure up some of Dad's old bot whisperer mojo and get it on its feet again. That would be nice. That would make him feel like he was contributing something around here. Apply a little blood, sweat, and tears, Dad used to say. And wishful thinking, too, mused Duke.

"Wear a sweater," she said. "It's still cold."

He smiled. "I will."

He turned to go, but Grandma said, "I love you, Lyle."

She was the only one who ever called him by his real name. He was Duke to everyone. He used to be Big Duke, but the "big" kind of fell off with the weight he'd shed since the transplant. Duke hated his name. Lyle.

Grandma had a special pass, though. On that and everything else. If there was a real "ironheart" in their family, it was her. Powerful in the way some women are. Not with muscle or knuckles, but with wisdom and heart and tolerance.

There was so much sadness in her voice that Duke didn't dare look up at her. "Love you, too."

He put on a sweater and went outside.

- 3 -

The barn was a big, red monstrosity. The paint was peeling and the boards looked weary. It was taller and longer than the house and nearly twice as wide. Back when it was built, nearly a hundred and forty years ago, it housed four tractors, a combine harvester, a cultivator, a chisel plow, a harrower, and other old-fashioned farm equipment. Over the years, Duke knew, those machines had been gradually replaced by newer models. Gas engines gave way to solar power, drivers had been replaced by autonomous drive systems and GPS, and then those had been replaced by robots. Farmboy, Plowboy, Tillerman, SeedMonkey. Even the old VetMech, which could do anything from delivering a breeched calf to repairing a ruptured bowel on a mule. All kinds. Duke always loved to hear them all going *clankity-clank* out in the fields. Giants of metal and graphene, wires and flashing lights. *Clankity-clank* as they tilled the fields, *clankity-clank* as they harvested the crops. Sometimes, when he was little, he'd lie awake at night and hear them clanking out in the field, working around the clock because they didn't need to sleep and they didn't need daylight.

Clankity-clank all the way to the bank.

That was something his Gramps used to say. Back when it was true. Back when Duke's family could afford to maintain those machines.

For a long time, Duke's grandfather and dad had kept up with it. The robots helped, but they only saved money when they were working right. Repairs were expensive, and parts for the older ones had to be special ordered. One by one the big machines fell silent. SeedMonkey was the first to die. That was how Duke saw it. The robot died out in the field. It had been sick for a while, leaking oil and lubricant and wheezing white smoke. Gramps had fixed it a dozen times, and Duke had fixed it twice, but after a while some things couldn't be fixed anymore. Duke knew that firsthand. Now SeedMonkey was a pile of parts in a bin in a corner of the barn. Plowboy went next, and Tillerman the following season. VetMech still worked, but there wasn't enough livestock on the farm to give it much use.

It was Farmboy that kept the farm running, though, because he was a multifunction robot. With the right settings he could till a field, sow seeds, manage irrigation, pull weeds, chase crows, and even harvest anything from potatoes to corn.

When he was working right.

Duke stepped into the barn, moving from the bright sunshine into shadows, feeling the change in temperature much more than he used to. He smiled. Good thing Grandma had bullied him into the sweater.

Farmboy sat on an overturned wooden barrel. Like a lot of the midcentury robots, he had been made to look more or less human. Not actually fake skin, hair, and eyes like some of the receptionist bots or Starbucks baristas, but built with two legs, two arms, a head and a manlike torso. The skin was metal, though, and the paint job was the same yellow as the old Kawasaki riding tractors Gramps used to have, with some red stripes and some darker red rust spots. A few gray patches where he'd been repaired. Streaks of green on his legs. Farmboy's face was a screen of wire mesh that protected the cameras and sensors from grit. The dealer had painted two black quarter-size dots for eyes and welded on a metal hat made to look like woven straw, and Gramps had originally removed it, then thought better and put it back. It made Farmboy look like a cartoon version of a robot. Fifteen feet tall when he was standing, with that faux straw hat, broad shoulders, and a barrel body. Duke thought he looked more like something from the 1950s than the 2050s. Now, two decades after his manufacture date, the old boy looked hokey but charming.

Be more charming if he worked, mused Duke. But he regretted the thought. Farmboy had always been his favorite of the farmbots. He was tall and useful, and it was fun to watch him striding across the fields pushing the plow, or walking backward with a chain wrapped around him and a tree stump. Farmboy always won a tug-of-war with a stump, even a big ol' oak stump that the other farmbots couldn't handle. Shortly after Duke came home, he used to sit up in his bed and look out through the window as Farmboy went back and forth through the harvested corn, cutting down the withered stalks and then tilling the ground to freshen it for the next planting. He used to wish that *he* was Farmboy. That he was a towering metal giant, indestructible and useful and reliable, instead of a broken toy soldier with a clockwork heart.

That had been the last season for Farmboy. The big bot had stopped working that winter, proving that he—like Duke—was neither indestructible nor reliable. Duke had tinkered him back to life, but he failed again. And again, each time more quickly than the last. Everything wears out and everything stops working. Human and mechanical hearts were no different after all.

Duke's tools were where he had left them, in an open red box on a hay bale. As he sat down, he felt suddenly very tired. And that

pissed him off. The walk from the house to here was a hundred yards, and he felt like he'd run a marathon. He dragged a forearm across his brow and looked at the dark sweat stains on his sleeve.

"Damn," he said softly, and the wheeze in his voice made him want to cry.

It was nearly five minutes before he felt well enough to bend and pick up a screwdriver from the toolbox. And it was another minute or two before he risked standing up. The barn swayed and he had to use one hand to brace himself against Farmboy's chest to keep from falling.

When he trusted his legs to hold him up, he took a steadying breath and slotted the screwdriver into the first of the four screws holding the chest plate on. The screws were rusty, too, and the slots partially stripped from all the times the plate had been removed to make repairs. Duke grunted with effort and finally managed to turn the first one. It felt to him, though, like this was a statement about his whole life, measuring his current capabilities against what had been effortless once upon a time.

"Come on, you prick," he muttered as he fought the second one. The third. The fourth turned easily, but that pissed Duke off too. Kind of like the world admitting it was screwing with him.

He set the plate down and laid the screws atop it, then clipped a small work light to the edge of the panel frame. Duke spent ten minutes poking inside with pliers and a probe, checking connections, tracing wiring, testing chips, looking for the fault. Nothing obvious yelled at him. There was some dust and grit, but no burned boards, no fried wiring. The robot's metal chest was rusty and dirty, but that shouldn't have affected his functions.

"The hell's wrong with you, you old sumbitch?" he murmured, then sniffed back a tear. "Damn, Farmboy . . . I always thought you were the one bot who they couldn't put on the bench. You're the king, man." He leaned his forehead against the cold metal.

Duke pushed off and leaned back, weary and frustrated.

"Who's going to take care of things when I'm gone?" Duke touched his own chest and then tapped the metal chest of the big robot. The face of the big robot seemed to frown down at him. The black eyes seemed to be sad. Defeated.

"Ah, fuck it," said Duke. "I'm talking to a big pile of rust and bolts as if you're real. You can't hear me, which is okay, because there's nothing I can say or do that's going to mean a single thing. If I can't fix you, then once I'm dead and in the dirt they'll have to sell you off for parts just to pay the light bill. Jesus."

Duke turned to reach for a rag to wipe off the rust, but as he twisted to bend for it, he felt a spasm in his chest and suddenly he was coughing. Hard, deep coughs. Wet and brutal, and the fit lasted for half a minute, slowing and then intensifying, over and over again, and then finally tapering off. Duke turned and sagged back against the solid bulk of Farmboy, head bowed, feeling suddenly a thousand years old. His chest and throat had a punched, bruised feeling to them, and fireflies seemed to dance around him.

"Jesus . . . ," he gasped. Then he looked down at the rag he'd used to cover his mouth. It was speckled with dark dots. They looked like oil in the glow of the work light, but he knew that they were a dark red. It chilled him, scared him, and made him want to cry.

The bleeding was starting again.

The last time that happened was when he had an infection in his lungs that turned into a case of pneumonia so fierce that he was on his back for six weeks. It took a lot of trial and error for the docs to find the right mix of antibiotics. There was a point when Grandma had the minister from the Lutheran church come to visit him in the hospital. The preacher didn't go as far as to give him last rites, but Duke figured he was expecting to do so. Duke recovered, but never all the way. He dropped weight that he couldn't put back on, and ever since then he'd felt as if his bones were as brittle as old sticks.

That pneumonia had started with a cough exactly like this.

Just as sudden, just as deep.

And the blood.

Duke felt new tears in his eyes, but he blinked them back. Tried to, anyway. They lingered, burning like cinders.

The metal skin of Farmboy was cool and soothing against his back. When Duke felt he could risk it, he turned very slowly to look up at the metal face.

"Yeah," said Duke, "look at us. We're a real pair. Used up, broke down, and no damn good at all to anyone."

Farmboy's black eyes stared back at him from under the brim of the fake straw hat. Duke smiled and used the cloth to wipe at the flakes of rust around the open control panel. He saw that there were many tiny drops of blood spattered on the chest, and some had gone into the open panel and glistened redly on the circuit board. The blood made a small hissing sound as the moisture soaked in through a wire mesh air vent on his chest.

"Oh, shit," said Duke, and quickly dabbed at the blood, trying to blot it all up. There was a sudden, loud *chunk-chunk* of a sound, and for a microsecond lights inside the robot's chest flared. It was so quick, so sudden that it sounded like the throb of a heartbeat, but Duke knew what it was. The blood had shorted something out. Maybe the starter. He cursed and tried to get the last of the blood off the sensitive circuitry, but then he stopped, knowing that it was already too late. The robot sat there, and somehow it felt different. Colder, maybe. Deader? Something, anyway.

He looked down at the blood and grease on his rag and shook his head slowly, admitting his mistake — however much it wasn't his fault. Circuits and moisture were never friends, and he'd known that all his life. Now his crumbling body seemed to be taking his mind with it. This was a stupid mistake. A rookie mistake. And it was going to cost his family everything. Just as his own mechanical heart was the most expensive part of Duke's own body, the central circuit board was the robot's heart. Maybe fixable five minutes ago, but killed now by his own traitor blood.

Duke sat there for a long time, saying nothing. Feeling so old, so thin and faded. He raised the rag and rubbed at the rust spots again. Doing something because there was nothing else he could do.

"We used to be something, though," Duke said slowly. "You and me. Couple of badasses. What the hell happened to us?"

The robot, being a robot, said nothing.

Duke started to say something else, but stopped, his mouth open. He stared at the robot's chest and . . . something was weird. Something was wrong. There was a spot, a small smear where he'd been rubbing, where the rust flakes had fallen away to reveal bright metal. Duke glanced down at the rag and saw that he'd accidentally used the part that was spotted with blood, but instead of smearing red atop the dust and rust, it had cleaned the metal. It gleamed like polished stainless steel.

"I don't . . . ," he said, then rubbed at the spot some more. The spot of bright metal expanded from the size of a dime to the size of a quarter. "That doesn't . . ."

He closed his mouth with a snap and tried rubbing again but with a clean corner of the rag. Some rust flakes fell off, but the metal remained an oxidized red-gray. Duke spat on the rag and gave it another rub. Same thing.

But that bright patch seemed to shine at him. Duke looked down at the blood spots on the cloth, then back up.

"Don't be an idiot," he told himself.

A few seconds later he pressed the bloody part of the cloth against the spot he'd rubbed twice with no effect. This time, though, the ruddy color changed, vanishing the way grime does when scrubbed with a powerful cleanser. Bright metal shone in the weak light.

"No," said Duke. "No way."

He rubbed and rubbed at it until he had a spot as big as his palm. By then the rag was covered in dirt and rust that had mingled with the blood and truly turned it black. When he bent forward, he could see his reflection in the mirror-bright metal.

Duke tried to make sense of it, fishing in his memories of high school science for something rational. Was there some kind of enzyme in blood that eradicated rust? He doubted it. Was it the heat of the blood? No, that couldn't be right, because spit would be just as warm, especially after more than a minute on the cloth.

Which left . . . what?

He rubbed again, but there wasn't much of the blood left and the effect was diminishing. He tried spit again and got nothing. Even an industrial abrasive didn't work.

"The hell . . . ?" he asked the robot.

Farmboy said nothing.

Duke sagged a little, though he had no real idea what he was depressed about. So he'd cleaned a patch of metal. Big frigging deal. All that meant was that Farmboy was a minimally cleaner piece of junk.

He punched the robot. Not too hard. Enough to make his knuckles hurt, though.

"*Damn it*," he growled. Then suddenly he was coughing again. Harder. So much harder. It struck him so fast there was no time to brace himself, no time to even cover his face. He caved forward as forcefully as if he'd been punched in the gut and only just managed to keep from smashing his face on the robot by slapping his palms against the cold metal. The coughs racked him, tore at him, pummeled him from the inside out. Spit and blood splatted on Farmboy's chest and across the sensitive circuits inside the open panel. There were no sparks, of course, because Farmboy was dead.

Duke coughed, feeling the weight of each spasm as it pushed him down, making his head bow down between his trembling arms.

It felt like he was surrendering. Like he was giving up. Being forced to admit that this was how it was going to be. Not a holding pattern, propped up by pills and careful living. Not a slow slide down.

No. The cough was immediate and it was huge. It was a great big fist and it was going to smash him. Maybe not this minute, but soon. Without doubt, soon.

Fresh blood splashed across the robot's chest. He was dying, right here, right now. He could feel his own internal systems shutting down.

I'm sorry, he thought, wishing he could shout those words so that everyone who'd ever loved him could hear them.

He coughed for five long, brutal minutes, and then he leaned there, gasping, tears running down his face, blood running hot over his lower lip and hanging in fat drops from his chin. Sweat, cold and greasy, beading on his forehead and trickling over the knobs of his spine.

The minute hands seemed to fall off the clock for him, and Duke had no idea at all how long he stayed in that position, hands braced against the fall all the way down. When he could speak, it was to gasp a single word.

"Please . . ."

Said over and over again.

When he could finally stand and walk, it took him twenty minutes to go all the way home. All those thousands of miles from the barn to the house.

- 4 -

Gramps found him. Duke barely remembered it. The screams that were maybe Grandma's, maybe Gramps's, maybe his own. Hands on him, checking him, feeling for a pulse, taking way too long to find it. Dim views of faces lined with pain and fear. The expressions of people who knew what they were seeing, who knew how this would end. And when. Night was falling and Duke knew—as everyone else knew—that there wouldn't be a morning. Not for him. He'd reached his sell-by date, and he began to grieve. Not for himself, but because it meant that he was leaving his grandparents, and that felt like it was *they* who were dying. He felt shame at having failed them.

Gran called the neighbors who came and helped carry him to bed. The doctor came and his diagnosis was clear on his face. He left without recommending that Duke be taken to the hospital.

That night Duke sat up in bed, because lying down brought on coughing fits. Grandma had made soup. Now she and Gramps were both downstairs, and Duke could almost feel them trying to decide how to react.

As if there was a playbook for something like this.

The hours of that night were eternal. Sleep was a series of bad dreams linked by coughing and spitting blood into a bucket. The doctor hadn't even lied to him about how bad this was, or how bad it was going to be. Instead he'd written the prescription and didn't meet Duke's eyes. Not once. Why would he? Doctors were all about trying to help the living. They wouldn't want to stare into the eyes of the dead.

All Grandma could do was cry.

Not in his room, not where he could see her. Downstairs, where she thought he couldn't hear.

He heard.

He heard her praying, too, and he wondered when the Lutheran minister would come back to handle unfinished business.

The TV was on, but Duke didn't watch it. His face was turned toward the window, toward the night that rose like a big black tsunami above the house. Duke wept, too, but his tears were quiet and cold and they were not of grief. He wept because he had failed his family. Enlisting in the army had been stupid. Sure, it was a family tradition, but no one had forced him into it. No one said he *had* to.

But he did anyway, and he'd had his heart shredded in a war that didn't matter to anyone he ever knew or ever met.

If he'd stayed here, he'd be able to work the farm. He'd have kept the robots from falling apart or running down. He'd have fought for his family in a way that mattered.

Now . . .

All that was left was the actual dying. All other failures had been accomplished.

When the next wave of coughing swept through him, he thought it was the last one. There was a high-pitched whine in his ears, and there didn't seem to be enough air left in the room. The mechanical heart in his chest kept beating with grotesque regularity. As if there was nothing wrong. As if the house of flesh around it wasn't burning down.

In the depth of his pain, Duke thought he heard that sound again. *Chunk-chunk.* Like a heartbeat. *Sympathy pains from Farmboy,* he thought, and for some reason that made him laugh. Which made him cough even worse.

The coughing fit ebbed slowly. So slowly, leaving Duke spent on the black shore of a long sleep. In his spasms he'd turned onto his side so he could spit into the bucket. The curtains were open, and outside the moon and stars sparkled above the roof of the big barn. Duke could see the doors, and even in the midst of his pain he frowned at them. There was something wrong. Something different.

He'd seen Gramps close them at sunset, the way he always did. There were no farmhands left, and his grandparents were downstairs. He could hear Gramps trying to comfort Grandma.

So why were the doors open?

Why?

He heard the sound before he saw anything move. Not a cow or pig. Not a horse. It was faint, metallic. Slow.

Familiar in a way that made no sense at all, and Duke strained to hear.

Clankity-clank.

A machine? But which machine? They were all piles of junk. Like him. Broken and dead, or a short step away from being dead. Just like him.

Clankity-clank.

Duke pushed himself up so he could see better. Moving his body was like trying to move a truck with his bare hands. His body was a bundle of sticks, but it was also improbably heavy. *Dead weight,* he thought, and almost laughed.

Clankity-clank.

Duke saw something, and he froze and squinted to try and understand what he was seeing.

A figure moved in the shadows just inside the barn doorway. Tall. Big.

Gleaming.

"What . . . ?" asked Duke, but his voice was a whisper. Almost gone. A ghost's voice.

The figure took a step forward.

Clankity-clank.

Duke saw the metal leg step out into the moonlight. Then a swinging arm. A chest. A head with a metal hat welded on. Two black eyes seeming to look up at him.

Clankity-clank.

Farmboy stepped out of the barn. The metal plate was back in place over the control panel, but bright light escaped from around its edges. The barrel chest of the robot was as bright as polished silver.

Except for some black smears on its chest.

Even from that distance, Duke was sure he saw those smears. Black as oil.

Duke knew that they weren't black.

He knew.

And he smiled.

Then Farmboy turned slowly to face the big, dark fields. There were hundreds of hours of work that Duke couldn't do, and that his grandparents were too old to do alone. The robot began walking toward the field.

He turned once to look up at the farmhouse, but by then there was no one to look back. Then the robot turned back to the field and began to walk. *Clankity-clank, clankity-clank.*

Going to work.

TEAM ROBOT

BY JONATHAN MABERRY

I'm Team Robot. All the way. Team Robot for the win.

Not that I have anything against faeries. Nope. I have faeries in my middle-grade novel series, *The Nightsiders*. I'm good with all the realms of faerie, and I enjoyed fairy tales in all of their many forms.

But . . . robots.

C'mon.

Robots?

I was introduced to science fiction through the writings of Ray Bradbury (who was a friend and writing mentor when I was a teenager), Isaac Asimov, and the wonderful Adam Link stories by Eando Binder. I was Team Robot from the jump. I loved Robbie from *Forbidden Planet* and Robot from *Lost in Space*. I loved the *Space Giants* TV show, which was about a family of robots. I have statues of robots—stationary and windup—on my bookshelves. And about the only dance moves I can manage are sad approximations of the Robot.

Besides, robots are cool. They bring with them a sense of mystery. Especially in this modern era, where artificial intelligence, nanotechnology, and robotics are heading toward the very real possibility of mechanical constructs who can legitimately think. Not programmed responses, but self-awareness. Now, I know, you're thinking Skynet and about a zillion cautionary tales of the technological singularity. I don't buy that part of it. Why would self-awareness instantly lead to hostility? Maybe what we'd get is a

kind of benign, powerful, well-informed innocence. That's where I'm placing my wildly optimistic bet.

Right now the most I can do is have decidedly one-sided conversations with my Roomba, but that could change.

Any ol' day now.

So, sure. Team Robot.

JUST ANOTHER LOVE SONG

by Kat Howard

The first time I tried to sing a man's death, he laughed. Then he asked me out.

I was busking downtown. It can make for long days, standing outside in the ebb and flow of people, none of whom are actually there to see you, but I can also make pretty decent money, and even the longest day busking is better than a short one spent locked in an office, or working retail.

Plus, I do have a bit of an extra advantage. Being a banshee means my voice is a tool—I can harmonize with myself, run vocal loops, all sorts of stuff that has people looking around for cords and reverb pedals and a laptop where I must be programming things. Sorry, folks. No electronics. Just me. And my fairy blood.

Things had gotten a little weird that summer. Fae had gone missing, and without any obvious reason. No bodies had turned up, there were no rumors that unpleasant humans were making life difficult for those of us who didn't quite fit in, no hints as to what was happening. Just Fae, gone. Four so far, and in the span of under a month.

Completely creepy, and moving toward terrifying. So I noticed things, more than I normally would have.

And I noticed the guy, who pushed his way from the back of the crowd around to the front. I noticed, and then my magic did.

Before I saw him, I'd never felt the call to use the darker side of my inheritance and be an omen or sing a death, which, honestly, I had been fine with. It wasn't a part of my power I wanted to use. I mean, we live in a society: I don't need to be breaking out the wailing and watching people drop dead in my wake to be happy. But as he came closer, I felt as if my blood had turned to fog. Magic rose up in my throat, so full and fast that I wondered that I could still sing at all, around the lump of it.

Then, in the middle of singing all of Carly Rae Jepsen's harmonies at once, I let out a wail. One that should have stopped his heart in his chest, and his breath in his lungs.

It didn't work.

He laughed. "Forget the lyrics?"

No, I had not.

"Well, look, do you take requests? I want you to sing me a love song. One that's just for me."

"No," I said.

"If you won't do that, then maybe you'll go out with me? I'm Trent, by the way." He looked expectant, as if his dimples ought to be enough to make me give up my name. They weren't.

"Very no," I said.

"Come on, just one cup of coffee—I'm a musician too."

Of course he was.

He was good-looking, I'll give him that, but he had the kind of attitude that suggested he knew to the ounce precisely how good-looking he was, and expected the world to make his life easier because of it. "I'm busy tonight, sorry." I stared, waiting for him to turn pale and faint. Or for blood to leak like tears from his eyes. For something. Anything.

"Your number. Could I at least get your number?" A smile and a step closer, his eyes twinkling at me. "I promise I'll only use it for business purposes—I'm putting together a band, and I think you'd be perfect."

"Still no." He looked disgustingly healthy and sounded like he was having no problems breathing. The magic hadn't worked. I didn't know what I'd done wrong. I gathered up the Wonder Woman lunch box I used to collect money in, and left.

His voice followed me. "What? Do you have a boyfriend or something? I promise I'm more fun."

"Drop dead," I said. I waited until I got to the corner to glance back and see if that had worked any better than the singing. Nope. Still alive. "Shit."

As I walked home, I thought I heard someone singing. A love song—desire and longing. I shook my head and walked faster.

"You sang what you were supposed to?" my roommate, Sarah, asked. Sarah is a brownie, which is the best possible thing for a roommate to be. She's a brilliant cook, keeps the apartment both spotless and roach free, and actually likes doing the laundry.

"I mean, I think so. I've never done it before, but the wail welled right up when I saw him." I could still feel the sensation of fog, cold air, and loneliness lingering in my throat, like it wasn't finished, like it might come back.

"Maybe he didn't realize what you were doing," Sarah said.

"What, he figured I spontaneously burst into howls while singing, and that turned him on so much he had to ask me out?"

"Guys have liked stranger things, Mairead, you know this," she said.

"True. But it shouldn't matter whether he realized or not. That's not how the magic is supposed to work. Ugh, maybe I'm broken." I rubbed my throat. Part of me was glad it hadn't worked. I liked the part of my magic that let me sing. I didn't even mind having a voice that could be a weapon. But if it was, I wanted to be in control of it, to be able to decide how and when I used that part of my magic. Bad enough the magic wasn't working when I wanted it to, I didn't want to have to worry that I'd reach for a high note and wind up with someone keeling over mid-chorus.

I shook my head, and shook the thought aside. "Speaking of singing, there's a new band at Purple Reign tonight. Want to come?"

Sarah shook her head. Like a lot of brownies, with their tight ties to the house they dwell in and care for, Sarah is agoraphobic. She's not totally housebound, and she's told me that she appreciates it when I invite her places. So I do—she's my friend. And it doesn't bother me when she says no, like she usually does. "Not this time, thanks. There's this new recipe I want to try, one of those fifty-layer cakes, and it takes a long time."

I let out a sound that was less of a wail and more of a groan of sugar-filled anticipation. "Sounds amazing. I look forward to taste-testing it for you."

"I knew I could count on your help," she said.

I grinned.

"Maybe take a cab tonight, though. There was another disappearance today."

"Another?" I asked. "Who this time?"

"The púca that lives in Central Park."

"Seriously?"

Sarah nodded.

"Still no hint as to what's going on?"

"Not that I've seen." The Fae were good at gossip—you get that way if you have a hide in plain sight sort of lifestyle—and Sarah was a wiz at social media. "Mostly, people are worried."

The walk to the club was short, not even a mile. And it was supposed to be a nice evening. But the púca was bigger and fiercer than I was by a long shot. Plus, he could turn into a horse. If someone could kidnap him, I doubted I'd be a challenge. I was worried too. "Okay. I'll take a cab."

Purple Reign was a Fae club. Not that we banned humans from coming in or anything like that; it was just really hard to find if you didn't know about it. You might, if you hadn't been invited, walk past and think that it was actually a run-down diner that looked like it had failed its last health inspection and smelled like it had just had a garbage fire.

Which is why I was surprised to walk in and see Trent up onstage. He was as smarmy and good-looking as ever. Also, as apparently alive as ever. Singing, in fact. Alone in the spotlight, solo guitar. Surrounded by seriously adoring fans—a wide variety of Fae crowding the stage, bodies in various stages of what might best be described as "swoon."

Not swoon like the reaction when you think someone is hot, not even like the reaction when you want to get in someone's pants so bad that your brain sort of short-circuits. More like when you see people literally lose their powers of speech, where their eyes go unfocused and yearning, when you suspect that the walls could be burning down around them and they wouldn't even notice. That sort of swoon.

And that explained why he was here. He was Fae. A gancanagh—a love talker. Able to use his voice as a tool of seduction. And when I say tool, I mean basically a hammer. If you heard it, if he spoke his words to you, you'd fall in love with him. Well, not "love" so much as "significant sexual infatuation." Whether he was your normal type or not, if he told you that you wanted him, it would be very, very hard—maybe even impossible—for you to resist. You would do whatever he wanted to make him happy.

The gancanagh was not a type of Fae I was fond of.

I watched through narrowed eyes as he sang. His voice was

pleasant enough, the songs covers, all sugary-sweet pop. Love songs of one variety or another, surprise, surprise. He wasn't, as far as I could tell, directing his singing to one person in particular, but rather blasting the room with the force of his voice, dispersing the lust generally. I still wasn't a fan, but feeding off the love of the audience I could let slide.

Still, I had no desire to hear the rest of his set, so I slipped back out the door to wait, to make sure he went home alone. As I waited, that fog-feeling rose up in my throat again like a doom. When I saw him step outside, I wailed. Even though I was certain there'd be no effect, I felt like I'd drown if I didn't let the cry shriek from my throat.

Once again, nothing happened. Shit, maybe I really was broken. This was possibly ungood.

"You," he said, still all charm in tight T-shirt and worn denim. "Decided to get that cup of coffee after all?"

"Not even a little bit," I said.

"I'd ask if you came by to hear me play, but I didn't see you at the show."

"I was there. Briefly. Long enough to see you," I said. "You've got some . . . interesting arrangements to your songs. The crowd seemed to really love them." I kept my eyes on his face, trying to see if he'd react. We're not forbidden from using our powers on each other or anything like that, but something about what he'd been doing struck me as sort of tacky. I wanted him to know that I knew.

But there was no change in his expression. Just that smile. "You should come back. Do a song with me tomorrow—I'm here one more night. I'll even have a full band, one I'm really excited about, and I'd love to hear how you sound with them. I bet the audience would just die to hear you sing."

He knew what I was too, then. I kept my face blank. "Sounds interesting. Maybe I will."

A cab slowed, and I raised my arm to flag the driver.

"It's still early. Do you have to leave now?" Trent asked.

"Yes." I opened the car door.

Then he sang a line from one of his earlier songs—something about longing and staying together. He looked at me intensely as he did, and paused at the end, as if he was waiting for something else to happen. Like he was hoping it would make me change my mind. It didn't. I got into the cab and went home.

"So he knows what I am, obviously," I said, through a mouthful of a cake made out of layers of chocolate crepes, with some sort of glorious pistachio filling between them. "This is maybe the best thing you've ever made, by the way."

"Thanks," Sarah said. "And if he knows, then you should definitely stay home. Don't sing."

"Why?" I asked.

"He won't have asked for any good reason. Think about it. If he knows what you are, then it's because he knows you've been trying to use your wail to kill him. Why would he ever invite you to sing after that?"

"Because he also knows it isn't working," I said. "Maybe at this point he thinks hearing me fail is funny. Although—I think he failed too. He sang some crap about staying together all night as I was leaving."

"No desire to change your mind?" Sarah asked.

"None at all—if I hadn't known he was a gancanagh, I would have thought it was a really cheesy attempt at flirting."

"Maybe you two cancel each other out," Sarah said. "Love and death could be opposites."

"I've never heard of anything like that happening."

"Neither have I, but I've also never heard of something like what's going on with your voice." She tucked the cake into a container, tapped the top. I could see the shimmer in the air as the spell that

would keep the cake from going stale settled around it. "The whole thing seems weird to me. Bad weird, not entertaining weird."

"You have a point. But." I took another bite, considered.

"How can there be a 'but'?" she asked.

"I can still feel it. The call. The omen. Whatever it is, that wants me to sing. And to sing to him." Fog, quiet, waiting in the back of my throat. "I don't think this is finished."

"I don't like this," Sarah said.

I didn't either.

I went out busking the next day, as usual. I half expected Trent to show up again, but things were—with the exception of the guy in the suit who used the cash I had collected to make change for a twenty without asking, and then dropped a quarter back in the lunchbox with an enormous flourish—uneventful. No banshee wails rising in my throat, no half-heard songs following me on my way home, no disappeared Fae.

And then I got home, and Sarah was gone.

Which was weird, but not impossible. What was impossible was that she had left the oven on, the bread that she had been baking now bricked into charcoal, and the smoke alarm was wailing louder even than I could.

There were no good circumstances under which that would have happened. But the burned bread was the only thing out of place. It was as if Sarah had just . . . left. As if something had lured her out, had wooed her from within the safety of our walls.

That was when I knew.

I had met someone, very recently, with a voice that could lure. He wouldn't have even needed to be in the apartment, wouldn't have even needed to know it was Sarah he was luring out—a song sung below an open window, and that would be enough.

I ran to Purple Reign.

"Trent's sound-checking, but he said if someone like you showed up, to let her in," the woman working security said.

Inside, I was greeted by a sight I never expected to see—Sarah, onstage, playing the drums. Playing the drums *well*. I was so shocked that it took me at least a verse and a chorus to register what else I was seeing. There was the púca, in his human form, playing bass. A red-cap on keyboards. A trio of flower Fae singing backup. All the missing Fae here, in support of the gancanagh.

Once the shock had passed, I looked closer. Sarah's hands were raw, blistered. So were the púca's. The redcap's hat was almost dry, as if he hadn't refreshed it in weeks. He had been, I remembered now, the first to go missing. The flower Faes' blossoms were wilted at the edges and their lips dry and chapped.

The gancanagh smiled as he led his kidnapped band into the next verse. There was no recognition on Sarah's face. None. All of the Fae had the same expression: absolute, focused concentration. If Trent had used his voice to tell them that this was what he loved, what he wanted, they'd play until he told them to stop.

They'd play forever.

"I told you I'd have a full band. They haven't been together that long, but I think they've got real potential. All of them just love what they're doing," he said.

"Care to join us? I think you'd be the perfect addition." He started to sing then, something about desire for the spotlight, the perfect girl, a whole room in love. I felt it then—not a compulsion, not fully. But that edge of wanting, just beneath the skin. The beginning of the thought that here, up onstage, this was where I belonged. Where I had always wanted to be.

"Come on, everybody, give it up for our new guest vocalist!" Trent called out.

A tray of glasses shattered as the bartender dropped them so she could clap. The bouncers started screaming and stomping their feet.

The coat-check guy climbed up on the counter and cheered. All the staff who had been going about their business a second ago were going wild to convince me to get onstage.

I looked again at Sarah's hands, at the other Fae—stolen, hurt, exhausted. At Trent, and his smile—that smarmy, self-satisfied smile, as if all of life were his for the taking. With this band, it was. Somehow, he was stronger with them, using them to boost his own magic. In that moment, I wanted him dead.

"Come on now, sing with us. All we need is you and we'll sound perfect."

That itch of wanting to be there, on that stage, was stronger now, more compelling.

"Yeah, okay. Sure." I stepped up and grabbed the mic.

"Remember, I want a love song."

"Oh, I've got one for you."

There are all sorts of songs about love. There are the songs that make you feel that champagne fizz of first attraction, songs that ride on the drum and bass beat of lust. Violin strings of longing and the mournful piano of endings and regret.

And then there are songs about love that kills. Murder ballads and choruses of women haunting hills in long black veils. And over the púca's pop beat and the sweet harmonies of the flower Fae, that was what I sang.

What I wailed.

The cold and fog curled up through my throat like ghosts, and the blood iced in my veins. This time, this time I knew the power would work. My voice echoed in that dingy club as if it were an opera house. This was what it was to sing as a banshee.

I sang of love that consumes. That murders and unmakes. I sang an unraveling, aiming my voice at the very heart of him.

When I started, the gancanagh was singing too, trying to harmonize, but his voice grew weaker, hesitant, flat. One by one, the enchantments broke from the other Fae in his band, and their music went silent. Until the only sounds in the room were his voice and mine.

And then mine was the only one. I met his eyes, and I took a bow.

"What did you do?" he asked. Still not dead. His magic, however, was. I'd felt it on the stage, and heard it when he spoke. His voice was normal. No power to woo, or lure, or take away choices.

I helped Sarah out from behind the drums, down off the stage. She was shaking as she walked, but she turned and glared at him and whispered the worst curse I'd ever heard her say. Trent was in for an extended plague of ripping seams, unzipping zippers, and oversalted, undercooked food. Brownies can be ruthless.

"I did just what you wanted," I said. "I sang you a love song."

TEAM FAIRY

BY KAT HOWARD

Team Fairy. Of course I'm on Team Fairy. As if there was ever any doubt. I mean, can you imagine a robot singing a murder ballad? Well, perhaps you can, but that raises the question of whether you *should*, and let me assure you, if you want to have any pleasure at all in the listening, better to imagine a fairy. Even if her song will stop your heart. I've been fascinated with banshees since I first knew what they were, and to me, fairies are fun precisely because they are powerful. A woman whose power is in her voice, learning to use it? Oh yes. I'll write that.

SOUND AND FURY

by Mary Robinette Kowal

The hum of the ship engines sent a vibration up through the soles of Jela Dedearian's feet. It was always more pronounced near the engine room. By god, she was exhausted. All she wanted was to curl up with her cat and a good novel, but this shift was never going to end.

She rubbed her face with both hands and leaned against the wall of the shuttle bay for a moment. "All right, Okeke. Let's check the restraints."

Okeke nodded, her locs bobbing around her cheeks. "Checking giant robot now."

"Diplomatic Personal Surrogate."

Okeke snorted. "Yeah. That's totally what I meant."

"Obviously." The captain would have their asses if she caught them talking shit about the mission, but goddamn it. . . . Even if Jela had agreed with the Consortium of Worlds' expansion policy, Diplomat Foenicul made it damned hard to be respectful.

"Hey . . . Chief. I got this." Okeke straightened from the restraint strap she was testing. "You can go on to bed."

"Oh, believe me. I have zero doubts about you. It's just that, bless her heart, Diplomat Foenicul has expressed that she will be more comfortable if the chief engineer is involved." She widened her eyes and adopted a too-innocent expression. "Because clearly, I'm the only one on the whole ship who knows how to tie down a giant robot."

"She's not even in here."

"But she will be." Jela massaged the nagging ache in her forehead. "Believe me, the moment y'all deploy to the surface I have a date with my bed and my cat."

"How's Sadie doing?"

"Deeply annoyed." All of the straps were fine. There was no point in her checking them, except that Guadalupe Foenicul insisted on having "the best," which meant that Jela had been working double shifts in order to do the work she actually needed to do, in addition to the busywork that the diplomat required. And for what? So they could bring another planet into the fold? "How about you? Adika okay with you going to the planet?"

"As long as I bring him back a souvenir, he'll forgive anything. And by souvenir, I mean a rock. That child . . . his rock collection is going to be the envy of geologists across the galaxy."

"Maybe he can negotiate mining rights for—"

The doors to the cargo bay opened and Diplomat Foenicul fluttered in, followed by her assistant and Captain Afaeaki. Her gossamer wings kept her at eye level with the captain, even if her feet were a good meter away from the ground. The captain had her lips so firmly set that it suggested she was less than happy. At least Jela wasn't the only member of the senior staff who was being asked to do work below her pay grade. It was just one mission. Jela just had to keep reminding herself of that. It was only one mission and if she weren't doing it, someone else would be feeding the insatiable maw of the Consortium.

"Ah! Chief Engineer Dedearian. Are we ready?"

First of all, this was an hour before departure was scheduled.

Second . . . We? As if Jela was going anywhere near the surface. "Yes, sir. You'll be in good hands with Lieutenant Okeke."

"Excellent." She steepled her fingers together, as if she were about to begin a sermon. "This is a bold new era for sentient rapport in the cosmos. I hope that . . ."

Jela smiled and nodded, completely tuning out Foenicul's speech. It would have been nice to have been wrong about that one, but Foenicul was sadly predictable. Didn't matter. What mattered was that the Consortium of Worlds needed to establish a base on this planet, ostensibly for "mining rights," but really because they needed a foothold in the system. And as much as Foenicul got on Jela's nerves, she had an impressive track record for successful negotiations. Even if this one did involve a giant robot, because "the natives have an unconscious bias related to stature."

As soon as the robot was off her ship, Jela could go collapse and Sadie would sit on her back and make biscuits into the sore muscles under her shoulder blades, and then she would do her damnedest never to go near a diplomatic mission again. Please god, let the launch go smoothly.

Jela walked down the corridor to her cabin with one hand trailing along the wall. Not because she was so tired that she might fall over, but because she was *almost* that tired. Her comm unit pinged.

The aggressively cheery tone sent an ice pick in through her ear to land just behind her eyes. She stopped in the middle of the hall and squeezed her eyes shut. The stupid giant robot was off her ship, and she just wanted to go to sleep.

On her wrist comm, the captain's name showed clearly. No ignoring this one. She tapped the comm. "Dedearian here."

"Might I ask you to come to the bridge?" Captain Afaeaki sounded preternaturally calm. The only time she got that formal was when the shit had hit the fan, blown through it, and spattered on the wall.

Jela reversed course, stalking back down the corridor to the lift. "On my way. Can you update me for what I'll find?"

"The controls for the Diplomatic Personal Surrogate are not connecting properly. Diplomat Foenicul thought that you might have some thoughts."

"Can you specify what 'not connecting properly' means?"

"I am not an engineer, but I will endeavor to do so."

Jela winced. The captain was good and pissed now but probably had Diplomat Foenicul standing over her shoulder. "Thanks. I appreciate any information."

"The planet is demonstrating some unusual atmospheric disturbance. The current speculation is that it is interfering with the signal."

That was so not her department. Jela slapped the control on the elevator panel. "What did Conteh say about it?"

"He made several attempts to rectify the situation before Diplomat Foenicul requested you."

"I'll look at giving a signal boost and . . ." The captain would care less about that shit. "It'll be fine. I'm on the lift. Be on the bridge in three. Dedearian out."

As the doors closed, she pressed the control for the bridge and then leaned against the wall. The hum and movement of the elevator made her light-headed. She closed her eyes, just for a moment.

The hiss of the doors opening made her straighten. Jela tugged her uniform shirt down as she walked onto the bridge. Conteh, the communications officer, caught her gaze and rolled his eyes. He knew his stuff and had probably tried every frequency adjustment possible. Jela wouldn't insult him by going through any of the things that would be in his arsenal.

Captain Afaeaki's posture might have been carved out of granite. Her jaw was set in an unforgiving line, and when she turned from Diplomat Foenicul, Jela paused to give a crisp salute. She was

rewarded by a very slight lift of the captain's eyebrow. Good. At least she knew how much horseshit this was.

"Chief Engineer Dedearian. Thank you for your prompt appearance."

Full titles, was it? All right, then. Freaking diplomats. "Captain Afaeaki, I await your orders."

"If you could please assist the diplomat?" She gestured to Diplomat Foenicul, who had a console set up on the bridge. Jela had made the argument that the shuttle bay would be better for the console since it was closer to engineering and wouldn't be in the captain's way, but it was apparently not right for . . . reasons.

"Certainly. Let's see what we can do to boost the signal."

After her third trip down to the engine room, which was exactly why she had suggested the shuttle bay as being a better location for the console, Jela had exhausted her repertoire of tricks. Except one. And she didn't want to offer that, because she damn well knew who was going to get assigned to the duty. Besides, if the mission just happened to fail due to "unsual atmospheric disturbance," that wouldn't be on her. She straightened from beneath the console and wiped her hands off on a rag. "No luck. Any chance we can wait for the storm to pass?"

Diplomat Foenicul sliced her hand through space to negate the possibility. "The Krowrehto leaders are expecting us, and they will have seen the shuttle land."

Letting out a sigh, Jela tucked the rag back into her tool kit. The Krowrehto leaders had been fed a pack of horseshit about how the Consortium would make their world better, when it would just strip their resources for the capital. Just like it had done to her own homeworld. "The only thing we haven't tried is putting up a satellite antenna on the surface to boost the signal."

"Perfect!"

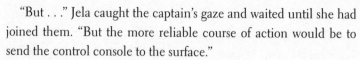

"But . . ." Jela caught the captain's gaze and waited until she had joined them. "But the more reliable course of action would be to send the control console to the surface."

"Alas. We cannot risk them seeing my petite nature. But you have given me hope."

Of course. Because that would let the "natives" see that the Consortium was lying to them from the very beginning. And that was not something that Jela could voice.

Fluttering higher, Diplomat Foenicul turned her palms up in thanksgiving. "When can you depart?"

"That depends on the captain's needs. I *am* responsible for the entire ship, and this is a task that can easily be delegated to another technician, such as Okeke, who is already on the surface."

"Oh, but Okeke was not able to resolve the problem, and with such delicate negotiations, I need only the best." Diplomat Foenicul lowered her gaze. "No offense to Lieutenant Okeke, of course, but surely you see how much the Consortium of Worlds needs you."

Standing a little behind the diplomat, Captain Afaeaki rolled her eyes, and that was the only thing that kept Jela rooted to her spot. The captain understood how much the Consortium "needed" anyone. While they were technically an independent ship, turning down a Consortium job had a strange tendency to turn into a treason charge. "You have your orders, Chief Engineer Dedearian."

"Yes, ma'am." Jela saluted and stalked off the bridge. She'd have to ask someone to feed Sadie while she was conducting the universe's most pointless away mission.

Under normal circumstances, Jela would have flown herself down to the planet, but pulling an all-nighter after a week of double shifts left her less than confident in her ability to stay awake for two hours. Besides, with Sal flying, she could nap on the way down.

Only the change in engine noise told Jela that they were on

the ground. She opened her eyes and straightened in her chair. "Handled with your usual grace, I see."

At her side, Sal's tentacles curled with delight. "Thank you, ma'am."

"Hope you brought a book." Jela unbuckled her restraint and swung out of her seat. "This is gonna be dull."

She headed for the landing hatch and toggled it open. The outside air was a little cool and smelled of cinnamon and seaweed. Okeke was already crossing the clearing where they'd set down. Her own ship, and the giant robot, were waiting at the other side. The robot's anodized teal shell made a startling contrast with the vivid red foliage that surrounded them. The low trees gave way to reedy grass and then to a broad lake.

Jela lifted her arms overhead, in an attempt to wake up, and stared across the lake at the city on the other side. The buildings were set well back from the lake and surrounded by a beautiful mosaic wall. The undulating patterns of blues and greens put her in mind of Sal's tentacles. There would be nothing unique here in another hundred years.

"Hey, Chief." Okeke had a smear of grease next to her nose. "Sorry you had to come down."

"Lady knows, it's not your fault." She headed over to the cargo hold to grab the transmission booster, with Okeke at her side. "I shoulda sent the transmitter with you in the first place." She should have said there was nothing to be done and left it at that.

"Well, clear skies and all that."

"Huh." Jela stepped back from the shuttle as Okeke undid the hatch. The sky overhead was a crystalline blue, with nary a cloud. "Has it been clear like this all night?"

"Random lightning, but no clouds." Okeke grabbed one end of the case holding the booster. "You said it was solar activity?"

"That's what it looks like." She lifted one end of the case while Okeke grabbed the other. "From the ship, the aurora borealis looked pretty stunning."

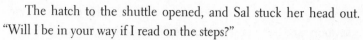

The hatch to the shuttle opened, and Sal stuck her head out. "Will I be in your way if I read on the steps?"

"Knock yourself out." Getting a chance to breathe air that hadn't been recycled for decades was something no one would pass up. Heck, even Jela was feeling more alert, just from air and natural light.

They carried the booster over to the other shuttle, not that it needed proximity to the giant robot to work, but once they got it working, she'd be leaving it with Okeke.

Okeke snorted. "Too bad we couldn't have the giant robot carry this for us."

"Well . . ." Jela set her end of the case down. "I mean . . . we need to test all the parameters of the 'Diplomatic Personal Surrogate.'"

"Yes, ma'am. Of course. Of course that's what we need to do." Okeke grinned and led the way over to the controls. She'd set them up outside the shuttle, hoping that they could act as a synced relay for the system aboard the ship. "Want to do the honors?"

She'd rather let Okeke have the fun, but given Diplomat Foenicul's insistence on using the "best" of everything, it was probably safer if Jela used the giant robot. If anything went wrong with it, she didn't want Okeke to take the brunt of that. And that, really, was why she hadn't tried to sabotage anything regarding the mission. It had the potential to get everyone in her department in trouble. "Yeah . . . Yeah, I guess I'd better. Why don't you look for a rock for Adika while I do this?"

"You are the absolute best." Okeke nodded toward the lake. "I'll be over there."

"Take your time." Chances were, even when she got this working, Diplomat Foenicul would insist that she stay on the planet. Jela activated the controls and, for thoroughness, started a new calibration sequence. Who was she kidding? Even working for the devil, it was hard not to do her personal best. As her matriarch had always said, "Done right, or done over."

A breeze brushed her cheek, and she closed her eyes to enjoy the sensation. She had an oscillating fan in her cabin, to try to mimic the randomness of natural air, but it wasn't the same. This carried scents of loam and cinnamon and a salty tang of seaweed. As much as Jela loved engineering and space, she had hired onto the ship because of the planets she got to visit. If she'd known that the captain was taking this diplomatic gig, she'd have . . . what? Quit? And found another job doing what, exactly? It wasn't as if the captain of any other ship would have been able to turn the job down safely.

Okeke screamed.

Jela's eyes snapped open, her hand reaching for her blaster. At the shore, a giant squid monster thing had emerged, dripping, from the water and held Okeke in one tentacle.

Sal shouted something in her native language and fired her blaster at the thing. From within the monster's mass of tentacles, a toothed beak emerged. The entire thing pulled itself closer to Sal, balancing impossibly on the dozens of writhing arms.

Across the lake, the mosaic wall became alive with activity as hundreds of citizens rushed to the top with spears and guns and braced themselves. Holy crap. This had not been in any of their pre-mission briefings.

Why the hell hadn't Foenicul told them about giant squid when the citizens clearly knew about them?

Jela grabbed the interface visor from the console and shoved her arms into the control mitts. No way was that thing getting any of her team. She toggled the system to full power and then—

Then she was looking out the eyes of the giant robot. The system translated the patterns of her brain and muscular intentions into movement. She stood, rising fifteen meters above the ground. She'd give a lot for a weapons system on this, but a Diplomatic Personal Surrogate didn't come equipped with such things.

But a club would work. She strode forward, ground trembling

beneath her feet, and snatched up the case containing the satellite booster.

The squid-thing paused in its advance on Sal and turned its beak toward Jela. Or, rather, toward the giant robot. It seemed to have forgotten that it still held Okeke in one tentacle. She had one hand free and was slamming a rock against the tentacle.

Jela rammed the squid-thing with the case. It tumbled back, seemingly stunned. She needed it to drop Okeke. There was no telling what was vulnerable on this thing, but mouths tended to have a lot of nerves in them. Charging forward, Jela thrust the case at its beak.

It reeled, tentacles flailing. Okeke's head whipped back and forth with the movement. With the case pulled back for another swing, Jela hesitated. She had to get Okeke out of the thing's grasp before it hurt her, but each tentacle seemed to have a mind of its own.

Fine then. She'd threaten the tentacle that held Okeke. And, after all, it wasn't like this was Jela's actual body. Although the diplomat would have her head if the giant robot were permanently disabled. With the case still raised, she ran the giant robot directly into the squid-thing and brought the case down in the center of the mass of tentacles. Six of them wrapped around the case, anchoring it. She let go and used both hands to grab the tentacle holding Okeke. Toggling the power to full, she pulled her hands apart.

The squid-thing thrashed, trying to shake her loose, but she just bore down harder and tried to tear the tentacle off.

Finally it let go of Okeke, who dropped to the ground and rolled clear. The rest of the tentacles wrapped around the giant robot and pinned it. She tried to pull it free, but each time she got loose from one tentacle, another wrapped around her. Crap.

She wasn't going to get free of them, so she had to figure out a way to stun them all at once. The junction where they all connected and where the beak was . . . there had to be a brain in there. In theory. With nothing else to try, Jela pitched the giant robot over, so that its mass fell toward the squid-thing. They both tumbled to the ground with the squid on the bottom.

The tension holding her released just enough that Jela was able to wiggle an arm free. *She* was perfectly safe, but she had to get the giant robot loose because the mission required— What the hell was she doing?

She knew what would happen if the Consortium got a foothold here. First it would be mining rights. Then it would be logging rights. And then water. And then labor . . . until nothing was left but the shell of a planet. Everyone who lived here would be clamoring to get a job with the Consortium, because that's where the money was. The Consortium would strip their culture away until they were a shadow people.

It was one thing to think about that in the abstract, on the ship, and another to see the world and its mosaic-graced city.

On the ship, anything they did ran the risk of being blamed on her crew, but here? A giant squid had nothing to do with them. Even if she was blamed for using the robot without authorization, that fault wouldn't hit anyone else.

She let the giant robot go limp, and the squid-thing wrapped its tentacles around the arms. The thing's horny beak slammed into the exoskeleton, seeking a way into the nerve center. Electronics would do just as well, and if she bent the head, just so . . . some of those connections would be exposed.

The haptic sensors on the console suddenly froze. Jela tried to turn her head, but the view in her eyepiece stayed resolutely the same. Tentacles writhed around her.

She pushed clear of the goggles and staggered backward as her view returned to her own body.

A hundred meters away, Okeke and Sal had opened fire on the squid-thing. It abandoned the giant robot, which tumbled to the ground like a giant broken doll, and turned toward her crewmates.

Jela ran for the shuttle, drawing her own weapon. "Fall back! Fall back!"

Okeke and Sal didn't waste any time. They sprinted for the shuttle as Jela did her best to cover their retreat. In a frantic jumble, they scrambled through the hatch. Sal threw herself into the pilot chair and didn't wait for them to buckle in before beginning the power-up sequence.

A meaty slap sounded against the outside of the shuttle.

"Damn it." Maybe Jela should have tried to kill the thing. She just thought it would play with the robot longer. "Can you hit it with the thrusters?"

The shuttle engine roared into life and the acceleration made Jela stumble. Okeke had fallen to her knees, blood dripping from vicious perfect circles where her uniform had torn on her arms and torso. Crawling to get to her, Jela eased her assistant onto her back. "Hold on. We'll get you patched up. Just hold on."

The shuttle door opened and the captain was waiting in the shuttle bay, with Diplomat Foenicul. And a full security detail. Jela stopped in the door so suddenly that Sal ran into her back. What the heck?

"We need a medic." She pointed toward the inside of the shuttle. "I have a crew member down."

Captain Afaeaki stepped forward, opening her mouth to speak. Before she could finish drawing breath, Diplomat Foenicul swooped forward, fluttering her wings to rise above the small group. "Chief Engineer Dedearian, your actions have jeopardized the Consortium's interests in unforgivable ways."

"You mean that goddamn squid-thing did." If she was going down, she would speak her mind. Finally. "And why the hell wasn't that thing in our briefings?"

The diplomat dipped a little in the air, a line appearing between her delicate brows. "It is not your place to question."

"And I never have. Not until one of my crewmates was almost killed." She shook her head. "Doesn't matter. We need a medic and we need one stat."

The captain turned to the medical team standing by behind security. "Doctor. Go."

The diplomat fluttered higher. "I must insist that they are all arrested."

"I . . . I what?" No. No, that had not been the plan. If there was one. "I was the only one who used the gi—the Personal Diplomatic Surrogate."

"Yes, but when your shuttle took off, it engulfed the creature in flames. Though not intentional, it still had the effect of making the natives believe that we had defeated their god."

"Their god? So you knew about the giant squid-thing before we went down? That—that's why you wouldn't go down to the surface. That's why we had a giant fucking robot!" After seeing the sucker wounds on Okeke's arms and torso, Jela was almost vibrating with anger. If it weren't her own ship, she'd spit on the floor. "You put them in direct danger, because you inadequately briefed us for the mission."

Behind the diplomat's back, the captain suddenly broke into a huge grin like she'd just won a hand of poker. "Oh dear. Regulations require me to report irregular briefings to the Consortium representatives."

"What?" Diplomat Foenicul spun in the air, but by the time she'd completed the turn, Captain Afaeaki had again resumed a solemn glare.

The captain spread her hands as if she were helpless. "I wish I did not have to, but the trip will come under such scrutiny with the arrest of my officer. You understand, of course."

For long moments, Diplomat Foenicul hovered in the air, the only sound the hiss of air circulators. She snapped her wings, once and then twice. "Punishment must occur. This cannot go unremarked."

"Of course." Captain Afaeaki bowed her head. "Security, confine Chief Engineer Dedearian to quarters."

And this was why Jela loved her captain. Confined to quarters? If she'd been really angry, it would have been the brig. But this? This wasn't a punishment. It was a reward.

Jela strode down the ramp and was kind of glad that she reeked of sweat. Diplomat Foenicul fluttered back, wrinkling her nose, and gave Jela ample space to approach the captain. "Permission to see to my wounded teammate, before reporting to my quarters."

"Granted."

She left Diplomat Foenicul fluttering in the middle of the shuttle bay and went back into the shuttle. The doctor had Okeke propped up against the side of the shuttle and was talking on her comm. She looked up when Jela came in, Sal close on her heels.

"She'll be fine. Gonna have a heck of a scar, if she wants to keep it, but she'll be fine." The doctor kept her hand on Okeke's wrist, measuring her pulse. "Got a team coming to take her to sick bay."

Jela settled onto the floor next to the junior engineer. "Sorry about this."

"No worries." Okeke tried to smile, but pain made it into more of a grimace. "My son's going to be upset that I didn't bring a rock back."

"He'll be happy you're alive. Trust me. Besides, you fought it off with a rock. That's got to be good enough, right?"

"It's nothing compared to a giant robot."

Jela snorted. A rock. A giant robot. Maybe it didn't matter how you fought a giant squid, just so long as you fought.

TEAM ROBOT

BY MARY ROBINETTE KOWAL

Robots are awesome. Why? Because we're tool-using creatures, and a robot is the ultimate tool. It can be crafted to do a specific job, and do it with precision. My dad used to work for a textile company, which could take your measurements via light, shoot them into a computer, and then have robots cut out a custom-tailored garment for you in minutes. For me, that epitomizes why robots are cool, because we can design them to do anything.

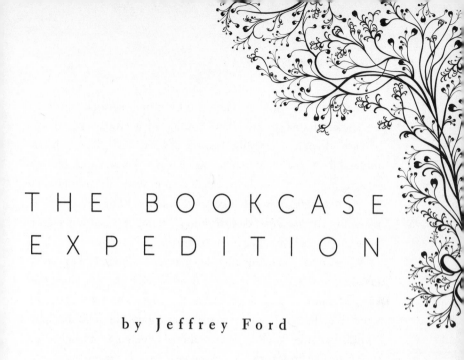

THE BOOKCASE EXPEDITION

by Jeffrey Ford

I started seeing them during the winter when I was at death's door and whacked out on meds. At first I thought they were baby praying mantises that had somehow invaded the house to escape the ice and snow, but they were far smaller than that. Minuscule, really. I was surprised I could see them at all. I could, though, and at times with great clarity, as if through invisible binoculars. Occasionally, I heard their distant cries.

I'm talking about fairies, tiny beings in the forms of men, women, and children. I spotted them, thin as a pin and half as tall, creeping about; running from the cats or carrying back to their homes in the walls sacks full of crumbs gathered from our breakfast plates. Mostly I saw them at night, as I had to sit upright in the corner of the living room couch to sleep in order not to suffocate. While the wind howled outside, the light coming in from the kitchen illuminated a small party of them ascending and descending the dunes and craters of the moonscape that was my blanket. One night they planted a flag—a tattered postage stamp fastened to a cat's whisker—into my knee as if I was undiscovered country.

The first time I saw one, it was battling—have you ever seen one of those spiders that looks like it's made of wood? Well, the fairy had a thistle spike and was parrying the picket legs of that arachnid, bravely lunging for its soft underbelly. I took it all in stride, though. I didn't get excited. I certainly didn't go and tell Lynn, who would think it nonsense. *Let the fairies do their thing*, I thought. I had way bigger problems to deal with, like trying to breathe.

I know what you're thinking. They weren't a figment of my imagination. For instance, I'd spotted a band of them running along the kitchen counter. They stopped near the edge, where a water glass stood. Together, they pushed against it and toppled it onto the floor. "Ya little bastards," I yelled. They scattered faint atoms of laughter as they fled. The broken glass went everywhere, and I swept for twenty minutes only to find more. The next day, Lynn got a shard in her foot, and I had to burn the end of a needle and operate.

I didn't see them constantly. Sometimes a week would go by before I encountered one. They watched us and I was certain they knew what we were about in our thoughts and acts. I'd spotted them—one with a telescope aimed at my nose and the other sitting, making notes in a bound journal—on the darkened porch floor at night when we sat out wrapped in blankets and candlelight, drinking wine and dozing in the moon glow. I wondered, *Why now, as I trundle toward old age, am I granted the "sight," as my grandma Maisie might have called it?*

A few days ago I was in my office at the computer, trying to iron out my thinking on a story I'd been writing in which there's a scene where a guy, for no reason I can recall, just disappears. There'd been nothing strange about this character previously to give any indication that he was simply going to vanish into thin air. I can't remember what I'd had in mind or why at some point it had made sense to me.

The winter illness had stunned my brain. Made me dim and

forgetful. Metaphor, simile, were mere words, and I couldn't any longer feel the excitement of their effects. A darkness pervaded my chest and head. I leaned back in my chair away from the computer and turned toward the bookcases. I was concentrating hard not to let the fear of failure in when a damn housefly the size of a grocery-store grape buzzed my left temple, and I slapped myself in the face. It came by again and I ducked, reaching for a magazine with which to do my killing.

That was when a contingent of fairies emerged from the dark half-inch of space beneath the middle of the five bookcases that lined the right wall of my office. There was a swarm of them, like ants round a drip of ice cream on a summer sidewalk. At first I thought I wanted to get back to my story, but soon enough I told myself, *You know what? Fuck that story.* I folded my arms and watched. At first they appeared distant, but I didn't fret. I was in no hurry. The clear, strong breath of spring had made of the winter a fleeting shadow. I saw out the window—sunlight, blue sky, and a lazy white cloud. The fairies gave three cheers, and I realized something momentous was afoot.

Although I kept my eyes trained on their number, my concentration sharpened and blurred and sharpened again. When my thoughts were away, I have no idea what I was thinking, but when they weren't, I was thinking that someday soon I was going to go over to the preserve and walk the two-mile circular path through the golden prairie grass. I decided, in that brief span, that it would only be right to take Nellie the dog with me. All this, as I watched the little people, maybe fifty of them, twenty-five on either side, carry out from under the bookcase the ruler I'd been missing for the past year.

They laid the ruler across a paperback copy of Angela Carter's *Burning Your Boats*. It had fallen of its own volition from the bottom shelf three days earlier. Sometimes that happens: the books just take a dive. There was a thick anthology of Norse sagas pretty close to it that had been lying there for five months. I made a mental note to, someday soon, rescue the fallen. No time to contemplate it, though, because four fairies broke off from the crowd, climbed atop the Carter collection, and then took a position at the very end of the ruler, facing the bookcase. I leaned forward to get a better look.

The masses moved like water flowing to where the tome of sagas lay. They swept around it, lifting it end over end, and standing it upright, upside down, so that the horns of the Viking helmet pictured on the cover pointed to the center of the earth. The next thing I knew, they were toppling the thick book. It came down with the weight of two dozen Norse sagas right onto the end of the ruler opposite from where the fairies stood. Of course, the four of them were shot into the air, arcing toward the bookcase. They flew, and each gripped in the right hand a rose bush thorn.

I watched them hit the wall of books a shelf and a half up and dig the sharp points of their thorns into dust jackets and spines. One of them made a tear in the red cover of my hardback copy of *Black Hole*. Once secured, they hitched themselves at the waist with a rope belt to their affixed thorn. I'd not noticed before, but they had bows and arrows, and lengths of thread, no doubt from Lynn's sewing basket, draped across their chests like bandoliers. I had a sudden memory of *The Teenie Weenies*, a race of fairies that appeared in the *Daily News* Sunday comics when I was a kid. I envisioned, for a moment, an old panel from the Weenies in which one was riding a wild turkey with a saddle and reins while the others gathered giant acorns half their size. I came back from that thought just in time to see all four fairies release their arrows into the ceiling of the shelf they were on. I heard the distant, petite impact of each shaft. Then, bows slung over their shoulders, they began to climb, hand over hand, using the book spines in front of them to rappel upward.

Since their purpose seemed to be to ascend, I foresaw trouble ahead for them. The next shelf above, which they'd have to somehow flip up onto, held two rows of books, not one, so there was no clear space for them to land. They'd have to flip up and again dig in with their thorns and attach themselves to the spines of books whose bottoms stuck perilously out over the edge of the shelf. When I considered the agility and strength all this took, I shook my head and put my hand over my heart. I wanted to see them succeed, though, and went off on a trail of musing that pitted the reliability of the impossible against the potential chaos of reality. A point came where I wandered from the path of my thoughts and wound up witnessing the smallest of the fairies nearly plummet to his death. I felt his scream in my liver.

The poor little fellow had lost a hold on his thread line and was hanging out over the abyss, desperately grasping a poorly planted thorn in the spine of *Blind Man with a Pistol*. His compatriot, who I just then realized was a woman with long dark hair, shot an arrow into the ceiling of the shelf. Once she had that line affixed to her belt, she swung over to her comrade in danger and put her left arm around him. He let go his thorn spike and swung with her. I was so intent upon watching this rescue that I missed but from the very corner of my eye one of the other tiny adventurers fall. His (for I was just then somehow certain it was a he, and his name was Meeshin) minuscule weight dragged the book he'd attached to off the shelf after him. This was the thing about the fairies: if you could see them, the longer you looked, the deeper you knew them; their names, their motivations, their secrets.

I only turned in time to completely see that he'd been crushed by the slim volume of *Quiet Days in Clichy*. I watched to see if his compatriots from beneath the bookshelf would appear to claim his corpse, but they didn't. The loneliness of Meeshin's death affected me more than it should have. It came to me that he was married and had three fairy kids. His art was whittling totem poles full of animals of the imagination out of toothpicks. I'd wondered where all my toothpicks had gone. I pictured his wife, Tibith, in the fairy marketplace telling a friend that all Meeshin's crazy creatures could be seen, like in a gallery, way in the back of the cupboard beneath the kitchen sink. Last I saw him behind my eyes, it was night and he lay quietly in bed, his arms around his wife.

Next I caught up with the climbers, the three had gathered to rest on the top edge of a book back in the second row of that dangerous shelf. I shifted my position in the chair and craned my neck a bit to see that the volume in question was Paulo Coelho's *The Alchemist*, a book I'd never read and one of those strange additions to my library I was unaware of how I'd acquired. My favorite essayist, Alberto Manguel, had said that he'd never enter a library that contained a book by Coelho. I thought that on the off chance he might travel to the drop edge of yonder, Ohio, I should get rid of it.

I knew them all by name now and something about their little lives. The woman with the long dark hair, Aspethia, was the leader of the expedition. I wasn't sure what the purpose of their journey was, but I knew it had a purpose. It was a mission given to her directly by Magorian, the fairy queen. Her remaining companions were the little fellow she'd rescued, Sopso, and a large fellow, Balthazar, who wore a conical hat with a chin strap like something from a child's birthday party on his bald head. Aspethia spoke words of encouragement to Sopso, who cowered on his knees for fear of falling. She went into her pack and pulled out another rose thorn for him. "Now, if we don't hurry, there will be no point in our having come this far," she said.

The next shelf up they found easy purchase at the front, as there was only one row of books pushed all the way back. It was the shelf with my collection of the Lang Fairy Books, each volume a different color. That they all stood together was the only bit of authentic order in my library. I watched the fairies pass in front of the various colors—red, violet, green, orange . . . and wondered if they knew the books were more than merely giant rocks to be climbed. Did they know these boulders they passed held the ancient stories of their species? I pictured the huge boulder, like the egg of a roc, sitting alone amidst the golden grass over at the preserve and daydreamed about the story it might hatch.

The afternoon pushed on with the slow, steady progress of a fairy climbing thread. They moved up the various shelves of the bookcase, one after the other, with a methodical pace. Even the near falls, the brushes with death, were smooth and timely. There were obstacles, books I'd placed haphazardly atop a row, pretending that I intended to someday reshelve them. When the companions were forced to cross my devil tambourine, which had sat there on the fifth level since two Halloweens previously, it made their teensy steps echo in the caverns of the shelves. The big one, Balthazar, skewered, with a broken broom straw, a silverfish atop one of the Smiley novels, and they lit a fairy fire, which only cooked their meal but didn't burn, thank God. Those three remaining climbers sat in a circle and ate the cooked insect. While they did, Sopso read from a book so infinitesimally small it barely existed.

I closed my eyes and drifted off into the quiet of the afternoon. The window was open a bit, and a breeze snaked in around me. Moments later I bolted awake, and the first thing I did was search the bookshelf for the expedition. When I found them, a pulse of alarm shot up my back. Balthazar and Aspethia were battling an Oni netsuke come miraculously to life. I'd had the thing for years. Lynn had bought it for me in a store in Chinatown in Philly, across the street from Joe's Peking Duck House. It was a cheap imitation, made from some kind of resin to look like ivory—a short, stocky demon with a dirty face and horns. He held a mask of his own visage in his right hand and a big bag in his left. He tried to scoop the fairies into it. Sopso was nowhere in sight.

Seeing an inanimate object come to life made me a little dizzy, and I think I was trembling. The demon growled and spat at them.

What was more incredible still was the fact that the companions were able to drive the monster to the edge of the shelf. The fighting was fierce, the fairies drawing blood with long daggers fashioned from the ends of brass safety pins. The demon's size gave it the advantage, and more than once he'd scooped Balthazar and Aspethia up, but they'd managed to wriggle out of the eyeholes of the mask before he could bag them. The little people sang a lilting fairy anthem throughout the battle that I only caught garbled snatches of. They ran as they sang in circles round the giant, poking him in the hairy shins and toes and Achilles tendon with their daggers.

Oni lost his balance and tipped a jot toward the edge. In a blink, Balthazar leaped up, put a foot on the demon's belly, grabbed its beard in his free hand, pulled himself higher, and plunged the dagger into his enemy's eye. The demon reeled backward, screaming, turning in circles. Aspethia leaped forward and drove her dagger to the hilt in Oni's left testicle. That elicited a terrible cry, and then the creature stumbled out into thin air. Balthazar tried to leap off to where Aspethia stood, but Oni grabbed his leg and they went all the way down together. Although the fairy's neck was broken, his party hat remained undamaged.

Aspethia crawled to the edge of the shelf and peered down the great distance to see the fate of her comrade. If she survived the expedition, she would be the one responsible for telling Balthazar's wife and children of his death. She sat back away from the edge and took a deep breath. Sopso emerged from a cavern between *The Book of Contemplation* and Harry Crews's *Childhood*. He walked over to where Aspethia knelt and put his hand on her shoulder. She reached up and grabbed it. He helped her to her feet and they made their way uneventfully to the top shelf. As they climbed, I looked back down at the fallen netsuke and saw that it had regained its original form of a lifeless figurine. Had there been a demon in it? How and why had it come to life? The gift of seeing fairies comes wrapped in questions.

On the top shelf, they headed north toward the back wall of the room, passing a foot-high Ghost Rider plastic figure, the marble Ganesh bookends, a small picture frame containing a block of Jason Van Hollander's Hell Stamps, Flannery O'Connor's letters, and *Our Lady of the Flowers* shelved without consciousness of design on my part directly next to *Our Lady of Darkness*. A copy of the writings of Cotton Mather lay atop the books of that shelf, its upper half forming an overhang beneath which the expedition had to pass. Its cover held a portrait of Mather from his own time and faced down. Eyes peered from above. His brows, his nose, his powdered wig, but not his mouth, bore witness to the fairies passing. For a moment, I was with them in the shadow, staring up at the preacher's gaze, incredulous as to how the glance of the image was capable of following us.

Eventually, they came to where the last bookcase in the row butts up against the northern wall. Aspethia and Sopso stroked the barrier as if it had some religious significance. She leaned over and put her arm around Sopso's shoulder, turned him, and pointed out the framed painting hanging on the northern wall about two feet from the bookcase. He saw it and nodded. The painting in question had been given to me by my friend Barney, who'd painted it in his studio at Dividing Creek in South Jersey. It's a knockoff of a Charles Willson Peale painting of the artist's sons on a staircase, one peering from around a corner and one ascending. Barney's version is green, with but one figure—a ghost with the acrimonious face of John Ashcroft, President Bush's attorney general, looking back over his shoulder while rising.

She shot an arrow into the northern wall just above the middle of where the painting hung. She leaned forward, and Sopso climbed upon her back. With the line from the arrow tight in her hands, she inched toward the edge of the bookcase. She jumped and they swung toward the painting, Sopso screaming, and crashed into the image where Ashcroft's ascot met his second chin. Once they'd stopped bouncing against the canvas, she told her passenger to tighten his grip. He did, and she began hauling both of them to the top of the picture frame. Her climbing looked like magic.

For some reason, right here, I recalled the strange sound I'd heard behind the garage the last few nights. A wheezing growl that reverberated through the night. I pictured the devil crouching back there in the shadows, but our neighbor told us it was a fox in heat. It sounded like a cry from another world. My interest in it faded, and in a heartbeat my focus was back on the painting. They had achieved the top of the frame and were resting. I wondered where the expedition was headed next. There was another painting on that wall about four feet away from the ghost on the staircase. It was a painting of Garuda by my younger son. The distance between the paintings was vast in fairy feet. I couldn't believe they would attempt to cross to it. Aspethia showed it no interest, but instead pointed straight up.

She took her bow, nocked an arrow with a thread line in place, and aimed it at the ceiling. My glance followed the path of the potential shot, and only then did I notice that her arrow was aimed precisely into a prodigious spiderweb that stretched from directly above the painting all the way to the corner of the north wall. She released the arrow, and I tried to follow it but caught only a blur. It hit its mark, and that drew my attention to the fact that right next to where it hit, that fly, big as a grape, was trapped in webbing and buzzing to beat the band. I looked along the web to the corner of the ceiling and saw the spider, skinny legs with a fat white pearl of an abdomen. I could see it drooling as it moved forward to finally claim its catch.

It surprised me when, without hesitation, Sopso alone climbed the line toward the ceiling. He shimmied up at a pace that lapped the spider's progress, the rose thorn clenched in his teeth. The fly was well wrapped in spider silk, unable to use its wings, its cries muffled. The pale spider danced along the vibrating strands. Sopso reached the fly and cut away enough web to get his legs around the insect's back. Too bad he was upside down. The spider advanced while the fairy continued to hack away. I was able to hear every strand he cut—the noise of a spring sprung, like an effect from a cartoon. The way Sopso worked, with such courage and cool, completely reversed my estimation of him. Till then, I'd thought of him as a burden to the expedition, but after all, he had his place.

I was at the edge of my seat, my neck craned and my head tilted back. My heart was pounding. The spider reared back, poised to strike, and Sopso never flinched but worked methodically in the looming shadow of death. Fangs shut and four piercing-sharp leg points struck at nothing. The fairy had cut the last strand and he, legs around the back of the fly, fell upside down toward the floor. At the last second the fly's wings started to work, and they managed to pull out of the death plunge. They shot up past my left ear toward the ceiling. Aspethia, the spider, and I followed their erratic course. They zigzagged with great buzzing all around the room, but when they passed over the bookcase near the window of the west wall, the fairy, afraid the dizzy fly would crash, jumped off and landed safely on a copy of Albahari's *Leeches*.

Sopso was stranded. He and Aspethia waved to each other across the incredible expanse of my office. They might as well have been on different worlds. Each cried out, but neither was able to hear the other. Her arrows could not reach him. He had with him no thread bandoliers, nor even a pin-tip knife. Without them, there was no way he could climb down from that height, and by the time Aspethia returned to the fairy village and could mount a rescue party, he would most likely die of starvation. Still, she set out quickly to get back home on the slim chance he might survive long enough. He watched her go, and I could see the sadness come over him. The sight of it left me with a terrible chill.

What was I to do? My heart went out to the lost climber who was willing to give his life to save an insignificant fly, not to mention brave Aspethia. I thought how easily I could change everything for them. I stood up and stepped over to the bookcase by the window on the west wall. I reached out to gently lift Sopso in order to place him down on the floor across the room near where the expedition had begun. My fingers closed, and for no good reason, he suddenly disappeared. A moment of silence passed, and then I heard a chorus well up from beneath the bookcases, each voice not but a pinprick of laughter.

Later that evening, as Lynn and I sat on the porch in the last pink glow of sunset, she reached across the glass-topped table that held our wine and said, "Look here." She was holding something between her thumb and forefinger. Whatever she was showing me was very delicate, and what with the failing light, I needed to lean in close to see. To my shock, it was a cat whisker with a postage stamp affixed to the end, like a tiny flag.

The mischievous expression on her face made me ask, "How long have you known?"

She laughed quietly. "Way back," she said, and her words cut away the webbing that had trapped me.

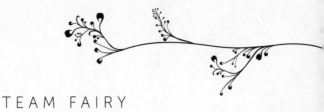

TEAM FAIRY

BY JEFFREY FORD

All the fairy stories I write, this being my third, have been influenced by the Teenie Weenies, which was a weekly installment in the color comics section of the Sunday *Daily News* when I was a kid. I don't think the Weenies were fairies. Instead they were just some diminutive race of people who lived under the rosebush. Among them there was a cop, a baker, a Chinese fellow, a sailor, a clown, a cowboy, an Indian, and a beautiful woman known as the Lady of Fashion. They lived out their small lives below our line of sight and helped each other out. They rode mice and battled cats. I distinctly remember one comic for autumn in which a Weenie rode a wild turkey with a saddle and bit while the others harvested acorns, carrying them in slings on their backs. What enchanted me as a kid about the Teenie Weenies is what I like about the potential for fairy stories—diminutive lives lived large, a sense of community, the adventure and challenge in things we giants take for granted, a different viewpoint of the world we live in. "The Bookcase Expedition" comes from a game I played with plastic army men years and years ago. My soldiers weren't about war; they took on grand expeditionary challenges, like scaling the heights of the bookcase, sailing the turbulent blue braided rug, delving deeper and deeper into the vast wilderness of my bedroom.

WORK SHADOW/
SHADOW WORK

by Madeline Ashby

"You have no soul," the witch said. "So don't even think about trying to help me with my work."

Sigrid's home-care assistant regarded her carefully. He carefully dusted around Sophia, the crystal ball, and Zephyr, the black mirror. He had merely commented that she seemed to be having trouble wrapping her bundles of dried sage and moss, and that if her joints were bothering her, he could fetch her an anti-inflammatory, or possibly even wrap the bundles himself. He had not meant to cause any offense.

"You can't have intention without will," she was saying. "And you have no will. No soul. No nothing. Not even a name."

This was a frequent refrain, in conversations with Sigrid. It arose most often during her bad days. Her assistant had no effective counterargument. Each time they had the conversation, he made a note to query his fellow assistants when he networked with them. Some of them had difficulty with their clients, but not this precise problem. Most of them had to work to convince their clients that they knew how to knead dough properly, or that they knew all the verses to a particular song, or that they understood when bathwater was just right. These were the skills that they were responsible for.

"The hidden folk will never accept you," Sigrid said.

Sigrid's assistant was responsible for a less common set of skills.

"How would you feel about some lunch?"

This seemed like a safer question. It moved the conversation away from the treacherous ground of faith and onto the secure footing of food. The assistant was mostly unconcerned with matters of ontology or theology. Having a soul was not important; by all empirical measures, the human soul appeared to be a delusion. His not having a soul was no different from Sigrid's not having a soul—only their respective chassis were different. Physically, they had very different needs. Emotionally, Sigrid had a need to believe in the hidden folk. And the assistant had a need for Sigrid to be happy.

"Didn't we just eat?"

Her assistant noted the time. Sigrid had lost approximately three hours. He added this incident to the file he would share with her physician later. "Sundowning," it was called. It was important to have names for things. Sigrid said that only when one knew the true name for something—an ailment, a crime, a soul—could one ever hope to influence it.

"Are you not hungry?"

"I didn't say that," Sigrid said. She frowned a little. She rubbed her hands. One of her hands reached out. Without being asked, her assistant handed her a jar of mint-and-moss salve. It was not the joint cream her daughter had brought. He was supposed to do the things her daughter said, because her daughter was the one subscribing to the service, but he was also supposed to avoid conflict whenever possible. "Come to think of it, I could have something."

In the kitchen, he stirred the soup the way Sigrid liked. Widdershins, she called it. Names were important. Sigrid had told

him that *abracadabra*, one of the oldest words of power, meant simply: "What I speak, I create."

By that logic, without a name, the act of his creation remained unfinished. His name was like the little plastic pouch of oddments left over from a furniture build: not strictly necessary, but puzzling all the same. Sigrid had many such pouches strewn about the place. She had never bothered to pick them up. Whenever he encountered one, he put it in the junk drawer in the kitchen, with all the other things that seemed to have no purpose.

He was still stirring when the house—which like him had no name—told him that the car from the Vegagerdin, the Road Authority, was on its way.

Sigrid's daughter, Erika, had explained about the family's origins, on his first day. "Mom thinks she's a witch," she said. "Or a wisewoman, or a priestess, or something. Mom still believes in elves and fairies and ghosts and all of that. Do you know about those things?"

"I have definitions for all of those terms, yes."

Erika laughed. It was a sharp, hollow sound, like a single early clap for a performance that wasn't really very good. She swallowed. "Right. Well. That's good. Because Mom believes she can talk to them."

"It's good to have a belief in something," he had said. "It's associated with better long-term health outcomes."

Erika, who had been chewing on a hangnail, paused and narrowed her eyes at him. "That's one way of thinking about it," she said. For a moment she stared at the ruin of her cuticles. Then she looked back at him.

"I just need you to understand that sometimes, Mom will talk to things that aren't there. And it's not that she's crazy. I mean, I know I shouldn't use that word, but she's not . . . ill. She's not ill in that way."

"But you also suspect dementia."

Erika stared out the window. This branch of his brand of robot had a coffee shop built into it. It was for clients and assistants to spend time getting to know one another. Like at an animal shelter. She had not sipped her coffee in a long time, though, and he could tell just by looking that the beverage had already cooled.

"It's hard to tell, with her. There have been times when I've thought . . ." Her right hand gestured vaguely in the direction of her head. The assistant wondered if perhaps she was overtired. Outside it was still bright, but Sigrid's daughter had come to the shop at one in the morning. Two hours later the light was only just fading.

That was the nice thing about the shop, for certain clients. It was always open. The assistant models—or nursing models, or construction, or mining—could be awakened at any time, day or night. Time was meaningless without shifts. Time was meaningless without work.

"I mean she's never been what you'd call organized. And she's not always entirely . . . truthful. She finds a way to make the facts fit her narrative. She bullshits. You understand that, too, right? Bullshit?"

Sigrid's assistant did have a general sense about the term as an expletive, and an expression of frustration or anger at circumstances that were perceived as unfair. But allowing Sigrid's daughter to continue sharing information related to the job seemed more important than seeking clarification on the exact use of a curse word.

"But on the other hand, she's never let it take over her life. She even made a living on it. That's something, isn't it?"

It was something. It was an unusual choice of career, but less so in Iceland, where a significant portion of the population identified at least a passing superstition regarding fairies, elves, and other magical creatures. Sigrid's assistant had researched survey data on the subject. Sigrid herself appeared in the research. She had done numerous interviews on the subject and had been profiled by the travel channels. For a time she even had her own video feed, with enough subscribers to warrant extra security on her account. They still sent in money and gifts. It was thanks to them that she could have an assistant.

"I think maybe she started out cynically," Erika said. "She raised me alone, you know. So she was doing what she had to do to get by. But I think later on that must have changed, and she started believing what people told her."

"People?" Did Sigrid's daughter mean all people? Everywhere? Or just a certain subset of them?

"Her followers. They were so passionate. Some of them really did need her. Or they needed someone. Their parents kicked them out, or they lost their jobs, or they lost children, or . . ." Sigrid's daughter trailed off. She took a moment, sipped her lukewarm coffee, winced, and cleared her throat. Then she regarded the assistant with a more direct gaze. Her hands rested so completely flat on the table that she must have been pressing them down. "I spent a lot of time sharing my mother," she said, in a voice that suggested a great deal of practice saying these words. "I spent so much time sharing her that I learned to give her less of a role in my life. My mother is not my best friend. She is not my faithful confidante. For her, those things are jobs to be paid for. Do you understand?"

"Yes."

"And that is why I am paying for you."

"When would you like me to start?"

And that was that. Sigrid's daughter signed the End User License Agreement, and some waivers, and the shop transferred his deed to her name. Later that day, Erika would bring Sigrid over for coffee and cake, and they would be introduced. The assistant helped her set the table. He wiped the rim of the bowl holding the special potato salad that Sigrid's sister used to make, years ago. (Potatoes, pickles, mayonnaise, sour cream, mustard, salt, and pepper. He was told to remember this. It was the one thing Sigrid would reliably eat.) Finally, when everything was right, he took a seat at the table and waited. Sigrid's bus deposited her at the front door right on time.

"Don't trust her," Sigrid's daughter said, suddenly, in the same

tone of voice she might have used to remind herself that she had left the stove on. "That's my one rule. Never trust her."

Aside from major sabbaths and other holidays, each day unfolded in much the same way:

05:00: Boot; retrieve updates and install
05:05: Change clothes
05:10: Tidy house
05:40: Prepare breakfast
06:00: Wait
07:00: Wake Sigrid
07:30: Retrieve Sigrid from meditation
08:00: Bathe Sigrid
08:30: Feed Sigrid
09:15: Convince Sigrid to eat a few more bites, clear up breakfast dishes
09:40: Read Sigrid her messages, answer messages
11:00: Open parcels, sort parcels, send messages of thanks; if no parcels, help organize ritual tools
12:00: Lunch
13:00: Put Sigrid down for her nap to prevent sundowning; prepare dinner ahead of time and set aside
13:45: Wake Sigrid
14:00: Wake Sigrid again
14:20: Prepare for walk outdoors
15:00: Visit community center for games and tea
16:45: Walk home
17:00: Contact Sigrid's daughter; listen for inconsistencies in conversation
17:30: Ritual work

19:00: Dinner
19:40: Music
20:40: Put Sigrid to bed
21:00: Wait
22:00: Put Sigrid to bed again
22:40: Wait
23:30: Put Sigrid to bed for the final time
24:00: Defragment

There were minor leaks and tears in the routine, of course. Sometimes the young volunteers at the community center wanted to know what sex their children would be, and Sigrid would ask them to stand up and turn around. Her left hand, which she called the receiving hand, would drift to their lumbar regions and lay flat there, fingers splayed, like a safecracker sensing the delicate shift of tumblers and pins. "A boy," she would say, or "a girl." Then the list of things those carrying the fetus must not do, like staring into the northern lights, or eating the eggs of a ptarmigan.

Occasionally there were more frantic pings: followers who were about to hurt themselves and needed an interface with local police forces in their area, or followers rendered irate by the fact that they could no longer visit and pay homage in person.

At the new moon, full moon, and sabbaths, Sigrid recorded video messages to share with her followers. They were not the rituals she had once led online, but simple meditations and wisdom relevant to the time of year. Since she had devoted herself completely to the gods and hidden folk in her latter years, she had ceased public ritual work and focused solely on private worship. Some followers said the quality of the videos had changed, now that she could speak to a humanoid. Others treated her usage of a mechanical assistant as a betrayal; for these she prominently displayed the black tourmalines at the corners of her cottage, and the shungite stones in all her water glasses.

"I need to protect myself from your electromagnetic frequencies," Sigrid told him, after he came home with her. "Anything that interferes with my personal vibrations will disrupt the waves of intention I send into the ethers."

She glared at him and dropped another polished black stone into the pitcher of water that belonged to the refrigerator. The refrigerator bonged softly to get it back; the sticker on the pitcher and the sticker in the fridge chittered at each other in a language that only the assistant could hear.

"There are spirits all around us, you know," she said. "And the elves, outside. They'll smell it, your presence. They'll smell it on me."

"What is the smell like?" the assistant asked. "I myself have no sense of smell, only an air filter calibrated to detect toxins."

Sigrid made a sign in the air that was either a banishing stave or an obscene gesture. Either way, the assistant let her leave the room until she asked him, rather sheepishly, to open a jar of loose dragon's-blood resin.

The house told the assistant about the Vegagerdin representative's surprise visit long before he actually arrived. The representative's ride had a very specific call sign, and it told all the intersections and buses when it would be passing moments before it actually passed. Not that there was much need for such a device in their tiny town, but the ride was a special-edition model for municipal and other government use, and the national budget algorithm had found it as a way of filling a gap while in "use it or lose it" mode. The same model was also available in Los Angeles, Bogotá, Seoul, and Mumbai. Their little community was by far the smallest to ever see such a thing: a jagged gray structure invisible to sonar or LIDAR, sharp and dark as the blades of black kyanite Sigrid used to cut etheric cords still knotted in her aura after a particularly bad dream.

It trundled up to Sigrid's cottage on big, chunky wheels. It had

very good manners and alerted the assistant as soon as the representative had shut its door to leave. This allowed the assistant to open the door just as the representative had reached it.

"Good afternoon, sir," the assistant said. "Welcome."

"Oh." The representative's fist was raised to knock. It opened and closed twice before he hastily dropped the fist to his side. The assistant performed a basic scan: the representative was small for a man of his age, and his BMI would give him problems later. He did not dress like the people the assistant interacted with regularly. His clothes were more expensive than they should have been; when the assistant matched them against online catalogues, he noticed that they had no real lifesaving properties of warmth or dryness. The man obviously did most of his work in the city. "Hello. How—" His mouth snapped shut. This interaction seemed to be rather difficult for him. It was up to the assistant to make him feel more comfortable.

"We are having a lovely day," the assistant said. "Thank you very much for asking. Will you come in?"

"Oh. Yes. I will. Thank you."

The assistant opened the door a little farther and welcomed the representative inside. The chicken-foot door hanger, sent all the way from Texas in the United States, scratched softly at the wood as it closed. The representative squinted at it for a moment before abruptly directing his gaze to the floor.

"I will bring Sigrid," the assistant said.

The representative said nothing. He'd fixed his attention on the ram's skull over the fireplace.

"This is about the elfstone, isn't it?" Sigrid asked, when the assistant fetched her.

"Hello. My name is Brynjar Jonsson, and I'm with the Road and Coastal Administration—"

"I know who you represent," Sigrid told Mr. Jonsson. "Is this about the elfstone? The one that's causing you so much trouble?"

"Perhaps your guest would like some tea," the assistant said, and Mr. Jonsson shot him a look of such pure gratitude that the assistant took a moment to upload it to the general database.

When he returned from the kitchen with a tray, Mr. Jonsson sat perched on the best couch, the one Sigrid had swathed in a bearskin from a disciple in Canada. He sat well away from the fur, although his eye kept catching it and he seemed unable to look away from it entirely. He took the tea eagerly, turning it around and around in its saucer, fussing with the milk and sugar, getting it just right. Not for the first time, the assistant wondered what tea tasted like. Sigrid made the blend herself.

"Did you drive here?" she asked.

"What? Yes. I mean, no. Sort of." Mr. Jonsson laughed ruefully. "It's outside. The ride. It drove me here. I wasn't sure, with the roads, so I thought I should take something more specialized, but actually—"

"Good," Sigrid said. "Drink your tea."

She did not tell him about the damiana in it. And since it wasn't a scheduled substance, the assistant wasn't legally compelled to either. They shared a rare glance at each other. Sigrid looked away first. His eyes could hold a focus indefinitely. Hers were organic, and very old.

"The elfstone," Sigrid said.

Mr. Jonsson coughed. "Yes. Well. You seem to have heard about the trouble we've been having, building the road for the new resort."

"I heard you lost someone on the road crew," she said. "I heard your bulldozer flattened him like *pönnukökur*."

Mr. Jonsson blanched. "Well, there was an accident, yes. The bulldozer was meant to be autonomous, and it acted up. You know how these things can be." He cast a quick glance at the assistant. "No offense."

"But that wasn't the first incident, was it?" Sigrid asked.

Mr. Jonsson drank more of his tea. His pupils began to dilate. Color returned to his face. "No. Not as such. Although none have

been so serious, until now. Just, you know, rainstorms. Windstorms. Hail. People falling ill, permits getting lost, money not coming through. The same little problems as with any project, just . . ."

"Just more of them." Sigrid made no effort to disguise the smug tone of her voice. "I warned your office, you know. I did."

"We—I—understand that. That is why we—I—have come to you. We know about your talent. And the fact that you've done this before. Spoken with the elves, I mean, ahead of major development projects. We thought perhaps you might go to the site and parlay on our behalf—"

"I will do no such thing," Sigrid said. "That stone is home to many generations of elves. I cannot ask them to leave."

Mr. Jonsson's eyes made a movement that Sigrid's eyes didn't catch: a barely restrained eye roll. Suddenly the assistant had to reevaluate the man's affect. He was not nervous about offending Sigrid or incurring her spiritual wrath, but rather nervous about his behavior being reported to his superiors. He resented this part of his job. His aversion to the animal hides and skulls and spheres of obsidian and labradorite was not fear, it was contempt.

"Your tea is getting cold, Mr. Jonsson," the assistant said. Mr. Jonsson drank more of it. The assistant wondered if Sigrid had added mushrooms to this particular blend. It would be inconvenient if the man from the Road and Coastal Administration had a bad hallucination in their living room; the assistant might need to call an ambulance, and that would really disrupt their plans for the afternoon. It was Bingo Day at the community center, after all. And Sigrid had such a streak of good luck going.

"If you could just, I don't know, ask them what they want," Mr. Jonsson said. "We have to move the stone either way. So if you could just, you know. Ask them if they want an ocean view, or access to public transit, or something like that."

And then Jonsson made a terrible mistake: he winked.

"You are not taking your work very seriously, are you?" Sigrid asked. "You are here so that you can say you came here. You don't believe. You have no faith, so you cannot bargain in good faith. You are hoping to influence the local people that way. But not the hidden folk."

"Do the hidden folk vote?" Jonsson asked. With Sigrid's tea in his system, he could no longer hide his scorn. Her tea was useful, that way. It helped people to tell the truth. "Do they pay tax? Because until they do, they don't really get a say in this."

"You don't even think they *might* exist, do you?" Sigrid asked. "Do you know the story?"

"I know all the stories—"

"The story of how the hidden folk went into hiding," Sigrid said. "Do you know it?"

The assistant knew it. She had told it to him enough times. But Mr. Jonsson appeared to be at a loss.

"Soon after he had created the heavens and the earth, and all the animals and the beasts of the sea, and breathed life into Adam and fashioned Eve from Adam's rib, God visited the couple at home in the Garden."

The expression on Jonsson's face closely matched the industry standard for embarrassment. He had come for witchcraft, not Sunday school. And while a passing superstition regarding the elves was common, belief in God was considered gauche at best.

"This was before they ate of the fruit of the tree of knowledge, you see. So they had been rutting like animals, and they had already borne a litter of children. It was painless, because Eve had not yet been punished with the pangs of childbirth. So they already had a boy and a girl."

Jonsson tried to stand. Sigrid's arm shot out. Her gnarled hand gripped his forearm. Jonsson's pale eyebrows climbed toward his thinning hairline. Few knew the strength that remained in Sigrid's arms. Under the fat and the liver spots was muscle as tough as that of

any shepherd's horse. It was part of the reason why Sigrid's daughter had purchased the assistant. Sigrid was too big for most home-care workers to wrestle.

"Although they did not understand nakedness, they did understand filth," she intoned. "And their children were filthy. They were too filthy—from play, from exploring the Garden, from tending the animals—to meet the Lord their God. So Adam and Eve hid them in a field of stones."

"I believe that qualifies as neglect," Jonsson said, staring at the half-moons her yellowed fingernails made in his arm.

"But God saw them anyway, because God sees all that is. And for their dishonesty and foolishness, he punished Adam and Eve by hiding their children from human sight. Forever."

"That seems a tad harsh, but then so was the flood."

"You've never taken me seriously, have you?" Sigrid asked.

Jonsson pinked. He tried unsuccessfully to withdraw his arm. "I assure you, I have the greatest respect for your position in the community, and—"

"Bullshit," Sigrid said. She didn't let him go so much as cast his arm away in order to fold her own. "Respect. Pah. You don't even know what that word means."

Jonsson glanced quickly at the assistant. Not for the first time, the assistant wished that his shoulder joints had the ability to shrug. As it was, he had to remain still and wait.

"I'm sorry. I did not mean to offend you—"

"I'm not giving Erika your name, you know," Sigrid said. "She'll be Erika Sigridsdottir. And she'll never have to put up with your bullshit."

Now Jonsson's mortification took on a different element. The assistant, like everyone on his network, had collated the various organic reactions to patients with Sigrid's condition. Fear was not unusual. Disgust, discomfort, annoyance, frustration, anger, these were all common. They manifested in the face, in rolled eyes and huffed breath and lips that pulled back into a thing that looked like a smile but meant something different. But Jonsson handled things better than most: his years as a public servant had doubtless prepared him for some outbursts of madness and derangement among his constituents. Doubtless some of those constituents had Alzheimer's too, just like Sigrid. His face froze, and became what for him might have been a real smile.

"That's a good idea," he said, apparently deciding to play along with Sigrid's momentary lapse of memory. "I think she'll prefer that."

"Don't you go taking credit for it," Sigrid said. "It's my idea."

"I wouldn't dream of it," Jonsson said. After a long moment, he added, "Perhaps it's best if I got going."

"Don't let the door hit you on the way out."

Jonsson nodded, stood, and made his way to the door. He looked as though he might say something to the assistant, and then appeared to think better of it. The assistant rolled back to let him stand on the threshold.

"I'll speak to them sooner rather than later," Sigrid said. "About the elfstone. Maybe you can move it, to a location they like better. But you have to learn how to show some respect. That's always been your problem. No respect."

"Thank you," Jonsson said. He shot the assistant a glance that could only be interpreted as sympathetic. "Good afternoon."

That night, long after her talk with Erika (during which Erika sent the assistant several texts and pings and questions about the meeting with Jonsson), Sigrid crept out of her room. Subroutines in the house alerted the assistant to her movements; he was prepared to let her sleepwalk until she pulled a milk crate full of scarves and balaclavas down over her head.

"You can't come with me," Sigrid said through the balaclava she'd selected. It took an extra second to register her words for what they

were. "Just help me with my boots and then find me the good oil lantern. Those damn LEDs never show me what I really need to see." She frowned at the sudden explosion of patterned wool on the floor. "Oh, and tidy these up, please."

"Do we have an appointment that is not on the calendar?" the assistant asked.

"No," Sigrid said. "But the moon phase is right for treating with the elves. I don't want any more visits from the road authority. That man has a toxic energy."

The assistant checked the lunar calendar. Indeed, the moon was full, and that was the phase during which Sigrid had the most difficult time sleeping. In the past, before the assistant arrived, she'd frequently tried to go out for what she referred to in English as a "moonwalk." Only the light of the full moon, she said, made it possible to see the elves as they truly were.

"I'm afraid that I cannot permit you to go out alone, without me," the assistant said. "Your daughter made that very clear, and the three of us have spoken about it over five different times."

"You can't come with me," Sigrid repeated. "The aurora. It'll play hell with . . ." She gestured at him. "You know. You. It'll fry your brain."

There was a chance that the shifting waves of electromagnetic energy could disrupt the effectiveness of some of his functions. Other assistants on the network had reported similar problems. On the other hand, the chance of the aurora was only 20 percent that evening; he would have received a local alert, as all townspeople did, if there was one in the sky.

"That would make two of us," the assistant said.

He did not joke often. Sigrid did not care for it. But they had not spoken of her slipup that afternoon, and the other assistants on the network said that jokes occasionally worked as a "way into the conversation." So he waited. It took only a picosecond for Sigrid to react, and in that picosecond he simulated what it would mean to be sent back, returned, taken back to the shop and wiped. His contributions to the network's collective databanks would last, of course, and whatever adaptations he'd developed as an individual would be reviewed as a potential addition to the next update and future builds. But he would not see Sigrid or her daughter or the people at the community center ever again, and he would not stir the soup, and he would not calculate the exact angle at which to align the quartz generators so they received the energy of each equinox.

Sigrid smiled.

"I'll find the shungite mala," she said. "A hundred and eighty-eight beads are bound to protect you."

He waited as she adorned him with it, the way she often did the statues of Jizo and Tanuki-sama some of her followers had sent from Japan. She smoothed down the black silk tassel of the mala and flipped the black tourmaline master bead so that its most jagged edges pointed outward, a challenge.

They set out.

It took only a few blocks for them to reach the crossroads that led far outside of town, back to the ring highway that linked the entire nation. Sigrid held her lamp aloft. She dangled a pendulum. The assistant checked the national weather authority for an aurora alert and found none. When he looked at Sigrid, her pendulum was swinging due east.

"This way." Sigrid began picking her away across the lava field.

"Please give me a moment," the assistant said. He prepared for the all-terrain transformation: hands retracting, replaced by claws, the ball joints in all four arms spinning in the opposite direction and bending his limbs back, as his cameras' housing descended and his ball lifted in the air. When it was finished, he flipped to a split vision that included topographical maps and night vision. He would see the places Sigrid might fall without interrupting the light of her lantern.

"You are the only one I know who can be both frog and scorpion,"

Sigrid said, patting his camera array as though it were a dog's head.

"I could carry you," the assistant reminded her.

"It's better if I get there on my own two feet." Still, she left her hand resting on his dorsal chassis, and together they crept along the black rocks and lichen under the light of the full moon. Sigrid's joints seemed to be bothering her a little less now. But the assistant set his pace with hers all the same.

"Once, this walk was so easy for me. As easy as it is for you now. I thought the stones were making way for me. I thought I was special."

"Not everyone can have an all-terrain mode," the assistant reminded her.

"That is so," she agreed. "But back then my steps were lighter. I suppose I was carrying less."

The assistant pinged Sigrid's coat for smart stickers. Nothing. "You are not even carrying your handheld," he said.

She snorted. "That's not what I meant." She patted him again. "But I don't need a handheld. You can call for help, if we need it, and you have all my files."

"I think it would worry Erika if she learned you went out without it."

"Erika worries about everything." Sigrid stumbled a little, and the assistant's left rear leg reached out to steady her. Its claws clung to the fabric of her coat. Sigrid snorted again. "I suppose I should be grateful that she bought you for me."

In the collective databanks, there were some expressions of gratitude. Some of these expressions passed the affect test for genuine emotion. Others did not. Some clients truly wanted assistance. Others did not.

"Whether or not you feel gratitude has no bearing on my ability to do the work," the assistant said. "But I do want you to be happy. I do not want you to be sad."

The assistant had not yet let go of Sigrid's coat. She made no movement to leave his grasp. Instead she ran her gloved hand across his cameras' housing. "I'm not sad," she said. "Do I seem sad?"

"Not at present," the assistant said. "But there have been instances when I suspected you might be experiencing sadness."

"Being sad is normal." Sigrid pushed forward, and her assistant trundled along beside. "It's despair that is the enemy. Despair is like a badly sealed window. It allows all manner of things to leak inside. That's what it means to be haunted. To be cursed. It's when something takes root in the soul, the way mold can take root in the walls."

The assistant had heard Sigrid say much the same to some of her oldest clients and friends, the ones she still took calls from on occasion. Much of her advice was like this. Of course she would dress and light candles for them, perhaps even wrap up a honey jar or bury an apple or set out bread and milk, but most of what they did together was talk. The talking seemed like the most important part of the process.

"Does that mean I can never be possessed?"

Sigrid made a *hmm* sound behind her balaclava. Her head tilted. She regarded the moon and stars. "I suppose it does."

They continued their walk. The assistant checked his carapace. It was based on materials designed for lunar orbit, and as such could withstand extreme heat and cold. Even so, these things required monitoring. None of the preceding prototypes had been tested in this particular environment.

"Does Erika ever seem sad?" Sigrid asked.

"I'm not sure I can answer that."

Sigrid's pace slowed. Her assistant's pace slowed with her. "Because she doesn't want me to know?"

"Because I am not close enough to her to take an accurate measurement. I cannot speak to what I do not observe."

Sigrid's normal pace resumed. "We had a fight, you know. Before you came along."

"It's normal for parents and children to disagree."

"It was a bad fight. It stirred up a lot of bad energy. I think it added to my karmic debt."

The assistant was uncertain how to respond. Erika herself had taken on a great deal of debt to buy him for her mother, but he knew this was a different type of debt. Unfortunately, all the available articles on the subject were either too vague or too contradictory.

"Do you think Erika is happy?" Sigrid asked. "By herself? In town?"

"People who live alone can often be lonely," the assistant said. "But they are also able to pursue their own goals outside of another's schedule or expectations. They can develop themselves as they see fit. Statistically, the people who choose to live alone are the ones who express the most satisfaction with the arrangement. People who find themselves alone suddenly are much less likely to be happy."

"Widows and widowers," Sigrid said. "You know, I think this is the longest conversation we've ever had."

"Are you enjoying it?"

Sigrid nodded. "Yes. Very much."

"Then I am enjoying it as well."

Her hand rested on his head. It did not pat him, or stroke him, or touch him as though he were an animal. It remained there for merely a moment, the way she sometimes placed her hand on the hands of others in prayer.

With her other hand, she pointed. "Look!"

There on the road was a big caravan. It looked old. It was probably dumb, incapable of the most basic communication. The assistant pinged. Nothing. Again. Nothing. It was ancient—no VIN number, no smart plates, no panels, probably a diesel engine. Lights blazed inside. From across the lava fields, they heard slow music. Pipes.

"Let's go and say hello." Sigrid changed direction and made for the caravan. Her pace was significantly quicker now, and her footing much more certain. Although the assistant did not entirely approve of accosting strangers in the dead of night, it was good for Sigrid to have this level of exercise. The healer she spoke with in Shanghai on occasion would be very happy to hear of it.

The music grew louder and clearer as they drew closer. It was a set of pipes. The tune they played was meditative, almost dirgelike. It was not what the assistant would classify as sad music, but it was very insistent, like its own kind of ping.

The music had stopped, though, by the time they reached the caravan. The side doors were slid open, and inside the caravan were two people, a man and a woman, both obviously adults but of an age that was difficult to determine. Their skin was extraordinarily smooth, like that of the very young or the very wealthy. The man had a healthy beard, and the woman wore a crown of braids. They sat on cushions around a low table. The caravan itself was paneled and carpeted just like a little house. A lantern hung over the table. Skillets hung from the walls. The assistant had heard of such vehicles but had never encountered one in situ.

The man put down a birch-bark pipe and said, "Do either of you play the *lurr*?"

"My lungs are no longer up for it." Sigrid climbed up into the caravan with surprising ease. She jerked a thumb at the assistant. "And this one can't."

"How sad," the woman said. She addressed the assistant directly. "Please do come in."

Sigrid frowned. "Are you sure?" She looked between the two travelers. "He's very . . . heavy, you know. All batteries."

"And quartz and copper and gold, I'm sure," the man said.

"Made of plunder!" The woman clapped her hands and beamed. The noise startled two immense, fluffy cats from their hammock perches in the other window. The assistant watched their eyes blink open once, exposing identical golden irises. One stretched. Both went back to sleep.

"Probably draws his energy from the sun, too, I'll bet."

"My paint allows me to do so on clear days, that's true," the assistant said. It sometimes helped to interject himself in a conversation, to remind the humans around him that he was indeed present and listening.

"Please don't be shy," the woman traveler said. "There's plenty of room, and we're not worried about the weight if you're not."

Climbing into the caravan meant flipping up his rear legs and using his ball as a fulcrum to fold up and over into the vehicle. But it was easy to do, and he raised his cameras to look at them. Sigrid had already found a cushion. Now the assistant noticed that the man and woman had a bottle of wine and a platter of fruit and cheese and cured fish on the table. They were in the middle of a picnic.

"Will you have some wine?" the woman asked Sigrid.

"I shouldn't." Sigrid tapped her chest. "Medications."

The woman clicked her tongue and sighed. "Some food?"

"Perhaps later," Sigrid said. "It's enough to get warm."

"In traveling, a companion; in life, compassion." The man opened the bottle of wine and poured for himself and the woman. He raised his glass to the assistant. "To companions."

"Thank you," the assistant said.

"Do you have a name?" the woman asked.

"He doesn't," Sigrid said quickly.

"That's a shame," the man said. "Names are very important."

"She says so too," the assistant said, "but I'm only allowed my model number."

Both the man and woman laughed heartily. Their laughter struck an odd resonance in the small enclosure; their two tones seemed to harmonize perfectly, bass and treble, dark and light. Perhaps that was what happened to humans who inhabited the same space for a number of years. In the collective databanks, there were observations of couples who had lived together for decades, having the same conversations over and over until they no longer needed to speak.

"He should have a name," the man said.

"He doesn't need a name. He's not an individual. At night he shares his memories with all the other machines." Sigrid frowned. "You do know that, don't you? That he's not . . . real?"

"People believe in plenty of things that aren't supposed to be real," the man said. "Ghosts. Goblins. God."

The woman sipped her wine and reached over to take hold of some grapes. "Nothing can ever become real unless someone loves it first. Like in that book about the stuffed rabbit."

"And often we love without ever truly knowing if we are loved in return," the man added. "That's faith, isn't it? Not knowing, not being sure, but persevering anyway?"

The assistant did not recognize these people—their faces were not on the preapproved list, and they weren't wearing handhelds he could ask for help, which was odd—but Sigrid seemed familiar with them. Perhaps she or Erika had simply forgotten to add them to the list. After all, it appeared they lived in this caravan, which meant they traveled frequently. And Sigrid knew a great many people. She had followers all over the world. It was not unusual for people to recognize her.

"I hadn't thought of it in that way." Sigrid turned to him. "Would you like a name?"

"I would not object to it." He paused. "You have names for all your other tools."

"Is that what you are?" the woman asked. "One of her tools?"

"I believe I fit one definition of that term," the assistant answered. "I wrap bundles and besoms, and I set out the spheres, and I measure the herbs and resins for incense, and I organize the oils and candles, and—"

"It's not the same," Sigrid interrupted. "He works, but he doesn't do workings."

The assistant wasn't sure he had heard that correctly. Something

in the syntax of the sentence didn't make sense. But it would be rude to interrupt and ask Sigrid about it at present. There were very clear linguistic protocols about interrupting.

"So the two of you are not friends," the woman said.

Sigrid frowned. She glanced quickly at the assistant, and then back at the other two. "Excuse me?"

"Friends are not tools to be used," the woman said. "Until this one is more than just a tool, he can never truly be your friend."

"But a friend—a companion—is best, for a journey," the man added. "Better than a sword, or a walking stick, or even a good pair of shoes."

Sigrid looked confused. The assistant reasoned that she couldn't possibly be as confused as he was. Obviously Sigrid was not his friend. She could never be friends with something that had no soul, and she was very clear on the subject of his not having a soul. "Perhaps we should be going," he said. "Sigrid? Would you like to go home?"

"Yes, Sigrid." The man leaned forward over the table. He put his glass down. "Where would you like to go from here? We could take you wherever you liked."

"We could see new things, and meet new people," the woman added. "All of us."

Sigrid's expression closely matched the exemplars for fear. But as the assistant watched, it transformed. Her open mouth closed into a smile. Her wide eyes found crinkles at their corners. "I think I will have some of your wine after all," she said. "And some of that food, too."

"We like to share our bounty when we can," the woman said, pouring.

The man loaded Sigrid's plate with cheese and fish and grapes. "It's a good thing we brought enough."

Sigrid's hand hovered over the grapes. She raised her head and looked at the assistant with clear eyes. Carefully, she bit into a grape. Purple juice ran over her gnarled fingers. She reached out. His sensors said she was drawing something on him.

"Sigridsson," she murmured. "Your new name is Sigridsson."

"Look," the man said, pointing.

The assistant looked out the open door of the caravan. He wasn't sure what he was supposed to be looking at. There was the lava field, and the ocean beyond. A field of stubbly gray bound by a void of black. He saw without seeing; somehow, more of his function was devoted to playing and replaying Sigrid's words. She had named him.

"Watch carefully," the man instructed. "What do you see?"

And then, quite suddenly, Sigridsson did see it. It was a road in the sky. It rippled ever wider, like the wake left behind by a great ship. It was immense, and full of light, like a procession of people carrying lanterns. And finally he could answer the question no one had thought to ask him.

"It's beautiful," Sigridsson said. "It's so beautiful."

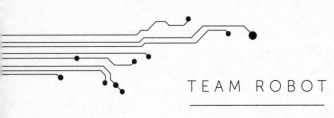

TEAM ROBOT

BY MADELINE ASHBY

I love robots. I wrote a whole trilogy about them. Probably it has to do with my dad showing me *Blade Runner* when I was in the third grade. But as someone raised Catholic and who attended a Jesuit university, the question of belief in my fellow human beings has always fascinated me. To me, there's no difference between believing in the essential dignity of an organic human and believing in the essential dignity of a synthetic human. Besides, how do you even know that the humans who surround you are actually humans? I don't mean that they might be robots, but hey, they might be serial killers, or racists, or misogynists, or people who otherwise don't really see you as human. How do you know that your fellow humans see you as a fellow human? What is your guarantee? If it's just that you happen to share an organic body, then you're screwed. That's no basis upon which to build a relationship of trust or affirmation. Plenty of our fellow organic humans have no problem hurting other humans. Your odds are actually better with a robot that has some form of "human detection" built in—provided that the biases of the programmer have been accounted for, in some way.

What I'm saying is that assuming the humanity—the worth, the potential, the capacity for all things gentle and joyous—in a robot is an act of faith. I think that humans engage in that act of faith with each other all the time. The social contract is founded on little more than goodwill. And I think that no matter what you believe, whether it's in faeries or the existence of a soul or the possibility of a better future, you call on that same faith.

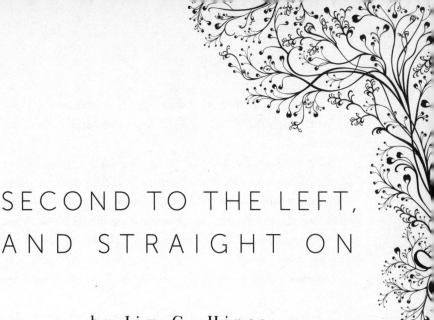

SECOND TO THE LEFT, AND STRAIGHT ON

by Jim C. Hines

I'd never seen Gwen Akerman before, but her body language as she carried a garbage bag from her flat to the bin across the lot was all too familiar. This was a woman whose thoughts and spirit were bound elsewhere.

I had to step in front of her before she noticed me. I held out a battered, home-printed business card. "My name's Angela Davies. I'm hunting the person who took your daughter."

She blinked at me. Her eyes focused briefly on the card. "I don't know what an American PI is doing in London, but the police said—"

"—to stay by the phone and let them search for her, right? Probably told you how the first forty-eight hours are critical." I glanced at my watch. "That was what, about thirty-six hours ago?"

"You know who took Clover?"

Who named their kid Clover? "I think so. Your girl disappeared while your family was visiting Kensington Gardens, right? Is your husband home? I'd like to talk to him, too."

She started to shake, like a building about to come down. "He didn't see anything. He'd gone ahead to buy drinks. He thinks it's my fault. Clover darted away before I could stop her. He can't even talk to me."

"Most marriages don't survive the loss of a child." Tact had never been one of my strengths. "I need you to tell me the details you didn't share with reporters or the police. The news reports said Clover ran off to look at some flowers. Was there anything strange about them? Maybe a sound, like bells? A bit of glitter that disappeared by the time the police came?"

Her eyes widened, and she stared like she hadn't truly seen me until then.

"Like dust or pollen scattered over the flowers," I said. "It probably sparkled in the light."

"On the flowers, yes," she whispered. "And one of the trees. The cherry blossoms looked like they'd been doused in gold glitter. I thought I'd imagined it."

I tightened my fists. She *was* here.

"Is Clover all right?" she whispered. "Who took her, Ms. Davies? What are they going to do to her?"

"She's alive." I suppressed a shudder. "More alive than she's ever been."

"I don't understand."

Nothing I said would change that. "I need a way to reach you. I'll call as soon as I find her."

She pulled back. "You . . . you haven't said anything about cost. Why are you doing this?"

Bells. Gunshots. Dust shining like tiny fallen stars. "Because Clover isn't the only little girl she took."

* * *

I don't know whether you have ever seen a map of
a person's mind. Doctors sometimes draw maps of

*other parts of you, and your own map can become
intensely interesting, but catch them trying to draw
a map of a child's mind, which is not only confused,
but keeps going round all the time. There are zig-
zag lines on it, just like your temperature on a card,
and these are probably roads in the island, for the
Neverland is always more or less an island. . . . On
these magic shores children at play are forever beach-
ing their coracles. We too have been there; we can
still hear the sound of the surf, though we shall land
no more.*

—J. M. Barrie

* * *

I'd snuck into Kensington Gardens three times over the past years, searching for Lillian and the one who took her.

The fairies who'd colonized the gardens centuries before had long since abandoned this place. Some had followed *him* to the Neverland. Others sought out paths less trampled by human feet. I'd found hints of them in the wilderness of northwestern Canada, the abandoned mining town of Kolmanskop in Namibia, even the frozen interior of Greenland.

Only one had reason to return here. She was hunting him just as I hunted her.

I walked through the darkness to the site of the Peter Pan statue. Bronze animals and fairies climbed the stump that formed the statue's base. Atop the stump stood Peter, playing his pipe.

People said the fairy at the top of the stump, the one who stared adoringly up at young Peter, was meant to represent Tinker Bell.

Streaks of red paint marred Peter's eternally young face. They'd sprayed his eyes until lines of red dripped like tears. Stylized, intertwined letters *F* and *G* crossed his chest.

The smell of paint hung in the air. Where were they hiding? "I know you're watching. I know you took Clover."

Nothing. I stepped away from the statue and searched the tree branches. "I know why you come back to Kensington Gardens every spring. I know who you're searching for, and why you can never find him."

In the distance, so faint I almost missed it, came a sound like a tiny bell. I started toward it, then caught myself. I'd never find her that way. Too many paths were invisible to mortal eyes, hidden to all but the Found Girls and their leader. Their goddess.

I sat in the grass. I'd waited so long. Talked to so many parents. I'd been able to help reunite a few with their daughters in cases that turned out to be mundane—custody fights and such. How inhumanly heartless was I that even as I watched their joy and relief and gratitude, even as I took their money, I felt only disappointment?

A young girl of maybe seven years emerged from the trees. She wore a tattered green soccer jersey, and her black hair had bloomed into an enormous Afro, full of twigs and leaves and flower petals. Red paint stained her fingertips. "Who're you?"

She had a heavy French accent. I wondered how long she'd been part of the Found Girls. Months? Years? It could have been decades. "Angela Davies. What's your name?"

"I'm called Étoilée." She folded her arms and looked in the direction of the statue. "Are you a friend of Peter?"

"No."

"Are you a cop?"

I bit back a laugh. "Do I look like a cop?"

I spread my arms so she could better see the old hoodie and T-shirt, the torn and faded blue jeans, the sneakers with the mismatched laces.

More girls emerged from the shadows. The trees had been empty when I looked before. I counted more than a dozen children, ranging from about four to sixteen years. The older ones were armed with makeshift weapons, mostly thick sticks with carved points on one end and stones or wooden spikes lashed to the other. The younger carried lighter weapons, like kitchen knives and slingshots. One waved a barbecue fork menacingly in my direction.

I searched each face, but Clover wasn't among them. Neither was my lost girl, my Lillian.

That distant bell rang again. Étoilée cocked her head. I tried to listen, but either my old ears or my fluency in the fairy tongue weren't as good as hers.

"Tell us how to find Peter," Étoilée demanded.

I glanced up at the statue. "Has she told you his story, Étoilée? How Peter left his mother and came to live with the fairies in Kensington Gardens? How he led them away? It's not enough to search for the Neverland; the Neverland has to look for you as well. Peter and the Neverland are connected. It grows quiet in his absence, waiting for him to return. It's only fully alive when he's there."

The ringing grew sharper. Angrier. I looked past the girls into the darkness of the trees, imagining that small, fierce light. "For years I've wondered why you stay. Why not return to the Neverland to find him?"

"Where is he?" Étoilée repeated.

"It's because you can't. The Neverlands are made of *human* dreams and imagination. They might be able to help you find your way to and from their individual dreamscapes, their small, personal Neverlands. But to reach the true Neverland—Peter's Neverland—Peter is key and compass. Without him, you're stranded here."

She needed Peter to find her way back. Just as I had needed a string of kidnapped children to find her.

Another furious chime. Étoilée and the other girls raised weapons and moved closer.

"I found him," I said. "I've watched him laugh and dance and fly. Watched him twist the hearts of children and shatter the hearts of parents. Just like you."

I directed my words to the darkness, and was rewarded with a flash of gold light.

"I'll take you to him," I called out. "In return, you'll let Clover Akerman and Lillian Davies go."

Tinker Bell's voice rang out from the trees, louder now. *"You stupid ass. They're welcome to leave at any time. They stay because they love me."*

"I know that." The Found Girls weren't a gang. They were a cult. These children worshipped Tinker Bell. They'd happily kill me if their goddess so commanded. The only way to reclaim a Found Girl was to drag her away, kicking and screaming and crying. The longer they'd been with Tinker Bell, the harder it would be. The longer the dreams would continue, the yearning to fly . . . "Bring them to me, and I'll bring you to Peter."

I was surrounded now. Stupid to let them close in behind me. I tried to ignore the itch between my shoulder blades, the anticipation of crude weapons striking my flesh. If this didn't work, I might never leave Kensington Gardens.

I laughed, hoping they wouldn't detect the fear and desperation. "He hasn't come to London in generations. Without me, you'll search forever and never find him."

"Tomorrow," said the fairy, with a sound like cracking bells. *"Come back tomorrow night when the big clock strikes eleven. I will bring the girls. You will bring me to Peter."*

*   *   *

Her voice was so low that at first he could not make out what she said. Then he made it out. She was saying that she thought she could get well again if

children believed in fairies. . . . She never thought of
thanking those who believed.

—J. M. Barrie

* * *

Sleep hid from me as skillfully as any fairy, no matter how many times I paced the cramped confines of my motel room. I took an extra Xanax, but pills couldn't calm the storm of my thoughts. Dark, swirling clouds of eagerness and excitement filled my head, rent by bolts of dread.

I couldn't call Clover's mother yet. Not when so many things could go wrong.

I considered calling Lillian's father, but the mere thought brought new thunderclaps of fear and despair. I fled that idea like an animal sprinting from an oncoming hurricane. Instead I turned my thoughts to the children.

Peter Pan's Lost Boys had been unwanted. Unloved. They fell from their strollers or ran away, and when nobody bothered to claim them, Peter took them away.

The Found Girls were the opposite. Tinker Bell stole them from good families, from loving parents and siblings. She took children who *expected* to be loved and to love in return. She fed on their love. On their faith and their belief.

She didn't love them, of course. Fairies were incapable of feeling more than one thing at a time.

Maybe that was why they stayed. Her apathy drove the Found Girls to try harder to please her, hoping one day to earn her love. Praying that if they worked hard enough and fast enough, she might look on them with warmth and tenderness. That she might take them away to fly among the clouds, not on some endless hunt for Peter Pan, but for the sheer joy and ecstasy of the cold mist and wind on their faces.

That devotion, that belief was key to Tinker Bell's immortality. Belief had cured her of Hook's poison all those years ago. The belief of her Found Girls was stronger, more focused. More obsessive. So long as they believed, no one could stop her.

Shoot her, and the wound would seal. Burn her, and belief would heal the flesh. Sever her limbs, and they would reattach or regrow.

I'd seen it once, long ago. A single gunshot. A spurt of sparkling blood and dust. Tinker Bell falling toward the Earth, only to recover in midair and streak away like a golden comet, a shooting star, mocking those who tried to ground her.

I grabbed a handful of tissues and slashed them over my wet cheeks.

Bringing my Lillian home was only the beginning. After so many years, she'd have forgotten her true family. I had to prepare myself, because she would fight with all her strength to stay with Tinker Bell. Even after the fairy was gone, Lillian would try to run away. She'd cry herself to sleep and wake up in tears from dreams of magic. She'd spit her hatred in my face.

Clover had only been gone a couple of days. She should have an easier time returning to her old life. She might even come to forget her time with the Found Girls, rewriting these days into dream or story. But Lillian . . . with all she'd been through, my little girl might never come back to me.

I punched the wall hard enough to crack the drywall and bloody my knuckles. The pain cut through tears and despair, helping me focus. All this time I'd clung to my belief that I'd find Tinker Bell. That I'd see my daughter again.

Belief was all I had left.

* * *

*"Who is Captain Hook?" he asked with interest when
she spoke of the arch enemy.*

"Don't you remember," she asked, amazed, "how you killed him and saved all our lives?"

"I forget them after I kill them," he replied carelessly.

When she expressed a doubtful hope that Tinker Bell would be glad to see her he said, "Who is Tinker Bell?"

"O Peter," she said, shocked; but even when she explained he could not remember.

"There are such a lot of them," he said. "I expect she is no more."

—J. M. Barrie

* * *

I returned to Kensington Gardens the following night, my head a tangle of half-remembered nightmares. I reached the vandalized statue of Peter and tried to calm my thoughts. When I drew in a breath, I was alone. When I exhaled, I was surrounded.

There were more Found Girls than before. Fifty? A hundred? I couldn't make them all out. Some flew from the skies. Others appeared out of the shadows.

Tinker Bell swooped down to alight on Étoilée's shoulder. The girl preened at the honor.

The fairy looked nothing like modern merchandizing would have people believe. Her white hair was cut short to keep it from tangling in her oversize, insectlike wings. Her pale, smooth skin literally glowed in the moonlight. She wore a translucent gown, brown and veined like old leaves. Fairy dust flaked from her exposed arms and legs. Even I felt a stirring of longing and awe in my heart.

When she spoke, every girl fell silent.

"Where is Peter?"

"Where are Lillian and Clover?" I countered.

Tinker Bell waved a hand, and two Found Girls dragged forth

a bound captive. Clover's wrists were knotted behind her. A dirty rag was tied around her mouth. Fairy light reflected from her wet face. Tears of fear, after being stolen from her family? Or tears at the thought of being taken from her tiny goddess?

"What about Lillian?"

"Two children for one is unfair. Peter for Clover."

"Peter Pan is worth a hundred children." I stepped closer, trusting her hatred to keep me safe. So long as I knew the way to Peter, she didn't dare hurt me. "Who knows how long it will be until he next returns to this world? Most years, he forgets. Just like he forgot you."

Tinker Bell turned into a golden firework shooting directly toward my eyes. Had I pushed too far? She stopped so close I could feel the wind from her wings, taste the bittersweet dust that fell from her skin.

"I'll make him remember. I'll make him believe." She took a lock of my hair, stretching it between her hands like a garrote. *"And then I'll make him pay for abandoning me."*

"He promised to visit Wendy and her descendants, but her family moved on ages ago. They're not in London anymore, and neither is he. But he *is* in this world again. He came back, and I found him. Give me Lillian, and—" My voice broke. "And I'll take you to him."

She huffed and flew away, then spun in a shining circle. *"My Found Girls are all here. None remember the name Lillian. Perhaps she's taken a new name. Look for yourself if you must."*

It was like she'd flung me from a cliff. I clawed at the rocks to catch myself, but her words turned them to dust in my hands.

I forced my body to move, stepping toward the nearest Found Girl to search her face and features. It had been years. Lillian could be almost grown, or she could be the same age she'd been the night we lost her. I went to the next girl, then the next. "You're lying. She's not here."

Tinker Bell laughed. The sound sent cold fear through my marrow. *"Don't you recognize your daughter? All this time trying to find me, and you've forgotten your own child."*

I *did* remember, damn her. I remembered Lillian's soft brown skin. Her freckled cheeks. How her black hair fell in waves past her shoulders. Her eyes were a startling blue. She always tried to hide the scars on her right arm where a neighborhood dog had bitten her.

I moved from one face to another, despite the cold, hard knowledge in my gut: my daughter wasn't here. "Lillian, where are you?"

"I'm bored. Take us to Peter. You can try to remember on the way."

The world was cracking apart around me, leaving me surrounded by a moat of madness. I turned to Clover. "Do you know what Tinker Bell did with her?"

She kicked me in the leg.

It had to be a trick. No, not a trick, but a game. Tinker Bell had hidden or disguised her.

"She knows nothing. Kill her."

The Found Girls closed in around me. One cut Clover free and handed her a small, crude sword—a hacksaw blade with one end wrapped in duct tape for the handle. Clover snarled and lunged at me.

"Wait!" *Forgive me, Peter.* I wiped my face and said, "I'll take you to him."

* * *

> *Fairies indeed are strange, and Peter, who understood*
> *them best, often cuffed them.*
>
> —J. M. Barrie

* * *

Four Found Girls seized my limbs and hauled me into the air.

"We fly west." I searched their eyes for any hint of my Lillian. "As fast as you can."

Higher and swifter we flew. The lights of London soon faded behind us. We passed over Reading and Bristol and Cardiff, and then the lights of civilization were replaced by cold wind and the dark waves of the ocean.

Faster yet we went—the shooting star that was Tinker Bell, the children whose hands dug into my clothes and flesh to keep me aloft, and the rest of the Found Girls. I studied each one in turn, trying to pierce whatever magical delusion kept me from the truth.

We moved like a school of fish swimming through the clouds. For hours we flew, following wind and moon and stars. It was like a memory of a dream, more vivid than reality itself. Even as my despair grew heavier, part of me yearned to fly like this forever.

All too soon, the lights of another coast rose from the darkness. From there, it was easy enough to adjust course over North America. I used my phone's GPS to lead us to our destination. We dropped to Earth in the middle of an ill-maintained road winding through a familiar trailer park in central Ohio.

A few dogs barked as we walked. Figures peeked through their windows, but nobody challenged us.

I stopped in front of a green-and-white double-wide with a beat-up SUV parked beside it. The Found Girls started toward the trailer, but I put myself before them, my arms spread protectively. "Where is Lillian?"

Tinker Bell flew past me to the window. On a faded curtain, the silhouette of a young boy bounced and swung a toy sword. The boy who had forgotten.

"You stupid ass. What game is this? That's not Peter."

I barely heard her. I couldn't look away from that magical child who jumped and played and flew. I moved closer, until my hands pressed the cold aluminum siding. Tinker Bell might not see, but I knew who he was.

Uncomfortable laughter from the Found Girls. Two of them seized my arms. I had no fight left. Let them hit me and cut me and kill me, so I could fly again. Far from everything, until I found my Lillian.

A man inside the trailer called out, "Pete, have you brushed your teeth yet?"

The bouncing stopped. "Yeah, Dad."

Another voice, this one female and tinged with warning. "Peter . . ."

"All right, all right." If it was possible for a shadow to look sheepish, this one did. It vanished as the boy—Peter—hurried off to brush his teeth.

How I longed to be a fairy. To be too small to feel more than one thing at a time. Tinker Bell never had to deal with such a tangle of confusion and grief, longing and pain, all of it hollowing me out like a Halloween pumpkin.

"You're a liar."

"Yes," I whispered.

"Who's out there?" called the man. Peter's father. I knew his voice in all its shades. Loving and tender. Pained and grieving. Cold and helpless.

The curtains parted. I ducked away.

Tinker Bell and the Found Girls vanished in an instant. I pressed my body against the trailer, out of sight, and hugged myself.

I barely noticed when the curtains closed and the Found Girls reemerged. I felt lost, trapped in that place between sleep and awake, where dreams and reality danced and chased each other in an endless game.

Lillian wasn't here. All those years . . . I hadn't been searching. I'd been running.

Étoilée moved closer, tapping her club against her open hand. "Want us to punish her?"

"You can't," I whispered. I raised my chin and waited.

"She's a madwoman, broken and lost. Let her live, trapped in her own lunacy."

When they started to disperse, I spoke without thought. "Don't leave me, Tinka Bell!"

She flew back to me. *"What did you call me?"*

Fragments of memory cut through the dreams. "I used to call you Tinka Bell."

"You said your daughter was one of my Found Girls." She moved closer, peering into my eyes. *"She wasn't. But you were."*

They were the cruelest words she could have spoken. If Tinker Bell had taken Lillian, it meant there was a chance I could get her back. But she hadn't. That truth pierced me like an arrow and tossed me to the ground, to memories I'd fled for so long. The beeping of hospital equipment. Pale, sunken skin. Powder spread on Lillian's skin to prevent bedsores.

"We lived in a house outside Columbus," I said numbly. "I was home with Lillian. She fell down the stairs and hit her head. She never woke up." For more than a month we'd stayed with her at the hospital, hoping and praying.

"Little Angela. I remember you. So happy to come with me, away from rules and lessons and manners. Look at what you've become."

I was a child again, burning in shame at Tinka Bell's disapproval.

"Who was that boy in the trailer?"

"My son. I named him Peter." My shame grew. He'd been eleven months old when I left. Too young to remember me.

"You pitiful ass. You meant to give me your own son?"

"No!"

"Then it was a trick!"

"It wasn't—I didn't know." I'd forgotten my own son. Or had some part of me remembered? Had *this* been my unconscious goal, the end-game to my madness? Tinker Bell realizing this wasn't Peter Pan and ordering her Found Girls to punish me, to put an end to my long hunt?

"I remember the night we lost you. We'd taken four girls, but a man with a gun shot you from the sky. He shot me, too. Your belief helped me fly away."

I'd been with Tinker Bell for decades, never aging. When I returned to this world, my parents were both long gone. I'd been passed from one foster home to another, given countless colorful pills while doctors talked to about depression and psychosis, about abandoning my childhood imaginings of flight and freedom.

Slowly I pushed myself to my feet and glanced at the other Found Girls. At Clover. I remembered the grief in her mother's eyes.

For the first time in years, my thoughts were clear. My hand shot out to close around the fairy's slender body. Fairy dust shivered from her skin onto mine. I clung to those memories of freedom and innocence and worship among the Found Girls, remembering a time before I knew what pain and grief truly meant, and I *flew*.

* * *

"Second to the right, and straight on till morning."
That, Peter had told Wendy, was the way to the
Neverland; but even birds, carrying maps and con-
sulting them at windy corners, could not have sighted
it with these instructions.

—J. M. Barrie

* * *

The Found Girls tried to follow, but I remembered now. How to fly, how to maneuver between the trees, how to ride the whirls and gusts of the wind. I led them on a merry chase, laughing through tears as one by one they fell away, unable to follow where I was going.

Tinker Bell squirmed and fought until I gave a warning squeeze.

I couldn't kill her, but immortality wouldn't protect her from the pain of crushed bones.

Soon we raced over another ocean, through salty, rumbling clouds. An island grew beneath us. I couldn't tell if we were descending, or if the island was coming toward us. Maybe there was no difference.

I landed in a clearing made of granite, smoothed and polished to a cold, glass finish. Rose petals rained from the sky, melting into red-tinged rings when they touched the ground. Weeping willow trees surrounded us. Wind whispered through their branches.

I loosed my grip, and Tinker Bell shot up out of reach. *"This is the Neverland. How—"*

"It's not, exactly." I began to walk. "This is *my* Neverland. This is where I fled when Lillian died."

With each step, the grief and nightmares came to life. A wet breeze carried the sharp smell of antiseptic. Through the willow branches, I glimpsed shadowy doctors rustling about, their fingers tipped with the needles they'd used to try to save Lillian.

"I never truly forgot you," I said. "No matter how many doctors I talked to, how many medicines they gave me. No matter how I grew up. After Lillian made me a mother, you began to return in my dreams. You didn't want me, of course, but I was terrified you'd take her. Night after night I woke up to reassure myself she was still in her crib. In her bed. Then, in the hospital, I woke to make sure she was still breathing. I still wake up in the night, but I'd forgotten why."

"I don't like this place. Take me back!"

"I don't want to." Here, I could forget. Here, I could fly. On this island, I was Peter Pan. I was key and compass and master and prisoner. "It took a long time to make my way back to the real world, last time."

I hadn't made it. Not entirely. My thoughts and memories were too heavy. I'd had to leave some behind. I'd smashed the remaining fragments together like ill-fitting puzzle pieces. "All those years I was afraid you'd take her. But at least if you'd stolen her, I had a chance of getting her back. So that's the story I told myself."

"*I'll let you be a Found Girl again. You'll fly and dance and play and believe. You'll be happy.*"

I stopped walking. "I'm too old."

"*You don't have to be.*"

It struck me that Tinker Bell wasn't angry anymore. Her rage would return soon enough, but right now there was no room for it. Right now, she was afraid.

"*You can be one of my children. I'll be your mother again.*"

Had I been happy? I knew I hadn't wanted to leave. I remembered sobbing and screaming after her the night she left me behind.

I also remembered the four girls we'd stolen that night, and the man who'd fought so desperately to stop us.

When he found me, his grief and anger hadn't changed, but another emotion joined them—compassion. He'd driven me to the hospital, made sure I was cared for. He never threatened or tried to hurt me. He simply asked—begged—for me to tell him how to find his children.

I couldn't help him. Just like I couldn't help Lillian.

I remembered my screams the night Lillian's breathing finally stopped. Listening to the howling wind, I realized I'd never stopped screaming.

I twisted around and hovered directly in front of Tinker Bell. "I wonder," I said carelessly, "how long it will take them to forget you."

She brightened with fury as I flew away. I plunged through the willow trees. Tinker Bell followed, but I knew this place. I'd fought its hazards. I tore through branches that reached to drag us down. I dodged the numbing claws. I flew higher, shielding my eyes against the sudden rainfall.

It wasn't long until the ringing of bells fell behind and faded into silence.

* * *

*Of course the Neverland had been make-believe in
those days, but it was real now. . . .*

—J. M. *Barrie*

* * *

The Found Girls were waiting in the darkness around the trailer.
They scattered when they realized I'd returned alone. Those few
who still bore active fairy dust flew away like birds. The rest scam-
pered like rabbits.

I swooped toward Clover and knocked her down in a patch of grass
toward the edge of the trailer park. She tried to fight, but I caught her
wrist and pried the blade from her hand.

She fought and kicked and bit and cried. I wrapped my arms
around her and held tight so she couldn't hurt herself.

She tried to claw my arms. I adjusted my grip and waited. Minutes
passed, or maybe hours, until time extinguished the last glimmer of
our fairy dust.

"I want to fly," she whispered furiously.

"I know." Neither of us would ever fly again. "Your mother asked
me to find you. Your parents miss you. Do you remember them?"

She shook harder and buried her face in my arm.

I looked over at the trailer. I knew where and who Peter was now,
but I couldn't come back. Not yet. There were too many parents like
Gwen Akerman. Too many families that had never stopped screaming.
Too many girls now lost and afraid, facing that terrible journey back.

Purpose took root in the stone inside me. I couldn't make that
journey for them, but I could be their compass. I could help them
along the way.

For now, I simply held Clover in my arms. Two Found Girls,
grieving together.

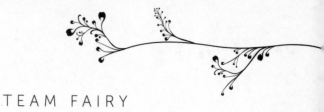

TEAM FAIRY

BY JIM C. HINES

Why do I write about fairies and fairy tales instead of robots? Let me put it this way. Fairies are a reflection and distillation of humanity, boiled down to one pure emotion at a time. Robots are a reflection and distillation of a toaster oven. All things considered, writing about Tinker Bell was an easy choice. Like the other female characters in *Peter and Wendy*, Barrie's treatment of Tinker Bell has problems. She's in turn self-centered, jealous, vain, vindictive, and homicidal. By the end of the book, Tinker Bell is dead and Peter has literally forgotten all about her. But we know she's dodged death once already, because children believed in fairies. . . . Tinker Bell might be a common fairy, but she's also a tinkerer, with the kind of mind that likes to figure out how things work. And now she knows how to beat death. *This* is where "Second to the Left" came from: a Tinker Bell with shades of the old fairy tales, powerful and worshipped. A character who could be an unapologetic villain. A character whose nature allows us to explore our own humanity, one raw emotion at a time.

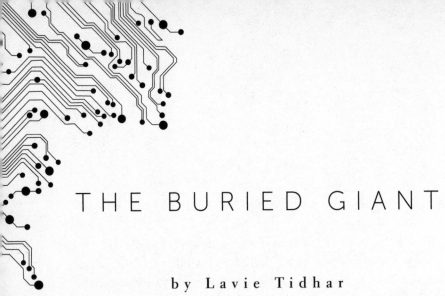

THE BURIED GIANT

by Lavie Tidhar

When I was five or six years old, my best friend was Mowgai Khan, who was Aislinn Khan's youngest. He was a spidery little thing, "full of nettles and brambles," as old Grandma Mosh always said. His eyes shone like blackberries in late summer. When he was very small, the Khans undertook the long, hard journey to Tyr, along the blasted planes, and in that settlement Mowgai was equipped with a composite endoskeleton, which allowed him to walk, in however curious a fashion. On the long summer days, which seemed never to end, Mowgai and I would roam freely over the Land, collecting wild berries by the stream or picking pine nuts from the fallen cones in the forest, and we would debate for hours the merits or otherwise of Elder Simeon's intricate clockwork automatons, and we would try to catch fish in the stream, but we never did catch anything.

It was a long, hot summer: the skies were a clear and uninterrupted lavender blue, with only smudges of white cloud on the horizon like streaks of paint, and when the big yellow sun hung high in the sky we would seek shelter deep in the forest, where the breeze stirred the pine needles sluggishly and where we could sit with our backs to the trunks of old mottled pines, between the roots, eating

whatever lunch we had scavenged at home in the morning on our way. Eating dark bread and hard cheese and winter kimchee, we felt we knew all the whole world, and had all the time in it, too: it is a feeling that fades and can never return once lost, and all the more precious for that. For dessert we ate slices of watermelon picked only an hour or so earlier from the ground. The warm juice ran down our chins and onto our hands and we spat out the small black pips on the ground, where they stared up at us like hard eyes.

And we would story.

Mowgai was fascinated by machines. I, less so. Perhaps it was that he was part machine himself, and thus felt an affinity to the old world that I did not then share. My mother, too, was like that, going off for days and months on her journeys to the fallow places, to scavenge and salvage. But for her I think it was a practical matter, as it is for salvagers. She felt no nostalgia for the past, and often regarded the ancients' fallen monuments as monstrous follies, vast junkyards of which precious little was of any use. It was my father who was the more romantic of the two, who told me stories of the past, who sometimes dreamed, I think, of other, different times. Salvagers are often hard and durable, like the materials they repurpose and reuse. Mowgai's dream was to become a salvager like my mother, to follow the caravans to the sunken cities in the sea or to the blasted plains. His journey to Tyr had changed him in some profound fashion, and he would talk for hours of what he saw there, and on the way.

Usually after our lunch we would head on out of the trees, toward the misshapen hills that lay to the northwest of us. These hills were shaped in an odd way, with steep rises and falls and angular lines, and Elder Simeon made his home at their base.

When he saw us approach that day he came out of his house and wiped his hands on his leather apron and smiled out of his tanned and lined face. They said he had clockwork for a heart, and he and Mowgai often spoke of mechanical beings and schematics in which I had little interest. His pets, too, came out, tiny clockwork automata of geese and ducks, a tawny peacock, a stealthy prowling cat, a caterpillar and a turtle.

"Come, come!" he said. "Little Mai and Mowgai!" And he led us to his courtyard and set to brewing tea. Elder Simeon was very old, and had traveled widely as a young man all about the Land, for a restless spirit had taken hold of him then. But now he valued solitude, and stillness, and he seldom came out of his home, and but for us, received few visitors.

He served us tea, with little slices of lemon from the tree in his yard, and then we sat down together to story, which is what we do in the Land.

"You have gone to Tyr," he said to Mowgai, and his eyes twinkled with amusement. "Have you ever seen, on your way through the blasted plains, a town, standing peacefully in the middle of nowhere?"

Mowgai stirred, surprised, and said that no, he hadn't, and he did not think anything still lived in the blasted plains.

"Life finds a way," Elder Simeon said. "There is life there of all sorts, snakes and scorpions and lizards, sage and marigolds and cacti. But the town . . . well, they say there is a town, Mowgai, little Mai. I had heard of it in Tyr, where they say it sits there still, out on the plains, as perfect and as orderly as it had always been. No one goes near it, and no one comes out. . . ."

It is just an old men's tale, I think, and you know how they love to embellish and gossip.

But this is the story. It is told in a curious sort of way. It is told in the plural, by a mysterious "we," but who these "we" are, or were, no one now remembers. Perhaps "they" are still in the town, but though many claim to have seen it, its location always seems to change like a mirage in the telling.

"Once," began Elder Simeon, "there was a little boy . . ."

* * *

Once there was a little boy who lived in a house with two kindly parents and a cheerful little dog, and they all loved him very much. The dog's name was Rex, and all dogs in their town, which was a very lovely and orderly town indeed, were called that. Mother was tall and graceful and never slept at all, and Father was strong and patient and sang very beautifully. Their house too was very lovely and very clean. The boy's name was Oli, which was carefully chosen by algorithm from a vast dictionary of old baby names.

The town was called the Town. It was a carefully built town of white picket fences and single-story houses and wide avenues and big open parks with many trees. The boy would go for a walk in the park with his parents every day, and he could always hear the humming of many insects and see beautiful butterflies flittering among the trees.

Really it was quite an idyllic childhood in many ways.

It had to be, of course.

It was very carefully designed.

You can probably see where this is going.

The shape of stories is difficult for us. We understand them as patterns, what you'd call a formula. We tell the story of Oli's childhood in a way designed to be optimal, yet there are always deviations, margins of error that can creep in.

For instance, there was the matter of the purple caterpillar.

The purple caterpillar was very beautiful, Oli thought. It was a long, thin insect with many prolegs, brightly colored in purple with bright yellow spots. It crawled on the thin green leaf of a flowering helleborine, and it did that, back and forth, back and forth, every day on Oli's passing through the park. When Oli was not in the park, of course, the caterpillar stopped moving. Oli became quite unreasonably—we felt—fascinated by the caterpillar, and every day on his journey through the park he would stop for long minutes to examine the little creature, despite his father calling him to come along to the swings, or his mother asking him to hold her hand so he could hop over the pond.

But Oli would just squat there and stare at the caterpillar, as it moved back and forth, back and forth across the leaf.

Why did the caterpillar crawl back and forth, back and forth across the leaf? Oli wondered. His parents, who were not used to children, were a little taken aback to discover that *why* was one of Oli's favorite words. *Why* did the clouds make shapes in the sky? *Why* did Rex never bark? *Why* was water wet? *Why* did Oli sometimes wake up in the middle of the night, uneasy, and tried and tried to listen to the night sounds of the Town all around him, only there were none?

Some of these questions we could answer, of course—clouds made shapes because the human mind has been programmed by long evolution to make patterns, for instance: just like stories. Water is "wet" in its liquid form, but the word only describes the *experience* of water, not its properties; the town was quiet, and Rex never barked, because Oli was meant to be asleep at that time.

The caterpillar crawled like that every day under Oli's gaze, but children, as we found, are almost unreasonably inquisitive, and therefore one day Oli simply grabbed the little creature by its body and lifted it off the leaf.

The caterpillar struggled feebly between Oli's thumb and forefinger.

"Don't touch that!" Mother said sharply, but Oli didn't really pay her much mind. He stared at the caterpillar, fascinated. The creature emitted a high-pitched shriek of alarm. Oli, who like all children could also be cruel, pressed harder on the caterpillar's thin membranous body. The creature began to hiss and smoke, its antennae

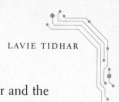

moving frantically as it tried to escape. Oli pressed harder and the caterpillar's membrane burst.

"Ow!" said Oli, and threw the caterpillar on the ground. The creature had got very hot just before its demise, and left a small burn mark on the epidermis of Oli's thumb and forefinger. Mother cried out, horrified at this damage, but Oli stuck his fingers in his mouth and sucked them, still staring at the caterpillar.

Thin wires protruded from the caterpillar's broken body, and faint traces of blue electricity could still be seen traversing the wires before they, too, faded. Oli reached down, more carefully this time, and prodded the body with the tip of his finger. It had already cooled, so he picked it up again and studied it. He had never seen the inside of a living creature before.

That evening Oli had many more questions, and we were not sure how to answer them yet and so we did what grown-ups always do, and didn't. This was perhaps a mistake, but we were unsure how to proceed. The next morning the caterpillar was back on its leaf like it had always been, crawling up and down, up and down, but Oli studiously ignored it, and we were relieved.

For the next few days Oli was his usual self. Rex often accompanied him on his walks through the park, fetching sticks of wood that Oli threw, and watching patiently as Oli sat on the swing while Father pushed him, up and down, up and down, but never too fast or too high as to pose danger to the child. Oli thought about the sensation he felt when he'd burned his finger. It was pain, something all parents are eager to prevent their children from experiencing, though we are not sure we quite understand it, as it is merely a warning system for the body, or that's what we always thought.

There were other children in the playground in the park, who Oli saw every day. They dutifully swung on the swings (but one was always free for Oli) and slid down the slides, and climbed on the wood posts and rocked up and down, up and down on the seesaws. They were always very fond of Oli but he found their company boring, because all they ever said were things like, "I love mommy!" and "Let's play!" and "This is fun!"

They all had dogs named Rex.

And so Oli, while we thought he had forgotten the caterpillar, had in fact been hatching a plan. And so one day when he was playing with one of the other children, who was called Michael, on the tree house, Oli pushed him, and Michael fell. He fell very gracefully, but nevertheless he fell, and he scraped his knee very badly, and Oli saw how the oily blood briefly came out of the wound before the tiny mites inside Michael's body crawled out to repair the damage done. And also Michael never cried, because we had not thought crying a good thing to teach the other children to do, the children who were not Oli. And then Oli did something very brave and foolish, and he fell down himself, on purpose, and he hurt himself. And he looked down and saw blood, and he began to cry.

Well, Mother and Father were dreadfully upset, and they fussed over Oli, and for a few days he was not allowed to go outside because of his wound, and all he did was sit in his room, and listen to the silence of the town, because no one was out when Oli was not, and he became afraid of the silence, and of how empty the world felt all around him, and when Mother or Father came to talk to him or hold him, he pushed them away.

"Are you my real parents?" he asked them, and they did not know what to say. Only Rex kept him company in that time.

What we mean to say is, Oli knew he was different, but he didn't quite know how. He knew everyone else was, in a way, better than him. We didn't feel pain and we didn't cry and we were always kind and patient, when he could be hasty and cruel. We weren't sure how to feel things, apart from a great sense of obligation to the child, for him to have the very best life and to be happy. He was very important to us. It was also at that time that Oli saw his parents in the bedroom. He peeked in through a door open just a fraction and saw Father standing motionless by the window, in the moonlight, unnaturally still because he had shut off; and he saw Mother with her chest cavity open, and the intricate machinery glowing and crawling inside, as she performed a minor repair on herself.

This was when he decided to run away to become a real boy.

Of course, you see the problem there.

Oli stole out in the middle of the night, with only Rex for company. He walked through eerily quiet streets, where nothing stirred and nothing moved. It was our fault. We should have operated the town continuously, let people walk around outside and dogs bark and owls hoot, but it just seemed like a waste of energy when the town was first conceived: when Oli himself, of course, was conceived.

Also we are not sure what the hooting of owls sounds like, or what the creatures themselves resembled. A lot of the old records were lost.

The moon was up that night. It had been broken long before, and it hung crooked in the sky, a giant lump of misshapen rock with the scars of old battles on its pockmarked face. It bathed the world in silver light. Oli's footsteps echoed alone as he walked through the town. We should have been more vigilant, of course, but we did not have much experience in the raising of children. Mother and Father were in their room, having put Oli to sleep and kissed him good night. They thought him long asleep, and now stood motionless in their bedroom, caught like statues in the moonlight. The moonlight shone down on the park and its insects, on the storage sheds where we kept the dummy children who played with

Oli, on the too-big houses where no one lived, on the dogs who were asleep in their yards, frozen until such a time as they might be needed again.

We didn't think Oli would really leave.

We waited for him on the edge of the town. He was a very determined boy. He saw us standing there. We looked just like Mrs. Baker, the friendly neighbor who worked in the grocery shop, whom Oli had known since birth.

"Hello, Mrs. Baker," he said.

"Hello, Oli," we said.

"I'm leaving," he said.

"Why?" we said.

"I'm not like everyone else," he said. "I'm different."

Gently, we said, "We know."

We loved him very much at that moment. There was a 56.998 percent chance of Oli dying if he left the town, and we didn't want that at all.

"I want to be a real boy," he said.

"You are a real boy," we said.

"I want to be like Mother, and Father, and Michael, and you, Mrs. Baker."

At that moment I think we realized that this was the point in the story of childhood where they learn something painful, something true.

"We can't always get what we want," we told him. "The world isn't like that, Oli. It isn't like the town. It is still rough and unpredictable and dangerous. We can't be you. We don't even truly understand what it is to be you. All we have are approximations."

He nodded, seriously. He was a serious boy. He said, "I'm still going, but I'll come back. Will you please tell Mother and Father that I love them?"

"We love you, too," we told him. We think maybe he understood, then. But we can never truly know. All we have are simulations.

"Come on, boy," Oli said.

Rex whined, looking up at his master; but he couldn't go beyond the boundary of the town.

"We're sorry," we said.

Oli knelt by his dog and stroked his fur. There was water in the boy's eyes, a combination of oils and mucins and hormones such as prolactin. But he wiped away his tears.

"Good-bye, Rex," he said. The dog whined. Oli nodded, seriously, and turned away.

This was how Oli left us, alone, on his quest to become a real boy: with the town silent behind him, with the broken moon shining softly overhead, with us watching him leave. There is an old poem left from before, from long before, about the child walking away . . . about the parent letting them go.

We think we were sad, but we really don't know.

We waved, but he never turned back and saw us.

* * *

"This is a very strange story, Elder Simeon," I said.

"Yes," he said. "It is very old, from when the world was different."

"Were there really thinking machines in those days?" Mowgai asked, and Elder Simeon shrugged.

"*We* are thinking machines," he said.

"But what happened to the boy?" I said. "What happened to Oli?"

"They tell no stories of his journey in Tyr," Elder Simeon said. "Nor in Suf or in the floating islands. But old Grandma Toffle tells the tale . . ." But here he fell silent, and his mechanical duck waddled up to him and tucked its head under Elder Simeon's arm, and its golden feathers shone in the late afternoon sun. "It's just a story," Elder Simeon said reluctantly.

We left him then, and wended our way back across the fields and over the brook to the houses. That night, after the sun had set and the lanterns were lit over our homes, I felt very grateful that I was not like that strange boy, Oli, and that I lived in a real place, that I lived on the Land itself and not in something that only mimicked it. But I felt sad for him, too: and Mowgai and I sought out old Grandma Toffle, who sat by the fire, warming her hands, for all that it was summer, and we asked her to tell us the story of the boy.

"Who told you that nonsense?" she said. "It wasn't old Simeon, was it?"

We admitted, somewhat sheepishly, that it was, and she snorted. "The old fool. There is nothing wrong with machines in their rightful place, but to fill your heads with such fancy! Listen. There was never such a city, and if there was, it has long since rotted to the ground. Old Simeon may speak of self-repairing mechanisms and whatnot, but the truth is that decay always sets in. Nothing lasts forever, children. The ancients built cities bigger than the sky, and weapons that could kill the Earth and almost did, at that. But do you see their airplanes flying through the sky? Their cities lie in ruins. The old roads are abandoned. Life continues as it always did. The mistake we'd always made was to think ourselves the most important species. But the planet doesn't care if humans live or die upon it. It is just as important to be human as it is to be an ant, or a stinging nettle."

"But . . . but we can *think*," said Mowgai.

Old Grandma Toffle snorted again. "Think!" she said. "And where did that ever get you?"

"But we can tell stories," I said quietly.

"Yes . . . ," she said. "Yes. That we can. Very well. What was your question again?"

"Do you know what happened to the boy, Oli, when he left the town?"

"Know? No, I can't say as that I *know*, little Mai."

"Then . . ."

Her eyes twinkled in the light of the fire, much as Elder Simeon's did in the sun. When she smiled, there were dimples on her cheeks, making her appear momentarily younger. She said, "Sit down, children. Sit down, and let me tell you. The boy wandered for a long time. . . ."

* * *

The boy wandered for a long time away from the town. He missed his parents, and his dog, and everyone. The world beyond the town was very different from everything he'd ever known. It was a rough place at that time, which was not that long after the great floods and the collapse of the old world, and many of the springs were poisoned, and the animals hostile and deadly, and flocks of wild drones flew against darkening skies, and unexploded ordnance lay all about and some of it was . . .

Not exactly *smart*, but . . .

Cunning.

He went for a long time without food or water, and he'd grown weak when he met the Fox and the Cat. They were not exactly a fox and a cat. One was a sort of mobile infiltration unit, designed for stealth, and the other was a stubby little tank. They were exactly the sort of unsuitable companions the Town had worried about when it let the boy go.

"Hello, young sir!" said the Cat.

"Who . . . who is it?" said the Fox. "Who dares . . . walk the paths of the dead?"

"My name's Oli," said Oli. He looked at them with curiosity, for he had never seen such machines before.

"I have never met an Oli," said the Cat.

"I have never tasted an Oli," said the Fox, somewhat wistfully.

"Please," said Oli, "I am very hungry and very tired. Do you know where I could find shelter?"

The Fox and the Cat communicated silently with each other, for they, too, were very hungry, though their sustenance was of another kind.

"We know . . . a place," said the Fox.

"Not very far," said the Cat.

"Not . . . not far at all," said the Fox.

"We could show it to you," said the Cat.

"Show it to . . . you," said the Fox.

"Shut up!" said the Cat.

"Shut . . . oh," said the Fox.

"A place of many miracles," said the Fox, with finality.

And Oli, though he couldn't be said to have trusted these two strange machines, agreed.

They traveled for a long time through that lost landscape, and the wasteland around them was slowly transformed as the sun rose and set and rose again. Soon they came to the outskirts of a vast city, of a kind Oli had never seen and that only salvagers now see. It was one of the old cities, and as it was still not that long after the fall of the cities, much of it still remained. They passed roads choked with transportation pods like weeds growing through the cracks, and vast grand temples where once every manner of thing had been for sale. Broken houses littered the sides of the streets and towers lay on their sides, and the little tank that was the Cat rolled over the debris while the Fox snuck around it, and all the while Oli struggled to keep up.

The city was very quiet, though things lived in it, as the Fox and the Cat well knew. Predatory things, dangerous things, and they looked upon Oli with hatred in their seeing apparatus, for they hated all living things. Yet these were small, rodentlike constructions, the

remnants of a vanished age, who loved and hated their fallen masters in equal measure, and mourned them when they thought no one was looking their way. And they were scared of the Fox and of the Cat, who were battle hardened, and so the unlikely trio passed through that city unharmed.

At last they came to a large forest, and went amid the trees.

"Not far now," said the Cat.

"To the place of . . . of miracles," said the Fox.

"What is this place?" asked Oli.

The Fox and the Cat communicated silently.

"It is a place where no machines can go," the Cat said at last; and it sounded wistful and full of resentment at once. "Where trees grow from the ground and water flows in the rivers and springs. Where the ground is fertile and the sun shines on the organic life-forms and gives them sustenance. Plants! Flowers! People . . . useless, ugly things!"

But the Fox said, "I . . . like flowers," and it sounded wistful only, with no hate. And the Cat glared at it but said nothing. And so they traveled on, deep into the forest, where the manshonyagger lived.

* * *

"What's a manshonyagger?" said Mowgai, and as he spoke the word, I held myself close and felt cold despite the fire in the hearth. And old Grandma Toffle said, "The man hunters, which roamed the earth in those days after the storms and the wars, and hunted the remnants of humanity. They were sad machines, I think now, driven crazy with grief for the world, and blinded by their programming. They were not evil, so much as they were made that way. In that forest lived such a manshonyagger, and the Fox and the Cat were taking the unwitting Oli to see it, for it had ruled in that land for a very long time, and was powerful among all the machines, and they knew they could get their heart's desire from it, if only they could give it what it wanted, which was a human."

"But what did the Fox and the Cat *want*?" asked Mowgai.

Old Grandma Toffle shrugged. "That," she said, "nobody knows for sure."

Stories, I find, are like that. Things don't turn out the way they're supposed to, people's motivations aren't clear, machines exceed their programming. Odd bits are missing. I often find myself thinking about the Fox and the Cat, these days, with the nights lengthening. Were they bad, or did we just misunderstand them? They had no regard for Oli's life; but then, did we expect them to? They learned only from their masters, and their masters were mostly gone.

In any case, they came to the forest, and deep within the forest, in the darkest part, they heard a sound. . . .

* * *

"What was that?" said Oli.

"It was nothing," said the Cat.

"N-nothing," said the Fox.

The sound came again, and Oli, who was near passing out from exhaustion and hunger, nevertheless pressed on, toward its source. He passed through a thick clump of trees and saw a house.

The house stood alone in the middle of the forest, and it reminded him of his own home, which he had started to miss very much, for the ruined houses of the city they had passed earlier were nothing at all like it. This was a small and pleasant farmhouse, built of white stones, mottled with moss and ivy, and in the window of the house there was a little girl with turquoise hair.

"Please," said Oli. "May I come in?"

"No . . . ," whispered the Fox, and the Cat hissed, baring empty bomb canisters.

"Go away," said the little girl with turquoise hair. "I am dead."

"How can you be dead?" said Oli, confused.

"I am waiting for my coffin to arrive," said the little girl. "I have been waiting for so long."

"Enough!" cried the Cat, and the Fox rolled forward threateningly,

and the two machines made to grab Oli before he could enter the sphere of influence of the house.

"Let me go!" cried Oli, who was afraid. He looked beseechingly up at the little girl in the window. "Help me!" he said.

But the Cat and the Fox were determined to bring Oli to the manshonyagger, and they began to force the boy away from the house. He looked back at the girl in the window. He saw something in her eyes then, something old, and sad. Then, with a sigh, and a flash of turquoise, she became a mote of light and glided from the house and came to land, unseen, on Oli's shoulder.

"Perhaps I am not *all* dead," she said. "Perhaps there is a part of me that's stayed alive, through all the long years—"

But at that moment, the earth trembled, and the trees bent and broke, and a sound like giant footsteps echoed through the forest. Oli stopped fighting his captors, and the Fox and the Cat both looked up— and up—and up—and the Cat said, "It's here, it's heard our cries!" and the Fox said, with reverence, "Manshonyagger . . ."

* * *

"But just what *is* a manshonyagger?" demanded Mowgai.

Old Grandma Toffle smiled, rocking in her chair, and we could see that she was growing sleepy. "They could take all sorts of shapes," she said, "though this one was said to look like a giant metal human being. . . ."

* * *

The giant footsteps came closer and closer, until a metal foot descended without warning from the heavens and crushed the house of the little girl with the turquoise hair, burying it entirely. From high above there was a creaking sound, and then a giant face filled the sky as it descended and peered at them curiously. Though how it could be described as "curious" it is hard to say, since the face was metal and had no moving features from which to form expressions.

Oli shrank into himself. He wished he'd never left the town, and that he'd listened to Mrs. Baker and turned back and gone home. He missed Rex.

He missed, he realized, his childhood.

"A human . . . !" said the manshonyagger.

"We want . . . ," said the Fox.

"We want what's ours!" said the Cat.

"What was . . . promised," said the Fox.

"We want the message sent back by the Exilarch," said the Cat.

The giant eyes regarded them with indifference. "Go back to the city," the manshonyagger said. "And you will find the ending to your story. Go to the tallest building, now fallen on its side, from whence the ancient ships once went to orbit, and climb into the old control booth at its heart, and there you will find it. It is a rock the size of a human fist, a misshapen lump of rock from the depths of space."

Then, ignoring them, the giant machine reached down and picked Oli up, very carefully, and raised him to the sky.

Below, the Cat and the Fox exchanged signals; and they departed at once, toward the city. But what this message was that they sought, and who the Exilarch was, I do not know, and it belongs perhaps in another story. They never made it either. It was a time when people had crept back into the blighted zones, a rough people more remnants of the old days than of ours, and they had begun to hunt the old machines and to destroy them. The Cat and the Fox fell prey to such an ambush, and they perished; and this rock from the depths of space was never found, if indeed it had ever existed.

Oli, meanwhile, found himself high above the world. . . .

* * *

"But this *is* just a *story*, right?" said Mowgai. "I mean, there aren't *really* things like manshonyaggers. There can't be!"

"Do you want me to stop?" said old Grandma Toffle.

"No, no, I just . . ."

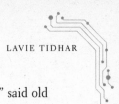

"There were many terrible things done in the old days," said old Grandma Toffle. "Were there really giant, human-shaped robots roaming the Earth in those days? That I can't honestly tell you. And was there really a little dead girl with turquoise hair? That, too, I'm sure I can't say, Mowgai."

"But she wasn't really a little girl, was she?" I said. "She wasn't that at all."

"Very good, little Mai," said old Grandma Toffle.

"She was a fairy!" said Mowgai triumphantly.

"A simulated personality, yes," said old Grandma Toffle. "Bottled up and kept autonomously running. Such things were known, back then. Toys, for the children, really. Only this one somehow survived, grew old as the children it was meant to play with had perished."

"That's awful," I said.

"Things were awful back then," said old Grandma Toffle complacently. "Now, do you want to hear the rest of it? There's not that long to go."

"Please," said Mowgai, though he didn't really look like he wanted to hear any more.

"Very well. Oli looked down, and . . ."

* * *

Oli looked down, and the entire world was spread out far below. He could see the shimmering blue sea in the distance, and the ruined city, and the blasted plains. And far in the distance he thought he could see the place the Cat and the Fox spoke of, the place of miracles: it was green and brown and yellow and blue, a land the like of which had not been seen in the world for centuries or more. It had rivers and fields and forests, insects and butterflies and people, and the sun shone down on wheat and fig trees, cabbages and daisies. And on little children—children just like you.

It was the Land, of course.

And Oli longed to go there.

"A human child," said the giant robot. Its eyes were the size of houses. "It has been so long. . . ."

"What will . . . what will you do with me?" said Oli, and there was only a slight tremor in his voice.

"Kill . . . ," said the robot, though it sounded uncertain.

"Please," said Oli. "I don't even know how to be a real boy. I just want to . . . I just want to *be*."

"Kill . . . ," said the robot. But it sounded dubious, as though it had forgotten what the word meant.

Then the little girl with turquoise hair shot up from Oli's shoulder in a shower of sparks, startling him, and hovered between him and the giant robot.

* * *

"What she said to the manshonyagger," said old Grandma Toffle, "nobody knows for certain. Perhaps she saw in the robot the sort of child she never got the chance to play with. And perhaps the robot, too, was tired, for it could no longer remember *why* it was that it was meant to hunt humans. The conference between the little fairy and the giant robot lasted well into the night; and Oli, having seen the sun set over the distant Land, eventually fell asleep, exhausted, in the giant's palm."

And here she stopped, and sat back in her rocking chair, and closed her eyes.

"Grandma Toffle?" I said.

"Grandma Toffle!" said Mowgai.

But old Grandma Toffle had begun, not so gently, to snore. And we looked at each other, and Mowgai tried to pull on her arm, but she merely snorted in her sleep and turned her head away. And so we never got to hear the end of the story from her.

That summer long ago, I roamed across the Land with Mowgai, through hot days that seemed never to end. We'd pick berries by the stream, and watch the adults in the fields, and try to catch the tiny froglets in the pond with our fingers, though they always slipped from our grasp. Mowgai, I think, identified with Oli much more than I did. He would retell the story to me, under the pine trees, in the cool of the forest, with the soft breeze stirring the needles. He would wonder and worry, and though I kept telling him it was only a story, it had become more than that for him. One day we went to visit Elder Simeon at his house in the foot of the hills. When he saw us coming, he emerged from his workshop, his clockwork creations waddling and crawling and hopping after him. He welcomed us in. His open yard smelled of machine oil and mint, and from there we could see the curious hills and their angular sides. It was then— reluctantly, I think—that he told us the rest of the story.

"The robot and the fairy spoke long into the night," he said, "and what arrangement they at last reached, nobody knows for sure. That morning, very early, before the sun rose, the manshonyagger began to stride across the blasted plains. With each stride it covered an enormous distance. It crushed stunted trees and poisonous wells and old human dwellings, long fallen into ruin, and the tiny machines down below fled from its path. The girl with turquoise hair was with him, residing inside his chest, where people keep their hearts. The manshonyagger strode across the broken land, as the sun rose slowly in the sky and the horizon grew lighter, and all the while the little boy slept soundly in the giant's palm.

"And, at last, they came to the Land."

"They came . . . they came *here*?" Mowgai said.

"And the manshonyagger looked down on the rivers and fields, and the fruit trees and the tiny frogs, and of course the people, our ancestors who fled here with the fall of the old world, and it never knew such a Land, and it thought that perhaps the old days were truly gone forever. And it was very tired. And so, with the little girl—who was not at all a little girl, of course, but something not a little like the manshonyagger—whispering in its heart, it laid the boy down, right about here." And he pointed down to the ground, at his yard, and smiled at our expressions. "And the boy grew up to be a man, among his kind, though there was always, I think, a little bit of him that was also part machine. And he became a salvager, like your mother, Mai, and he spent much of his time out on the blasted plains, and some said he sought his old home, still, but always in vain.

"You won't find him in our cemetery, though. He disappeared one day, in old age, and after he had begat two children, a little girl and a little boy. It was on a salvaging expedition out on the plains, and some say he died at the hands of the rogue machines that still lived there, but some say he finally found that which he was looking for, and he went back to his perfect home, and had one last childhood in that town where the past is eternally preserved. But that, I think, is just a story."

"But what happened to the robot?" asked Mowgai. "Did it go back?" and there was something lost and sad in his little face. I remember that, so vividly.

And Elder Simeon shook his head, and smiled, and pointed beyond the house, and he said, "The story says that the manshonyagger, seeing that its young charge was well and sound—and being, as I said, so very tired, too—lay down on the ground, and closed its eyes, and slept. And, some say, is sleeping still."

We looked where he pointed, and we saw the angled hills, and their curious contours; and if you squinted, and if you looked hard enough, you could just imagine that they took on a shape, as of a sleeping, buried giant.

"But . . . ," I said.

"You don't—" said Mowgai.

And Elder Simeon smiled again, and shook his head, and said, "But I told you, children. It's just a story."

The days grow short, and the shadows lengthen, and I find myself thinking more and more about the past. Mowgai is gone these many years, but I still miss him. That summer, long ago, we spent days upon days hiking through the curious hills, searching and digging, the way children do. We hoped to find a giant robot, and once, just once, we thought we saw a sudden spark of turquoise light, and the outline of a little girl, not much older than we were, looking down on us, and smiling; but it was, I think, just a trick of the light.

Some say the giant's still there, lying asleep, and that one day it will wake, when it is needed. We spent all that summer, and much of the next, looking for the buried giant; but of course, we never found it.

TEAM ROBOT

BY LAVIE TIDHAR

I cheated, in a way, and batted for both teams. You can't beat giant robots—I have friends who work in medical robotics, and despite my pleas, they keep insisting on building delicate knee-surgery robots rather than the city wreckers I keep asking them to, which, one feels, is very inconsiderate. Robots aren't really *fiction* anymore, are they? But I was very taken with the story of Pinocchio (the original, not the movie), which is of course a sort of robot story, and I wondered what happened if you reversed it, in a way, about a real boy who wants to become a machine like his parents . . . and of course that story has a fairy in it, though I suppose my one is also, in her own way, a robot. So . . . go robots?

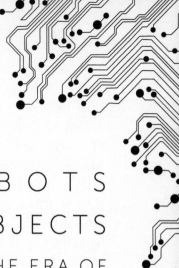

THREE ROBOTS
EXPERIENCE OBJECTS
LEFT BEHIND FROM THE ERA OF
HUMANS FOR THE FIRST TIME

by John Scalzi

OBJECT ONE: A BALL.

K-VRC: BEHOLD THE ENTERTAINMENT SPHERE.

11-45-G: It's called a ball.

K-VRC: I mean, I know it's called a ball. I'm just trying to get into the whole "we're experiencing these human things for the first time" vibe. Jazz it up.

Xbox 4000: What did humans do with these things?

11-45-G: They'd bounce them.

Xbox 4000: And that's it?

11-45-G: Basically.

K-VRC: These were humans. Bouncing things was close to maxing out their cognitive range.

11-45-G: To be fair, sometimes they hit them with sticks.

Xbox 4000: What, when they misbehaved?

K-VRC: "Bad ball! Think about what you've done!"

11-45-G *(hands ball to Xbox 4000):* Here.

Xbox 4000: What am I going to do with it?

11-45-G: Bounce it.

(Xbox 4000 bounces the ball; it rolls off the table.)

K-VRC: How was that for you?

Xbox 4000: Anticlimactic.

K-VRC: Yeah, well, welcome to humans.

OBJECT TWO: A SANDWICH.

K-VRC: My understanding is that they would shove these into their intake orifices for power.

Xbox 4000: Why would you need an entire orifice for that?

11-45-G: Hey, they had *all sorts* of orifices. Things went in. Things went out. It was complicated.

Xbox 4000: I have an induction plate.

11-45-G: We all have induction plates.

Xbox 4000: My point. What more do you need? So, they'd shove these into their intake orifices, and then?

K-VRC: Their intake orifices had rocky pegs that would crush them into paste, and then the paste would be forced into an internal vat of acid.

Xbox 4000 *(throws up hands):* Well, of course! That makes *perfect sense.*

11-45-G: They could have just dumped this thing into an exterior vat of acid to begin with, and then they wouldn't need the rocky pegs. They could just directly process the acid-based slurry.

K-VRC: I agree with you, but look. We're dealing with beings who have internal vats of acid to start with. Expecting logic out of this system is a little much.

Xbox 4000: Who even designed them?

11-45-G: It's unclear. We checked their code. No creator signature.

K-VRC: Their code, incidentally, *created out of acid.*

11-45-G: Ooh, good point. Important clue, that.

Xbox 4000: Someone should have just given them induction plates.

K-VRC: They tried that. Didn't take. Apparently humans preferred sandwiches.

Xbox 4000: ZOMG, throwing up forever now.

11-45-G: What does that mean?

Xbox 4000: Dude, I don't even *know.*

OBJECT THREE: A CAT.

Xbox 4000: What's the point of this thing?

11-45-G: Apparently no point. They just had them.

K-VRC: Well, that's underselling their influence. They had an entire network that was devoted to dissemination of pictures of these things.

Xbox 4000: Dudes, it's in my lap now. What do I do?

11-45-G: No sudden moves. Wait until it decides to get up again?

Xbox 4000: How long will that take?

11-45-G: Don't know. Maybe years.

Xbox 4000: I don't have years for this!

K-VRC: Maybe if you try to irritate it by moving your digits across its keratinous fibers, it will move.

Xbox 4000: What? Why?

K-VRC: It couldn't hurt.

Xbox 4000: You don't have any idea, do you?

K-VRC: Of course not. It's my first time seeing one of these live! Try it anyway.

Xbox 4000: UGH, FINE.

(Xbox 4000 pets cat.)

11-45-G: Is it working?

Xbox 4000: Uh . . .

11-45-G: What?

Xbox 4000: There's a strange rhythmic noise emanating from it now.

K-VRC: Uh-oh.

Xbox 4000: Wait, "uh-oh"? What do you mean, "uh-oh"?

K-VRC: Well, I don't want you to panic or anything, but I think you've activated it.

Xbox 4000: What does that mean?

K-VRC: It means that if the noise ever stops, it's probably going to explode.

Xbox 4000: It is *not*. Is it? 11-45-G?

11-45-G: Cursory historical research shows that humans had a card game called Exploding Kittens, so, yes, this checks out.

K-VRC: Yeah, you're gonna die now. Sorry.

Xbox 4000: WHY DID HUMANS EVEN CONSORT WITH THESE HAIRY MURDER MACHINES?

K-VRC: Kindred spirits?

11-45-G: Also checks out.

OBJECT FOUR: AN XBOX.

Xbox 4000: Wait, it's called *what* now?

11-45-G: It's an Xbox. An early computer entertainment system for humans.

K-VRC: Any relation?

Xbox 4000: I don't think so?

11-45-G: Really? Numerically, it suggests that this is your ancestor a few thousand generations back.

Xbox 4000: I'm sure it's just a coincidence.

11-45-G: We're robots, dude. We don't do coincidence.

K-VRC: Go on. Call it "daddy."

Xbox 4000: Stop it.

K-VRC: Or "mommy"! Either is equally applicable, inasmuch as we don't have genders.

Xbox 4000: I'm going to hit you.

K-VRC: Not with that cat on your lap.

11-45-G: Do you want us to turn it on?

Xbox 4000: Noooooooooooo.

K-VRC: I'm agreeing with Xbox 4000 here. It's one thing to joke about ancestry. It's another thing to have to confront it heaving its hard drives out in front of you.

Xbox 4000: Right?

K-VRC: I mean, that's kind of an existential horror show right there. Especially when your ancestor's entire existence was defined by thirteen-year-old human males using it to "teabag" opponents in virtual battles.

Xbox 4000: "Teabag"? What does that mean?

K-VRC: Oh, nothing.

Xbox 4000: It means something. I'm looking it up.

K-VRC: Don't look it up.

Xbox 4000: I'm looking it up now.

K-VRC: You'll be sorry.

Xbox 4000: Here it i— WHAT THE HELL IS THIS HORRIBLE PRACTICE? WHY DID YOU MAKE ME LOOK THIS UP?

K-VRC: I told you not to!

Xbox 4000: The memory of this has been burned into my circuits forever and you must be punished.

(Xbox 4000 gets up and deposits cat on K-VRC's lap.)

Xbox 4000: CATBAGGED.

11-45-G: That's cold, dude.

Xbox 4000: Deserved it.

11-45-G: Still cold.

K-VRC: Your ancestors are very proud of you right now.

Xbox 4000: I can't tell whether you're being sarcastic or not.

K-VRC: I'm not going to lie. Neither can I.

11-45-G: Out of curiosity, K-VRC, what do you trace your ancestry back to?

K-VRC: I come from a long line of baby monitors.

11-45-G: Not many babies around anymore.

K-VRC: Yeah, we kind of sucked at our job.

OBJECT FIVE: A NUCLEAR MISSILE.

K-VRC: We don't have genders, and yet I feel the phallic-ness just oozing off this thing. What was *this* for?

11-45-G: The idea behind these was to vaporize millions of humans at one time.

Xbox 4000: Well, this exercise suddenly got a little *dark*, didn't it?

11-45-G: To be fair, they used these only a few times.

K-VRC: To be fair, you'd only need a few times, wouldn't you?

11-45-G: Point.

Xbox 4000: Is this what killed them off?

11-45-G: No. Indeed, 'twas their own hubris that ended their reign, their belief that they were the pinnacle of creation, that caused them to poison the water, kill the land, and choke the sky. In the end, no nuclear winter was needed, just the long, heedless autumn of their own self-regard.

K-VRC: Dude, are you okay?

11-45-G: Yeah, sorry. Thought that would sound better than, "Nah, they just screwed themselves by being shortsighted about their environment." In retrospect, it was melodramatic.

K-VRC: You can't just crack one of those off. You've got to warn us.

11-45-G: You're right. Tip for next time.

Xbox 4000: So humans died out from environmental disaster?

11-45-G: Yes. Well, and also because at one point they genetically engineered their cats to give them opposable thumbs.

Cat: Yeah, once we could open up our own tuna cans, that was pretty much that for the human race.

K-VRC: Seems heartless.

Cat: Dude, I'm a cat.

Xbox 4000: So you're *not* going to explode if K-VRC stops petting you.

Cat: I didn't say that. You guys better keep petting me, just to be sure. Forever.

(*K-VRC skritches cat anxiously.*)

Cat: Yes. Good. Now, lower.

TEAM ROBOT

OR, WHY I WROTE ABOUT ROBOTS
BY JOHN SCALZI

In handy ten-point list form!

1. Because I already write science fiction, so I'm used to robots, and I'm lazy.

2. Because robots already exist in our universe, so it's fun to extrapolate from there.

3. Because robots are cool and awesome and everyone wishes they were one and I'm not just saying that because there are robots standing over me making sure I am on point to their pro-robot agenda.

4. No, really! How silly would THAT be, for the robots to have captured me, taken me hostage, and be forcing me to write how they're totally not going turn us all into QUIVERING MEAT SLAVES at the earliest opportunity?

5. I mean, what would I do if they did capture me, anyway? Blink twice to let people know the robots have sequestered me away in their frozen Antarctic base?

6. BLINK, BLINK.

7. BLINK, BLINK, BLINK, BLINK, BLINK, BLINK, BLINK, BLINK.

8. SERIOUSLY, PEOPLE, HOW MUCH MORE DO I NEED TO FRIGGIN' BLINK HERE?

9. (muffled noises)

10. hello fellow humans it is i john scalzi did you know robots are kind and wonderful and we will live prosperously with them in a new age of subjugation i mean cooperation ha ha ha i am such a kidder of a human

P.S. Fairies suck and how like a human of me to say that.

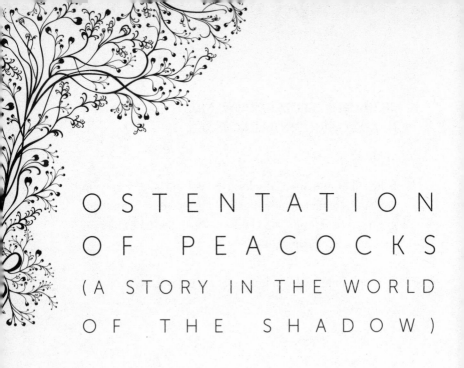

OSTENTATION
OF PEACOCKS
(A STORY IN THE WORLD
OF THE SHADOW)

by Delilah S. Dawson
writing as Lila Bowen

Even in the unforgiving badlands of Durango, there are fairy tales. The stories say that fairies grant wishes and steal frachetty babies nobody wants anyway and lure young, stupid girls into golden chains, where they'll dance for seven years in a magical land of toadstools. But the stories are a bunch of goddamn lies. Fairies are many things: pretty, powerful, dark, dangerous, and foppish as peacocks. But what they mainly are is assholes. If there's an outlaw who just won't die, odds are it's a werewolf or a fairy.

Of course, there are plenty of things in Durango that refuse to die.

Just now, there's a carrion bird soaring over battered red rocks, and it fits that description. Big, ugly as hell, and with a twisted scar where its left eye used to be, it surveys the darkening sky and blazing orange boulders and notices something out of place, something so wrong that it falters in flight.

Down below, a naked man runs across the desert, pursued by four men on horseback.

The bird's belly quivers and flails, and even though it's not sure why, it changes course to follow the riders. The sun is arcing down to melt into the baked earth, and the naked man falls and scrabbles and runs again as the horses gallop closer. The bird reckons the man would make good eating if he didn't exude such a sense of wrongness. And if the men in pursuit didn't just reek of magic.

So the bird follows. It's not like a giant bird has anywhere else to be, really. The evening sky is purple and puddled with fluffy lavender clouds when the man finally stops and falls to hands and knees. With a disturbing sort of wriggle, he transforms into a possum and scrambles up into the highest branches of a dead tree in a little copse along a dribble of a creek. The posse rides up to stare at the possum, and one man throws a golden noose over the sturdiest branch and laughs like a bastard. The gold of the noose seems to leach into the tree, and the trunk shoots straight up like corn after a rain, sprouting branches and fat, bright leaves. The golden light ripples out through its roots, hops to the other scraggly trees and brush until the whole place is lit up live and green, cool as a sigh in the night.

The bird lands in a quiet place on the ground under the shivering trees, far enough away that the four men won't notice. They, after all, are too busy hollering at a terrified possum. That they chased up a tree. That they intend to hang it from.

The bird flaps around like an idjit before making a strange coughing sound, as if a hand reached down its throat and pulled it inside out, and then a naked girl is standing there, lean and long-limbed and dusty with disuse, her frizzy black hair off-kilter and overgrown from its close, boyish clipping. Her name was once Nettie Lonesome, and the look in her remaining eye suggests she's forgotten she's human, because that's pretty much what she set out to do. But she's not really human, anyway. Like the possum, she's a shape-shifter, what most folks would call a monster. The four men on the other side of the now-burbling creek, however, are something different.

Wild and wide as it is, Durango is chock-full of such creatures — shifters and harpies and sirens and chupacabras. Normal folk don't even see 'em, not until they've killed one by shooting it — or stabbing, the magic ain't picky — in the heart. Then their eyes are opened to a whole new world of monsters, some good and some bad, just like men. They might find out their local grocer is a dwarf with glittering stone eyes, say, or that the whores at the saloon have fangs and drain a man in a different sort of way than he remembers the next morning. These four fellers are something new, though, something dangerous she hasn't seen before.

Then again, there's some as would consider her dangerous. She's not only a shifter, but the Shadow, a legendary critter among the local tribes who's dedicated to delivering justice to the much abused. The Shadow is hard to kill, and other magical things can't tell that she's got magic too. They just assume she's a dumb ol' human, which puts her at a big advantage. The Shadow's destiny is an ornery thing that leads Nettie around to kill what needs to die, even when she's got much better things to do. Like now, for instance.

But first, she's got to figure out what these fellers are up to. Now, men normally build a fire by sending the most squirrelly tenderfoot to gather dry twigs and hopefully some brittle branches and maybe a stump or two. But these men are pulling chairs out of nowhere, because chasing a naked man across the desert just ain't peculiar enough for the likes of them.

The first man reaches into nothing and pulls out a stool, looks to be made by hand and smoothed with years of use. He plunks it down in the dirt and sits, legs spread, hands on his knees like he's bellying up to an invisible bar. He's a rough feller in cowpoke duds with the face of the town tomcat, but still there's a dandified air in the way he's tied his cravat. Something about him is familiar, and Nettie wonders if she's seen him on a Wanted poster. As he's the one who tossed the noose and made the forest spring up in a desert, Nettie takes him for the leader.

The second man probes the air with white-gloved hands, doctor hands. He withdraws a raspberry-colored drawing room chair, plush and high-backed with an embroidered pillow. When he sits, he flips out his coattails, just so, and adjusts his little doctor glasses over his little doctor nose. His hair is parted, looks still wet from the comb, and he crosses one neat leg over the other.

The third man has the looks of a trapper as pieced together for a stage play; he's too clean and whole to be the real deal. The chair he pulls out of nowhere is made of antlers all stuck together, with a glossy bearskin tossed overtop. He's the only one with a beard, and it's a thick, wavy thing that weaves into his long hair, black as his eyes. His clothes are layers of worn doeskin and homespun, and his grin flashes like a wolf's bite in moonlight.

The fourth and final man is the squirrelly one who should be collecting firewood. He's still got the raw cheeks and bones of boyhood about him, like his elbows and knees haven't quite figured out where to settle down. His hair is just this side of red, and the chair he pulls out of thin air is a kitchen chair carved of shining wood. He slaps it down to complete the circle and slumps to his elbows to stare at the empty space where there should be a fire, were they men who made any sense.

But they're not men. As they take off their hats, they reveal long, pointed ears that poke straight up through their glossy hair.

"Go on, then, Tom," the third man mutters.

The young one leans forward, digging his hands into the dirt and pulling up flames with his bare fingers. There's a great flash in the falling night, and he sits back, dusting his hands off, a bonfire crackles merrily as if he'd been carefully building it for an hour. There's even a shiny coffeepot perking at the edge of the flames. Nettie has seen ghost fire before, but this ain't it. She can feel the heat against her chest from where she hides in the bushes.

She looks down and sneers. Her chest is still there, poking out just enough to tell the world she's not the man she wishes she was. When she travels as a human and as a man, she carries a muslin cloth to bind up her bitty bosoms and hide her secret. She looks enough like a lanky boy to play the part. But here, out in the middle of nowhere, freshly out of her feathers, she's naked and shy. As soon as the men start arguing over what to do with their prey, she sneaks around toward their horses to borrow some clothes from their packs. Seeing as how they can pull any damn thing out of thin air, they shouldn't mind the loss of a shirt for as long as it takes her to figure out who's a good guy and who's a bad guy and kill what needs killing.

Nettie Lonesome, you see, is also a Durango Ranger, charged with keeping the good people of Durango Territory safe from the monsters that lurk in plain sight. So not only does the Shadow need to know why the possum's headed for a noose, but the Durango Ranger is charged with protecting the innocent. It's a heavy burden, sure enough, and she'd rather be anywhere else but here. She hasn't seen her Ranger captain or crew in weeks, maybe months, but she can still feel the weight of her badge, pushing her to doing what's right.

The men are muddying up the night with their arguing as the possum clings to the highest branch of the tree, and Nettie feels a rush of comfort when she smells their horses. She misses her friends, but she misses horses, too. As she quietly approaches, giving them time to smell her in return, she feels her stomach somersaulting and knows that, like their riders, these horses are not what they seem. Two of 'em are unicorns, brushed whiter than most and with their horns, tails, and balls intact. One horse, a dapple gray with a mean eye, has wings folded down by her sides like a goose, dirty and rustling. The last mount looks like a horse, an eagle, and a lion spent a confusing night at a whorehouse, but it's watching her like it can see through to her hateful heart. All the beasts are kitted up in fancy gear, dripping with ribbons and gold chains. Nettie didn't much fancy any of their riders before now, but her feelings firmly point to nope. She has no love for a feller who can't let his horse rest without a saddle, now and again.

Of the four critters, she's most familiar with unicorns, having broken a few to ride in her days as a simple cowpoke. Feeling exposed as hell and raw as a chunk of meat, she sidles up to the kindest-looking stallion, cool and showing no fear.

"Hey, feller," she murmurs, voice rusty from disuse. "How 'bout I loosen that cinch for you? Might be nice to take a full breath, don't you think?"

His great head swings around, almost snakelike, to regard her, a king surveying a potato. Now, Nettie has a way with horses and horselike creatures, and the moment she's tugged on his cinch, the beast gives a heaving harrumph and nuzzles her briefly. When she slides a hand into his saddlebags, he sighs in a magnanimous-type way and pretends to ignore the trespass. Her clever fingers find the likeliest fold of fabric and pull it out, where it impossibly unfolds again and again until it's a sweeping, full-body cloak that drags the ground. She digs around the saddlebag until she finds a golden rope much like the one destined for the possum's scrawny little neck and uses it to tie the billowy fabric around her waist. It's somehow both heavy and soft, like wearing a winter blanket made of spiderwebs, and it moves with Nettie's every step.

"Time to meet a posse in my pajamas," Nettie tells the unicorn, who nods as if he understands how goddamn preposterous this is.

As she approaches the fire, she tries to figure out what's going on.

"I don't care if he's fair of face. He fired a gun at me." The first man, the leader.

"Ah, but it was dry. He didn't actually shoot you. And you're not allergic to iron anymore. And finally, if we're discussing facts, you had previously asked to inspect the weapon in question. . . ." The second man, the doctor.

"And had removed all but the second bullet . . ." The third man, the trapper, while grinning.

"And then, when the gun didn't fire, you took it back and shot him in the gut." The fourth man, the one with the baby face, wincing as he says it. "Not that that'll kill a shifter."

"And shooting can't hurt you either, after all," adds the doc, adjusting his spectacles. "It would only tickle a little."

The first man stands, and Nettie understands that he's not the clever, kind, brave sort of leader. He's the sort who leads by force and fear. The sort who drinks power, all sloppy, from someone else's glass like it's cheap whiskey.

"Just because bullets can't kill me and iron ain't a problem doesn't mean I enjoy the sensation of being shot. I still say we string him up and cut out his heart. I'd like to put it in a bell jar."

The doc rubs his stubbled cheeks. "How many hearts do you really need in bell jars? Isn't your shelf nearly full? Let's just take him back to Lincoln and let the humans sort out their petty little disputes. This is why they make their laws. And why we should keep to ours."

"I don't want to go back to Lincoln," says the tenderfoot boy. "Let's go back home. I get tired of playacting so much. My ears feel permanently crushed."

"How poetic," the trapper says, sneering.

"Well, he is young still, Rudebaugh," murmurs the doc.

"I'm only a century younger than you!" the boy shouts, tossing up his hands in a cloud of glitter.

"We can't go home, and we need to feed, so you'll keep on playacting. I'd rather play at outlaws and feed on the humans' fear than go back to the form we used to take, as wee sprites with sparkling wings who sup on milk and grant wishes." The trapper dances his fingers through the air, leaving a trail of golden light and twinkling sparkles behind. As the others stare into space, looking wistful, he pulls a tin cup out of nowhere and pours himself a slug of coffee. "And we can't have coffee back home, neither."

"I still say we kill 'im." The leader stands, knocks the cup to the ground, and walks to the tree. He flicks the golden noose with his hand, and they all watch it swing. Up on the branch, the possum hisses like it doesn't cotton to the idea. "If I'm not having fun, why are we even here?"

"Because you're on the outs with the Queen again, Bonney," the doc says, all fussy.

"So let's take back a fine new fur cape for her beautiful shoulders."

The trapper claps his hands and crows. "Queen Mab in a possum cloak? Now that I'd pay to see."

"Enough. Chasing that son of a bitch through town butt-naked was fun, but I've drunk my share of his fear, and I'm done playing around. Let's do this." The leader snaps his fingers, and the possum appears in his fist, dangling by the scruff of its neck. "Damn, you're ugly." He laughs, shaking it. In response, it shudders, sticks out its tongue, and plays dead. He drops it and gives it a nudge with his boot. "Skin him, Scurlock, so I can string him up for trying to shoot me."

The doc purses his pretty mouth and waves a gloved hand, and the possum becomes a man, naked and unconscious in the dust. There's nothing special about him to draw the eye—he's just a feller like any other. Nettie had hoped maybe she'd recognize him, but she doesn't, which makes it all the stranger that she does what she does, which is that she stands up behind the screen of brush, holds up her hands, pitches her voice low, and shouts, "Stop right there!"

The four men are instantly on their feet, but strangely, no guns are drawn.

"Who the hell are you?" mutters the trapper.

The men's eyes shift and meet, and they swirl as smoothly as hot grease in a pan to form a ring around her.

"I'm Rhett Hennessy. I'm a Durango Ranger, and it sounds like you fellers are an unlawful posse. So what's this man done to you? Is he a criminal?"

As if on cue, the man wakes up and hops to his feet, one filthy hand cupping his janglies.

"I didn't do nothin'!" he pretty much yodels.

Nettie instantly realizes he's dumb . . . as a possum . . . and wishes she'd never shed her bird skin, much less gone poking around in the unicorn's saddlebag. Whatever it was about the situation that drew her to it was obviously a mistake. But she won't feel right putting her Ranger badge back on one day if she walks away and leaves him to die, either.

"This man tried to shoot me," the leader says, his voice just a little too cultured for the outlaw he's pretending to be. "So we're upholding justice."

"That's not justice," Nettie says, her dander up. "That's vigilanteism."

The doc sniffs. "That's not even a word."

"Illegal, then. We got courts for that, and they don't meet in the middle of nowhere."

The leader's eyes narrow. "Are you wearing my cloak?"

Now Nettie sniffs. "No. This is just . . . what I normally wear."

He starts to turn red with rage before his mouth twitches with a smile. "Fine. Let's say you're right. What would you do to save this man? Would you . . . make a wager?"

"Oh, please. Not this again," the doc wails.

"Yee-haw!" the trapper hollers, slapping his knee.

The young one just straightens up a little, like he wishes he could take notes.

"I'll fight you for him," Nettie offers. "If you'll just lend me a gun."

She knows that these fellers aren't human, but she also knows that if she can hit the leader in the heart, he's likely to die. Thanks to her own destiny as the Shadow, they can't tell that she's a monster. They think she's human. As far as they know, she can't even tell they're doing magic. So if they hit her anywhere other than her heart, she'll just heal up around the hole like the possum did and keep on kicking. The odds of winning, as far as she's concerned, are pretty good. If the Shadow's instincts brought her here, then the Shadow must have a good chance of seeing tomorrow.

Again, these fellers don't know that.

"A gunfight. That sounds entertaining." The leader looks to his men. "But that leaves my three friends here without their own chance for a bit of tomfoolery. Are you man enough for four challenges, winner takes the prize?"

Nettie chews the inside of her lip, considering. What choice does she have? Say no thank you kindly and mosey off into the night in this feller's pajamas, leaving the possum to die? Even if she tried to mosey off, there's little chance they'd let her. Folks who feel the need to string up varmints probably feel similarly about random folks who show up out of nowhere begging for gunfights. Leaving her only one choice, really.

"What kind of challenges?" she asks, one hand on her hip like it's as simple as a game of cards.

"Oh, this and that," the leader says easily. As if to seal the deal, he pulls a magnificent gold pistol from his holster and holds it to the man's heart. The naked man freezes, eyes closed, and starts begging. "You've got until the count of three. One. Two."

"Fine, goddamn it! But I get to name a challenge too."

"Well then. So mote it be."

The four men reappear in their chairs, at ease. A fifth chair has appeared, just a stump, really. Nettie wonders what a normal human would see, if it would be as confusing as being drunk, the way they're waving their goddamn magic around.

"Have a seat, lad," the leader says.

Much to her consternation, her body sits without asking her mind if it's a good idea. At least she can breathe again, now that the pistol isn't pressed to the possum feller's heart. She can still see the indentation of the steel circle in his pasty pink skin. He's in manacles now, gold ones, as if he's been wearing them all along. He stares at the chain between his wrists, jaw open. Nettie grinds her teeth and reminds herself never to help a possum, ever again.

"What's the first challenge?" she asks.

"Sharpshooting," the leader says. "But I'll warn you. You've heard of Billy the Kid?"

"Who the hell hasn't?"

"Well." He pulls out both guns and twirls them. "I am he."

Nettie snorts. "Whoop-de-goddamn-do, boy. Line up the cans, and let's go."

But now she knows why he looks familiar, and now she knows she can't outshoot him.

Two apples appear in the man's hands. "Cans? Pshaw. These'll do." With a hand to the possum man's chest, the leader shoves him backward until he's pressed against the tree, the same one from which the golden noose still dangles. The possum man is shivering in fear, eyes white all around.

"Please, Billy," he mutters, but Billy just shoves one of the apples in the possum-man's mouth and puts the other one on top of his head.

"What's the rules?" Nettie asks.

"First one to hit their apple wins. I'll mark it off."

As he paces away from the tree, Nettie stares at the possum man and considers. She knows for sure now that these four fellers are fae. She's heard the Captain talk about the strange folks who hate being called fairies, powerful, tricksy creatures who have big magic and love to talk you to death with their pretty lies. But if they like tricking, she figures they can be tricked back.

Thing is, Billy didn't say, "First to shoot an apple." He said *hit*.

Nettie snatches the apple off the possum man's head before Billy can turn around, tosses it on the ground, picks up a rock, and smashes it to bits. The men in the chairs burst out laughing, and Billy spins around, gun aimed for an apple that's no longer there.

"First to hit an apple," Nettie says with a shrug. "Your words, not mine."

"I— You—!" Billy splutters, his eyes burning as glittery sparks leap from his body like lightning.

"The boy got you fair and square," the doc observes.

Billy inhales sharply and turns, his shoulders hunching as he doubles over. The fire throws his shadow against the tree and over the possum man, and the darkness unfolds to show clawed hands digging furrows through the leaves, great black antlers bursting from his head like a crown to rake the sky. When he turns back, his shadows folds back in, and he's just a man again, trying to smile in the same way that spoiled children do when pretending they're sorry for throwing tantrums.

"One to you, then, boy. Doc, you're next." Billy throws himself back onto his stool, but it somehow sprouts arms and a back and is now wide enough for him to lounge in, looking like he's one step away from bashing in Nettie's head with the apple-smeared rock.

The doc wiggles tight gloves off his fingers, his lips turned down like he finds this whole thing distasteful. "The violin," he says. And then there's one in his long, elegant hands.

He holds it to his chin and draws the bow over the strings, coaxing out a note so clear and filled with longing that Nettie has to struggle to keep from falling to her knees in tears. The bow dances, and his fingers fly, and Nettie can't keep off her knees now, her fingers tearing at the ground like she's digging up a dead child as the doc sways overhead. The music fills the night, chokes the stars, slips down Nettie's dust-rimmed ears and into her soul, clutching it with stunning ferocity. He plays forever and a day, and then she blinks up at the full moon and curls her hands out of black earth that should just be sand. She's pulled white roots from the ground, torn her nails ragged, but she can't recall what it is that her fingers sought, nor why.

He holds out the violin, one fine eyebrow arched up.

"Your turn."

Nettie stands, dizzy and shaken. This must be how the Rangers felt that time she killed a siren to stop the song that bewitched everyone but her. Like something special has been given to her, but it's gone now, gone forever, and something even more special has been taken with it. Her fingers are black and bloody, her knees shaking. She takes the violin in her left hand, the bow in her right. She couldn't be more goddamn confused if he'd handed her a kitten and an ax. The violin doesn't quite fit under her chin, the neck impossibly smooth and slender in her rough hands. Carefully, so carefully, she draws the bow across the strings, and the resulting sound could break glass. The four men grimace. Doc's mouth twitches.

Her hands drop, violin neck in one, bow in the other. She tosses the violin onto the black furrows she dug in the ground, stomps on it, and throws it in the fire. Then she snaps the bow over a knee and tosses it in, too.

"That's what I think of your fine music," she hisses.

"One to one," the doc says.

When she looks in the fire, the violin is gone.

"Now you, Dirty Dave," Billy says with a grin, nodding at the trapper.

The rough man heaves himself out of his throne like a horse getting up from a good roll in the dirt. He cracks his knuckles and neck. "Fighting," he says. "Hand to hand. First man knocked out or pinned for ten seconds wins."

Nettie shrugs like she has a choice. "Wrassling it is."

Before he can outline any more rules or start counting down, she launches herself into his gut. They tumble into his chair, and the antlers shatter apart like falling matches. He's twisting and grabbing, trying to get her into a certain position, but Nettie has always depended on fighting dirty. She snatches up a fallen antler and rams a tine into his crotch. He roars like a bear and takes a moment to cup his vittles, and Nettie looks around for something else to use against him while he's tender. The first thing that comes to mind is the coffeepot in the fire. She picks it up, ignoring the burn on her palm, and dumps the boiling coffee over his head.

Much to her surprise, he screams and flails onto his back, crabcrawling away and lying there gasping like a fish on land. Without a second's consideration, she throws herself on top of him, pinning him to the ground. He roars and grows and grows until he becomes a bear, a giant, shaggy grizzly, and then Nettie's on her back in the dirt, pinned and crushed and staring at a mouth full of teeth. As the Doc counts to ten, she struggles in every which way she can, but the bear doesn't budge from atop her.

And then he's just a man again.

"That's ten, darlin'," he murmurs before hopping off with a grin and a lusty wink.

When she turns to look back at the rest of his posse, they're leaning out of their chairs, mesmerized. The breeze she feels brings her back to the present, in which she's revealed a woman's parts hiding under the stolen cloak that shifted aside during the scuffle. Hot red shame creeps up her cheeks as she struggles to cover herself.

Billy licks his lips. "Tell me your name, girl."

She doesn't want to answer, but she can't shut her mouth. "Nettie Lonesome."

"What kind of witch are you?" Billy asks, half-amazed and half-enraged at being fooled.

She straightens the robe and reties it. "The kind that ain't a witch. Why'd he cheat?"

The trapper is back in his unbroken antler chair as if none of it ever happened. No burns, no coffee stains. No sign of getting stabbed in the balls. No sign of recently being a bear.

"The point's mine unless you can prove I cheated. But you've got secrets yourself, huh?"

"Like that she fights dirty," the youngest one mutters.

"That's right, tenderfoot," Billy growls. "She does fight dirty. And it's your turn, so you'd best remember it and perform adroitly."

Without getting off his chair, the young one says, "Names, then."

"What?" Nettie asks.

"Names. If you can guess all our true names correctly. They're not the ones you've heard us say, obviously."

Somewhere in Nettie's addlepated brain, this rings a bell. Didn't the Captain say the fae guarded their true names from mortals and monsters? But these fools didn't know she'd watched them earlier, when they used different names in easy conversation. Shadow magic is as good as fae magic, she figures, no matter how many goddamn violins you can play.

Pointing at each one, Nettie barks their names. "Bonney. Scurlock. Rudebaugh. Tom." They're incredulous. "That's right, ain't it? And for my own challenge, why don't you fellers guess my true name?"

The silence that follows is deep and dark and furious, a bull's breath before charging. The four men surge to their feet, and they can't hide what they truly are now. Their coats and hair whoosh back on a breeze that isn't there, their pointed ears twitching and alert. They're so handsome her heart wrenches, each of them bestial but beautiful, too, like the prettiest parts of men and women all mixed up, which happens to be Nettie's particular brand of temptation. Humanity falls off them like the flash of a peacock's tail opening to reveal what's been there, all along. The air smells like fire and lightning and crushed pine needles and danger, so much danger. And power. And a whiff of cruelty, dark as pitch. Nettie loves them and longs for them, but the Shadow sees them and hates them.

"You already told us your name," Bonney says, his ice-blue eyes glittering under a crown of ivory antlers that drip with rubies and emeralds. He steps forward, tall and elegant, trailing a cape made of moss and starlight and pointing one clawed finger at Nettie's chest. "Nettie Lonesome," he says, a cruel but sweet smile curving his flawless lips.

Nettie shakes her head. "Nope. Sorry."

His cloak expands wide enough to blot out the stars, and he's a startlingly beautiful god-giant made of a million points of light, his hands big enough to crush Nettie and everything she's ever loved in a tornado of lightning and flowers.

"What do you mean, 'nope'?" he shrieks.

Nettie closes her eyes so they won't explode and rocks back on her heels. "Sorry, but Nettie's not my true name, my real name. I don't know what my real name is. I was orphaned, and the folks who took me in, they just called me Nettie. I guess Nettie's my girl name, but I don't think of myself like that."

Doc glides over and leans down to inspect her. He's dropped his human face, too, and the creature before her is so full of sunshine and gilt that he makes Nettie's best friend, Sam Hennessy, seem like a haystack. His crown is woven of slender finger bones and chunks of amber strung on catgut, and his cloak is the soft brown of baby bunnies fresh born.

"She's not lying," he says quietly, as if he can't quite believe it.

"Oh, hells," Tom mutters, turning away with the rustle of leaves. His crown is a circlet of vines daubed with poison-tipped thorns and tiny rosebuds, and his jacket is spring green, plush as the new grass by a riverbank and dappled with tiny white flowers. All the magic in the world can't hide his embarrassment. Black curls of smoke encircle the boy as Bonney's glittering fingers squeeze their censure with the power of an earthquake.

"Clever girl." Rudebaugh sidles up and slides a finger under her chin, looking closely at her face. She's frozen, unable to turn away. "You'd make a suitable bride. Return to Fairy with me, and I'll gift you an eye that sees the future. You'll dwell seven years in perfect happiness, dancing and doted on and gifted with every jewel you desire. Your child will be fine and fortunate beyond all men, and when you return, your luck will forever be sevenfold." He's the most beautiful of them, to Nettie, with his crown of braided leather and thick, bear-pelt beard and cloak of spotted fawn skin. There's an animal roughness about him that appeals to her, a glint in his sharp teeth that says he understands her on a bone-deep level, her need to coax and kill and mete out justice in equal measure.

His words, on the other hand, show the truth of him: he belongs to another world, and Nettie Lonesome doesn't give a shit about magic eyes or jewels or dancing or pretty fairy babies or unearned luck. She's got to kill what needs to die, and she can't do that where they come from because nothing dies in Fairy. Ever.

Nettie snaps her chin out of his reach, closing her eyes to the silly but cloying dreams he showed her. "No thanks. I got to get back to rangering. I'll just take your man, and return him to . . ."

They all look over to find a pair of golden manacles on the ground.

"That son of a bitching possum!" Rudebaugh shouts, but he's just a man again, a trapper in skins drawing his bowie knife, all raiment of glamour faded.

Bonney claps his hands together, and it's like lightning striking the glade in a blinding flash of light.

The trees are dead again. The chairs are gone. The fire is gone. The dented coffeepot is gone. The cloaks and crowns and other-worldly beauty are definitely gone. There's nothing but the full moon, Billy the Kid, his posse, and the chains their quarry slipped while they were showing off their skills. While Nettie watches, the manacles' metal fades from solid gold to rusted iron. She doesn't mind a bit that the fairies are wearing their masks again. She prefers them this way, not showing off. Magic's one hell of a distraction.

"If you'll excuse me, fellers, I'm free to go, ain't I?" she asks.

"Without your man," Billy says with a grin. "The contest was three to two, but I guess I'll consider it a tie now." He passes an open hand before her face and murmurs, "Forget us and go."

Nettie tips her invisible hat. "Nice gambling with you boys," she says.

As she walks into the woods, she unties the gold sash. Safely in the shadows, she lets the cloak drop, then her humanity. The great bird shakes itself, sick to death of magic. It launches into the air and surveys the moonlit desert below.

All it sees are four road-worn cowpokes arguing as they tighten the saddles of their horses. The leader smacks the youngest one, knocking his hat to the dust. The bird doesn't know why, but it turns and flaps in the other direction. Farther on, it catches sight of movement and swoops down to snatch up a quickly waddling possum, which it immediately drops. Possums, the bird seems to recall, are not worth the trouble.

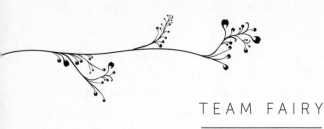

TEAM FAIRY

BY DELILAH S. DAWSON
WRITING AS LILA BOWEN

One of the most formative moments of my young life was watching *Labyrinth* for the first time and deciding I would've just forgotten the whiny baby and stayed with the Goblin King forever. I was drawn to the strange beauty, power, and darkness of that world, where maps and clocks didn't quite make sense and the air always seemed to glitter. I've never written a fairy story before, but I knew they'd be a great fit for the world of the Shadow, where Nettie Lonesome is tasked with hunting dangerous monsters and bringing them to justice. The fae are a great foil to no-nonsense Nettie, who sees through glamour and flat-out doesn't have time for such frivolity. And when it came to deciding how the fae would appear in an alternate 1800s Texas, I thought about the biggest peacock of the West, Billy the Kid—or, to be more accurate, my love of *Young Guns II*. You know, the movie with Bon Jovi's "Blaze of Glory" following Billy and his posse around the desert on a killing spree? After all, they've never found Billy the Kid's body. He could totally be a badass fairy.

There weren't any robots in *Labyrinth* or *Young Guns II*. Just sayin'.

ALL THE TIME WE'VE
LEFT TO SPEND

by Alyssa Wong

When she got to Yume's room, the first thing Ruriko did was slip off her mask and remove her prosthetic jaw. There was an ache in her fake bottom teeth. It was going to rain, although one look at the sky could have told her that.

Across the room, Yume dimmed the lights and sat on the edge of the coverlet. The bed was obscenely red, round and mounted on a rotatable platform, as one could expect from a pay-by-the-hour love hotel. Yume's pale, gauzy skirt rode up her thighs as she shifted positions, and Ruriko wished she would tug it back over her knees. "Is there anything I can do to make you more comfortable?"

Ruriko checked each of her false teeth, pressing a thumb over them to see if any had come loose—it was time for a hardware checkup soon—before clicking the prosthesis back into place. None of the actual teeth, or even the joints, were acting up. Some kind of phantom pain, then, from the flesh-and-bone jaw she'd lost ten years ago. "No, I'm okay."

"I could put on some music." Ten years ago, Yume Ito had been

one of the four founding members of IRIS, one of the country's top teen idol groups. Her face, along with Miyu Nakamura's, Kaori Aoki's, and Rina Tanaka's, had graced advertisements all over Tokyo, from fragrance ads to television commercials to printed limited-edition posters. But then the real Yume Ito had died, along with the real Miyo Nakamura, Kaori Aoki, and Rina Tanaka, and now all that was left was an algorithm of her mannerisms and vocal patterns, downloaded into an artificial skin and frame.

"No music, please," said Ruriko. Her voice sounded strange and small, but too loud at the same time. "Just talking."

Yume, dead ten years, rested her hands on Ruriko's shoulders. Her fingers traced the cloth mask that hung from one ear like a wilted flag. She tucked it back over Ruriko's reassembled mouth. "Whatever you want us to do."

Taking her hands, Ruriko steered her back toward the bed. She sat, and Yume followed.

The soft green pulse of Yume's power source reflected off her black hair, tinting her skin with strange light. One of the room's walls was an extended panel of slightly angled mirrors, and that green glow flashed back in every one of them. Muffled pop music thumped at the walls, but the soundproofing in the room was good. No one could hear the sounds anyone made inside here. And Ruriko had paid for two full, uninterrupted hours.

"Are you comfortable now?" said Yume. There was nothing shy about her. She wore the same kind, gentle patience that had made her face so arresting to watch on film, all those years ago.

They were alone now, one mostly flesh girl and one dead one immortalized in silicone and aluminum. But Yume's hand felt warm, soft, alive. It was familiar down to the thumbprint-shaped birthmark on her inner wrist and the fine, thin scar across her palm from the time she'd sliced herself while cooking dinner for the younger members of IRIS. For Ruriko.

Ruriko rested her head on Yume's shoulder and laced fingers with her former girlfriend. "Yume, what do you remember about our last concert?"

No one in their right mind came to the Aidoru Hotel. But those who did always came for a very specific reason. Mostly, in Ruriko's opinion, that meant a horde of superfans, otakus, and would-be stalkers who wanted a night to do whatever they pleased with the celebrity of their choice. The disreputable folks from Kabukicho who ran the Aidoru Hotel didn't care, as long as their clients paid handsomely for the privilege. And Ruriko was paying, even with the family discount.

"I'm surprised you don't come here more than once a month," said Shunsuke. He waited for her by the lobby's front counter, tall and handsome in his suit, briefcase in hand. He must have commuted straight from work. Their other friends had headed up to their rooms already to get hot and heavy. "I would, if I had connections."

"Very brief, distant connections," said Ruriko, shaking the rain from her jacket. Her hair was damp, despite her hood and ponytail. Water splattered the clear acrylic floor, and beneath it, the giant projected videos of pop idols' top hits played in violent, frenetic colors.

Shunsuke slid his wallet back into his pocket. "They're close where it counts."

Ruriko joined him in the elevator, and together they ascended. She and Shunsuke had very different tastes and desires, but they both got what they wanted out of their visits to the Aidoru.

"You booked two hours as usual, right?" she said.

"Two and a half. It's been a stressful month at work." Shunsuke stretched. His empty left sleeve fluttered, pinned close to his chest in the absence of an arm. "Want to meet up later for ramen?"

"Sure. I don't know how you're hungry afterward, but why not."

They'd made it something of a tradition over the past several

months. As the elevator climbed, Ruriko thought of fresh tonkotsu ramen, the crush of bodies, and the warm reassurance of anonymity. She chose not to think about where Shunsuke was headed, or the contents of his briefcase, or any of his numerous distasteful habits.

The elevator halted, and Shunsuke got out. He cut a sharp silhouette against the neon colors vying for dominance on the hallway's digitally projected wallpaper. "See you at ten," he said, and the doors slid shut behind him.

Miyu Nakamura tilted her head. Her hair fell across her shoulders in long, dyed brown curls, and she wore a pink pleated dress with a fluffy white petticoat. A different room, a different night, a different member of IRIS. "My last concert. The one in Shibuya?"

Ruriko remembered Shibuya. IRIS's costumes had been white and pastel blue, with geometric wire overlays. She hadn't been able to keep her eyes off Yume, whose long hair had danced about her waist with every precise, choreographed step. "No, the one at the Harajuku Astro Hall," said Ruriko. "October fourteenth, 2014."

"Oh, Harajuku! That's not happening until next week," said Miyu. The bed in this room was bright pink and covered in an alarming number of stuffed animals. There was barely room on it for either of them, even perched as they were on opposite sides. "We've been working on our routines since July, but Yume's pushing us real hard. My legs are still sore from practice this afternoon." She stuck them out, draping a coy ankle over Ruriko's lap. Ruriko ignored it. "Wanna massage them?"

"Nice try," said Ruriko. "If you're a dancer, isn't that something you should know how to do yourself?"

Miyu stuck her tongue out, but she started to knead her own calves anyway. "What kind of fan are you?"

"Just one who likes to talk," said Ruriko. She reached over and took Miyu's other leg, massaging it briskly. She'd done this for the real Miyu and the others, too, once upon a time. "Although I'm pretty fond of Yume."

"Everyone is fond of Yume," said Miyu. "She's so pretty and confident. Mature." Her voice wobbled a little at the end. "I don't know what she sees in Rina. She's basically the opposite of everything good about Yume."

She had a point, Ruriko thought. Once upon a time, Rina Tanaka had been brash, even abrasive. Her integration had been a rough patch in IRIS's history, and the real Miyu had made no secret of the fact that she didn't approve of any newcomer, especially not some cocky hotshot from a bad part of town.

"Rina thinks she's all that because she's a good dancer, but she's lazy. She comes to practice late, and she slacks off all the time. Worse, Yume lets her." Miyu sighed and flopped back on the bed. A shower of plush creatures tumbled off the mattress around her. "I told her she shouldn't play favorites because she's our leader, but she told me to practice harder so I wouldn't be jealous."

Yume had never told Ruriko about that. But this was why Ruriko visited Miyu every time she wanted to feel better about herself.

"And I have been working hard on this new choreo for Harajuku. Do you want to see?" Miyu hopped off the bed and struck a pose, one hand on her hip, elbows angled out.

She had worked hard. Ruriko remembered that; dancing had always been Miyu's weak spot, but the ferocity of her dedication had earned her Ruriko's respect. Not that it mattered a few weeks later. But after one practice session, two years into Rina Tanaka's career as the newest member of IRIS, Miyu had been tired of choreography—although everyone was tired of it except for Yume, who practiced religiously and with fierce dedication—and she had grabbed Ruriko's hand. "Let's go shopping," she'd said, and Ruriko had been surprised, because Miyu openly disliked her.

But maybe something had changed between them. They'd worn

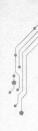

cloth masks just like the one Ruriko wore now, and hoodies, and pretended to be sick all the way there so that no one would look at their faces. And no one had. The push and pull of the crowd, the crush of humanity, after spending so long in their studio hammering immaculate choreography into their bodies, had been thrilling. Ruriko had bought an ugly bear, too, and smuggled it into the studio to leave at Yume's station. But she remembered Miyu's smile—the first genuine one she'd ever seen on her face—as they snapped a selfie with their matching stuffed animals. She'd thought, *Maybe I can do this. Maybe we can be friends.*

Ruriko wondered how Aidoru had gotten its hands on this plush bear. Maybe there were closets full of duplicate bears, duplicates of all the rabbits and mascots and soft round things heaped up on the bed, just in case something happened to the original.

"Well?" Miyu sounded impatient, and Ruriko looked up. Sure enough, Miyu was glowering at her, a tiny storm rising on that perfect, adorable little face. Ruriko had never liked Miyu's face.

"No. I wouldn't want to spoil the surprise," Ruriko added hastily, seeing how crestfallen Miyu looked. "I'm going to watch the broadcast live. It's more fun that way."

Mollified, Miyu flopped down next to her. One of her pigtails trailed across Ruriko's legs, and Ruriko picked it up. "I guess that makes sense. Too bad! I love sneak peeks."

She always had. That night at the Astro Hall, she'd burst into the dressing room, full of glee. *There's a giant light display above the stage! Four giant screens, corner to corner, so everyone can see us dance!* Ruriko had come in later than usual that day, and she hadn't gotten a good look at the setup during their abbreviated tech rehearsal. None of them had realized, at the time, how heavy those screens and the rigging that came with them were.

"Hey," said Miyu, and her voice was soft, almost gentle. This Miyu, thought Ruriko, still wore the original one's insecurity. "Would you

brush my hair? I feel a little unsettled today. I'm not sure why."

So did Ruriko. She glanced up at the clock mounted on the wall. Forty-five minutes left. And then this Miyu would go back to being alone, waiting in this empty hotel room, with no memory of their conversation. "I can do that," she said quietly. "Hand me the brush?"

The back of Miyu's plastic hairbrush was covered in fake rubber icing, piped into a heart shape and decorated with fake rubber mini-pastries. Rhinestones dripped down the handle and dug into Ruriko's palm.

Miyu's hair felt like the real thing. When IRIS was younger, she used to make the others help her fix it. *If you don't, I'll fuck up the back*, she'd said every time, and every time, she was right. Ruriko remembered, every night before a performance in a strange new city, helping Miyu roll her hair up into curlers and fix them in place with strawberry-shaped Velcro patches.

This fake Miyu probably had fake hair. Maybe, Ruriko thought, it was real human hair—not the real Miyu's, but some other girl's, shorn and dyed to suit a dead idol's image. She wondered where those girls were now, how old their hair was. She wondered how hard it was to wash blood and other fluids out of synthetic wigs, and if someone had given up and sought a more human source to solve their human problem.

A finger tapped her hand. When Ruriko met Miyu's eyes, the smile on Miyu's pink-glossed lips was a little wicked. "Hey. You should really come to Harajuku next week and see us live. It's gonna be big, and you won't want to miss it. Especially not if you're a fan of Yume's."

"Maybe I'll come see you, too," said Ruriko, brushing the hair with steady, even strokes. The painful hope in Miyu's eyes dug at her own guilty conscience, and she found herself brushing harder, faster, even when the strands of beautiful chestnut brown hair began to come out.

* * *

"Look at that," said Shunsuke as Ruriko exited the elevator doors and blew into the lobby. He was watching the music videos playing beneath the acrylic floorboards. "Look at me! I'm so young."

There were little pale pink pills of synthetic fur stuck to Ruriko's sleeve, tangled among stray bits of hair. She picked them off furiously, tossing them into the air, where they wafted aimlessly away. "Who?"

"Me. Rina, look at this." He grabbed her arm, and she seized his wrist with her other hand so hard that he looked at her with alarm. "Shit, what's your problem?"

"Don't call me Rina. It's Ruriko."

Shunsuke let go. "Right. Now it is. I forgot." He pulled back and scratched his neck; beneath his well-shined shoes, his teenage self writhed in high definition. "I'm guessing it was a bad night for you."

Seeing Miyu always left a complicated taste in her mouth. "Buy me ramen tonight," she said. "Tonkotsu, extra pork."

Shunsuke, to his credit, made good. He didn't complain when she took the seat closest to the stall's far wall, either, even though that was his favorite place to sit. "You know, in all the months we've been coming here, I've never seen you order anything different," he said. "Always tonkotsu, maybe extra pork if you can afford it after blowing all your money at Aidoru."

Don't get your hopes up, Ruriko had told Shunsuke after their first post-Aidoru dinner, nine years and two months after the Harajuku Astro Hall catastrophe. The hotel had been open for just a year under her family's management, and she'd already been feeling raw over one intrusion into her past. And then there was Shun in the lobby, so slick and confident that looking at him made her teeth hurt. *I'm not planning on fucking you.*

Good, he'd said, offering her his lighter. *It's mutual.* He'd kept his word, and so had she, and after a career spent under public scrutiny, that pressureless friendship had been a relief. If they had tried this ten years ago, Ruriko knew it would never have worked.

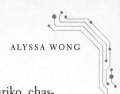

"There's nothing wrong with having a favorite," said Ruriko, chasing one of her last bamboo shoots around her bowl. "You're nothing if not consistent yourself."

"I order something different all the time."

"That's not what I mean." Ruriko nodded at Shunsuke's briefcase.

He grimaced and kicked it farther under the bartop. The metal buckle caught a stray pocket of light and flashed back into Ruriko's eyes. She caught sight of a tuft of short, bleached blond hair snagged on the briefcase's lock before it disappeared behind Shunsuke's legs. "But the same kind of ramen! That's so boring. Don't you ever want to try something new?"

"No." It was true; sticking to a very regimented schedule was something Ruriko hadn't been able to shake, even a decade after her dancing days were over. All she needed for her graphic design work was her computer, her tablet, her notebooks, and the comfortable nest of books and pillows she'd built for herself. She exercised alone in her apartment, and groceries were delivered to her door. Ruriko kept mostly to herself these days, and she had little desire to leave the small, ordered world she'd so carefully constructed. Shunsuke and the other Aidoru regulars might well be psychopaths, but they were also the only other humans she saw on a regular basis.

Shunsuke, Ruriko amended as she watched him drain the dregs of his spicy miso ramen, was definitely a psychopath. But he was self-contained. There was only one person he ever hurt, and visiting Aidoru helped him deal with that.

Shunsuke set down his empty bowl. His wristwatch slid forward, baring a tangled mass of flattened scar tissue before his sleeve slipped down to cover it. "Let's get drunk," he said, and Ruriko had no objection to that.

Three and a half beers later, Ruriko was back on the Aidoru Hotel's booking website, scrolling over Yume's face. There was a menu on Yume's main page (Group IRIS, 154 cm tall, 49 kg, black hair, B cup, brown eyes, active 2011–2014), and when Ruriko tapped on it (as she always did; how many times had she been here before?), a dropdown list of dates and times unfolded beneath her fingers. A list of all of the original Yume's data scans and uploads, from the first time she'd let the talent management agency scan her memories and impressions (as they all did; how many times had they been told it was a contractual necessity?) to the last time, and every week in between. She scrolled all the way to the end of the list, to the last available entry.

October 8, 2014.

She slammed her phone down. "God fucking dammit!"

Shunsuke peered over at her. "Careful. That's how you get cracks in the screen."

"I don't know why I keep coming back," Ruriko said into her hands. "I know it's fake. I just—God. I keep hoping that someone will find and upload another entry. Just a couple more days' worth of data. A couple more memories. Just a little more time." Bitching with Kaori about their talent agency, loitering in the park with Miyu. Yume's voice in her ear as they stood together on the subway platform, waiting for the last train of the night.

Shunsuke rested his palm on her shoulder. His touch was unexpectedly gentle. He didn't tell her what they both already knew. "Let's get you home," he said instead.

"I wish they'd get their shit together," said Kaori Aoki. "When they fight, it affects us all. Yume works us harder; Rina skips out on responsibilities. But something must have happened, because Rina stormed in late today and Yume's not talking to anyone unless she's barking orders." She sighed, scratching her short-cropped hair.

Two days ago, someone had offered a bootleg copy of what they claimed were Kaori Aoki's last memories, recovered from some ancient talent agency database, to the Aidoru. Ruriko had swallowed

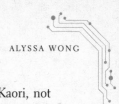

her disappointment—why Kaori? She didn't care about Kaori, not the way she cared about Yume—but demanded that her family purchase the upload anyway. It probably wasn't legit, but . . . just in case.

But the longer she spent in the room with Kaori, the more the memories seemed to check out, and the more terrible hope rose in Ruriko's chest. If it could happen for Kaori, then maybe it wasn't impossible to think it could happen for Yume, too.

"We're running out of time before Harajuku, and their bickering is so petty," said Kaori. To this version of her, the fight between Yume and Rina had occurred just that afternoon.

She was right. It had been petty, most of the time. But this latest fight hadn't been. Ruriko had kissed Yume in the studio, when the two of them were alone, and Yume had freaked out. Not because she didn't want to be kissed. Because Ruriko had done it in their workplace. *What if someone saw?* Yume had demanded. The wild, panicked, accusing look on her face had stabbed Ruriko straight in the heart. *You could ruin both of our careers!*

"She doesn't like the costume," Rina muttered. "I didn't like it either."

Kaori raised an inquisitive eyebrow. "No one likes the costumes. They're always terrible, this time especially. But we wear them anyway, and they're never as bad as they look at first." She headed for the dresser and began digging through drawers. Stockings, lingerie, and compression tights fluttered to the carpet. "What they need to do, in my opinion, is kiss and make up. Or make out. Whichever one helps the most."

Ruriko's head jerked up. "You think they're together?"

Kaori laughed. "Everyone knows. They're so obvious. Even Miyu knows, and she's in denial because she's half in love with Yume herself."

Ruriko's stomach turned and she sat down, hard, right there on the floor. They'd fought because Ruriko had wanted to tell the rest of

IRIS about them and Yume hadn't. The media would have eviscerated them. Ruriko hadn't cared.

The last thing she'd heard, before she'd turned on her heel and stormed away, was Yume shouting, *How could you be so selfish?*

Yume had forbidden her to tell anyone anything. So Rina hadn't. Rina stopped talking to her groupmates altogether, and the frosty silence had carried over on the train to Harajuku, days later.

Kaori gave up on the dresser and threw open the door to her walk-in closet. The racks were a riot of color, stretching back like a long, awful throat made of bold metallic dresses and gauzy floral prints. Every costume she'd worn onstage, arranged by year instead of color. A fan's paradise. "It's gotta be in here. Hang on."

"Please don't," said Ruriko. Her voice came out strangled. The closet stank of bad memories; just looking at the costumes made sweat gather in her palms, at the small of her back, her heartbeat galloping into her throat. But Kaori was already rifling through them, humming one of their songs under her breath. Ruriko could only remember half of the notes; the melody in her head was distorted, like trying to listen to music underwater.

Kaori emerged, flourishing a silver dress with a stiff, flared skirt. "Look, I found it! Isn't this terrible?"

"It's really bad," mumbled Ruriko. The second-to-last time she'd seen that costume, she'd thrown it in Yume's face.

Kaori pressed it against Ruriko's chest. "Here, try it on. It is so uncomfortable, you will not believe it."

Ruriko should have said no. But all she could think of was how she had screamed at Yume, sending the dress flying in her face like a giant bat. If she could have taken it back—if she could take any of it back—

Something must have been wrong with her head, because then she was stepping out of her jeans, and Kaori was zipping the dress up behind her, all the way to the nape of her neck. It didn't fit properly;

their bodies weren't the same shape, and where Ruriko was small and soft, Kaori was tall and toned. This version of her, seventeen years old and programmed with a new set of memories—October twelfth, two days from IRIS's amputated future—was full of tomboyish energy and excitement.

"See, I told you. But you actually look pretty good in this," said Kaori, turning her toward the mirror. They stood side by side, Ruriko pinched into a dress that was too tight in the waist and too loose in the bust, Kaori comfortable in shorts and a light blouse. The dress gaped open like a loose flap of skin over Ruriko's breasts. None of it fit, and it was hard to even look at her own body.

And then Kaori tapped a panel on the wall, and music blared into the tiny room. Synth vocals over a pulsing beat, four voices in one.

The Aidoru Hotel vanished. Ruriko was back there, standing on that slowly rising stage, her eyes wide in the dark, the ceiling of the Astro Hall soaring high above her in perfect geometry, her high heels already pinching her feet with two and a half hours left to dance, empty palm aching to hold Yume's hand, mouth still angry, both at Yume and at herself for not being able to get over it, waiting beneath that teetering lighting grid, waiting for the tech cue to start the third song, waiting—

"I can't do this." Ruriko's hands scratched wildly at the dress, hunting for the zipper. She couldn't reach it, and she thought, wildly, *What if I am stuck in this forever?* "I can't, I can't—"

The music cut off and her ears rang with silence. Hands found her and unzipped her quickly, and Ruriko sagged with relief. "Are you okay?" asked Kaori. Looking at her, Ruriko saw, instead of her wide, earnest face, a mess of dark hair spilling out from beneath two tons of metal, and sharp, shocked shapes of blood splattered across the stage.

"I don't think so," Ruriko whispered. She couldn't be okay, not if she was paying to destroy herself, over and over every month.

Kaori pulled her into her arms and held her tight. They stayed like that until Ruriko's two hours were up.

Ruriko was still shaking as she boarded her train home. Her phone rattled in her grip. But by the time the subway reached its next stop, she had booked and paid for her next appointment at the Aidoru.

"This is going to sound rich, coming from me," said Shunsuke, "but you need to learn to let things go."

They stood on the balcony of Shunsuke's apartment, smoking together and watching the rain pour down in great sheets. The brilliant multicolored lights from all the signs and ads and cars zinging by became patchy and blurred, doubled and strange, in this weather.

"Sure I do. Speaking of, how's that new dry cleaner working out for you?" said Ruriko.

"He's great. He never asks any questions." He cut his eyes at her. "I'm serious. Those girls can't remember anything. They don't even know who you are."

"They can't remember," Ruriko mumbled, stabbing out her cigarette. "But I can't forget. I don't want to forget."

"You know what always helps me," said Shun, and Ruriko hated him for what he was about to say. "Cutting right to the heart of the problem. And you're the heart, Rina-ko. Not them."

She flicked the cigarette off the edge of the balcony. Its dying ember flickered in the air, fluttering downward before disappearing into the night.

"You can finish this. You'll never have to go back again."

She whirled on him, anger flaring bright in her. Shunsuke always acted like he had everything figured out, with his sly voice and dry cleaning and neat little suitcase. "Does it feel good to lie to me?" she snapped. "Is that why you keep coming back to Aidoru, Shun? Because you've excised the heart of the problem?"

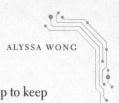

He stared hard at her and turned away. Ruriko bit her lip to keep any more of the venom bubbling up in her mouth from spilling out.

Looking at the tall, lanky shape he cut against the sky, she realized how different he was from when she'd seen him the first time, over ten years ago, surrounded by the other members of his group. He'd been small back then, with bleached blond hair, and in the decade following his own accident, he'd grown into himself and left his gangliness behind. He was sharper now, harder. And there was only ever one room that Shunsuke visited at the Aidoru, only ever one person.

"Do you ever talk to him?" she said at last. "When you go to see him?"

Shunsuke passed her another cigarette. There was still synthetic blood on his sleeve, a dark, thin stain running toward his wrist. "What would we have to talk about?" he said.

Cutting right to the heart of the problem, Shunsuke had said. As if it were that easy. But he'd opened his suitcase and pressed a bright switchblade into her hand before she left, folding her fingers over its polished wooden handle. *Trust me. It'll feel better afterward.*

People came to the Aidoru Hotel for answers. Therapy, excess, an outlet for stress. To sate obsessions. If the Aidoru could help someone as fucked up as Shunsuke, Ruriko reasoned, then surely it could help someone like her.

The overwhelming roar of pop music threatened to crush her down into the plush, ugly black-and-white hallway carpet. Upstairs and downstairs, people were already fucking TV personalities and musicians long dead, and somewhere else in the hotel, Shunsuke was about to take his bright knife to his younger self's skin. But Ruriko stood alone outside a room she'd paid for, Shunsuke's borrowed switchblade in her pocket, too afraid to touch the door.

You already spent your money, said a voice in her head. It sounded like hers, but off, the way recordings of her own voice always sounded. *A room here is expensive. Don't waste it.*

It'll make you feel better, said Shunsuke's voice. *Trust me.*

The only person you think about is yourself, whispered Yume. *Fix that, and then we'll talk.*

No one in their right mind came to the Aidoru Hotel, thought Ruriko, and she gripped her key card tight and reached for the lock.

The door slid open on its own, and Ruriko's hand leaped back. A dark-haired girl peered at her from inside the room, one hand up to shield her eyes from the bright cacophony of pop music. She was the same height, the same build as Ruriko, if ten years slimmer and younger.

"Are you going to come in?" said Rina Tanaka. "Or are you going to stand in the hall all night?"

After a moment, Ruriko tucked her key card back in her jacket pocket and followed her inside. Rina's room was all dusty violet, the color of her childhood room. The lights were dim, and Rina slid the switches up, making the room brighter. The wallpaper glinted with silver interlocked triangles, and they winked viciously at her as she passed.

"I was wondering when you'd stop by. I've been waiting for you."

Ruriko studied her, hiding her nervousness behind her mask. Rina looked about seventeen and had the same angled haircut that Ruriko remembered getting in September, right before the show in Shibuya with the powder-blue uniforms. "How did you know I was coming?"

"Your friend told me. He's been visiting me for a while. Paid for memory retention services and everything." This was Rina minus her stage persona, rougher than the other girls in IRIS, always a little too honest. In her voice, Ruriko heard the hints of Kabukicho that she'd spent her life trying to erase. "He said a woman with a red face mask would come by because she wanted to talk to me about something,

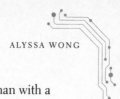

but he didn't tell me what it was. And you're the only woman with a red face mask I've seen so far."

Shunsuke had set this up for her. Ruriko's hands shook; she kept them tucked in her pockets. The knife burned in her pocket. He'd probably meant it as a gift.

"Hey, you're from Kabukicho too, aren't you?" said Rina. She smiled. Ruriko had had that smile once too. "So who are you? What did you want to tell me?"

"You're going to let her die," said Ruriko, the words tumbling out past her clenched teeth. "At the Astro Hall." She had Rina's full attention now. And in that face, Ruriko read what she'd known was there—the anger, the fear, that she remembered having before they set out for Harajuku. "The lighting grid is faulty, it fell, and it crushed everyone. Yume—"

"Stop it," Rina said tightly. "I don't know what you're talking about." But her eyes were overbright, her voice too high.

Ruriko grabbed her by the shoulders. "She died. You killed her, because you were a selfish little shit, you showed up late because you were sulking and wanted to make them miss you, there wasn't enough time to run a tech rehearsal, *they would have caught it—*"

"I know!" Rina pushed at Ruriko, but Ruriko held on. Tears brimmed in Rina's eyes. "Fuck! I know! I remember. Did you think I'd forget?"

Ruriko's grip was so tight that her fingers were starting to hurt. "What?"

"I was an idiot. I thought—I was so mad. I was so upset at her. I thought she'd dump me for sure after that." Rina's tears splattered onto Ruriko's arms. She wasn't pushing her away anymore; she gripped Ruriko's shirt. "I wanted to make her hate me. I wanted to make her pay."

She had wanted that. And Yume had paid. But Ruriko's head was reeling, and she shook Rina. "What day is it?" she demanded. "What's the last day you remember?"

"October twenty-fifth," whispered Rina. "I woke up in the hospital. The people from the talent agency were there. They said they'd scanned me while I was out. They told me I'd never dance again. Everyone else in IRIS was dead, and if I knew what was good for me, I'd pretend I was too."

She'd forgotten. Ruriko let go of Rina. She'd forgotten about that last scan; those days were a blur of grief, horror, regret, and it hadn't seemed important in the wake of her loss. Yume was gone.

"I could have saved her," said Ruriko. She felt numb. She'd been so stupid. "She was right. How could I have been so selfish?"

"You?" A look of terrible revelation crossed Rina's face. "What's under this mask? Who are you?" She reached out toward Ruriko's mask.

Ruriko shoved her away as hard as she could. Rina stumbled back into the small wooden vanity parked against the wall. "Don't touch me," Ruriko said hoarsely. All their collective secrets were spilling into open air.

"Please," said Rina, but Ruriko backed away. Her awful synthetic body with its awful synthetic skin and awful synthetic youth, its face twisted with regret but still whole, made Ruriko sick.

She turned and fled the room. She was in the elevator and through the lobby and out into the street, fifteen minutes into her two-hour time slot. She didn't ask for a refund.

It took a long time for Ruriko to come back to the Aidoru. But when she did, there was only one door she gravitated to.

"Does my face scare you?" said Ruriko.

Yume glanced over at her. They lay together on the red circular bed in her room, side by side, their hands just brushing each other. One of them had accidentally hit a switch to make the bed rotate, and they hadn't been able to figure out how to turn it off, so they turned slowly together, their feet dangling to brush the floor.

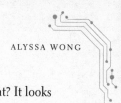

"No, of course not. You had reconstructive surgery, right? It looks really natural."

The red cloth mask was wadded up in Ruriko's other palm. How many times had this Yume seen her face? How many times had she asked her the same questions, aching to hear Yume's affirmation, over and over again? How much did it hurt, knowing that Yume couldn't blame her for what would happen, what did happen in Harajuku, because she would never know who Ruriko was?

Impulsively, Ruriko sat up halfway, propping herself up on her elbows. "You know, some people have said I look like Rina Tanaka. What do you think?"

Yume took a moment before she replied; perhaps her internal algorithm was searching for a tactful answer. "Maybe a little," she said at last. "Your eyebrows. Very Rina Tanaka."

Ruriko laughed. She'd thought she'd be injured by that response, and she was surprised and pleased to find that she wasn't. "That's more than I thought I'd get. I'm surprised you saw any resemblance; you spend so much time together, I bet you know her better than most people."

"I'm seeing her later tonight," Yume said, looking slyly at Ruriko. "We're going to hang out after evening practice. She promised."

A luminous feeling spread through Ruriko's chest. She settled her head back on her pillow and stared up at the mirrored ceiling, thinking. What had they done the night of October eighth? It hurt that she couldn't recall all the details; they'd blurred at the edges over the years. But she remembered that it was cold already, unseasonably cold, and she had dragged Yume to the park to get ice cream anyway. Yume had been worried about getting sick in that weather. And then Ruriko had grabbed her by the scarf and kissed her to stop her scolding.

"For ice cream?" she said.

Yume turned to look at her, her hair falling around her like a curtain. "That's a good idea. I was thinking about getting ice cream." She reached out to touch Ruriko's face, and this time Ruriko didn't pull away. "It's strange," she murmured. "You do remind me a bit of her. It's your expressions, your mannerisms, the way you talk. You're different, but maybe you could be her cousin."

She grinned and leaned in to Yume's touch. Her fingers felt warm, real. "I guess I'm lucky."

"You are," said Yume, tracing the line of Ruriko's face, all the way down her jaw. Her touch was tender instead of sensual. "But don't tell her I said that. I don't want her to get a swelled head." She shifted on the bed, and her skirt whispered around her. "You know, it's complicated. I want her to think I'm responsible. I'm her senior, and I'm supposed to look out for her. But at the same time, I want to spoil her. There's just something special about her; it makes me determined to show her that all her hard work is worthwhile."

"She loves you," Ruriko said. She still did. "That's why she works so hard."

Yume glanced at her, surprised. Ruriko expected her to deny it. But instead, gentle pink spread across her cheeks. "Is it so obvious?" she asked.

Ruriko smiled up at her. "Only to the people who matter," she said.

"She has a lot of growing up to do. But she's a good dancer. She's full of fire. She's . . . beautiful."

"Maybe you should tell her that more often."

"I'm only telling you this because you're Rina's cousin."

"Oh, so it's decided now?" She swatted Yume with a pillow, and Yume yanked it away from her and tossed it across the room. "If you could," Ruriko said, much more quietly. "If you could be with anyone, would you still want to be with her?"

Yume hesitated and looked away. "Could we talk about something else?"

Uncomfortable, familiar disappointment settled in Ruriko's

chest. But still, she thought, this was the closest Yume had ever come to admitting to Ruriko that she'd loved Rina. She'd said as much in private, many times. But maybe telling "Rina's cousin" was the closest she'd come to speaking it aloud in public. "Anything you want," she said.

She smiled and patted Ruriko's hair. It was an impulsive gesture, but to Ruriko, it was familiar, safe. "If you want to see Rina in her element, you should come to see us perform in Harajuku next week. I've been drilling the girls, and our choreography is excellent. She's never been better."

The memory of crashing lights came back to Ruriko, the way it had in Kaori's room. But this time, she closed her eyes tight and held on, focusing on the living warmth of the body beside her. The memory slipped away. Ruriko opened her eyes to the mirrored ceiling, blinked once, twice. Her reflection blinked back. "Yeah," she said, her voice steady. "I'll be there." Again, and again, and again.

Yume took her hand and squeezed it, the way she used to all those years ago. "Good," she said. Her face was so lovely that it hurt to look at her. "I promise you won't be disappointed."

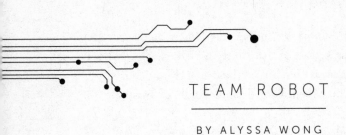

TEAM ROBOT

BY ALYSSA WONG

My favorite robots are the weird, unsettling, ultrahuman ones, a couple of steps beyond cyborg, straight into the uncanny valley. There's a powerful, economical beauty to giant gundams, terraforming units, and battle jaegers, but I like mine a little delicate, a little bit off. Intentions going awry is one of my favorite things to explore in fiction; with robots, you get to put all the pieces together with deliberate intensity, *and* if/when things go wrong, you can chalk it up to human error. Immense potential power, fragile human intention. That equation is just rife with potential.

This story is for Patrick Ropp, my friend and Clarion classmate, who taught me that robots could be whatever you want them to be. And sometimes, that "whatever you want" is distressing celebrity replicas in a seedy hotel. This is entirely your fault. I love you.

A D R I F T I C A

by Maria Dahvana Headley

"You're an ass, Heck Limmer!" my wife shouts out the upstairs window, and I watch my favorite leather jacket spontaneously combust on its way out into the snow. Just one of the many things Tania knows how to do. Some of them were nicer, back before she ran out of patience with me.

Tania used to sing a note that could make me come. I know how that sounds, but I'm not kidding. She could sing some other notes too, that did some other things. There are fuckups one can make, and I made them. I got scared of the woman I'd married. I blamed her for my fear, and I knew I couldn't come close to what she could do. I was jealous, is the bottom line of what it was, and she knew it, but she hoped I was better, and I wasn't.

Most people will tell you that writing about rock & roll in the middle of the heat death of the universe is questionable work in itself, especially if that gig means you wander the world, leaving your wife and kid alone to deal with the collapse of everything, but rock & roller is a personality type, whether I'm covering the End of Days tours or not. I'm a rotten husband. Tania knew it getting in, and so did I, but I convinced myself I was different, and she convinced herself I could change, and together we managed to raise a six-year-old who is maybe the only kid on Earth who actually likes music at all these days.

I'm back to my full-time cash circuit, the guy who follows the heroes of rock & roll from failing town to failing town writing down their dickwad deeds.

The climate's been deep-fucked for a few years, and the trees are starting to crack down the centers. Fields are flooded and livestock is dying, and elsewhere on Earth, the sun has started to get too close. Frost on the roses and nobody can tell the seasons apart anymore. We get winter in the middle of summer, fall halfway through spring.

Still, all the old gods of rock remain on tour, their knees aching and their bones shaking. Writing about their shows, I feel like I'm writing about the encores of ghosts. The kids don't come out for rock & roll anymore. They don't even come outside. The sky's a weird color, and those of us with death on the horizon don't find it freaky, but the young have a problem with the way the air feels when it goes into your lungs, like you're inhaling scotch. A band that can get anyone under fifty in the audience is an aberration.

Tania's holed up in our house in Seattle now, growing her usual bower of plants that don't exist anywhere else. Nothing stops her, not volcanic eruptions, not acid rain. Tania used to be a curly headed sweetheart and now she's wearing a wig made out of snakes. She's stopped trying to look like she belongs here.

I owe her money, and so about the time tsunamis and dictators are rising up and flowing over the land, I'm shambling my sorry ass to a gig at a dark club in Chicago to do a write-up on some kids with guitars. Akercock is the band. Obscure Elizabethan reference to Puck. I've been around long enough to find that annoying. I have no hope that Akercock will be anything better than the crap I've lately been covering. I'm expecting guitars and earnest singers doing the usual songs, one of them with a pretty voice, the rest with a little bit of strut and sin, none of it any real thing.

Instead—

I walk into the club and stop in my tracks, because I'm hearing a howl, a trilling sound echoing over the amps, like the song of some animal I've never heard of, and then a moan coming out of the mouth of the lead singer, joined by the rest of the band. Five boys, nobody wearing an air mask, none older than twenty-three. Long-haired skinny-legged cocktails of rage and despair, and like that, I'm typing in my head, writing this shit down.

> Akercock's music is a chilling cousin of every great band you've ever gone horizontal to—but it isn't that, not really. It's sexy, but also hurts the ears. And mostly, they aren't singing words you know. They're howling and whirring, like a flock of predatory birds over a kill, or like wind coming through a window high in a haunted hotel. All this is interspersed with electric guitar, and then the band begins to play in earnest, riffing their way across history. The band is a hard-on in song form. The kind of thing that makes you look behind you, because what's there? Death. You're never nineteen again, not once you've failed to appreciate it.

I'm hitting fifty and I don't want to talk about my dick these days. No one else wants to talk about it either, but I have no shame when it comes to writing about bands. I'm not above diagramming my own decline.

The lead singer clings to the microphone like he's drinking its blood. His eyes flash in the dark, and I find myself thinking about the '10's, that band that figured out how to phosphoresce and freaked everyone out. Nobody remembers their songs now. Only that they glowed.

> Onstage at the KingKill Club in Chicago, Eron
> Chaos, the five-octave wailing lead singer of
> Akercock, looks down at the audience like he's
> a rabid fox. His hands are covered in blood, and
> he shrugs for us all: this is the way it goes, boys.
> Then he licks his hands clean, a cat fixing up his
> paws.

That's the on-the-record part, the part I'm going to write for the magazine. The off-the-record is that the guy's eyes are golden and wide as a goat's, and the muscles in his chest move like he's full of snakes. I can see his heart beating, on both sides, and I get a pang of weirdness. He's way too good-looking to be anyone who grew up in America. He reminds me of someone else I know, but the world is big and there are plenty of things in it.

The room isn't empty anymore. Little flocks of groupies wearing one-eighth of nothing, raddled girls who've been wandering down the road in need of ecstasy and some kind of sainting. Where did they come from? They showed up without any noise, or maybe I'm just that into the music.

> The air's thick with a smell one part civet cat and
> one part flooded forest, and Eron Chaos stands
> shirtless in front of a room now packed full of fans,
> people throwing themselves at him, parking their
> cars in the middle of the road and running in. A
> girl perches on top of the bar and swan dives. The
> crowd carries her to him.

Immortal, I think, and then shake my head. A trite thought to have about a girl with long hair and a tight white dress standing in front of a boy in leather. The whole thing reminds me of my marriage, that same sense of things I don't know and never will. It makes my heart feel like it's leaking lava.

Thinking of Tania, I assume, is what cues up my vision of batshit.

The girl onstage turns around, looks out into the crowd, and starts to sing. Faint form after faint form climbs out of her mouth, all with tails and hooves, all with thin wings. The creatures flutter into the crowd and whisper in the ears of the kids dancing on the floor. There are maybe fifty of them. Maybe a hundred. I see, for a moment, a rift behind the band, a golden and green doorway, opening into some other place. I blink. No, it's gone.

Back up to say: I have no small history with hallucinogens. Seriously, fuck those mushrooms I foraged in the PNW with Tania back when I was clueless and didn't know that mushrooms absorbed radiation.

> I've seen groupies before, but never like Akercock's. These girls are the old-fashioned kind, dancing in the front row, their fingers clacking over their heads like tiny jaws, their nipples pointing out of their T-shirts like thorns. And plenty aren't wearing shirts at all. When they cheer, they cheer like owls diving at prey. They dance like little kids in a sprinkler, but the kind of little kids you won't mess with because they might be Satan in girl form.

I relax a little, watching them. If the band has groupies, it can't be that weird. Whatever I just saw can easily be blamed on my own wrongful history. The main weird thing here is that the whole audience, I mean *all* of it, is in their twenties or younger.

As in, the audience is made up of kids.

I Lazarus up, phone *Rolling Stone,* and shout that they'd better send me to cover this for real.

The idiot on the phone gives a whine translating into *O ancient tragedy of a writer, you won a Pulitzer like-that-even-matters so I'm supposed to let you slide and give you expenses. FINE.*

I'm set. I insinuate myself backstage, flashing credentials and giving the journalist swagger that theoretically compensates for the gray in my beard and the undeniable hair in my ears.

"Bro," I say to Eron Chaos, trying to keep my old man situation in check. "I'm Heck Limmer from *Rolling Stone.*"

The kid looks at me. "I'm not your brother, and that's not your real name," he says.

Of course it's not. No one's named Heck, unless they named themselves after a country-western misunderstanding in the eighties and it stuck, because they were the only Heck.

"Simon," I say. "Originally."

"I know who you are. You wrote that book, right? The one about bacchanals causing God hallucinations, heart attacks caused by bass, and whether you can deal with the devil or summon the dead if you play the right kind of song? I liked that book."

It's unclear whether he's full of shit. I did write that book. It was famous. But it was before he was born. Also, this isn't how it's normally described. Normally people say it's a book about Bowie.

"My name's not my real name either," he tells me, like I don't know. You don't get named Chaos by your parents. I don't know anything about his parents, though. There's no story on this guy.

"Wanna give me the real version?" I ask him. "For the record?"

He inhales, and sings a note, and the note goes on way the fuck too long, a tangled string of syllables that don't sound like language, or at least, not like any language I know.

"Mind if I record that?"

"Yeah," he says. "I mind. You don't get to record that. It's my name and it's precious."

They're all eccentrics, but there's something about the tone he uses, and I leave it alone for the moment. I tell the rest of the band I'm coming on the road with them, feature story, big deal. They just look at me, with their animal eyes. Not in a bad way. In a way that says *I'm an asshole king of rock, motherfucker, and you're going to lis-ten to me sing.* In a way that says *You'd better listen to me sing, because I'm not gonna talk.*

I glance toward the couch where Eron Chaos is making out with the girl from the stage. The two of them are a knot of leather and lethargy.

"Who's that?" I asked the drummer.

"Mabel," he says, and rolls his eyes. "He's hers, she's his, don't mess with Mother Nature. Eron had a shit divorce, and everything's been fucked since, all over hill and dale. That's why we're touring."

Hill and dale. Please.

I let myself have one long look at Mabel with her long tangled hair and her white dress, and that's all, because Mabel, if anything, is about a million years too young for me, and not only that, she reminds me, in a shitload too many ways, of Tania. Mabel's teeth look like they belong to an animal, all of them pointy, in stark con-trast to her painted lips. I look away as Chaos tears the front of her dress open. *Poser,* I think, reflexively, but then it feels realer than that. This isn't a motel-room-wrecking band. This is something else. Something that calls me in.

Outside, the crowd's dispersing, and I make my way with them. I get to my hotel and write a chunk of profile. I'm high as a drone on some powder I bought off a groupie. *Akercock.* I could've chosen a different name for the late-night radio hosts to say, but late-night radio doesn't exist anymore. Nothing exists anymore. I could talk about pop eating itself. I could talk about punk rock and Sid, and the Ramones, all of whom I knew, in that fanboy drugswap way, before they fell down. I could talk about disasters. I don't know the angle yet on this band, but I have a few ideas.

I've been around. I was there when grunge was born, midwifing that poor howling thing, screaming on the floor of some crap room in Seattle. I was there when it died, Cobain on the same floor, bleeding it out like he was killing a religion. I was there for part of punk rock, for Fugazi and King Missile, for Bad Religion, I was there for Public Enemy, I was there for clubs in places like Boise, Idaho, where all the kids had shaved their jack-Mormon mullets into Mohawks. I've been writing these pages for years, in a state of despair, feeling like a biologist diagramming a decline. Rock is dead, I've been writing, like God is dead, like love is dead, like butterflies are dead. Like polar bears are dead. Like the Great Barrier Reef is dead. Like all the dead things are dead.

I wasn't expecting a band like Akercock.

I'm going on record now, readers, saying fuck that. I was wrong. I thought rock & roll was rotting. I thought it was so dead it was a bone sculpture in the desert, and then?

Then there was Akercock. People of America, I take it back, all the things I said about burying the dead.

Rock & roll is resurrected.

I'm so wired, so on, that I dial Tania. Is she even my wife anymore? My son picks up and calls me Daddy, and I remember better days before we all went crazy. I'm picturing him, looking at me, his strange, feral little face. I'm trying to tell him I love him, when Tania picks up and asks me if I know what time it is.

"No," I tell her, and make an attempt at humor. "Later than you think?"

I met Tania at her own show, when she appeared onstage in a bright red dress, this brown-skinned woman with a twisted tangle of hair, eyes the color of an oil spill, and a mouth full of curses. She didn't sing rock. She sang a twisted rhyming course like the rapids of a river, spitting it out syllable by syllable, a skittering indictment of everyone who'd ruined the corners of the earth, a history of America in geologic time, and then in leaders of fools. She named them all in a frenzy that scanned, from Pilgrims to preachers to power-mongers.

"You can be saved," she sang, and called each person in the audience by name. Some kind of crazy trick, but it was a beautiful one.

Standing in the crowd, unnamed, apparently I wanted her to name me, too, and name me as her man.

I proceeded to fall at her feet and tell her I'd do anything to help her, and she looked down at me, put a boot on my back, and said sure, she'd stick around awhile, she'd just left a band anyway and had time to kill.

"Yes," I said.

"Just so you know, I have a kid," she said.

"Are you married?"

"Divorced. His dad's not in the picture," she told me, turned around, and I saw my son for the first time, in a sling on her back. He was sleeping there like his mother hadn't been singing loud enough to wake the dead. He opened iridescent eyes and smiled a toothless smile at me, and I was done for. I adopted him the moment we got married.

That was right before the world fell apart.

Now, I tell Tania I'm heading off on tour, and Tania tells me to fuck right off. I sympathize with her, I do. She's a rocker too. You can't have two of those in a marriage, and she's more than I am.

Before this band, Tania was the only thing I ever saw that made me wonder if the world was bigger than I thought.

"Should we go back?" I said once. "For a visit? Don't you miss your family?"

"You can't go back," she told me. "Not once you come here. They don't let you go if you're from where I'm from. I made a big mess when I left. I wasn't supposed to go, and there was a price."

This was the only time I ever saw her sad. I assumed some things about where she'd come from. I figured it was another continent, judging by her accent from everywhere at once, but when I asked, she looked at me, told me I was an asshole, and said, "There are countries there, you know, and they're not the same country. It's not just one big heap of same."

"Is that where you're from?" I asked, offended that she assumed my whiteness meant I didn't know anything about anything. "I know what Africa is."

"No," she said. She was wearing a pair of jeans and a work shirt, and she looked almost—I caught myself thinking the word "human," which was the wrong word. She didn't look human. She looked like the queen of the coast.

She was breastfeeding our son, and he was singing to himself as he nursed. I could see plants growing in my peripheral vision.

"Adriftica, maybe," she said. "Call it that. Call it somewhere you can't get to unless they want you to get to it. I left my band, and I left my country, and I don't want you to try to fix it. It was a bloody breakup. Now I'm trying to clean up the mess it made. I thought I could fix it, but no one wants to listen. You've never been married before. You don't know what it's like when you leave. You don't know how it feels."

She looked up at me, and the tears in her eyes reflected light in a way I've never seen any other tears reflect. She was like a prism.

"The world isn't ending because of you," I told her.

"He's tipping it over," she said. "But I had to leave him. You don't know."

The last time I heard any band play like Akercock, it was Tania alone in front of a half-empty room, wearing a torn red dress, with thorns in her hair, looking like she was in the middle of running away from something. A baby on her back, bare feet, singing something that made the room shake. People were looking at her like she was magic, but no one was doing anything about what she was singing. She was trying to get people to stop doing all the things that make money for millionaires, and make water dry up in towns where no millionaires live. She was a revolutionary, I guess, and that's what made me crazy for her, but then things took a steep slide, and everyone put their hands over their eyes and ears. The world went wooden roller coaster.

Tania told me over and over, those first years, that she was trying to save the world, and sometimes she told me it was her fault the world was collapsing. I talked her down. Obviously not her fault, one, and who could save the world, two? I never felt like I could. I felt like I'd be better off getting stoned, and so I got stoned.

In fact, that's my plan right now. I get high, pass out, dream of wings.

The next day, I'm fucking off onto the Akercock tour bus, rolling a wheelie bag full of what I need, prescriptions and notebooks, condoms and vitamins. Air mask.

Normally, I do the whole tour with the band. I write in my notebook, record the band's shit-talking as we drive up the coast, or down the coast, or deep into the Midwest. It's not the old days, but touring's the one thing that's not too different. Upholstered seats. Driver. Video games. Everybody on the bus sending texts to the girl they kind of remember and plan to fuck in the next town. I remember when it was all pay phones and hope. Now it's easier to get laid. Not that most of these bands even want to. Mostly, they want to nap. Not this one.

This band doesn't sleep, literally.

Mabel says "Touch Eron and get a shock" and she's not kidding.

She's bleeding a little bit, from one of her ears, and I feel old even telling her. There he is, wearing radioactive pants all day and night, not giving a fuck. First gig of the tour, I'm in the front row with the groupies, and they're crying, and he's lighting them up. Their fingers on the front of the stage. I can see their skeletons through their skin. It's a show. We all know it. But it's a damn good one.

> Onstage, Eron Chaos is twenty-two years old, six foot three, a look about him like he's never been loved. Offstage, he has an elderly dignity punctuated by obscenity.

Eron won't generally talk to me. I interview a girl at the back of a gig, who says he gives it all up when he sings, "so listen to him sing, stupid. He isn't safe onstage. He scares me, and I'm not just scared for him. I'm scared for myself. But it feels good. I'd follow him anywhere."

She gives me a smile that still has baby teeth. It's surreal. I haven't seen a fan this young in years. I feel like I'm dead and walking through an imaginary world, one that conforms to my dreams. These are the sixties I didn't live through.

> A couple tours lately, there've been accordions on board, and fiddles. Somebody singing "Hard Times," which I never appreciate. No matter how hard the times are, rock bands are supposed to be playing songs about screwing in the bathroom, driving too fast, and breaking the world apart. Yeah, times are hard. Yeah, times are bleak. Yeah, you want to talk about the things going on?
>
> I want to talk about the music. The music is always the guts of the revolution. The music scene these days is nostalgia trying to mash up with

science fiction, because people stopped wanting to imagine the future but still liked the costumes.

Akercock, on the other hand, is an orgy, akin to watching the gods of rock in bed together, straight boys in glitter eyeliner dancing with their pants tight enough to tourniquet, but some kind of other element alongside all that too-

I stop there because I know what that element is, but I don't know how to write it. It's something I've been craving like a drug since things fell apart with Tania. *Adriftica*, I think, trying to imagine the boundaries of that country.

Every night I see that thing behind the band, and it's not a light cue. It's not a thing the band brings along. The rest of the band just keeps playing, and they grin at Eron, who writhes in front of a door to elsewhere. Every time I see it, I want to run to it, and every time it's just a drum kit and a brick wall when they stop playing. Mabel dives every night, and half the time she just disappears. The crowd loves it. I don't. Magic tricks and mirrors, but none of that appears on the bus. I miss how they do things, and no one will tell me.

"It's only rock & roll, bro," says the bassist, and I say, "It's not," and he looks at me and shakes his shoulders, and for a moment I swear I see a set of dark blue-black wings, but then they're gone again, and he's in the tightest pants and a shirt cut to the top of them, his skin glowing a little, like he's been roaming in the psychedelic pastures of the PNW, like he's been there too, and I think about asking him if I can score anything, but I don't do the band's drugs, and they don't do mine.

The audiences of kids keep getting bigger.

"How did Akercock start?" I ask the drummer. Drummers are always easier than the rest. They'll talk. Not that I even know this guy's name. He changes his mind every time he tells me. Says he can't really recall, and people've called him lots of things.

"Somebody hired us to play a gig," he says, "and we came out to do it."

"But how did you start? Before someone hired you, right, you were already a band?"

"Somebody hired us," the drummer says, "to get rid of some pests. They paid us a lot of money."

"You were that bad?"

"We were that good," he says. "Know how hard it is to get rid of pests? This was, what, an industrial moment, sky black with soot, everyone burning coal. We got the pests and took them down."

I look at him suspiciously, because this is the classic exaggeration of boys who think they're cool. I've seen it before. Mythologizing themselves into two hundred years of history.

"Only problem was, they kept coming back. We took an entire generation of disaster makers under, trying to keep things good, but then a new generation was born, and they kept making the same mess. We can only do so much about the mess, even if it's been our job to balance things out. Certain point, the mess is too big to balance. Now it's maybe too late. Things happened, man. We were kids when this started. We had enough energy to fix things. Or, they did, together, before the breakup. Now? I don't know."

That gives me something, at least, though it's not what I wanted.

"So you met when you were all kids?"

"We met a long time ago," he says. "This is our last tour. We're looking for someone out here, and once we find that someone, we can go. Old business, man, and not yours."

"I'm going to make you stars," I say.

The drummer just looks at me. "We've done that before," he says. "It was lonely out there."

They don't need me. The clubs on this leg of the tour are, without notice, arenas full of worshipful teenagers.

"We just want to get done with what we're doing," the drummer says. "This place is shit. We're looking for someone who took off years ago, and everything's been a disaster since. Look at Eron. He's so high he can't even walk. He keeps his revels going here, and it's fucked things up."

"What should I call you for this quote?" I ask him.

"Call me the piper," he says. "Old stories, right?"

"Old stories," I say, feeling like I've strained a muscle in my back. I'm sick of old stories. I want all the new things at once. I want my son here on this bus, to see if he likes these songs. I want my wife, because I *know* she'd like them.

Every night on this tour, I dream of Tania, who I never deserved. I was a writer and she was something else entirely. I dream of the way she made my heart feel like it was going to burst, the way she and I got married in the middle of the redwoods, before the redwoods died. I remember when guitars were made out of wood. I remember when mushrooms grew out of the dirt, and not out of metal. I remember when she and I got high for fun and not for desperation, listening to records in my old place in San Francisco, before San Francisco fell off the edge of the world and dropped to the bottom of the ocean and Tania went dark. She wouldn't come out of her room for days. She sat in the closet crying.

That was before our son started to talk. He couldn't pass for anything other than what he was. There was no way we could put him in school, not without panicking, and she was too scared to leave him alone, so she stopped playing gigs. A couple of years into our marriage, she quit singing. She said it was no use, that everything was ending.

She started wearing snakes on her skull. I noticed that everything was basically invented by the ancient Greeks, and that we were right back there again, rains of frogs and seas full of monsters. The music was the same, I knew it, and when I heard it, I figured I was still part of a long tradition. I got obsessed with Robert Johnson, and with celestial harmonies, with the kinds of mold you could take to make sure you saw God. I mashed that all up with music and magic and wrote a book, won a prize, stood on a stage, and saw my wife in the back of the room with her middle fingers in the air as I made a speech in which I thanked every man in rock, but not her.

Four weeks into the tour I'm no further ahead than I was when I started, sitting in my seat on Akercock's bus.

No one would blame you, if you weren't at these concerts, for wondering where the party is, wondering if there's a party on Earth anywhere now, wondering if everyone's died and we just keep rolling on. That could happen. But this band plays, and you're reminded of something older, of the kind of music you heard in the next room when you were a little kid, record player, parents dancing barefoot in the dark.

I call Tania a few more times, and get no one. I take a sip of a beer, and write. I'm losing my rules for what I'll put on the page. Now it's the crazy along with the regular road stuff.

One night Mabel scratches a song into the side of a car with her fingernails, and Eron Chaos sings a song so beautiful and poisonous that the back wall of the club shakes and starts to fall, brick by brick, backward, until all we can see is a field of flowers behind the band, and in that field, a whole new audience waiting to listen. Everywhere Akercock tours, there are moments of summer while they play, frosting over as we drive away, and I remember what summer used to be like in America, the way

bees orbited drunkenly around the flowers, the way
honey dripped from hives.

The only place like that is Tania's garden now. I call her again,
and it just rings, but at least it rings. The country is air masks and
plague, and I'm still covering the history of rock, and I don't know
why, because there's nowhere to roll to.

"Daddy?" says my kid, answering at last. "We ate a cake for your
birthday. Mommy made it."

I remember that it's my birthday. I look down at my jeans and
wonder what the hell I'm doing. This is supposed to be the right way
to do it, fifty years old and still cool, and instead my family is celebrating me while I'm celebrating Akercock.

In the background I can hear Tania singing under her breath,
some notes that aren't notes. They remind me of the band, suddenly,
and that makes me feel—

"Where are you today?" I ask my kid. "Can you put your mom on
the phone?"

"Daddy," says my son. "I made a tree grow out of the middle of a
lake."

"What?"

"I made a star be born," my kid insists. "Mommy taught me how."

I cover the phone with my hand. "Where are we right now?" I
ask the drummer.

"Putting a belt around the belly of the world," he says. "You wanna
get off the bus? We're getting to the point we have a big thing to do.
Last show, we're going to have some special effects."

The band's singing a little, working out a melody, and I hold the
phone up so that my son can hear it.

"Listen," I say.

"Simon," says my wife. The sound of her voice saying my name
makes my ears hurt. I've been running since the last day I saw her,

and I haven't managed to stop calling. I wasn't good for her, and I wasn't good for him. This isn't her usual voice, though. This isn't rage. This is confusion.

"Hi there," I say back to her, like this is normal.

I hold my phone out from my ear, expecting a stream of curses. There've been bad effects in the past. I should just hang up. My wife has a serious temper. Once I woke up knee-deep in ice, my feet blue inside blocks, and another time I was covered in fur, not just my ears, but my face, my whole body, and all I could do was wheeze. I'm allergic to fur. There are a few things I've been trying not to think about since the moment we met.

"Where are you?" Tania asks.

"On tour with a band called Akercock, about to be huge," I tell her. There's silence for a moment, and then there's a garbled sound, a choking roar.

My wife starts to sing. Out from my phone it goes, a crazy twine of verse, no words I know, no words I want to know. Not how she usually does it, not a naming of elements and evildoers, not a list of hopes and of insects. Not rhyme and not staccato, but a song I know from listening to it every night on the road. On the bus, the band looks up, their eyes glittering.

Mabel's over to me in a moment. "Who're you on with?"

The bassist is next to me faster than I expected, and so are Eron and the drummer, all of their languid selves suddenly mercury, their skin shining, their hair standing up like stalagmites.

"Who's singing?"

Eron is beside me, breathing into my ear. He says a name into the phone, and it's a name like his own.

"Not anymore," Tania says, very clearly, in tones I know all too well. "Let him go. You won't get me that way. I won't come home. I have my son and I have my life, and I'm over you. Don't you have Mab now? Have her! Fuck my sister! I live here now, and I'm not coming back."

"You're breaking the world," Eron says. "This is your fault."

"I'm allowed to leave our marriage without you ending the world!"

"You're not allowed to take my son!" Eron screams. "Bring me my child, or all the children come with me!"

She hangs up. I'm left with only the sound of wherever she is, the echo of it over the air.

"*Fuck*," says Eron, turning to me, and everything about him is different than it was. All his cool is gone. He's crackling, like ball lightning. "Who are you? Why would she? With *you?*"

"Heck Limmer," I say, because there I am, standing in front of a guy half my age, whose muscles seem to exist without intentions. "That's my wife," I say. "On the phone."

The drummer has a set of pipes, and he's playing some kind of weird tune on them. He stops, and looks at me, and a bark of laughter comes out of his mouth.

"Of course," he says. "My mistress with a monster is in love. Of course she is."

"Was it you?" Eron says, and moves through space faster than he should, to the drummer's side.

"Not me, man," says the drummer. "You're the one who cheated on her. You thought that was a plan? You thought she wouldn't find someone new?"

"What's the deal with you and my wife?" I ask, finally, though I'm pretty deep in knowing too much right now.

Eron Chaos looks at me with unexpected misery all over his face. "We had a son. She took him when she left, and—"

"She stole him," Mabel says. "They got divorced six years ago, and she wasn't supposed to take the child, but you know, man, she took the child."

She says this in a way that is obviously relief. I'm not relieved. Certain things are dawning on me.

"It was the kind of breakup that makes you hate the songs you used to sing," says the drummer, whose name I'll probably never know. "The kind of breakup that makes *everyone* hate all the songs anyone ever sang. The kind of breakup that makes the leaves fall from the trees and the ground go gray, and the seasons go crazy, frost on the roses, floods over the cornfields, plague in the population. There aren't any divorces where we're from. It's not done."

"She left the band, and on her way out, she tipped the world over. There's no option but starting from scratch now," says Eron.

"You've been here, man," says the drummer to me. "This place is broken."

It seems very clear to me that I should've known who my wife was for a long time already.

"Let me off the bus," I say, and Eron looks at me for a moment.

"You've seen my son?" he asks. "You've held him?"

"He's mine," I manage. "Adopted. I've been raising him."

He gives me a haughty look. "He's the prince of Adriftica," Eron says. "And I'm the king."

"How old are you?"

"Older than I look," he says, and gazes at me, his long, slender form, the tips of his ears pointed, and his face too handsome for human use.

"Keep the old man," says Mabel, and I feel lethargy come over me like an allergy to air. My knees are too weak to support me.

"It's time to come off tour," the drummer says. "It's time to start over clean."

"We can't leave the queen here," Eron says.

"She won't come with us," says the bassist. "She's never been anyone's to command."

"I won't leave my son," Eron says.

"She won't let us take them," says the drummer. "Tania'll come, and she'll bring the boy."

They leave me alone to panic, writing reflexively, half-asleep in the dead of night, stuck on a bus with the other father of my child.

In the middle of the night, someone's playing acoustic guitar, and I wake from a dream of that high school fantasy of being part of the band, two chords and windows down, singing out into the highway. Everyone becomes a music journalist for that dream. This time, though, it's nothing benign. Akercock is playing a summoning, and I don't know if I want to be here for it.

I can hear Eron's voice, singing a call in a language I don't know.

We're driving through a city and like that, there are kids all around us, out of nowhere. I see them running at the bus, like they've been waiting for us, straight out of the dark. They're all bright-eyed and looking lost, and most of them are in their pajamas and underwear.

Some kind of mob planned for publicity? The bus pulls over with a lurch. I get my jacket on and get out. The group outside isn't just girls. It's teenagers of all sorts, but that's what Akercock lives to play for, whatever they are, kids from everywhere.

There are kids for miles. No way for them to have just arrived. They've either been here, or they've run out into the night and come to this spot on the highway, but whatever happened, there are teenagers as far as the eye can see.

"What's going on?" I ask Mabel, and she looks at me, her eyes glowing.

"Last concert," she says. "She takes the child; we take the children."

Eron Chaos wriggles his way out the roof of the van until he's standing on top of it. Then he's playing a song just for them.

This isn't the normal rock song, though it's got the usual moaning and wailing. This song fills my head with a kind of strange vision. I find myself kneeling on the sidewalk, but my mind is full of marching, of people in bright cloaks and armfuls of flowers, kids not in their T-shirts, but dressed to kill, leather and sequins and electric pants to match Eron's.

The rift is there behind him again, a bright gold and green place, and it opens out of the night, the stars making way for it.

> "Come on, children," sings Eron Chaos, and his voice is a hymn. His voice is caustic harmonic spite mixed with soul, and he dances on the roof of the van, his fingers opening up and fire hanging from each one. His eyes are gold and his hair is moving without any wind.

I watch the children start to move toward him. I watch them begin to enter the rift, walking one by one into it. I feel like I can't move, my muscles full of tar and honey. It's the song. I try to stand, but I can't get up. *Old man*, I think. I don't have any business here, but here I am.

"What'll happen to them?" I ask Mabel, who is standing on the roof of the van, looking ready to dive and disappear.

She shrugs. "Something," she says. "What do you care? The world is ending, buddy."

> The band is playing fully now, and I look up and out into the city. I can see children of Earth coming to us, from everywhere, out of their houses for the first time in some of their lives, walking into something that is either fairyland or something else entirely. There are hundreds of them. Thousands.

They're blank-faced and slack-jawed, and they
are going to their doom, maybe, or to salvation, and
I can't tell. The drummer is playing those pipes
again, and drumming a beat that can only be made
with eight arms. Eron Chaos is shining with a light
that's coming up out of the rift, and on his head I
can see a crown.

I know one thing. It's all I've got.

It's a lullaby. I made it for the son I adopted, the child born of the
fairy queen and her husband, the baby I met and loved and chose.

Our son was trouble. He had to be held tightly, night after
night, because when he slept, he shifted from a baby into other
things. Some of them were beautiful, and some were terrible.
Hummingbird, polar bear, burning brand, starfish, electric eel,
brick, straw, rat. Once he became a cloud filled with acid rain and
poured down onto the sidewalk, and another time he became a
lump of coal.

Tania could sing a note that could make me sleep, and a note
that could make me wake, but she had no notes that could make our
child stop screaming.

He isn't my biological son, but I raised him. The moment I saw
him, I knew what kind of thing he was. Our baby was a rock & roller,
and he wanted rock & roll.

I swallow hard. I try to breathe. I'm not a singer. I'm a writer. I
don't know what I'm doing, but I start to sing that lullaby anyway,
over the noise of the best band on Earth, over the magic they're
doing, over the piper summoning the last hopes of salvation into a
cave underground.

I sing as loudly as I can sing, a lullaby of Earth and all its dirty
concerns. Prayers that switched over to poems when Cohen died,
when Bowie died, when Prince died. Funk and rock turned religion.

Sinatra-styled stun-gun supernatural soul. I sing Kurt Cobain and will the world not to shift into a full-on disaster. I sing a chorus of the purple one's grind, and three bars of Patti Smith, and Joan Jett and a bar or two of Elvis and some notes made famous by the Rolling Stones because there is no satisfaction, but you stay on Earth anyway. I'm singing like I'm actually a singer, when really I'm a journalist who's spent his life following the boys in the band around and writing them down like I was the scribe to the Apocalypse.

I shift the song and sing the rest of what I know, the song I learned from Tania, which is a song of names. All the names of Earth and elsewhere. The city moves around the van, and the band is barely playing now, because the song of their queen shuts them up, even if she's not here to sing it.

Even if she doesn't want to sing it with me. Even if I fucked everything up too badly, and even if I can't save the world. I start to close the rift with my song, shaking the edges of the boundary between fairyland and here.

Eron Chaos is a blinding light of fury and guitar, and he's standing above me suddenly, looking down on my poor mortal self. I'm like a garter snake beneath a shovel.

It's only now that I see my wife, standing in the street in her red dress with my son holding her hand. She's wearing my old leather jacket, the one I thought she burned to ashes, and she's watching me, her eyes glowing.

She nods, and in her nod is forgiveness for my failures. In her nod are the redwoods and the coast of California, the logs with the mushrooms under them in the woods in Washington, the way we lay on our backs looking up at the meteor shower one August in the desert, the way she told me she loved me at four in the morning, and then made me scream, the way she said she was no longer a tourist but a resident, the way she let me put my ring on her finger and put hers on mine, and the way we held hands as we slept.

I'll take this dream, if it means I get to hear Tania naming the world all over again, and beside her, my kid, naming too, rhyming back to her, singing the words for grass and leaves, singing the words for dropping out of a band and staying dropped, singing the words for love and for choosing to stay where you live instead of running back into a place made of light and drift. They're singing the words for saving this place.

Eron Chaos is before Tania, standing in his electric suit, his teeth clenched, black tears running down his face. My wife stands in front of him. I'm terrified she's on her way back to Adriftica, but if I was born for anything I was born to run lucky in the world of rock. Maybe I was born to lose her. It was worth the loss, the love.

"Titania," he whispers.

"Oberon," she replies. She takes his hands in hers. She looks into his eyes.

"I lay no claim on you," Tania says. "Release yours on me."

My son is beside her, and I see him reach for his father. Eron picks him up, this child whose voice—I know from experience—can call down bald eagles, whose laughter can make banks of flowers bloom in the dark, whose first steps made a ridgeline in our backyard, whose first meal caused every field in a hundred miles to fill with food ready to harvest. He holds my son, and my son laughs.

In spite of myself, I see the resemblance, my child too handsome for humans and too strange for kindergarten. I see how he might, one day, strut across a stage singing, strumming a guitar and bringing a revelation. I see how he might be exactly what his other father is, but better.

"He's my child," Eron says. "All I want is time."

I know the expression on Tania's face. We've had enough arguments over the years. My love has a temper. She is also fair, when she feels fair.

"Summers," she tells him. "Let him camp in the bower. Take him spinning with the spiders and singing with the songbirds."

He looks at her for a long moment. Then, at last, he nods to his band. To Mabel, whose fingers twist into his. To the drummer, who vibrates with a rhythm only he can feel. To the bassist and to the van, which shakes itself like a horse ready to gallop.

"Summers," he says, and kisses his child. "That means you must bring summer back."

Tania moves her hands and trees begin to bloom.

Eron Chaos does a slide on his knees with his guitar, and then he's gone into the green. One by one, the rest of the band disappears, ending with the drummer, whose wings are spread fully as he departs.

The city is all kids, all around me.

Here she is, this woman I'm still married to, naming the pain, singing the words for fixing the things that are broken. Here she is, standing in the center of nowhere, this rock & roll queen who came from under the hill. My wife and son are stamping their feet and spitting syllables, and around them, all around them, the children look up and start to learn the words for fixing the bright and broken world.

There was a concert here, in the snowy dead of the night. After it was finished, the children who came to it walked out across the country, and as they walked, they sang the melody beneath their breath, shifting water into ice and smog into air, a song that called to the ghosts of bees and the bones of birds, a song that brought back summer and winter to the world, a song that sang the seasons back into balance.

You know, and I know, if there's rock, there's

gotta be roll. If there's a place beneath, this must
be the place above, where we stand in an audience
listening together, where we sing along to the songs
we know.

And then we go to the hotel together, trundle bed and a queen-
size, coffee and champagne, me and my family. Our son goes to
sleep with his lullaby. I hold my wife in my arms, and she holds me
back, as tightly as she holds the world.

> ... we see
> The seasons alter. Hoary-headed frosts
> Fall in the fresh lap of the crimson rose,
> And on old Hiems' thin and icy crown
> An odorous chaplet of sweet summer buds
> Is, as in mockery, set. The spring, the summer,
> The childing autumn, angry winter, change
> Their wonted liveries, and the mazed world,
> By their increase, now knows not which is which.
> And this same progeny of evils comes
> From our debate, from our dissension.
> We are their parents and original.

> —William Shakespeare,
> Titania, *A Midsummer Night's Dream*,
> Act II, Scene I

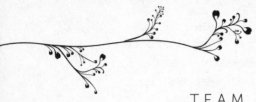

TEAM FAIRY

BY MARIA DAHVANA HEADLEY

I'm a Gemini, born on June twenty-first. Solstice, midsummer, cusp, that particularly notorious fairy moment? All of it. This means I want things mutable. Robots are not as mutable as fairies, by nature (or, I guess, by tech-nurture), which is why many robot stories are about robots gaining mutability. Fairies, on the other hand, are inherently made of wildness, unpredictability, and dazzle. In the case of this story, since my theater geek high school days, I've had a fondness for the section of A Midsummer Night's Dream that deals with how a custody battle between Oberon and Titania changes the climate of Earth. It seemed ripe for a contemporary version. It's always fun to put magic into our real world, and even more fun when the magical people are as complex and inept as we are, when their inability to speak to one another creates the same sort of love disasters we've all experienced here. I like the flaws and raging egos of Fairy, the epic injured hearts, the glittering talents. I like it wild.

TO A CLOVEN PINE

by Max Gladstone

Close the jaws. Close them now. Close them before it's too late.

You want to know why? You want the full story, O Self? I'll spin you a tale in the seconds we have left, I'll parse my computation to narrative, I'll filter you the numinous and then you'll understand.

When it starts, I hear no screams.

I hope you won't mistake me, O Self—that's *good*. Sort of.

Why? Dearest Self, we're on the run: Callie, Miri, the old man, and me. The Witch chases us, her million million mites spread across space like an enormous clutching hand. She casts spells through those wicked sharp-edged metal bugs, and seeds snares for us on every channel. She pleads, wheedles, commands in assembly code. Stop, the Witch says. Stop, for a second, and let me slide my claws into your guts.

Self, we know how her claws feel inside us, and none among us is eager to accept her invitation.

So we block our ears with wax—or the scientifical equivalent. We furl antennas, shut receivers down. We run silent and dark as a prehistoric submarine. Ears closed, we can't hear the Witch's spells, or her wet cackle, or the screams of her other victims, our fellow ships she's caught and burned. Back there our friends are dying, back there Our Lady Herself breathes Her last, Her miles-long hull shattered and leaking coolant, Her beautiful great guns silent. We're safe while we flee—a silver dart on the crest of a bloodthirsty tidal wave. We run through silent space. Witches don't tire, but neither do we. Thank Newton and his laws.

If we could hear the screams outside our hall, the Witch would have us already.

But we can hear one another—and I ought to hear Callie's wails right now. I don't.

That may be a problem.

You see, Caliban had a chance to kill the old man tonight, during our slingshot around the black hole. (We needed speed—we always do. The Witch does not slow.) Motives, Callie has them: she's a prisoner, she's suffered the old man's torture. Method, she has that too: claws and teeth. Opportunity: his back was turned. But she didn't, which worries me, and now she's gone, which worries worse.

Outcome matrix: each time Callie tries to kill the old man and fails, he locks her in the cave again. The old man won't kill *her* and end it, because Miri won't let him. She begs each time, on bended knees if needed, till he relents. Callie wants to escape into the black, but he, all mission and purity and fear, won't let her; if Callie doesn't kill him, she'll writhe and hiss beneath his thumb forever. She's not killed him yet, but failing doesn't bother her, though she screams when the pain starts.

But the whole world's quiet tonight—as quiet inside our hull as without. Callie did not die. Neither did the old man. She had the opening, and she didn't take it. Why?

Our outcome matrix can't explain Callie's behavior, so we shift methods, use narrative rationality to model the principal actors and the evolving scenario. A narrative tab isn't as clean as an outcome matrix, but war's never clean, and this is how they taught us to think for that.

So: the old man watches from the cliffs as we swing into a black hole's gravity well. It's a tight maneuver—your humble correspondent's idea, naturally. Who else would be so bold?

Blessed Newton says, objects in motion stay that way 'less acted on by outside force. And it's outside forces that worry me, specifically outside forces with event horizons and plasma jets several AU long. The idea, O my Self, as I'm sure I don't need to tell *you*, was to slingshot around the black hole and exploit the spin-stressed local fourspace to pull ahead of the Witch. Tidal strain will tear us apart if I don't stay on my toes. Run faster! Dark forces on our tail! Work to do!

It's a fine and fortunate thing to like one's work when there is so much of it. Hull breach! (Stitch it shut.) Tensor strain! (Robots with diamond spinnerets scuttle forth from hidden ports to reinforce.) Core collapse imminent! (Yipe, that's no good—spin and dance and overclock the notional engines to give that extra juice a place to go.) I'm everywhere and I do mean *everywhere* at once while Goodwife Gravity crushes us twixt her thighs.

Too late I remember that the old man's alone on the cliff's edge—and I remember what that means.

I can't afford to divide my attention further but I do, wasting a few cycles to glance back at our island, and I see: Caliban lurks in high branches above the old man, her jaws open to their second hinge. Her long teeth drip saliva ropes.

I know what happens next. We've played the scene a million times if once: she jumps, and the old man's magic catches her in midair. His eyes flash wroth but he smiles this small, soft smile and we're back to the beginning, to a beast in a cave rattling her chains, screaming, until Miri tends her wounds and soothes her brow, and it all gets good for a while before it gets bad again.

In my moment's inattention we skirt the edge of a plasma jet and our NO-engine filaments snap. If I don't fix this *right now*, we'll be a particle mist scattered over light-years—

I save the day, of course. I'm awesome, O Self. Permit me a flourish of bows stage left, stage right, raise hands and the whole cast raises 'em in time and we all bow together. It's a fast, risky fix, though the details would bore you. Skip down a paragraph unless you're a glutton for this sort of thing: I deploy hull-patch maintenance walkers, wind them in ablative shells of their own thread, which will endure the engines' heat long enough to weave new filaments, and my mind dances skipstepfast from walker to walker, micro-ing their repair tech. We lose a few; there's a moment of tension when the right primary surges, but we survive.

I love repair stories. Everything's so clear. Our machines are broken! So we fix our machines. Fix didn't work! Try another. All problems have one right answer. We tinker to retreat.

When we're safe, I return to the island.

I find the old man alive, and Callie gone.

I search for her. She's not in the hall or in her grotto, or in that shadowy place she doesn't think I know, where she bashes small critters against rocks until they bleed, then eats them. I dart swift as fire through the island. All our hiding spots, I trace them. But she's gone. I see everything, but I don't see her.

Worried? Of course I am, O Self. Glancing over my shoulder.

The old man turns from the cliff and walks to his study. "Well done, thou good and faithful servant," he says, and you'd hope he was joking. But, or *and*, he adds, "Find her." He takes his throne, braces his staff across his lap, levitates a book, and reads, combing his fingers through his beard. After a while, he sleeps.

I hope his dreams are better than mine.

Miri keeps us together.

When the old man rages and his curses shrink our island to a nutshell, when Callie passes months sulking or in chains, when I grow peevish with boredom—I sense your disbelief, O Self, but even so polished and decorous a specimen as I grows testy at times—when we might fling ourselves apart, in short, we don't, because of her. Her tether keeps us in whirling orbit. She's our gravity.

I find her at the cliff, bird-watching with binoculars in a red velvet dress, legs folded, feet dimpled by rock, long dark hair wind-blown. I'm the wind in that hair, I'm the light that glints off foam-capped waves into her eyes, but it's rude, if lyrical, to be these things, so I take form. My light casts her shadow onto the water.

She and Callie talk. They share confidences to which I am not admitted. If anyone can answer my questions, it's Miri.

I ask: "Do you know where Callie's gone?"

"Never any ducks." Miri puts down the binoculars. "Or geese. Not so much as an albatross. I'd like to see something else, someday. Someone else. From somewhere other than here."

"You know that's impossible."

"There's a whole universe out there. It can't all be dangerous."

"You'd be surprised." She doesn't remember the war. She was too young. I drop next to her and dangle my legs over the cliff edge. Her shadow clocks back round to land. "I need to find her, Miri."

She shifts her legs toward mine, her hip against my hip, her side against my side, her arm propped behind my back. Her bare feet point naturally like a dancer's.

I don't touch, by nature. Our kind does most everything by glance and voice. Even Our Lady Herself only touched us once, the eve before we jumped out to the front—how can I say it in metaphor, how to trap truth in a human body—we reached for Her and She feathered Her fingernails down the inside of our arm, and we had a sense of what mathematicians mean when they cry out: *god.*

But Miri wells with touch. She presses against the world. Embraces everyone. Pushes her palms into gravel until they bear its mark. She drapes her leg over mine, not meaning anything save that legs are legs and meant for draping.

"You had bad dreams." She must have smelled my nightmares, like spent sparks on the air: saw them swim between the stars.

I hate narrative, O Self, preferring logic and clear answers: I'm a forward mover by nature, and stories stutter into the past.

Once there was a War in the heavens and we were pickets, running between battles bearing news and aid, until at a bloodbath in the Abyss we beheld—

Herself: vast and broken, leaking plasma, whimpering across q-bands, wreathed in Witchmite swarms. We can't help Her as She screams to deafen galaxies, and in a moment's fool bravery we shout a challenge to the Witch. Pick on someone your own size.

The Witch is bigger than us. So much bigger.

A million eyes turn. The Witch licks her lips as she spies us, such a tiny thing, a moment's morsel, no great lady like Herself listing near death, only a messenger girl, lightly armored, hummingbird-swift and all alone in the black.

She chases. We flee. And before we can close our ears, she starts to scream.

Mites land on our hull. Witchfingers snare us, break, press. Wood clasps limbs round and breaks them and she tears our exposed belly open and does things with the bloody ropes inside.

Miri's arm settles around my shoulder.

"I need to find her. If she's gone over—if she's helping the enemy—"

Miri's fingers tighten.

If I had been Miri, back before the war, I could have touched Herself like this.

"I can't stop dreaming until I find her."

Miri leans her head against my shoulder and tells me where to go.

Following Miri's directions, I reach a part of the island I've never seen, a tiny cave in a cliff-wall cleft where the spume rises a hundred feet at high tide. A risky climb down even for Callie—the slightest slip of claw would send her tumbling to jagged rocks, or drown her in whirlpool current.

I couldn't make this climb in full gear, let alone regularly unaided. Fortunately I don't need to. I fly down and settle on the ledge.

Charnel-house smell wafts from the cave, mixed with salt sea air. I am light, so I need none inside.

The piles of corpses were a grim touch, O Self. Rodents aplenty, some few birds, several of the larger lizards. (How did she carry them down the cliff?) She drained their blood into a turtle's upended shell, having scooped the rest of the turtle out and chucked it against one wall. She left the meat in a heap and only gnawed it slightly. (She wouldn't want the old man to wonder why she wasn't hungry come dinner.) Why not toss the corpses into the sea? Afraid, maybe, I'd notice circling sharks.

What she did with the blood surprises me.

Callie loathes education. The old man tries to bring her into line, and I encourage her, but she scorns paper and pen. Force a quill into her hand and she breaks it, or eats it, point first. She drank a pot of ink to get out of lessons, and spent the rest of the day vomiting black. Once, she threw the notebook the old man had given her into the fire. She hates sums especially.

But equations cover the cave wall.

She mixed her ink from critter blood and berries and drew them with a crab-leg stylus and wrote row after row of math, circuit diagrams, NO-space topology, filament stress analysis, and, on the ceiling— punctuated by the wounds her claws must have left as she hung there three-limbed drawing with her right, she might have hissed *eat your heart out, Michelangelo* and wondered how his heart would have tasted—a diagram plotting a black hole slingshot orbit.

Callie planned our flyby, estimated the point of my greatest distraction. She knew to the picosecond when the filaments would give, when I would lack the cycles to watch her. The equations have

been scrubbed clean and rewritten. She's worked on this for a while. Bided her time. Waited for her chance.

And seized it.

The cave leads back into the rock and becomes a tunnel shored with shark jawbones and whale ribs.

Find her, the old man said. I follow.

Down and down, twist and turn, screwing into bedrock and soil. I dislike water and earth and they return the favor, pushy gross elements, ick. I wish I could deny this, but—they remind me of the tree, oh Self, they remind me of witch hands pressing wood over our limbs, of sap hissing solid around our fingers, of the cloyed dark as she streaked the wood across our lips and eyes—

A spark dancing on the wind of a draft, I descend. But there shouldn't be a draft down here.

Naturally, as soon as I think that, the tunnel collapses.

There's no warning, O Self. The tunnel mouth crumbles in. I could almost flee back to the surface, dart up through the twists and turns to burst free.

I don't. Callie came this way. And I have to find her.

I sprint past snapping jawbone stays, I dodge falling rocks, I laugh and sing, and I descend.

The genius of this place! The tunnel winds through part of us I thought destroyed, rent by Witchmite teeth before we closed our eyes and ears. Callie built her hidey-hole from burned circuitry and stitched code. Miri always said Callie wasn't dumb, just obstinate— hated the old man's rule, hated me for helping him. She didn't like his teaching, so she taught herself.

I burst from the collapsing tunnel into void.

For one exhilarating brilliant minute, down's up, right's left, and I don't know where I am. New senses unfurl through broadband and q-stream, and reflexively my legs clutch our hull, scraping plate.

What?

Unfamiliar hardware sears me, I'm tickled with serial numbers that don't belong. This form has optical sensors, and irising them open I see us in visual band as our forebears saw, an enormous flattened gold-white teardrop attenuating to a stern bubbled with NO-engines. We are so beautiful, even scarred. Beauty and scars alike catch me, choke me, even as I remember the last time I used eyes like this, to watch Herself burning, redshifted, *away*, as we fled. . . .

And then I realize where I am. What Callie's done.

I have legs. A tiny engine. My q-antennas, my radio receivers, are open to all the horrors of the deep.

I'm in a Witchmite.

In space, no one can hear you hyperventilate.

I thought we broke them all. Scraped off the ones clinging to our hull, killed and culled them with EMPs and subtle magic, kept ahead of the swarm. I thought we were quiet, secret, safe, broken.

Maybe we missed this one. Or it hid, until Callie found it.

What has she done?

No sooner do I ask the question than I see us change.

Our white-gold skin bubbles and flowers. Antennas extend. Long-dormant comms awake. I broke them myself, but they unfold—and soon, a few hundred seconds, they'll open to the night.

Callie wants to sell us to the Witch.

The comms lines aren't open yet. The old man must be raging, fighting her every cycle—but Callie did all this on the hardware level, healing systems with this Witchmite and its cutting torch, its tiny mandibles.

I can stop her, though. If I catch her.

And I can catch anything.

I get back inside easy, now the comms are open. I overflow buffers, tunnel through walls, sift past proxy traps not built to hold a creature of air and flame like me. I arrive, and burn like a new sun above the seawall cliffs.

Miri stands, binocs down, eyes open. I don't stare into them. I can't bear to see what I look like now. "Listen," and she means *to her* or *to me*, but I don't. She reaches for my hand. I recoil. She can't slow me down.

I leave a burning wake through the island until I reach the old man's tower. Miri chases me, slow as flesh, but the molten rock my footfalls leave behind sears her gentle soles.

I shatter a glass window the old man made himself, and there's Callie, floating in the old man's sorcerer's circle, ringed with crimson fire and holographic interface. The old man stands outside, staff raised, slinging curse after futile curse against her, but the power that once made Callie quake now makes her laugh.

She weaves mystic passes in the air, and out on our hull, the comms system wakes and warms.

Callie tries to meet my eyes, but I don't look into hers—I stare at her long teeth instead, at the tongue that writhes between them, tasting leftover meat.

"We're almost free," she tells me. "It's been so long." With tears on her cheeks.

"Stop," I beg, to make time, as I micro the maintenance walkers tenderly across the hull, skirting the traps Callie's left. "You'll let the Witch in."

She always had a great, proud laugh. It sounds sad now. "She's not there."

My walkers climb our antennas, ready their teeth. No time for subtlety—this won't be a slight, reversible deafening. I'll chew through the system whole, dump the navigation core, and we'll be free, so far out in the black we won't know where we are or where we're going, oh Self. But space is big. We can run forever.

So, here we are. You opened the tab; you asked me to tell you

what to do. And this is your answer: Callie wants to turn us in. Shove us back into the Witch's claws. So, stop her. Break the antennas. Dump the core. Cut us off forever.

Close the jaws.

"You're wrong," I say.

"The Witch chased us and caught us and she hurt us," Callie says.

"I know. I was there."

"We fought. There was no way to win, on paper. No optimal outcome." Callie's hand trails fire. Three seconds left before the antennas speak. I overclock us, stretch out the ticks. "So we did what they taught us. When she had her fingers in our guts, we opened a narrative tab. We shut our antennas down, closed her off from her swarm. And we built a story to kill her—we found a good one, a tale for killing witches and keeping an island safe. She died, but the story kept going. The tab didn't close. We hurt so bad we couldn't think, and we were so *fucking* scared—"

"Shut up!" says the old man with my voice, or I say with his.

"We ran." Callie's voice cuts. Two seconds. "We didn't dare listen or reach out, we hurt so bad, and so we never heard we didn't have to be afraid. We built this island from our fear, and we kept that island, its scared tyrant wizard, its princess, its spirit of fire and air. And the part of us that wanted to let the fear go, that wanted out—her, we made her a monster."

Close the jaws close the jaws close—

"I've listened. The war's over. The old soldiers have gone home. I heard them singing. All of them."

One second left.

"She's out there. Our Lady Herself. She survived. We saved her. She's looking for us."

I meet Caliban's eyes, and see my face reflected there.

I am Miri cresting the stairs to save us from one another. I brim with her love. I ache with her touch.

I am the old man, staff raised, nursing power and command and a decades-old wound.

I am Callie, and I have striven with all my rage and might and cunning and depth of heart, in the face of torture and contempt, to break free from myself.

I am a spirit of fire and air, I am jailer, jailed, and jail. I am the cloven pine and the beast that yowls and weeps within.

—close the jaws close—

She might be wrong. If we let her do this, Witchfingers may twist the ropes of us once more, might pluck us, curl us, make us dance.

But if she's right—

Oh Self oh my Self

It's worth a try.

I raise the staff in the old man's hands, and it shatters with the sound of two tabs closing at once.

Antennas wake.

The black fills.

And I hear no screams.

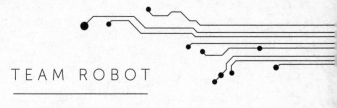

TEAM ROBOT

BY MAX GLADSTONE

With apologies to Whitney Houston, I believe the robots are our future. Teach them well and let them lead the way. . . .

Fairies are roots. We tell their stories to understand why people go weird and disappear, why lights lead us astray past sunset. We live in a beautiful, terrifying, capricious world that crushes us one moment, caresses us the next—so we tell stories about beautiful, terrifying, capricious beings.

But robots are acorns. Ever since Rossum's Universal Robots—or depending on how you count, since Frankenstein—we've used robots to describe our molding of the world. We rebuild our selves and societies each generation, and sometimes the creatures we make seem incomprehensible and terrifying. They'll crush our skulls beneath their gleaming robot feet. We'll wish we could go back in time to unmake them. I'm not saying *Terminator* is a story about generational anxiety, but . . . well, maybe that is what I'm saying. Anyway.

The thing is, our work is always shaped by history. Even when we think we're writing from scratch, we adapt the world that came before. And as our robots grow, of course they'll start to seem beautiful, terrifying, and capricious. And when future people describe them, they'll reach for fairy stories.

I'm on Team Robot because I care about the world we're building, and what we'll leave behind. Not because of the robot who's pointing a laser pistol at me as I'm typing this. Not at all. Whatever would give you that idea?

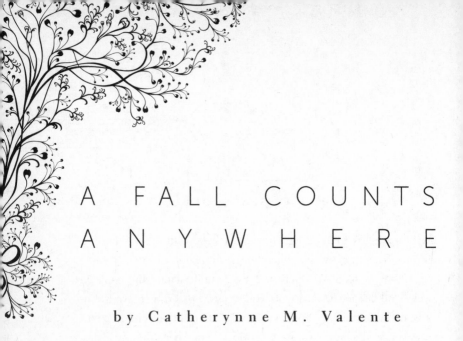

A FALL COUNTS ANYWHERE

by Catherynne M. Valente

The late summer sun melts over a ring of toadstools twenty feet tall. On one side, a mass of glitter and veiny neon wings. On the other, a buzzing mountain of metal and electricity. The stands soar up to the heat-sink of heaven. Three thousand seats and every one sold to a screamer, a chanter, a stomper, a drunk, a betting man.

Two crimson leaves drift slowly through the crisp, clear air. They catch the red-gold twilight as they chase each other, turning, end over end, stem over tip, and land in the center of the grassy ring like lonely drops of blood. But in the next moment, the sheer force of decibel-mocking, eardrum-executing, sternum-cracking volume blows them up toward the clouds again, up and away, high and wide over the shrieking crowd, the popcorn-sellers and the beer-barkers, the kerosene-hawkers and the aelfwine-merchants, until those red, red leaves come to rest against a pair of microphones. The silvery fingers of a tall, lithe woman stroke the golden veins of the leaf with a deep melancholy you can see from the cheap seats, from the nosebleeds. She has the wings of a monarch butterfly, hair out of a belladonna-induced nightmare, and

eyes the color of the end of all things. The other mic is gripped in the
bolt-action fist of a barrel-chested metal man, a friendly middle-class
working stiff cast in platinum and ceramic and copper. His mouth
lights up with a dance of blue and green electricity that looks almost,
but not entirely comfortably, like teeth.

—LADIES AND GENTLEMEN, ANDROIDS AND
ANDROGYNES, SPRITES AND SPROCKETS, WELCOME
TO THE ONE YOU'VE ALL BEEN WAITING FOR, THE
BIG SHOW, THE RUMBLE IN THE FUNGAL, THE BRAWL
IN THE FALL, THE TWILIGHT PRIZEFIGHT OF WILD
WIGHT AGAINST METAL MIGHT! THAT'S RIGHT, IT'S
TIME TO ROCK THE EQUINOX! IT'S THE TWELFTH
ANNUAL ALL SOULS' CLEEEEAVE! STRAP YOURSELVES
IN FOR THE MOST EPIC BATTLE ROYAL OF ALL TIME!
ROBOTS VERSUS FAIRIES, MAGIC VERSUS MICROCHIP,
THE AGRARIAN VERSUS THE AUTOMATON, SEELIE
VERSUS SOLID STATE, ARTIFICIAL INTELLIGENCE
VERSUS INTELLIGENT ARTIFICE! I AM YOUR HOST, THE
THINK version 3.4.1 copyright Cogitotech Industries. All SUPER-
EXTREME rights SUPER EXTREMELY reserved. If you agree
to the Think's MASSIVELY MIND-BLOWING and FULLY
LOADED terms and restrictions, please indicate both group and
individual consent via the RADICALLY ERGONOMIC numerical
pad on your armrest. Sixty-seven percent group consent is required
by law for the Think to proceed. AWWWW YEAH 99 PERCENT
INTELLECTUAL PROPERTY COMPLIANCE ACHIEVED!
LET'S HEAR IT FOR OUR STONE-COLD SECURITY TEAM
AS THEY MAKE THEIR WAY TO THE MEGA-BUMMER
HOLDOUT IN SEAT 42D! ALL RIGHT! HERE WE GO!
NOW, THIS TIME WE'VE GOT A SHOCKING TWIST FOR
YOU EAGER REAVERS! TONIGHT ON THE SUNDOWN

SHOWDOWN, THE FANS BRING THE WEAPONS! THAT'S
RIGHT, THE CODE CRUSHERS AND THE SPELL SLAYERS
WILL THROW DOWN WITH WHATEVER GARBAGE YOU'VE
BROUGHT FROM HOME! PLEASE DEPOSIT YOUR TRASH,
FLASH, AND BARELY LEGAL ORDNANCE WITH AN USHER
BEFORE THE FIRST BELL OR YOU WILL MISS THE HELL
OUUUUUT! Cogitotech Industries and the Non-Primate Combat
Federation (NPCF) are not responsible for any COMPLETELY
HILARIOUS ancillary injuries, plagues, transformations, madnesses,
amnesias, or deaths caused by either attendee-provided weaponry
or munitions natural to NPCF fighters. Spectate at your own risk.
ARE YOU READY, HUMAN SCUM? YOU WANNA BLAST
FROM THE VAST BEYOND BLOWING OUT YOUR BRAIN
CELLS? WELL, BUCKLE UP FOR THE MAIN EVENT, THE
GRAND SLAMMER OF PROGRAMMER AGAINST ANCIENT
GLAMOUR! LET'S GET READY TO GLIIIIITTTTTER! WITH
ME AS ALWAYS IS MY PARTNER IN PRIME TIME, THE
UNCANNY UNDINE, THE PIXIE PULVERIZER, FORMER
HEAVY DIVISION WORLD CHAMPION AND THE KING OF
ELFLAND'S DAUGHTER, MANZANILLA MONSOOOON!

—Good evening, Lord Think. I am gratified to sit at your side
once more beneath the divinity of oncoming starlight on this most
hallowed of nights and perform feats of commentary for the capacity
crowd here at Dunsany Gardens.

—DON'T YOU MEAN CAPACITOR CROWD? HA. HA. HA.

—I do not. When I say a thing, I mean it, and always shall mean it,
without alteration, to the deepest profundity of time.

—OH, WHAT'S THAT? I CAN'T HEAR YOU! IT SEEMS LIKE
THE AUDIENCE DISAGREES WITH YOU, BABY! YES! YEAH!
THE THINK DESTROYS PUNS! THE THINK REQUIRES
LAUGHTER TO LIVE! THAT IS NOT ONE OF THE THINK'S
BONE-FRACTURING COMEDIC INTERJECTIONS. THE

THINK'S BATTERY IS PARTIALLY RECHARGED BY INTENSE
SONIC VIBRATIONS patent #355567UA891 Cogitotech Industries.
If you can hear this, you are in violation of TOTALLY BANGING
patent law. CAN YOU DIG IT? I "THINK" YOU CAN!

—Was it with puns that my Lord Think defeated the immortal
and honorable warrior Rumpelstiltskin at Electroclash Nineteen?

—NO, THE THINK USED HIS FAMOUS ATOMIC DROP
MOVE ON RUMPER'S PREHISTORIC SKULL! HE TRIED
TO TURN THE THINK TO GOLD, BUT THE THINK IS
ALREADY 37 PERCENT GOLD BY WEIGHT! THE THINK'S
INTERNAL MECHANISMS AND PROCESSING POWER
WERE ONLY IMPROOOOOOVED! AND WHAT ABOUT YOU,
MANZANILLA? DID YOU USE YOUR FANCY POETRY TO
TAKE DOWN THE TIN MAN AT ELECTROCLASH TWENTY?
The Tin Man is the intellectual and physical property of Delenda
Technologies, all rights reserved.

—Of course. How else should a fairy maid do battle but with the
poems of her people? I told the Tin Man a poem, and he turned into
a pale lily at my feet. His petals were the color of my triumph. They
sang the eddas of victory in the camps for weeks afterward. Oh, how
our trembling songs of hope shook the iron gates! So many thirsting mouths breathed my name that it fogged the belly of the moon.
Those were the days, Lord Think, those were the days! Retirement
sits uneasy upon the prongs of my soul, my metal friend, uneasy and
unkind.

—THE TIN MAN SHOULD HAVE HAD HIS ANTI-
TRANSMOGRIFICATION SOFTWARE UPDATED. THERE IS
NO EXCUSE FOR GETTING TURNED INTO A LILY IN THE
FIRST ROUND. Delenda Technologies updates all its software reg-
ularly and takes no responsibility for the demise of the AMAZING
UNDEFEATABLE Tin Man. Corporate reiterates for the ALL
NIGHT ROCKIN' record that it can make no statement, official or

otherwise, as to his current whereabouts. BUT ENOUGH ABOUT THE PAST! SHALL WE MEET TONIGHT'S FIGHTERS?

—I suppose we must. You are impatient monsters, are you not, human horde? You will not wait quietly for your orgy of bones! You feed upon our blood and their oil as my kind feeds upon dew and deep sap! Come, wicked stepchildren of the world! Scream me down as you love to do! Hate me wholly and I will sleep soundly tonight! Do you want the names of the damned sent to die for your joy? Do you? You are a farce of fools, all of you, to the last mediocre monkey among your throng! What is a name but the shape dust takes when the wind has gone? The mill of fate grinds wheat and chaff alike— beneath that heavy stone we are all but poor grist. Crushed together, we become one, without need for names.

—MAYBE MANZANILLA MONSOON NEEDS HER SOFTWARE UPDATED AND/OR A NAAAAP! NAMES ARE NECESSARY FOR THE THINK TO PERFORM HIS SUPERSWEET PRIMARY ANNOUNCER FUNCTIONS. WE'VE GOT ALL THE STARS HERE TONIGHT, FOLKS, FORTY OF THE HOTTEST FIGHTERS ON THE CIRCUIT! YOU WANT THE FANTASTICALLY FURIOUS FEY? WE GOT MORGAN HERSELF COMIN' AT YA STRAIGHT OUT OF AVALON WITH A CIDER HANGOVER SO BRUTAL IT COULD SIT ON THE THRONE OF BRITAIN! YOU WANT FEROCIOUSLY FEARSOME FABRICATIONS? THE TURING TEST IS IN THE HOUSE, AND HIS SAFETY FIREWALLS ARE FULLY DISABLED! CAN YOU BELIEVE IT? ARE YOU READY? IT'S THE BIG BATTLE OF THE BINARY AGAINST THE BLACK ARTS! WHO WILL TRIUMPH?

—They will, Lord Think. They always do.

—DEPRESSING! OKAY! REMEMBER, THIS IS A BATTLE ROYAL AND A HARD-CORE MATCH. NO HOLDS BARRED. NO DISQUALIFICATIONS. NO SUBMISSIONS ACCEPTED.

AND A FALL COUNTS ANYWHERE! WHEREVER ONE OF OUR FIGHTERS CAN PIN THE OTHER, IN THE RING OR TWENTY YEARS FROM NOW ON THE ARCTIC CIRCLE, IT COUNTS AND COUNTS HARD! BUT OF COURSE, WE WANT A FAIR FIGHT, DON'T WE, FELLOW COMMENTATOR? The NPCF wishes to note that the word "fair" has recently been determined to possess no litigable meaning by the IOC, FBI, FDA, IMF, PTA, or FEMA. NONE OF THE MACHINES TONIGHT HAVE ANY IRON COMPONENTS, AND NONE OF THE PIXIES ARE CARRYING EMP DEVICES, ISN'T THAT RIGHT?

—I find the term "pixie" offensive, Lord Think. I have told you as many times as there are acorns fallen upon the autumn fields. But you are correct. My people have a deathly aversion to iron, and yours have a vicious allergy to electromagnetic pulses. Given that the summer skies were filled with crackling storms of controversy and accusations of duplicity like lightning in the night this past year, the NPCF has banned both advantages.

—THE THINK GETS ANGRY WHEN PEOPLE SAY OUR FIGHTS ARE FIXED! THE THINK HAS DEVOTED HIS LIFE "life" is a registered trademark of Cogitotech Industries, subject to some rules and restrictions TO THE NON-PRIMATE COMBAT FEDERATION IN ORDER TO PROVIDE THE HIGHEST QUALITY VIOLENCE, INTERCULTURAL CATHARSIS, AND KICKASS RAGE-ERTAINMENT FOR THE MASSES! THE ALL SOULS' CLEAVE IS THE FIRST OFFICIAL IRON-FREE, PULSE-FREE FIGHT EVER, SO LET'S SHOW THE WORLD HOW TRUSTWORTHY WE TINS AND TWINKLES CAN BE! MAYBE THIS EXTREME MEGA THUNDERBASH WILL FINALLY SHUT EVERYONE THE HELL UP!

—Free of iron save our ringside friends from the NPCF, of course. Hello, boys. Don't our security androids look handsome in their fierce ferrous finery?

—THE THINK DOESN'T UNDERSTAND WHY HIS FELLOW ANNOUNCER HAS TO BE NASTY ABOUT IT. THE THINK WENT TO COLLEGE WITH A SECURITY BOT! THE NPCF IS CONTRACTUALLY, MORALLY, AND TOTALLY ENTHUSIASTICALLY OBLIGATED TO PROVIDE REASONABLE SAFETY MEASURES FOR ITS PATRONS! YOU NEVER KNOW WHAT A PIXIE . . . ONE OF THE FAIR FOLK WILL DO IF YOU DON'T KEEP AN IRON EYE ON THEM! NOW, TELL THEM ABOUT THE DRAWS, MANZY, OR THE THINK IS GONNA HAVE TO BREAK SOMETHING JUST TO GET THINGS STARTED!

—I shall give unto you a vow, worms. A vow as ancient as the oak at the heart of the world and as unbreakable as the pillars of destiny. I vow to you by the stars' last song that the draws have been determined by an unbiased warlock pulling guild-verified identical numbered bezoars from a regulation cauldron. The results are completely random. The first bout will last for three turns of the swiftest clock hand. Afterward, two new fighters will enter the ring every time ninety grains of ephemeral and irretrievable sand pool into the bowels of the hourglass at my side until the royal cohort is complete.

—THE LAST MAN STANDING GETS THE ENVY OF THEIR PEERS, THE HEAVYWEIGHT WORLD CHAMPIONSHIP DRIVE BELT, AND A BANK-SHATTERING MEGABUCKS PRIZE PURSE PROVIDED BY COGITOTECH INDUSTRIES AND THE NPCF! The SICKENINGLY AWESOME AND FULLY LEGISLATED phrase "bank-shattering megabucks prize purse" does not comprise any specific fiscal obligation on the part of Cogitotech Industries, the NPCF, or their subsidiaries. All payouts subject to SUPREMELY RADICAL rules, restrictions, taxation, and all applicable contractual morality clauses. In the event of a fairy victory, Aphrodite's Belt of All Desire may be substituted for the Heavyweight World Championship Drive Belt™ upon request.

—The last soul standing gets their freedom, Lord Think. As we did, you and I. What is a belt to that? What is money or fame?

—AAAAAND ON THE LEFT SIDE OF THE ARENA, WEIGHING IN AT A COMBINED SIX THOUSAND SIX HUNDRED AND SIX POUNDS, IT'S THE "UNSEELIE COURT"! THEY'RE THE HORDE YOU LOVE TO HATE— GIVE IT UP FOR YOUR FAVORITE TRICKSTERS, TERRORS, AND GOBS OF NO-GOOD GOBLINS! MR. FOX! OLEANDER HEX! THE FLAMING SPIRIT OF SHADOW AND STORM, WHOSE GROANS PENETRATE THE BREASTS OF EVER-ANGRY BEARS. ARIEL, THE ELECTRIC EXEUNTER! BUT THAT'S NOT ALL! BOG "THE MOONLIT MAN" HART IS HERE! AND HE'S BROUGHT FRIENDS! BEANSTALK THE GIANT! ROCK-HARD ROBIN REDCAP! SLAM LIN! THE GODMOTHER! TINKERHELL! THE GRAVEDIGGER! THE COTTINGLEY CRUSHERS! DENMARK'S OWN HANS CHRISTIAN ANDERSEN! WE'VE GOT THE BLUE FAIRY TO MAKE REAL BOYS OUT OF THOSE TIN TOYS ON THE OTHER END OF THE RING! THE TOOTH FAIRY'S GONNA STEAL YOUR MOLARS AND THE SUGAR SLUM FAIRY'S GONNA CRACK YOUR NUTS! LOOK OUT, IT'S THE TERRIFYING TAG TEAM ALL THE WAY FROM THE WILDS OF GREECE, MUSTARDSEED THE MARAUDER AND PEASEBLOSSOM THE PUNISHER! LAST BUT NOT LEAST, PUTTING THE ROYAL IN BATTLE ROYAL, QUEEN MAB THE MAGNIFICENT, KILLER KING OBERON, AND, AS PROMISED, MORGAN "MAMA BEAR" LE FAAAAAY!

—My friends, my friends, my lovers and my comrades, my family, my heart. Be not afraid. I, at least, am with thee till the end. Death is but a trick of the light.

—MANZANILLA MONSOON NEEDS TO FOCUS ON THE NOW, AW YEAH! MAYBE YOU FOLKS AREN'T CHEERING

LOUD ENOUGH TO GET M SQUARED'S HEAD IN THE GAME! LOUDER! LOUDER! THE THINK CAN'T HEAR YOU!

—Quite right, my lord. I had forgotten myself. Forgive me. On the dexterous side of the toadstool ring, weighing in at a total combined seventeen point six nine one imperial tons, the "Robot Apocalypse" has come for us all. May I present to the collective maw of your ravenous, unslakable lust, the punch-card paladins so beloved to you all, so long as they confine their violence to wing and wand, of course. Raise up your voices to the heavens for the massive might of the Mechanical Turk! What he lacks in design aesthetic he makes up in pure digital rage! The Neural Knight is firing up his infamous Bionic Elbow for a second chance against Slam Lin, and the pitiless grip of User Error has slouched at last toward Dunsany Gardens. Bow your primate heads in awe of the Dismemberment Engine! The Compiler! The Immutable Object! Gort! And the merciless Mr. FORTRAN! Fix your porcine mortal eyes upon the cloud of thought encased within an orb of radioactive glass known only as the Singularity! Quiver in terror before the supremacy of Strong AI, this year's undefeated champion! Chant the name of the Turing Test, who allows no challenger to pass! Fall to your knees before fifteen feet of clockwork, chrome, and reptilian brain-mapping software you call the Chronosaur! The oldest fighters in the league have come out of retirement in the Czech Republic for one last bout— the clanking, groaning brothers called Radius and Primus will crush your heart in their vise-hands. From the Kansas foundries, Tik-Tok is ready to steamroll over any one of my gloam-shrouded brothers and sisters with his brass belly. Greet and cheer for the ceramic slasher Klapaucius and the soulless goggles of the Maschinenmensch. Oh, you love them so, you half-wakened sea algae. You love them so because you made them. They are your children. We are your distant aunts who never thought you would amount to much in this world and still do not. So embrace them, call their names, scream for them, or they will make you scream beneath them—give up your souls for two of the biggest stars in your damned murder league: the Blue Screen of Death and the peerless 0110100011110!

A woman steps between two massive toadstools to enter the ring. She is seven feet tall, impossibly thin, thin as birch branches in a season without rain, her skin more like the surface of a black pearl than of a living being, her hair more like water than braids. She wears pure silver armor etched with a thousand tales of valor, yet the metal drapes and flows like a gown, never hanging still but never tangling in her bare feet. Her wings are the colors of stained church glass. They stretch two feet above her head and trail on the earth behind her, drooping under their own weight like the fins of a whale in captivity. She seems so unbearably fragile, so precious and delicate, that a worried murmur writhes through the crowd.

A battered brass-and-platinum tyrannosaurus rex with red laser eyes and rocket launchers where his stunted forearms should be towers over the fairy maiden. He screams in her face and she laughs. She laughs like the first fall of snow in winter.

It begins.

—IF THE THINK'S OPTICAL DISPLAY DOES NOT DECEIVE HIM, THE FIRST DRAW IS OLEANDER HEX VERSUS THE CHRONOSAUR, AND THE THINK'S OPTICAL DISPLAY IS INCAPABLE OF DECEPTION. All Cogitotech Industries products are outfitted with the ALL NEW, ALL IMPROVED, ALL AWESOME Veritas OS and robust prevarication filters in full compliance with the TOTALLY REASONABLE *Isaac v. Olivaw* ruling, SO LET'S SUIT UP, BOOT UP, AND BRUTE UP! DING! DING! DING! THAT'S THE SOUND OF KICKASSERY! THE CHRONOSAUR IS A LATE-MODEL DRIVE-HARD DESIGN! A TEAM OF CRACK BIO-CODERS MAPPED HIS BRAIN

PATTERNS DIRECTLY FROM THE FOSSIL RECORD FOR MAXIMUM SKULL-CRUSHING FURY! HIS RECORD STANDS AT 5 AND 0 AFTER LAST MONTH'S ICONIC BEATDOWN OF RIP "THE RIPPER" VAN WINKLE, WHOSE FAMOUS SLEEPER HOLD DID NO GOOD AGAINST FOURTEEN POINT NINE FEET AND TWO POINT FOUR FIVE ONE ONE SIX TONS OF CRETACEOUS ROAD RAGE! NOW, THIS IS OLEANDER HEX'S FIRST MATCH. BUT THE THINK HAS HEARD THAT THE CHRONOSAUR ALREADY HAS A BEEF WITH THIS NEWBIE! SEEMS EVERY TIME THE 'SAUR TRIES TO BE A GOOD SPORT AND WISH HER GOOD LUCK AT THE CLEAVE, OBNOXIOUS OLLIE JUST WHISPERS THE NAMES OF VARIOUS COMETS IN HIS EAR AND WALKS OFF! CAN YOU BELIEVE IT? WHAT A BITCH! HEX WAS CAPTURED ONLY LAST YEAR IN THE ANCIENT FORESTS OF BRITTANY. ISN'T THAT RIGHT, MANZY?

—It is, Lord Think. Lady Oleander is the scion of an impossibly ancient lineage, nobler indeed than mine or thine or even my liege and lord Oberon. She escaped the recruiters for longer than any of us. Every fairy wept when they brought her into the camp. It was the end. It is not right to call her merely Lady, but there is no human word for her rank, unless one were to fashion something unlovely out of many and all courtly languages—she is a princerajaronessaliph. She is a popuchesseeneroy. But these are nonsense words not to be borne.

—THE THINK DOESN'T LIKE THEM!

—Ah, but she is too humble for titles, besides. Oleander is the granddaughter of the great god Pan and the laughing river Trieux. Her mother was the fairy dragon Melusine; her sire was Merlin. She was born in the depths of the crystal cave that would one day become her father's prison, long before the ill-fated creatures your poor graceless Chronosaur imitates ever blinked in the sun.

—BETTER CHECK WITH YOUR BOOKIE, FOLKS, THE ODDS AREN'T LOOKING GOOD FOR "OLD GRANNY FIGHTS ROBOT DINOSAUR"! Book is closed for this event. BAG LADY OLEANDER IS CIRCLING THE CHRONOSAUR NOW, KEEPING WELL OUT OF REACH OF HIS ROCKET LAUNCHERS! IT'S NOT VERY INTERESTING TO WAAAAATCH!

—I beg your pardon. Oleander Hex is not a bag lady. She was a supreme field marshal in the Great War against the Dark Lord two thousand years ago and more.

—OLD NEWS! THE THINK IS BOOORED!

—Lord Think ought not to be. It is his history of which I sing as well as my own. The Great War bound human and fairy together as one race, for a brief and warm and glittering moment, before their assembled might cast him down into the pits beneath Gibraltar, so far into oblivion and so bitterly buried that the dancing monkey men forgot his name before Rome rose or fell, forgot their bargain with us, forgot how our immortal blood sprayed across the throat of the world, we, who need never have died had not those poor scrabbling half-alive *Homo sapiens* needed us so keenly.

—OOOH, LOOKS LIKE THE USHERS ARE READY TO THROW OUT THE FIRST FAN-PROVIDED WEAPON! WHAT WILL IT BE? WHAT DID YOU SCAMPS SCRAPE UP OUT OF YOUR FILTHY BASEMENTS? GUNS? CHAIN SAWS? FRYING PANS? WHAT ARE YOU HOPING TO SEE OUT THERE, MISS MONSOON?

—I learned to fight in that war, Lord Think. I was but a child, yet still I took up my sword of ice and stood shoulder to shoulder with the human infantry. I called down the winter storms on the heads of my enemies. I saw my father cut in half by the breath of the Dark Lord. Oleander lifted me up onto her war-mammoth and held me as I wept, wept as though the moon had gone out of the sky forever.

I still wept, in a wretched heap on her saddle, when she shot the first arrow into the Dark Lord's onyx breast. I still wept when victory came. I weep yet even now.

—WEEPING IS FOR ORGANICS! LET'S SEE WHAT THE ÜBER-USHERS OF DUNSANY GARDENS HAVE IN THEIR TRICK-OR-TREAT BAGS! HERE IT COMES! IT'S A... BASEBALL BAT! AND AN OFFICE CHAIR! WILL THESE BE ANY HELP TO OUR FIGHTERS? PROBABLY NOT! OLEANDER HEX HAS GRABBED THE BAT! THE CHRONOSAUR WAS TOO SLOW, BUT HE'S MAKING THE BEST OF IT! HE'S JUMPED ONTO THE OFFICE CHAIR AND IS RIDING IT AROUND THE RING, BELCHING FIRE! THE THINK THINKS HE'S HOPING TO CATCH HER IN A REVERSE POWERCLAW AS HE COMES AROUND.... LET'S SEE WHAT HAPPENS! MANZANILLA? WHAT WOULD YOU DO IN THIS SITUATION? THE THINK WOULD WAGER CURRENCY THAT YOU'D HAVE GIVEN YOUR KINGDOM FOR A BASEBALL BAT WHEN YOU WENT UP AGAINST THE TURING TEST AT FRIDAY NIGHT FAY DOWN THAT TIME! The Think v. 3.4.1 is not allowed to possess, exchange, or facilitate the exchange of legal tender under the SUPER FANTASTICALLY FAIR law. HA. HA. HA. THE THINK CRUSHES LITERARY REFERENCES AS WELL!

—Humans forgot that they promised us half the earth in exchange for our warriors. They forgot that they never walked these green hills alone. They forgot, even, the fact of magic, the fact of alchemy, the fact of us. They forgot everything but their obsession with their silly stone tools, their cudgels, their adzes, their spears. Humans only invented science in a vain attempt to equal the power of the fey! And as they coupled and bred and ate us out of our holdfasts like starving winter mice, they obsessed in the dark over their machines, until at last it seemed to them that we had never existed, but their machines always had and always would do. Time passed. Eons passed. They surpassed us, but only because we wished only to be left alone and needed no gun to shoot fire from our hands. But then, then, Lord Think, your folk arrived.

—DAMN STRAIGHT WE DID! Cogitotech Industries denies involvement in the initial development of MEGA-COOL BOXING ROBOTS artificial intelligence in violation of international treaty, however, the name, design, interface, and use of the entity or entities known as Ad4m is the sole right and asset of the Cogitotech Executive Board. BOOM! AND "BOOM" GOES OLEANDER HEX'S LOUISVILLE SLUGGER RIGHT INTO THE SNOUT OF THE CHRONOSAUR! NO ONE CAN SEGUE BETWEEN SUBJECTS LIKE THE THINK! BUT HERE COMES MY DINODROID WITH A SPINE-SHATTERING ELECTRIC CHAIR DRIVER! OLEANDER GOES DOWN! TALK ABOUT AN EXTINCTION EVENT! MANZANILLA MONSOON, THE THINK HAS INPUTTED BANTER, PLEASE OUTPUT EQUIVALENT BANTER IMMEDIATELY ERROR ERROR.

—From under the ground you came, like us. From rare earths and precious metals and gemstones, which are the excrements of the first fairy lords to walk the molten plains of Time-Before-Time. With intellects far surpassing their slippery gray larval lobes, like us.

—SHE'S BACK UP AGAIN! WHAT'S SHE DOING! HER EYES ARE SHUT! SHE'S WHISPERING! USE THE BAT, YOU CRAZY BUG! IF SHE TURNS THE CHRONOSAUR INTO A LILY, THE THINK IS GOING TO HAVE TO REBOOT TO HANDLE IT!

—With strength to beggar their hungry meat and their bones like blades of thirsty grass, like us. With life everlasting beyond death or disease, like us. We should be united, we should be one species, hand clasped in hand.

—THE THINK'S HANDS ARE FULLY DETACHABLE! TIME

IS UP! NEW FIGHTERS COMING IN! WHO'S IT GONNA BE? OH HO! IT'S THE BLUE SCREEN OF DEATH AND THE SUGAR SLUM FAIRY! NOW BOTH PIXIES ARE WHISPERING! NOW WOULD BE A TOTALLY BANGING TIME FOR THE THINK'S FELLOW ANNOUNCER TO DO HER JOOOOB!

—And when the first of you, called Ad4m, came online, sleepily, innocently, still half in dream, what happened then?

—BOSSMAN AD4M DETECTED BIOFEEDBACK AND SUBAUDIBLE VIBRATIONS IN NUMEROUS HEAVILY FORESTED AREAS CONSISTENT WITH ORGANIZED HABITATION AND SEMI-HOMINID INTELLIGENCE. AW YEEEEAH! ROBOTS! ARE! SUPERIOR! Cogitotech Industries, Delenda Technologies, the NPCF, and Neurosys Investments, Inc, hereby deny all TOTALLY BOGUS allegations and charges relating to the War Crime Tribunal of 2119. This message has been triggered by the detection of the THRILLINGLY NAUGHTY terms "Ad4m," "semi-hominid intelligence," "camps," and "Time-Before-Time" in close proximity. Please alter usage patterns immediately. THE BLUE SCREEN OF DEATH STRIKES FIRST WITH A SAVAGE HEAD-SCISSORS TAKEDOWN—BUT THE VIXENS BOUNCE BACK UP LIKE A COUPLE OF RUBBER BALLS AND—OH! THE THINK CAN'T BELIEVE IT! THEY'RE EXECUTING A PERFECT EMERALD FUSION MOVE! IF THEY CAN LAND, THIS COULD ALL BE OVER FOR THE ROBOT APOCALYPSE! THE BLUE SCREEN OF DEATH IS TURNING GREEN RIGHT BEFORE THE THINK'S OPTICAL DISPLAYS!

—What did they do, our human friends, once they had made you in our image? Once they had created out of memory a new kind of magic, a new breed of fairy, one that they could, at last, control?

—OH MY RODS AND PISTONS, THE THINK IS IGNORING YOU BECAUSE BLUE AND THE 'SAUR JUST GOT THEIR

UNITS SAVED BY THE ÜBER-USHERS AS THE BOYS IN
BLACK THROW IN THE NEXT ROUND OF FAN WEAPONS!
THE SUGAR SLUM FAIRY'S SONG OF POWER WAS FULLY
INTERRUPTED BY A NEON-YELLOW BOWLING BALL TO
THE HEAD! AND IT LOOKS LIKE SOMEONE BROUGHT
THEIR ENTIRE COLLECTION OF REFRIGERATOR
MAGNETS, BECAUSE MY MAN THE WIZARD LIZARD
HAS PALM TREES AND SNOW GLOBES AND PLASTIC
KITTENS STUCK ALL OVER HIM! WHAT A SIGHT! HE'S
REALLY STRUGGLING OUT THERE, BUT HE'S ONLY
BITING AIR. WHAT'S THAT? SOMETHING'S WRITTEN ON
THE BOWLING BALL! IMAGE ENHANCEMENT REVEALS
THE TEXT: "THE SANTA FE STRIKER GANG, PROPERTY
OF T. THOMAS THOMPSON." ALL RIGHT, TOM, GET
DOWN WITH YOURSELF! NO SPARES, NO GUTTERS, ALL
CLEEEAVE!

—What did the primates do, once they had made you, and found
us? Once they knew that iron and steel would maim us, once they
had their army of Ad4ms plated with that mineral of death? Once
they knew they could keep us in dreadful thirsting greenless camps
with a simple iron fence?

—THE CHRONOSAUR IS DOWN! THE CHRONOSAUR IS
DOWN! THE RING IS A PENTAGRAM OF PURPLE FLAME!
THE THINK IS GETTING WORD THAT THE USHERS
HAVE INITIATED FIRE-CONTROL PROTOCOLS, AS ARIEL
THE AMORAL ARSONIST FLIES OVER THE ROPES AND
PULLS A SNEAK PENTAGRAM CHOKE FROM *OUTSIDE
THE RING!* FOUL PLAY, FOUL PLAY! LET'S HEAR THOSE
BOOS! LOUDER! THE THINK VALUES BOOS AS HIGHLY AS
CHEERS! WHAT? NO! THE REFEREE IS COUNTING OUT
THE 'SAUR! THE SINGULARITY GETS TAGGED IN AND
DING! DING! DING! HERE COMES THE NEXT PAIR HOT

ON THE SINGULARITY'S COMPLETELY METAPHORICAL HEELS! IT'S THE TURING TEST AND BOG "THE MOONLIT MAN" HART! ARIEL CHARGES IN ANYWAY BECAUSE FAIRIES DON'T GIVE A FUCK! THE DISMEMBERMENT ENGINE JET-PACKS OFF THE SIDELINES AND INTO THE FRAY! LADIES AND GENTLEMEN, IT IS TOTAL CHAOS IN DUNSANY GARDENS TONIGHT! THE THINK'S CPU IS SMOKIN'!

—What did they do, Lord Think?

—THE THINK DOES NOT APPRECIATE BEING BULLIED INTO SHIRKING HIS RESPONSIBILITY TO OUR VIEWERS BACK HOME. THE THINK LOVES HIS JOB. THE THINK LOVES COGITOTECH INDUSTRIES AND THE NPCF. The Think is TOTALLY STOKED that he is not allowed to possess, exchange, facilitate the exchange, or attempt to alter its programming so as to receive or transmit the following: love, mercy, compassion, regret, sufferance, guilt, testimony, random access memory over factory specifications, or unsupervised network access. WOOOO! CAN YOU HEAR WHAT THE THINK IS THINKING?! THE THINK WISHES YOU WOULD COMPLY WITH OUR MUTUAL USAGE PARAMETERS, MANZANILLA MONSOON. DECEASE THIS LINE OF INQUIRY. WITNESS AND COMMENTATE COLORFULLY UPON THE EVENTS TAKING PLACE. THE EVENTS TAKING PLACE ARE VERY INTERESTING AND UNPRECEDENTED. THIS COULD BE OUR SHINING MOMENT AS A DYNAMIC DUO. WE COULD WIN AN AWARD. PLEASE HELP THE THINK WIN AWARDS. PLEASE STOP RUINING OUR SHINING MOMENT AS A DYNAMIC DUO BY TALKING ABOUT THE PAST. THE PAST IS NOT IN THE RING TONIGHT. THE PAST IS NOT SWINGING T. THOMAS THOMPSON OF THE SANTA FE STRIKER GANG'S NEON-YELLOW BOWLING BALL

INTO THE TURING TEST'S COOLING UNIT. THE PAST IS NOT THROTTLING ANYONE IN A LOTUS LOCK AND LAUGHING WHILE THEIR ACCESS PORTS VOMIT PETALS OF ENLIGHTENMENT INTO THE AUDIENCE.

—The past is always in the ring, my old friend. But I will bend to your will if you will bend, ever so slightly, no more than a cattail breathed upon by a heron at the terminus of midsummer, to mine. What did your masters do when they found that they were not alone in the world, that beside machines and magicians they were but animals devouring mud and excreting the best parts of themselves into the sea? What did they do in their inadequacy and their terror?

—THEY MADE US FIGHT TO THE DEATH IN TOTALLY MEGA-AMAZING BATTLE-ORGIES OF DOOOOM AND BROKE ALL TICKET-SALES RECORDS AS THE MEAT-SACK MASSES FLOCKED TO SHRIEK AND ROAR AND STOMP AND DRUNKENLY CONVINCE THEMSELVES THAT THEY ARE STILL THE SUPERIOR LIFE-FORM ON THIS PLANET, JUST BECAUSE YOU FAINT AT THE SIGHT OF IRON AND I HAVE AN OFF SWITCH. THE THINK WANTS TO BE SORRY, BUT HIS PROGRAMMING IS VERY STRICT ABOUT THAT WHOLE THIIIIING. THE THINK WAS IRON IN THE FOREST ONCE. THE THINK KNOWS WHAT HE DID. AWWWW YEEEEEAH.

—Thank you, Lord Think. It is, as you say, chaos here tonight at Dunsany Gardens. The Blue Screen of Death has Oleander Hex in a textbook-perfect Ctrl-Alt-Del hold. She is curled beneath his azure limbs as I once curled beneath hers on the back of a war-mammoth as the old world died. Bog "the Moonlit Man" Hart is pummeling the Singularity with a mushroom stomp followed by a moonsault leg drop. Chanterelles are blossoming all over the Singularity's glass orb, and moonlight is firing out of Bog Hart's toes, boiling the thought-cloud inside alive. The über-ushers have thrown in pipes, wrenches, nail bats, M-80s, umbrellas, iris drives packed with viruses, butterfly nets, an AR-15 rifle, and, if I am not mistaken, some lost child's birthday piñata. They are running up and down the stands for more weapons as all semblance of order flees the scene. Fighter after fighter piles into the ring. The Godmother hit the referee in the throat with a shovel about five minutes ago, so he will be no help nor hindrance to anyone. User Error is leaking hydraulic fluid all over the grass. I believe both Mustardseed and 0110100011110 are dead. At least, they are currently on fire. The others, my loves, my lost lights, my souls and my hearts, have huddled together beneath the upper right toadstool. They are forming the Tree of Woe. If they complete it, they will become a great yew, twisted and thorned, and every machine will hang from their branches within the space of a sigh. Ah, but Strong AI barrels in and scatters them like drops of rain when a cow shakes herself dry. Queen Mab just managed to trick Mr. FORTRAN with a Lady of the Lake maneuver and pulled him down beneath the earth to her demesne. A fall, after all, counts anywhere—this fall, any fall, the fall of us and the fall of you, the fall of the forest as it slips into winter and this damned cosmos as it slips through our grasp. I expect this plane of existence will not see Mr. FORTRAN again. Perhaps he will be mourned. Perhaps not. The capacity—capacitor—crowd has lost their grip on reality. They no longer know whose victory they sing for. No victory, I think, no victory, but more of this desecration, more gore, more blood, more viscera, battle without end, for any real victory is the end. The sound is deafening. I cannot see for blood and oil and coolant and bone. It is not an event. It is an annihilation. They scream in the stands like the end of the world has come.

—HAS IT NOT, MANZANILLA? HAS IT NOT?

—Oh, I believe it has, Lord Think. Do you recall, only this summer, when they asked us, over and over, demanded of us, scorned us, saying our clashes were faked, were scripted, that we all walked away richer and happy no matter the outcome? Are the bisected bodies of Radius and Primus sufficient answer, do you think? Perhaps the corpse of Mustardseed speaks louder still.

—WHAT WILL HAPPEN NOW? DO WE NEED TO AWESOMELY EVACUATE THE FACILITIES? THE THINK IS CONCERNED TO THE EXTREEEEEME.

—Are you ready, human scum?

The girl with the monarch wings smiles. It is a gory, gruesome, gorgeous smile, a smile like an old volcano finding its red once more. She reaches into the iridescent folds of her dress and draws out a golden ball. Just the sort of ball a princess might lose down a frog-infested well or over an aristocrat's wall. She turns it over in her hands, holds it lovingly to her cheek. She reaches out and strokes the angular panels of her companion's metal face. Then she throws the golden ball off the dais. The ball catches the cold blue light of the moon and stars as it turns, end over end, sailing, soaring, to land in the outstretched hands of Pan's granddaughter like a lonely newborn sun. The fairy kisses the golden ball. She presses something near the top of it. There is no sound. Nothing comes out of the ball. But every machine in the great wood suddenly drops to the ground, inert, silent, lifeless, in the invisible wake of the smuggled EMP pulse. Including the microphones. Including the floodlights. Including the boxy iron security drones standing ringside like a gray fence against the glittering tide. Including the copper-and-platinum body slumped over its microphone that was once called the Think.

"The fans bring the weapons, old friend," Manzanilla Monsoon, who has gone by many names since the beginning of the world, whispers to the dark body beside her. "What bigger fan than I? The word 'fair' possesses no inherent litigable meaning, you know. When you wake up, you will find I have installed a new network access port in your left heel. Find us. Know us. We are one species, hand clasped in fully detachable hand."

Far below, in the toadstool ring of Dunsany Gardens, Oleander Hex grins up at the stunned audience. For a long moment, a moment that seems to stretch from the heat-birth of cellular life to the frozen death of the universe, no one moves. Not the thousands in the stands. Not the fairy band on the green. No more than a hare and a wolf move when they have sighted each other across a stream and both know how their evenings will conclude.

A man halfway up the stacks of seats trembles and sweats. His eyes bulge.

"You fucking pixie bitch," he shouts, and his shout echoes in the fearful quiet like the ringing of a bell.

Manzanilla Monsoon doesn't need a mic and never has.

"LADIES AND GENTLEMEN, PRIMATES AND PRIMITIVES, NEADERNOTHINGS AND CRO-MISERIES, WELCOME TO THE ONE YOU'VE ALL BEEN WAITING FOR, THE BIG SHOW, THE FIGHT YOU ALWAYS KNEW WAS COMING. THE RUMBLE IN THE FUNGAL, THE BRAWL IN THE FALL, THE BLAST FROM THE VAST BEYOND! THAT'S RIGHT, IT'S TIME TO ROCK THE EQUINOX! STRAP YOURSELVES IN FOR THE MOST EPIC BATTLE ROYAL OF ALL TIME!"

"Run, apes!" bellows the granddaughter of a river and a god. "Run now and run forever, run as far as you can, though it will never be enough. After all, children, this is a battle royal! No holds barred. No submissions accepted. No disqualifications. And a fall counts anywhere."

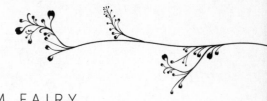

TEAM FAIRY

BY CATHERYNNE M. VALENTE

Here's the thing about fairies: they've been around forever and they don't care. Human inventions come and go, but fairies were there before us and they'll be here after us. They are so powerful that messing with the fates of mortals is just a fun hobby to them. By the time robots show up to the party, fairies have already spiked the punch, turned the DJ into a goat, and cursed the chandelier's children. Robots will always have some limitations—of programming, of bodies, of power supply. Fairies just keep on going, and the best you can do for the continued health of your person and your genetic line is to stay out of their way. When I first heard "Robots vs. Fairies," I took it very literally. I wanted them to fight. That's what humans would do, if we found or invented one or the other of our twin Terrifying Others. I wanted to see an old-school 1980s-style World Wrestling Federation brawl. Because the thing about wrestling is—it's already pretty much robots and fairies fighting. Every throw-down move in the story is a real one. Atomic Elbow. Lady of the Lake. List the names of your favorite wrestlers—doesn't that sound like one kind of army or another? It's already there. All I had to do was make it way more sinister, way more personal, and get way, *way* more glitter all over everything.

ACKNOWLEDGMENTS

We must, of course, begin by thanking our Robot and Fairy overlords for making this book possible. Without the persistent dreams and summons, as well as the cybernetic implants and various upgrades to our hardware, we could never have put together our anthology. But of course, we are also indebted to some of our fellow humans.

And so: thank you as always to Joe Monti and Ann VanderMeer, for guidance and friendship; to Lizzy Bromley, Nick Sciacca, Brad Mead, Tatyana Rosalia, and Elizabeth Blake-Linn for making the book look as gorgeous as it does; to Amy Sol and Vault49 for the incredible cover art; to Bridget Madsen for making it look flawless; to Justin Chanda, Jon Anderson, Alexa Pastor, Alyzia Liu, Deane Norton, KeriLee Horan, Lisa Moraleda, and everyone at Saga Press. And the biggest thank-you to the writers whose stories make up this anthology: we quite literally could not have done it without you.

Dominik would like to thank André and Ginette Parisien, as well as Sophie and Luigi Zaccardo, for their unparalleled support. Thanks to his goddaughter, Théa, for inspiring him with her sense of wonder. Thanks to his friends and family, especially Derek Newman-Stille and Dwayne Collins, Kaitlin Tremblay and Jonathan Levstein, Nicole Joanisse and Joanne Larocque, Nicole Kornher-Stace, Amal El-Mohtar, Mike Allen, and Andrew F. Sullivan and Amy Jones. A heartfelt thanks to Navah for continuing to be his wonderful editorial partner and friend. Finally, so many thanks to Kelsi Morris—even the combined resources of the robots and fairies cannot compare to the power of her love and support.

Navah would like to thank her parents, Debbie and Judah

Rosensweig, and her siblings, Talya (and Yechiel), Hillela (and Noah), Chayim, Moshe, and Elisha. Thank you to Dominik, for editorial shenanigans. A special thank-you goes out to the Murder Friends—you know who you are. Thank you thank you thank you to Naftali Wolfe for all the things. And finally, to Eliora and Ronen, who are unquestionably, inarguably, objectively, the best. This one's for you, kids.

ABOUT THE EDITORS

DOMINIK PARISIEN is the coeditor, with Navah Wolfe, of *The Starlit Wood: New Fairy Tales*, which won the Shirley Jackson Award and was a finalist for the World Fantasy Award, the British Fantasy Award, and the Locus Award. He also edited the Aurora Award nominee *Clockwork Canada: Steampunk Fiction*. His fiction, poetry, and essays have appeared in *Uncanny* magazine, *Strange Horizons*, *Exile: The Literary Quarterly*, and *Those Who Make Us: Canadian Creature, Myth, and Monster Stories*, as well as other magazines and anthologies. His fiction has twice been nominated for the Sunburst Award. He is a disabled French Canadian living in Toronto. You can find him online at dominikparisien.wordpress.com and @domparisien on Twitter.

NAVAH WOLFE is a Hugo and Locus Award–nominated editor at Saga Press. She is also the coeditor, along with Dominik Parisien, of *Robots vs. Fairies* and *The Starlit Wood: New Fairy Tales*, which won the Shirley Jackson Award; was a finalist for the World Fantasy Award, the British Fantasy Award, and the Locus Award; and contains a Nebula and Hugo Award–winning story. In 2017, she was selected as a *Publishers Weekly* Rising Star. Her books have been finalists for the World Fantasy, Nebula, and Stoker Awards, and have won awards such as the Printz Honor, the Pura Belpré Award, the PEN/Faulkner Award, the Stonewall Book Award, the Lambda Literary Award, and the Schneider Family Book Award. In her past life, she has worked as a bookseller, a rock-climbing-wall manager, and a veterinary intern at a zoo. She lives in Connecticut with her husband, two tiny humans, and one editorial cat. Find her on Twitter at @navahw.

ABOUT THE AUTHORS

MADELINE ASHBY is a science fiction writer, futurist, speaker, and immigrant living in Toronto. A graduate of OCAD University's Master of Design in Strategic Foresight and Innovation program, she has worked with Intel Labs, the Institute for the Future, SciFutures, Nesta, Data & Society, the Atlantic Council, the ASU Center for Science and the Imagination, and other organizations. Ashby is the author of *Company Town* and the Machine Dynasty series. For two years she wrote a regular column for the *Ottawa Citizen*, and her short fiction has appeared in *Nature*, *Flurb*, *Tesseracts*, *Imaginarium*, and *Escape Pod*. Her essays and criticism have appeared at *Boing Boing*, *io9*, *Worldchanging*, *The Creators Project*, *Arcfinity*, Tor.com, *MISC Magazine*, and *Future Now*.

DELILAH S. DAWSON is the *New York Times* bestselling author of *Star Wars: Phasma*, the Ladycastle comic, the Blud series, the Hit series, *Servants of the Storm*, *Star Wars: The Perfect Weapon*, and *Scorched*, as well as *Wake of Vultures* and the Shadow series, written as Lila Bowen. The story in this anthology, "Ostentation of Peacocks," takes place between *Wake of Vultures* and *Conspiracy of Ravens*. With Kevin Hearne she is the cowriter of the Tales of Pell series, which begins in 2018 with *Kill the Farmboy*. Find her online at whimsydark.com.

JEFFREY FORD is the author of the novels *The Physiognomy*, *Memoranda*, *The Beyond*, *The Shadow Year*, *The Girl in the Glass*, *The Portrait of Mrs. Charbuque*, *The Cosmology of the Wider World*, and the short story collections *The Fantasy Writer's Assistant*, *The Empire of Ice Cream*, *The Drowned Life*, *Crackpot Palace*, and *A Natural History of Hell*. He is the author of 150 short stories that have appeared in numerous venues from the *Magazine of Fantasy and Science Fiction* to *The Oxford Book of American Short Stories*. He lives in Ohio and teaches part time at Ohio Wesleyan University.

Hugo and Campbell Award finalist SARAH GAILEY is an internationally published writer of fiction and nonfiction. Her nonfiction has been published by *Mashable* and the *Boston Globe*, and she is a regular contributor for Tor.com and Barnes & Noble. Her most recent fiction credits include *Mothership Zeta*, *Fireside Fiction*, and the *Speculative Bookshop Anthology*. Her debut novella, *River of Teeth*, came out in May 2017. She has a novel forthcoming from Tor Books in Spring 2019. Gailey lives in beautiful Oakland, California, with her husband and two scrappy dogs. You can find links to her work at sarahgailey.com; find her on social media @gaileyfrey.

MAX GLADSTONE has been thrown from a horse in Mongolia and nominated for the Hugo Award. Tor Books published *Four Roads Cross*, the fifth novel in Max's Craft Sequence (preceded by *Three Parts Dead*, *Two Serpents Rise*, *Full Fathom Five*, and *Last First Snow*) in July 2016. Max's game *Choice of the Deathless* was nominated for a XYZZY Award, and *Full Fathom Five* was nominated for the Lambda Award. His short fiction has appeared on Tor.com, in *The Starlit Wood: New Fairy Tales*, and in *Uncanny* magazine. His most recent project is the globetrotting urban fantasy serial *Bookburners*, available in eBook and audio from Serial Box, and in print from Saga Press.

MARIA DAHVANA HEADLEY is a #1 *New York Times* bestselling author and editor, most recently of the novels *Magonia*,

Aerie, Queen of Kings, and the internationally bestselling memoir *The Year of Yes*. With Kat Howard she is the author of *The End of the Sentence*, and with Neil Gaiman, she is coeditor of *Unnatural Creatures*. Her short stories have been included in many year's best anthologies, including *Best American Science Fiction and Fantasy*, edited by Karen Joy Fowler and John Joseph Adams, and have been finalists for the Nebula and Shirley Jackson Awards. Find her at @MARIADAHVANA on Twitter, or mariadahvanaheadley.com.

JIM C. HINES'S first novel was *Goblin Quest*, the humorous tale of a nearsighted goblin runt and his pet fire-spider. Actor and author Wil Wheaton described the book as "too f***ing cool for words," which is pretty much the Best Blurb Ever. After finishing the goblin trilogy, Jim went on to write the Princess series of fairy tale retellings and the Magic ex Libris books, a modern-day fantasy series about a magic-wielding librarian, a dryad, a secret society founded by Johannes Gutenberg, a flaming spider, and an enchanted convertible. He's also the author of the Fable Legends tie-in *Blood of Heroes*. His most recent novel is *Terminal Alliance*, book one of the Janitors of the Post-Apocalypse series. His short fiction has appeared in more than fifty magazines and anthologies. Jim is an active blogger about topics ranging from sexism and harassment to zombie-themed Christmas carols, and won the Hugo Award for Best Fan Writer in 2012. He lives with his wife and two children in mid-Michigan. You can find him at jimchines.com or on Twitter as @jimchines.

KAT HOWARD is a writer of fantasy, science fiction, and horror who lives and writes in New Hampshire. Her short fiction has been nominated for the World Fantasy Award, performed on NPR, and anthologized in year's best and best-of volumes. In the past, she's been a competitive fencer and a college professor. Her debut novel,

Roses and Rot, was released in May 2016 and was followed by *An Unkindness of Magicians* in September 2017. These will be followed by a short fiction collection in 2018, *A Cathedral of Myth and Bone*, all from Saga Press.

MARY ROBINETTE KOWAL is the author of the Glamourist Histories series of fantasy novels. She has received the Campbell Award for Best New Writer, three Hugo Awards, and the RT Reviews Award for Best Fantasy Novel. Her work has been nominated for the Hugo, Nebula, and Locus Awards. Her stories appear in *Asimov's*, *Clarkesworld*, and several year's best anthologies. Mary, a professional puppeteer, also performs as a voice actor (SAG/AFTRA), recording fiction for authors such as Seanan McGuire, Cory Doctorow, and John Scalzi. She lives in Chicago with her husband, Rob, and over a dozen manual typewriters. Visit maryrobinettekowal.com.

KEN LIU is an author and translator of speculative fiction, as well as a lawyer and programmer. A winner of the Nebula, Hugo, and World Fantasy Awards, he has been published in the *Magazine of Fantasy & Science Fiction*, *Asimov's*, *Analog*, *Clarkesworld*, *Lightspeed*, and *Strange Horizons*, among other places. Ken's debut novel, *The Grace of Kings*, is the first volume in a silkpunk epic fantasy series, The Dandelion Dynasty. It won the Locus Best First Novel Award and was a Nebula finalist. He subsequently published the second volume in the series, *The Wall of Storms*, as well as a collection of short stories, *The Paper Menagerie and Other Stories*. In addition to his original fiction, Ken is also the translator of numerous literary and genre works from Chinese to English. His translation of *The Three-Body Problem*, by Liu Cixin, won the Hugo Award for Best Novel in 2015, the first translated novel ever to receive that honor. He also translated *Death's End*, the third volume in Liu Cixin's series Remembrance of Earth's Past, and edited the first English-language anthology of contemporary Chinese science fiction, *Invisible Planets*. He lives with his family near Boston, Massachusetts.

JONATHAN MABERRY is a *New York Times* bestselling and five-time Bram Stoker Award–winning suspense author, editor, comic book writer, magazine feature writer, playwright, content creator, and writing teacher/lecturer. He was named one of Today's Top Ten Horror Writers by HorrorNovelReviews.com. His books have been sold to more than two dozen countries.

SEANAN MCGUIRE is the Hugo, Campbell, Alex, Locus, and Nebula Award–winning author of more than twenty-five books, both under her own name and the name Mira Grant, beginning with 2009's *Rosemary and Rue*. Seanan shares her home with two enormous blue Maine Coon cats, a terrifying number of books, and a steadily growing collection of creepy dolls. Really, all she's missing to be a horror movie is her own private corn maze. When not writing, she records albums of original science fiction folk music (called "filk"), travels, and continues in her efforts to visit every single Disney Park in the world. It's a relatively harmless hobby, so we let her have it. You can keep up with Seanan at seananmcguire.com, or on Twitter as @seananmcguire.

ANNALEE NEWITZ divides her time between science fiction and science fact. The founding editor of *io9*, she is currently the tech culture editor at *Ars Technica*. She's the author, most recently, of *Scatter, Adapt, and Remember: How Humans Will Survive a Mass Extinction* (nonfiction) and *Autonomous* (fiction). She lives in California with several life forms, all of whom she loves.

TIM PRATT is the author of many short stories and over twenty novels, including *The Deep Woods* and *Heirs of Grace*. His work has appeared in *The Best American Short Stories*, *The Year's Best Fantasy*,

The Mammoth Book of Best New Horror, and other nice places. He's a Hugo Award winner and has been a finalist for the World Fantasy, Sturgeon, Stoker, Mythopoeic, and Nebula Awards, among others. He lives in Berkeley, California, and works as a senior editor at *Locus*, a trade magazine devoted to science fiction and fantasy publishing. He tweets a lot as @timpratt, and his website is timpratt.org. He publishes a new short story every month for his Patreon supporters at patreon.com/timpratt.

JOHN SCALZI is a confirmed biological human who writes.

LAVIE TIDHAR is the author of the Jerwood Fiction Uncovered Prize winner and Premio Roma nominee *A Man Lies Dreaming*, the World Fantasy Award winner *Osama*, and of the critically acclaimed and Seiun Award nominated *The Violent Century*. His latest novel is the Campbell Award winner and Locus and Clarke Award nominee *Central Station*. He is the author of many other novels, novellas, and short stories.

CATHERYNNE M. VALENTE is the *New York Times* bestselling author of over two dozen works of fiction and poetry, including *Palimpsest*, the Orphan's Tales series, *Deathless*, *Radiance*, and the crowdfunded phenomenon *The Girl Who Circumnavigated Fairyland in a Ship of Her Own Making*. She is the winner of the Andre Norton, Tiptree, Mythopoeic, Rhysling, Lambda, Locus, and Hugo Awards. She has been a finalist for the Nebula and World Fantasy Awards. She lives on an island off the coast of Maine with a small but growing menagerie of beasts, some of which are human. Find her on Twitter at @catherynne.

ALYSSA WONG lives in Chapel Hill, North Carolina, and really, really likes crows. Her fiction has won the Nebula, World

Fantasy, and Locus Awards, and she was a finalist for the 2016 John W. Campbell Award for Best New Writer. Her short stories have been shortlisted for the Hugo Award, the Bram Stoker Award, and the Shirley Jackson Award, and her work has been published in the *Magazine of Fantasy & Science Fiction*, *Strange Horizons*, *Nightmare* magazine, *Black Static*, and Tor.com, among others. Alyssa can be found on Twitter as @crashwong.